The French Powder Mystery

A Problem in Deduction

By

ELLERY QUEEN

Author of *The Roman Hat Mystery*

OTTO PENZLER BOOKS
New York

OTTO PENZLER BOOKS
129 West 56th Street
New York, NY 10019
(Editorial Offices only)

Simon & Schuster Inc.
Rockefeller Center
1230 Avenue of the Americas
New York, NY 10020

First Otto Penzler Books Edition 1995
Published by arrangement with Frederic Dannay Literary
Property Trust and Bank of Boston Connecticut

Manufactured in the United States of America

1   3   5   7   9   10   8   6   4   2

Library of Congress Cataloging-in-Publication Data
Queen, Ellery.
    The French powder mystery : an Ellery Queen mystery /
Ellery Queen. — 1st Otto Penzler Books ed.
    p.   cm. — (Otto Penzler's classic American library)
    1. Private investigators — New York (N.Y.) — Fiction.
    2. Fathers and sons — New York (N.Y.) — Fiction.
3. Police — New York (N.Y.) — Fiction.
    I. Title.   II. Series.
PS3533.U4T44 1995
813'.52 — dc20   94-30952
                                                              CIP

ISBN 1-883402-90-5

THE FIRST EPISODE

"Parenthetically speaking . . . in numerous cases the sole difference between success and failure in the detection of crime is a sort of . . . osmotic reluctance (on the part of the detective's mental perceptions) to seep through the cilia of WHAT SEEMS TO BE *and reach the vital stream of* WHAT ACTUALLY IS.*"*

—From A PRESCRIPTION FOR CRIME,
   By Dr. Luigi Pinna

CONTENTS

THE FIRST EPISODE

THE SECOND EPISODE

THE THIRD EPISODE

THE FOURTH EPISODE

THE LAST EPISODE

SOME PERSONS OF IMPORTANCE

ENCOUNTERED IN THE COURSE OF THE FRENCH INVESTIGATION *

NOTE: A list of the personalities involved in *The French Powder Mystery* is here set at the disposition of the reader. He is urged indeed to con the list painstakingly before attacking the story proper, so that each name will be vigorously impressed upon his consciousness; moreover, to refer often to this page during his perusal of the story. . . . Bear in mind that the most piercing enjoyment deriving from indulgence in detective fiction arises from the battle of wits between author and reader. Scrupulous attention to the cast of characters is frequently a means to this eminently desirable end.

ELLERY QUEEN.

WINIFRED MARCHBANKS FRENCH, *Requiescat in pace.* What cesspool of evil lies beneath her murder?

BERNICE CARMODY, a child of ill-fortune.

CYRUS FRENCH, a common American atavar—merchant prince and Puritan.

MARION FRENCH, a silken Cinderella?

WESTLEY WEAVER, amanuensis and lover—and friend to the author.

VINCENT CARMODY, *l'homme sombre et malheureux.* A dealer in antiquities.

JOHN GRAY, director. A donor of book-ends.

* The success of this device in his recent novel (*The Roman Hat Mystery*) has encouraged Mr. Queen to repeat it here. It was found useful by many of Mr. Queen's readers in keeping the *dramatis personæ* compactly before them.—THE EDITOR.

HUBERT MARCHBANKS, director. Ursine brother to the late Mrs. French.

A. MELVILLE TRASK, director. Sycophantic blot on a fair 'scutcheon.

CORNELIUS ZORN, director. An Antwerpian nabob, potbelly, inhibitions and all.

MRS. CORNELIUS ZORN, Zorn's Medusa-wife.

PAUL LAVERY, the impeccable *français*. Pioneer in modern art-decoration. Author of technical studies in the field of fine arts, notably *L'Art de Faïence, publi par Monserat, Paris, 1913*.

ARNOLD MACKENZIE, General Manager of French's, a Scot.

WILLIAM CROUTHER, chief guardian of the law employed by French's.

DIANA JOHNSON, a study in normal ebon.

JAMES SPRINGER, Manager of the Book Department; a mysterioso.

PETER O'FLAHERTY, leal head nightwatchman of the French establishment.

HERMANN RALSKA, GEORGE POWERS, BERT BLOOM, nightwatchmen.

HORTENSE UNDERHILL, genus *housekeeper tyranna*.

DORIS KEATON, a maidenly minion.

THE HON. SCOTT WELLES, just a Commissioner of Police.

DR. SAMUEL PROUTY, Assistant Medical Examiner of New York County.

HENRY SAMPSON, District Attorney of New York County.

TIMOTHY CRONIN, Assistant District Attorney of New York County.

THOMAS VELIE, Detective-Sergeant under the wing of Inspector Queen.

HAGSTROM, HESSE, FLINT, RITTER, JOHNSON, PIGGOTT, sleuths attached to the command of Inspector Queen.

SALVATORE FIORELLI, Head of the Narcotic Squad.

"JIMMY," Headquarters fingerprint expert who has ever remained last-nameless.

DJUNA, The Queens' beloved scull, who appears far too little.

Detectives, policemen, clerks, a physician, a nurse, a Negro caretaker, a freight watchman, etc., etc., etc., etc.

and

INSPECTOR RICHARD QUEEN

who, being not himself, is sorely beset in this adventure

and

ELLERY QUEEN

who is so fortunate as to resolve it.

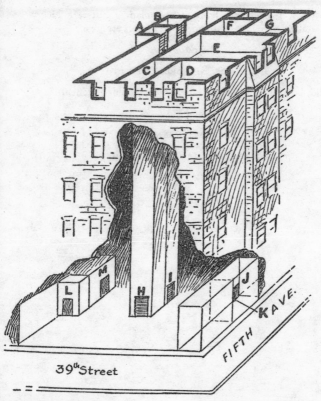

39ᵗʰ Street

A—Elevator shaft
B—Stairway shaft
C, D, E, F, G—French apartment
    C—Lavatory   F—Anteroom
    D—Bedroom   G—Cardroom
    E—Library
H—Ground floor door to elevator, facing 39th Street corridor

I—Ground floor door to stairway, facing Fifth Avenue corridor
J—Window containing Lavery Exhibition
K—Door to murder-window
L—O'Flaherty's office, with view of 39th Street entrance
M—Door from freight room

FOREWORD

EDITOR'S NOTE: It will be recalled by the readers of Mr. Queen's last detective novel * that a foreword appeared therein written by a gentleman designating himself as *J. J. McC.* The publishers did not then, nor do they now, know the identity of this friend of the two Queens. In deference to the author's wish, however, Mr. McC. has been kind enough to pen once more a prefatory note to his friend's new novel, and this note appears below.

I have followed the fortunes of the Queens, father and son, with more than casual interest for many years. Longer perhaps than any other of their legion friends. Which places me, or so Ellery avers, in the unfortunate position of Chorus, that quaint herald of the olden drama who craves the auditor's sympathetic ear and receives at best his willful impatience.

It is with pleasure nevertheless that I once more enact my rôle of prologue-master in a modern tale of murder and detection. This pleasure derives from two causes: the warm reception accorded Mr. Queen's first novel, for the publication of which I was more or less responsible, under his *nom de plume;* and the long and sometimes arduous friendship I have enjoyed with the Queens.

I say "arduous" because the task of a mere mortal in attempting to keep step with the busy life of a New York detective Inspector and the intellectual activity of a bookworm and logician can adequately be described only by that word. Richard Queen, whom I knew intimately

---

* *The Roman Hat Mystery,* by Ellery Queen; published by Frederick A. Stokes Company, 1929.

long before he retired, a veteran of thirty-two years' service
in the New York police department, was a dynamic little
gray man, a bundle of energy and industry. He knew his
crime, he knew his criminals, and he knew his law. He
brought to these not uncommon attributes, however, a
daring of method that put him far above the average
detective Inspector. A firm advocate of the more inspira-
tional methods of his son, he nevertheless was the practical
policeman to his fingertips. Under his long régime the
Detective Bureau, except for those stormy times when his
official superiors took it upon themselves by overhauling
the department to satisfy a theory or a press opinion,
garnered a record of solved capital crimes which to this
day is unique in the police history of New York City.

Ellery Queen, as may be imagined, deplored the more
unimaginative aspects of his father's profession. He was
the pure logician, with a generous dash of dreamer and
artist thrown in—a lethal combination to those felons who
were so unfortunate as to be dissected by the keen instru-
ments of his mind, always under those questing pince-nez
eyeglasses. His "life work" before his father's retirement
was hardly visible to the eye, unless his casual custom of
writing a detective story when the spirit moved him may
be termed a life work.* He occupied himself chiefly in a
student's pursuit of culture and knowledge, and since he
had an independent income from a maternal uncle which
removed him from the class of social parasite, he lived what
he characteristically termed the "ideal intellectual life." It
was natural for him to evince intense interest in crime, due

---

* It is interesting to note that "Ellery Queen" published many detective novels during his father's Inspectorship, but under his real
name, which is of course not Queen. These unrevealed stories, however,
should not be confused with the stories published under the name of
Ellery Queen, of which *The French Powder Mystery* is the second.
These latter are taken practically untouched from actual investigations
undertaken by the author and his father; which accounts both for the
nom de plume and the secrecy shrouding the identity of the Queens.

to his environment, which from childhood had been saturated with tales of murder and law-breaking; but the artistic element in his nature made him useless for routine police investigation.

I recall vividly a conversation between father and son one day many years ago which brought out their wholly opposed viewpoints on the subject of crime-detection. I relate the conversation here because it will crystallize the difference between the two men so clearly—a point quite essential to complete understanding of the Queens.

The Inspector was expounding on his profession for my benefit, while Ellery lounged in his chair between us.

"Ordinary crime-detection," said the old man, "is almost wholly a mechanical matter. Most crimes are committed by 'criminals'—that is to say, by individuals habituated by environment and repetitious conduct to the pursuit of law-breaking. Such persons in ninety-nine out of a hundred cases have police records.

"The detective in these ninety-nine hypothetical cases has much to go on. Bertillon measurements—fingerprint records, intimate photographs, a complete dossier. Moreover, he has a little file of the criminal's idiosyncrasies. We have not developed this phase of detective science so well as the London, Vienna and Berlin police, but we have at least laid a foundation. . . .

"A burglar who habitually makes use of a certain method of prying open doors and windows, or blowing safes, for example; a hold-up man who always wears a crude, home-made mask; a gunman who smokes and drops a certain brand of cigaret, purely from habit; a gangster with an inordinate fondness for women; a second-story man who always works alone, or one who invariably employs a 'look-out' . . . These idiosyncrasies of method are sometimes as definite clues to the identity of a criminal as his fingerprints.

"It seems peculiar to the layman," went on Inspector Queen, when he had inhaled deeply from his old snuff-box—a habit inseparable from the man—"that a criminal should constantly use the same *modus operandi*—always drop the same cigarette smoked the same way; always wear the same kind of mask; always indulge in a wild orgy with women after a 'job.' But they forget that crime is the criminal's business, and that every business leaves its indelible mark of habit on the business man."

"Your psychological policeman, by the way," grinned Ellery, "doesn't scorn the aid of informers, either, McC. Something like the little tick-bird that sits on the rhino's back and warns of approaching danger. . . ."

"I was coming to that," retorted his father equably. "As I said in the beginning, we have plenty to go on in the case of the hardened criminal. But most of all, despite my son's jeering attitude, we have come to depend upon the underworld's 'squealers,' 'stool-pigeons'—they're called less polite names, too—for the solution of routine crimes. It is an open secret that without the stool-pigeon a huge percentage of felonies would remain unsolved. They are as essential to the big city's police as a knowledge of the proper source-book is to the lawyer. It stands to reason— the underworld by its amazing grapevine inevitably knows who has pulled a big 'job.' Our problem is to find a 'stoolie' who will part with the tip for a fair consideration. It isn't always easy even then, by the way. . . ."

"Child's play," said Ellery in a provocative tone. And he grinned.

"I firmly believe," went on the old Inspector imperturbably, "that every police department in the world would collapse in six months if the institution of underworld informing were to come to an end."

Ellery lazily took up the cudgels. "Most of what you say, Sire, is only too true. Which is why ninety per cent of your investigations hold not a vestige of glamour for me. But the last ten per cent!

"Where the police detective woefully falls down, J.J.," he said smiling, turning to me, "is in the case of the crime whose perpetrator is *not* a habitual criminal, who has therefore left *no* handy fingerprints which will correspond with another set in your files, about whose idiosyncrasies *nothing* is known for the ludicrously simple reason that he has never been a criminal before. Such a person, generally speaking, is not of the underworld, and you can therefore pump your stool-pigeon to your heart's delight without eliciting the slightest morsel of useful information.

"You have nothing to go on, I am happy to say," he continued, twirling his pince-nez, "except the crime itself, and such clues and pertinences as that crime reveals upon observation and investigation. Obviously—and I say this with proper respect for my father's ancient profession—obviously to nab the criminal in such a case is the more difficult job by many headaches. Which explains two things—the hideously high percentage of unsolved crimes in this country, and my own absorbing avocation."

*   *   *

The French Powder Mystery is one of the older cases from the Queens' files—an actual case, as I have said, and one in which Ellery exhibited scintillating proofs of his unique talents. He kept notes of this case during the French investigation—one of his few practical habits. Subsequently, with the unmasking of the murderer, he wrote a book around the real-life plot, developing and embroidering the facts to fit a literary pattern.

I induced him to polish up the manuscript and have it published as the second novel under his pen-name—and this at a time when I was under his sacred roof in the Queens' Italian villa. For it will be recalled that Ellery, having renounced his old profession utterly, now that he is married and domesticated, has hidden his old cases in the depths of a filing-cabinet and nothing less than the detonation of a presumptuous friend's exhortations has been able to make him consent to a revivication of the mellowed manuscripts.

It should be borne in mind, in all fairness to Inspector Queen, that the old sleuth's comparatively small rôle in the French case was due to the enormous press of official business during that hectic season, and in no small degree to the heckling he was subjected to by the newly appointed civilian, Scott Welles, to the post of Commissioner of Police.

In closing, it might be pleasant to point out that the Queens are at this writing still in their tiny mountain-home in Italy; that Ellery's son has learned to toddle and say with innocent gravity, "gramps"; that Djuna is in perfect health and has recently undergone the stress of a cosmic love-affair with a little witch of a country girl; that the Inspector is still writing monographs for German magazines and making occasional tours of inspection through the Continental police departments; that Mrs. Ellery Queen has happily recovered from her recent illness; and finally that Ellery himself, after his visit last fall to New York, has returned to that "gem-encrusted" Roman scenery with gratitude in his heart and, he says, (but I doubt it), no regrets for the distractions of the West Side.

Which leaves me little else to write but a most sincere hope that you will enjoy the reading of *The French Powder Mystery* fully as much as I did.

J. J. McC.

NEW YORK
June, 1930

1

"THE QUEENS WERE IN THE PARLOR"

THEY sat about the old walnut table in the Queen apartment—five oddly assorted individuals. There was District Attorney Henry Sampson, a slender man with bright eyes. Beside Sampson glowered Salvatore Fiorelli, head of the Narcotic Squad, a burly Italian with a long black scar on his right cheek. Red-haired Timothy Cronin, Sampson's assistant, was there. And Inspector Richard Queen and Ellery Queen sat shoulder to shoulder with vastly differing facial expressions. The old man sulked, bit the end of his mustache. Ellery stared vacantly at Fiorelli's cicatrix.

The calendar on the desk nearby read Tuesday, May the twenty-fourth, 19—. A mild spring breeze fluttered the window draperies.

The Inspector glared about the board. "What did Welles ever do? I'd like to know, Henry!"

"Come now, Q, Scott Welles isn't a bad scout."

"Rides to hounds, shoots a 91 on the course, and that makes him eligible for the police commissionership, doesn't it? Of course, of course! And the unnecessary work he piles on us. . . ."

"It isn't so bad as that," said Sampson. "He's done some useful things, in all fairness. Flood Relief Committee, social work. . . . A man who has been so active in non-political fields can't be a total loss, Q."

The Inspector snorted. "How long has he been in office? No, don't tell me—let me guess. Two days. . . . Well, here's what he's done to us in two days. Get your teeth into this.

"Number one—reorganized the Missing Persons Bureau.

3

And why poor Parsons got the gate *I* don't know. . . .
Number two—scrambled seven precinct captains so thoroughly that they need road maps to get back to familiar territory. Why? You tell me. . . . Number three—shifted the make-up of Traffic B, C, and D. Number four—reduced a square two dozen second-grade detectives to pounding beats. Any reason? Certainly! Somebody whose grand-uncle's niece knows the Governor's fourth secretary is out for blood. . . . Number five—raked over the Police School and changed the rules. And I know he has his eagle eye on my pet Homicide Squad. . . ."

"You'll burst a blood-vessel," said Cronin.

"You haven't heard anything yet," said the Inspector grimly. "Every first-grade detective must now make out a daily report—in line of duty, mind you—a daily personal report direct to the Commissioner's office!"

"Well," grinned Cronin, "he's welcome to read 'em all. Half those babies can't *spell* homicide."

"Read them nothing, Tim. Do you think he'd waste *his* time? Not by your Aunt Martha. No, sir! He sends them into *my* office by his shiny little secretary, Theodore B. B. St. Johns, with a polite message: 'The Commissioner's respects to Inspector Richard Queen, and the Commissioner would be obliged for an opinion within the hour on the veracity of the attached reports.' And there I am, sweating marbles to keep my head clear for this narcotic investigation—there I am putting my mark on a flock of flatfoot reports." The Inspector dug viciously into his snuff-box.

"You ain't spilled half of it, Queen," growled Fiorelli. "What's this wall-eyed walrus, this pussy-footing specimen of a 'civvie' do but sneak in on my department, sniff around among the boys, hook a can of opium on the sly, and send it down to Jimmy for—guess what—fingerprints! Fingerprints, by God! As if Jimmy could find the print of a dope-peddler after a dozen of the gang had had their paws on the can. Besides, we had the prints already! But no, he didn't stop for explanations. And then Stern searched high and low for the can and came runnin' to me with some crazy story that the guy we're lookin' for'd walked himself straight into Headquarters and snitched a pot of opium!" Fiorelli spread his huge hands mutely, stuck a stunted black cheroot into his mouth.

It was at this moment that Ellery picked up a little volume with torn covers from the table and began to read.

Sampson's grin faded. "All joking aside, though, if we don't gain ground soon on the drug ring we'll all be in a mess. Welles shouldn't have forced our hand and stirred up the White test case now. Looks as if this gang—" He shook his head dubiously.

"That's what riles me," complained the Inspector. "Here I am, just getting the feel of Pete Slavin's mob, and I have to spend a whole day down in Court testifying."

There was silence, broken after a moment by Cronin. "How did you come out on O'Shaughnessy in the Kingsley Arms murder?" he asked curiously. "Has he come clean?"

"Last night," said the Inspector. "We had to sweat him a little, but he saw we had the goods on him and came through." The harsh lines around his mouth softened. "Nice piece of work Ellery did there. When you stop to think that we were on the case a whole day without a glimmer of proof that O'Shaughnessy killed Herrin, although we were sure he'd done it—along comes my son, spends ten minutes on the scene, and comes out with enough proof to burn the murderer."

"Another miracle, eh?" chuckled Sampson. "What's the inside story, Q?" They glanced toward Ellery, but he was hunched in his chair, assiduously reading.

"As simple as rolling off a log," said Queen proudly. "It generally is when he explains it.—Djuna, more coffee, will you, son?"

An agile little figure popped out of the kitchenette, grinned, bobbed his dark head, and disappeared. Djuna was Inspector Queen's valet, man-of-all-work, cook, chambermaid, and unofficially the mascot of the Detective Bureau.* He emerged with a percolator and refilled the cups on the table. Ellery grasped his with a questioning hand and began to sip, his eyes riveted on the book.

"Simple's hardly the word," resumed the Inspector. "Jimmy had sprinkled that whole room with fingerprint powder and found nothing but Herrin's own prints—and Herrin was deader than a mackerel. The boys all took a whack at suggesting different places to sprinkle—it was quite a game while it lasted. . . ." He slapped the table. "Then Ellery marched in. I reviewed the case for him and showed him what we'd found. You remember we spotted Herrin's footprints in the crumbled plaster on the dining-room floor. We were mighty puzzled about that, because from the circumstances of the crime it was impossible for Herrin to have been in that dining-room. And that's where superior mentality, I suppose you'd call it, turned the trick. Ellery said: 'Are you certain those are Herrin's footprints?' I told him they were, beyond a doubt. When I told him why, he agreed—yet it was impossible for Herrin to have been in that room. And there lay the prints, giving us the lie. 'Very well,' says this precious son o' mine, 'maybe he wasn't in the room, after all.' 'But Ellery—the prints!' I objected. 'I have a notion,' he says, and goes into the bedroom.

"Well," sighed the Inspector, "he certainly did have a notion. In the bedroom he looked over the shoes on Herrin's dead feet, took them off, got some of the print powder from Jimmy, called for the copy of O'Shaughnessy's fingerprints, sprinkled the shoes—and sure enough, there was a beautiful thumb impression! He matched it

* See *"The Roman Hat Mystery."*

with the file print, and it proved to be O'Shaughnessy's.
. . . You see, we'd looked in every place in that apartment
for fingerprints except the one place where they were—on
the dead body itself. Who'd ever think of looking for the
murderer's sign on his victim's shoes?"

"Unlikely place," grunted the Italian. "How'd it
figure?"

"Ellery reasoned that if Herrin wasn't in that room and
his shoes were, it simply meant that somebody else wore or
planted Herrin's shoes there. Infantile, isn't it? But it
had to be thought of." The old man bore down on Ellery's bowed head with unconvincing irritability. "Ellery,
what on earth are you reading? You're hardly an attentive
host, son."

"That's one time a layman's familiarity with fingerprints
came in handy," grinned Sampson.

"Ellery!"

Ellery looked up excitedly. He waved his book in triumph, and began to recite to the amazed group at the
table: " 'If they went to sleep with the sandals on, the
thong worked into the feet and the sandals were frozen
fast to them. This was partly due to the fact that, since
their old sandals had failed, they wore untanned brogans
made of newly flayed ox-hides.' * Do you know, dad,
that gives me a splendid idea?" His face beamed as he
reached for a pencil.

Inspector Queen swung to his feet, grumbling. "You
can't get anything out of him when he's in that mood. . . .
Come along, Henry—you going, Fiorelli?—let's get down
to City Hall."

* I had been brushing up on my Xenophon, and when I ran across
the passage relating to the Retreat of the Ten Thousand through
ancient Armenia, the shoe reference gave me an idea for a short story.
The incident is ridiculous in retrospect, although at the time I was
quite oblivious to its humor.—E. Q.

2

"THE KINGS WERE IN THE COUNTING-HOUSE"

It was eleven o'clock when Inspector Queen left his apartment on West 87th Street in the company of Sampson, Cronin and Fiorelli, bound for the Criminal Courts Building.

At precisely the same moment, some miles to the south, a man stood quietly at the library dormer-window of a private apartment. The apartment was situated on the sixth floor of French's, the Fifth Avenue department store. The man at the window was Cyrus French, chief stockholder of French's and president of its Board of Directors.

French was watching the swirling traffic at the intersection of Fifth Avenue and 39th Street with unseeing eyes. He was a dour-visaged man of sixty-five, stocky, corpulent, iron-grey. He was dressed in a dark business suit. A white flower gleamed on his lapel.

He said: "I hope you made it clear that the meeting was for this morning at eleven, Westley," and turned sharply to eye a man seated beside a glass-topped desk before the window.

Westley Weaver nodded. He was a fresh-faced young man, clean-shaven and alert, in the early thirties.

"Quite clear," he replied pleasantly. He looked up from a stenographic notebook in which he had been writing. "As a matter of fact, here is a carbon copy of the memorandum I typed yesterday afternoon. I left one copy for each director, besides this one which you found on the desk this morning." He indicated a slip of blue-tinted paper lying beside the desk telephone. Except for five books standing between cylindrical onyx book-ends at the extreme right of the desk, a telephone, and the memorandum, the glass top was bare. "I followed up the memos to the directors with telephone calls about a half-hour ago. They all promised to be here on time."

French grunted and turned again to look down upon the maze of morning traffic. Hands clasped behind his back, he began to dictate store business in his slightly grating voice.

They were interrupted five minutes later by a knock on the outer door, beyond an anteroom. French irritably called, "Come!" and there was the sound of a hand fumbling with the invisible knob. French said, "Oh, yes, the door's shut, of course; open it, Westley."

Weaver went quickly through the anteroom and flung open the heavy door. He admitted a weazened little old man who showed pale gums in a grin, and with an amazing celerity for a man of his years tripped into the room.

"Never seem to remember that locked door of yours, Cyrus," he piped, shaking hands with Westley and French. "Am I the first?"

"That you are, John," said French with a vague smile. "The others should be here any moment now."

Weaver offered the old man a chair. "Won't you sit down, Mr. Gray?"

Gray's seventy years sat lightly on his thin shoulders. He had a bird-like head covered with thin white hair. His face was the indeterminate color of parchment; it was constantly wreathed in smiles which lifted his white mustache above thin red lips. He wore a wing collar and an ascot tie.

He accepted the chair and sat down with a preposterously lithe movement.

"How was your trip, Cyrus?" he asked. "Did you find Whitney amenable?"

"Quite, quite!" returned French, resuming his pacing. "In fact, I should say that if we officially come to a complete agreement this morning, we can consummate the merger in less than a month."

"Fine! Good stroke of business!" John Gray rubbed his hands in a curious gesture; they rasped together.

There was a second knock at the door. Weaver again went into the anteroom.

"Mr. Trask and Mr. Marchbanks," he announced. "And if I'm not mistaken, there comes Mr. Zorn from the elevator." Two men passed into the room, and a moment later a third; whereupon Weaver hurried back to his chair by the desk. The door swung shut with a click.

The newcomers shook hands all around and dropped into chairs at a long conference table in the middle of the room. They made a peculiar group. Trask—A. Melville Trask in the Social Register—fell into a habitually drooping attitude, sprawling in his chair and playing idly with a pencil on the table before him. His associates paid little attention to him. Hubert Marchbanks sat down heavily. He was a fleshy man of forty-five, florid and clumsy-handed. At regular intervals his loud voice broke in an asthmatic wheeze. Cornelius Zorn regarded his fellow directors from behind old-fashioned gold-rimmed eyeglasses. His head was bald and square, his fingers were thick, and he wore a reddish mustache. His short figure completely filled the chair. He looked startlingly like a prosperous butcher.

French took a seat at the head of the table and regarded the others solemnly.

"Gentlemen—this is a meeting which will go down in the history of department store merchandising." He paused, cleared his throat. "Westley, will you see that a man is posted at the door so that we may continue absolutely undisturbed?"

"Yes, sir." Weaver picked up the telephone on the desk and said, "Mr. Crouther's office, please." A moment later he said, "Crouther? Who? Oh, yes. . . . Never mind looking for him; you can take care of it. Send one of the store detectives up to the door of Mr. French's private apartment. He is to see that no one disturbs Mr. French while the Board meeting is going on. . . . He is not to interrupt us—merely station himself at the door. . . . Whom will you send? . . . Oh! Jones? Good enough. Tell Crouther about it when he comes in. . . . Oh, he's been in since nine? Well, tell him for me when you see him; I'm very busy just now." He hung up and returned quickly to a chair at French's right. He snatched his pencil and poised it over his notebook.

The five directors were poring over a sheaf of papers. French sat staring at the blue May sky outside while they familiarized themselves with the details of the documents, his heavy hands restless on the table top.

Suddenly he turned to Weaver and said in an undertone, "I'd almost forgotten, Westley. Get the house on the wire. Let's see—it's eleven-fifteen. They should be up by this time. Mrs. French may be anxious about me—I haven't communicated with her since I left for Great Neck yesterday."

Weaver gave the number of the French house to the operator, and a moment later spoke incisively into the mouthpiece.

"Hortense? Is Mrs. French up yet? . . . Well, is Marion there, then? Or Bernice? . . . Very well, let me speak with Marion. . . ."

He shifted his body away from French, who was talking in a low tone to old John Gray. Weaver's eyes were bright and his face suddenly flushed.

"Hello, hello! Marion?" he breathed into the telephone. "This is Wes. I'm sorry—you know—I'm calling from the apartment—your father would like to speak to you. . . ."

A woman's low voice answered. "Westley dear! I understand. . . . Oh, I'm so sorry, darling, but if father's there we can't talk very long. You love me? Say it!"

"Oh, but I *can't*," whispered Weaver fiercely, his back rigid and formal. But his face, turned away from French, was eloquent.

"I know you can't, silly boy." The girl laughed. "I just said it to make you wriggle. But you do, don't you?" She laughed again.

"Yes. Yes. Oh, YES!"

"Then let me talk to father, darling."

Weaver cleared his throat hastily and turned to French.

"Here's Marion at last, sir," he said, handing the instrument to the old man. "Hortense Underhill says that neither Mrs. French nor Bernice has come down yet."

French hurriedly took the telephone from Weaver's hands. "Marion, this is father. I've just arrived from Great Neck and I'm feeling fine. Everything all right? . . . What's the matter? You seem a little tired. . . . All right, dear. I merely wanted to let you know that I'm back safely. You might tell Mother for me—I'll be too busy to call again this morning. Good-by, dear."

He returned to his chair, looked gravely around at the Board, and said, "Now gentlemen, since you've had a few moments to become familiar with the figures I thrashed out with Whitney, let's get to work." He brandished a forefinger.

*   *   *   *

At eleven forty-five the telephone bell jangled, interrupting a heated discussion between French and Zorn. Weaver's hand leaped to the instrument.

"Hello, hello! Mr. French is very busy just now. . . . Is that you, Hortense? What is it? . . . Just a moment." He turned to French. "Pardon me, sir—Hortense Underhill is on the wire and she seems disturbed about something. Will you talk to her or call back?"

French glared at Zorn, who was fiercely dabbing away

the perspiration on his thick neck, and snatched the telephone from Weaver.

"Well, what is it?"

A quavering feminine voice answered. "Mr. French, something dreadful's happened. I can't find Mrs. French or Miss Bernice!"

"Eh? What's that you say? What's the matter? Where are they?"

"I don't know, sir. They hadn't rung for the maids all morning, and I went up to see if anything was wrong a few minutes ago. You'll—you'll never believe it, sir—I can't understand—"

"Well!"

"Their beds aren't touched. I don't think they slept home last night."

French's voice rose in anger. "You silly woman—is that why you're interrupting my Board meeting? It was raining last night and they probably stayed overnight somewhere with friends."

"But Mr. French—they would have called, or—"

"Please, Hortense! Go back to your housework. I'll look into this later." He slammed the receiver on the hook.

"Foolishness . . ." he muttered. Then he shrugged his shoulders. He turned to Zorn again, palms on the table. "Now what's that? Do you mean to tell me that you'd stand in the way of this merger just because of a paltry few thousands? Let me tell you something, Zorn. . . ."

3

"HUMPTY-DUMPTY HAD A GREAT FALL"

French's occupied a square block in the heart of the midtown section of New York, on Fifth Avenue. On the borderline between the more fashionable upper avenue and the office-building district farther downtown, it catered to a mixed patronage of wealth and penury. At the noon hour its broad aisles and six floors were crowded with shop girls and stenographers; in mid-afternoon the tone of its clientele improved perceptibly. It boasted at once therefore the lowest prices, the most modern models, the widest assortment of saleable articles, in New York. As a result of this compromise between attractive prices and exclusive merchandise it was the most popular department store in the city. From nine o'clock in the morning until five-thirty in the evening French's was thronged with shoppers, the sidewalks surrounding the marble structure and its many wings almost impassable.

Cyrus French, pioneer department store owner, assisted by his associate Board, exerted the full financial strength of his powerful organization to make French's—an institution of two generations of French ownership—the show place of the city. In those days, long before the artistic movement had been communicated in the United States to the more practical articles of use and wear, French's had already made contact with its European representatives and held public exhibitions of art objects, art furniture, and kindred modernistic ware. These exhibits attracted huge crowds to the store. One of its main windows fronting Fifth Avenue was devoted to exhibits of periodically imported articles. This window became the focal point for the eyes of all New York. Curious throngs constantly besieged its sheathing of plate glass.

On the morning of Tuesday the twenty-fourth of May, at three minutes of the noon hour, the heavy unpaneled door to this window opened and a Negress in black dress, white apron and white cap entered. She sauntered about the window, seemed to appraise its contents, and then stood stiffly at attention, as if awaiting a predetermined moment to begin her mysterious work.

The contents of the window were arranged to illustrate a combination living-room and bedroom, of an ultra-modern design created by Paul Lavery, of Paris, according to a placard in a corner. This card acknowledged Lavery's authorship of the articles on exhibition, and called attention to "lectures on the fifth floor by M. Lavery." The rear wall, into which the one door opened by which the Negress had entered, was unrelieved by ornament and tinted a pastelle green. On this wall hung a huge Venetian mirror, unframed, its edges cut in an irregular design. Against the wall stood a long narrow table, exhibiting an unpainted grain highly waxed. On the table stood a squat prismatic lamp, made of a clouded glass procurable at that period only from a unique modern art-objects factory in Austria. Odd pieces—chairs, end-tables, bookcases, a divan, all of unorthodox construction, peculiar and daring in conception—stood about the gleaming floor of the window-room. The side walls served as background for several pieces of miscellaneous utility.

The lighting fixtures in the ceiling and on the side walls were all of the "concealed" variety rapidly gaining vogue on the Continent.

At the stroke of noon the Negress, who had remained motionless since her entrance into the room, stirred into activity. By this time a viscid mass of people had gathered outside the window on the sidewalk, awaiting the Negress's demonstration with hungry eyes and restless shoulders.

Setting down a metal rack on which were hung a number of simply lettered placards, the Negress picked up a long ivory wand and, pointing to the legend on the first placard, proceeded solemnly to one of the pieces on the east wall and began a pantomimic demonstration of its construction and properties.

The fifth placard—by this time the crowd had doubled in size and overflowed from the sidewalk—bore the words:

WALL—BED
This Article of Furniture
Is Concealed in the West
Wall and Is Operated Elec-
trically by a Push-Button.
It is of Special Design,
Created by M. Paul Lavery,
and Is the Only One of Its
Kind in This Country.

Pointing to the words once more, for emphasis, the Negress sedately walked to the west wall, indicated with a flourish a small ivory button set in a nacreous panel, and touched the button with one long black finger.

Before pressing it, she looked out once more on the jostling, expectant crowd before the window. Necks craned eagerly to see the marvel about to be revealed.

What they saw was a marvel indeed—so unexpected, so horrible, so grotesque that at the instant of its occurrence faces froze into masks of stunned incredulity. It was like a moment snatched out of an unbelievable nightmare. . . . For, as the Negress pushed the ivory button, a section of the wall slid outward and downward with a swift noiseless movement, two small wooden legs unfolded and shot out of the forepart of the bedstead, the bed settled to a horizontal position—and the body of a woman, pale-faced, crumpled, distorted, her clothes bloody in two places, fell from the silken sheet to the floor at the Negress's feet.

It was twelve-fifteen exactly.

4

"ALL THE KING'S HORSES"

The Negress uttered one horrified shriek, so piercing that it was distinctly audible through the heavy glass window, rolled her eyes wildly, and fell fainting at the side of the body.

The spectators outside still presented a tableau—they were stricken into silence, petrified with fright. Then a woman on the sidewalk, her face pressed immovably to the glass, screamed. Immobility became frenzy, silence a dull unpunctuated roar. The crowd surged away from the window, pushing madly backward, stampeding in terror. A child fell and was trampled in the crush. A police whistle blew, and a bluecoat ran shouting through the crowd, using his club freely. He seemed bewildered by the uproar—he had not yet seen the two still figures in the exhibition-window.

Suddenly the door in the window burst open and a lean man wearing a short pointed beard and a monocle ran into the room. His staring eyes took in the two motionless figures on the shining floor, traveled jerkily to the milling crowd outside and the policeman swinging his club, and returned with dazed disbelief to the floor. With a soundless oath he sprang forward, grasped a heavy silk cord in a corner near the plate-glass window, and pulled. A translucent curtain fell immediately, shutting off the view of the frantic people in the street.

The bearded man knelt at the side of the Negress, felt her pulse, hesitantly touched the skin of the other woman, rose and ran back to the door. A growing crowd of salesgirls and shoppers was collecting on the main floor of the department store, just outside the window. Three men— floorwalkers—rushed through as if to enter.

The man in the window spoke sharply: "You—get the head store detective at once—no, never mind—here he comes—Mr. Crouther! *Mr. Crouther!* This way! Here!"

A heavy-set, broad-shouldered man with a mottled complexion shoved his way, cursing, through the crowd. He had just reached the entrance of the window when the policeman who had dispersed the crowd on the sidewalk ran up and dashed after him into the window. The three men disappeared, the bluecoat slamming the door shut behind them.

The bearded man stood aside. "There's been a terrible accident, Crouther. . . . Glad you're here, officer. . . . My God, what an affair!"

The head store detective pounded across the room and glared down at the two women. "What happened to the coon, Mr. Lav-ery?" he bellowed at the bearded man.

"Fainted, I suppose!"

"Here, Crouther, let me take a look," said the policeman, unceremoniously pushing Lavery aside. He bent over the body of the woman who had tumbled from the bed.

Crouther cleared his throat importantly. "Listen here, Bush. This is no time to make an examination. We oughtn't to touch a thing until Headquarters is notified. Mr. Lav-ery and me—we'll stand guard here while you use the 'phone. Go ahead now, Bush, don't be an egg!"

The policeman stood undecidedly for a moment, scratched his head, and finally left the room with hurried steps.

"This is one sweet mess," growled Crouther. "What happened here, Mr. Lav-ery? Who in hell is *this* woman?"

Lavery started nervously and plucked at his beard with long thin fingers. "Why, don't you know? But of course not. . . . Good Heavens, Crouther, what are we to do?"

Crouther frowned. "Now don't go getting yourself all excited, Mr. Lav-ery. This is a police job, pure and simple. Lucky I was on the scene so quick. We gotta wait for the detail from Headquarters. Just take it easy now—"

Lavery regarded the store detective coldly. "I'm perfectly all right, Mr. Crouther," he said. "I suggest—" he weighted the word with authority—"that you immediately marshal your store forces to keep order on the main floor. Make it appear as if nothing out of the way has happened. Call Mr. MacKenzie. Send somebody to notify Mr. French and the Board of Directors. I understand they're having a meeting upstairs. This is—an affair of a grave nature—graver than you know. Go now!"

Crouther looked at Lavery rebelliously, shook his head, and made for the door. As he opened it a small dark man with a physician's bag stepped into the room. He glanced quickly around and without a word crossed to the side of the two bodies.

He favored the Negress with a scant glance and a feeling of the pulse. He spoke without looking up.

"Here—Mr. Lavery, is it?—you'll have to help—get one of the men outside to give you a hand—the Negress has merely fainted—get her a glass of water and put her on that divan there—send somebody for one of the nurses from the infirmary. . . ."

Lavery nodded. He went to the door and looked out over the whispering crowd on the floor.

"Mr. MacKenzie! Here, please!"

A middle-aged man with a pleasant Scotch face hurried up and into the room. "Help me, please," said Lavery.

The doctor busied himself over the body of the other woman. His movements concealed her face. Lavery and MacKenzie picked up the reviving form of the Negress and carried her to the divan. A floorwalker outside was dispatched for a glass of water and reappeared in a twinkling. The Negress gulped, groaned.

The doctor looked up gravely. "This woman is dead," he announced. "Has been for quite a while. What's more, she's been shot. Got it in the heart. Looks like murder, Mr. Lavery!"

"Nom du chien!" muttered Lavery. His face was sickly white.

MacKenzie scurried across the room to look down at the huddled corpse. He fell back with a cry.

"Good God! *It's Mrs. French!*"

5

"AND ALL THE KING'S MEN"

The window-door opened quickly and two men stepped in. One, a tall lank individual smoking a blackish cigar, stopped short, peered about him, and then, catching sight of the body, immediately advanced to the farther side of the wall bed, on the floor by which lay the dead woman. He favored the little physician with a keen glance, nodded and without further ado dropped to his knees. After a moment he looked up.

"The store doctor, are you?"

The physician nodded nervously. "Yes. I've made a superficial examination. She's dead. I—"

"I can see that," said the newcomer. "I'm Prouty, Assistant Medical Examiner. Stand by, doctor." Again he bent over the body, opening his bag with one hand.

The second of the two men who had arrived was an iron-jawed giant. He had stopped at the door, softly prodding it shut behind him. Now his eyes flickered over the frozen faces of Lavery, MacKenzie and the store doctor. His own face was cold and harsh and expressionless.

It was not until Dr. Prouty began his examination that this man vitalized into action. He took a purposeful step forward toward MacKenzie, but stopped suddenly as the door shivered under a violent pounding.

"Come in!" he said sharply, standing between the door and the bed, so that the body was hidden from the newcomers.

The door was flung aside. A small army of men surged forward. The tall man blocked their path.

"Just a moment," he said slowly. "We can't have so many people in here. Who are you?"

Cyrus French, flushed and choleric, snapped: "I am the owner of this establishment, and these gentlemen all have a right to be here. They are the Board of Directors—this is Mr. Crouther, our head store detective—stand aside, please."

The tall man did not move. "Mr. French, eh? Board of Directors? . . . Hello, Crouther. . . . Who is this?" He pointed to Westley Weaver, who hovered about the edge of the group, a trifle pale.

"Mr. Weaver, my secretary," said French impatiently. "Who are you, sir? What's happened here? Let me pass."

"I see." The tall man reflected a moment, hesitated, then said firmly, "I'm Sergeant Velie of the Homicide Squad. Sorry, Mr. French, but you'll have to abide by my orders here. Come in, but don't touch anything and let me give the orders." He stepped aside. He seemed to be waiting for something with unwearying patience.

Lavery ran forward, his eyes distended as he saw Cyrus French stride toward the bed. He intercepted the old man, grasped his lapel.

"Mr. French—please do not look—just now. . . ."

French petulantly brushed him aside. "Let me be, Lavery! What is this—a conspiracy? Ordered about in my own store!" He proceeded to the bed, and Lavery fell back, a resigned look on his mobile face. Suddenly, as if struck by a thought, he took John Gray aside, speaking in the director's ear. Gray paled, stood transfixed to the spot, then with an indistinct cry he leaped to French's side.

He was just in time. The store owner had bent curiously over Dr. Prouty's shoulder, taken one look at the woman on the floor, and collapsed without a sound. Gray caught him as he sank. Lavery sprang forward and assisted in carrying the old man's limp body to a chair on the other side of the room.

A nurse in white cap and gown had slipped into the room and was ministering to the hysterical Negress on the divan. She went quickly over to French, slipped a vial under his nose, and instructed Lavery to chafe his hands. Gray paced nervously up and down, muttering to himself. The store doctor hurried over to help the nurse.

The directors and the secretary, huddled together in a horror-struck group, moved hesitantly toward the body. Weaver and Marchbanks cried out together at seeing the woman's face. Zorn bit his lip and turned away. Trask averted his face in horror. Then, in the same mechanical motion, they moved slowly backward to a corner, glancing helplessly at each other.

Velie crooked a huge finger at Crouther. "What have you done?"

The store detective grinned. "Taken care of all the details, don't you worry. I've got all my men scrambled on the main floor and they've scattered the mob. Got everything well in hand. Trust Bill Crouther for that, Sergeant! Won't be much for you guys to do, that's a fact."

Velie grunted. "Well, here's something for you to do while we're waiting. Get a big stretch of the main floor roped off right around this section, and keep everybody away. It's a little late now, I suppose, to close the doors. Wouldn't do much good. Whoever did this job is miles away from here by now. Get going, Crouther!"

The store detective nodded, turned away, turned back. "Say, Sergeant—know just who the woman on the floor is? Might help us right now."

"Yes?" Velie smiled frostily. "Can't see how. But it

doesn't take much to figure it out. It's French's wife. Blast it, this is a great place for a murder!"

"No!" Crouther's jaw dropped. "French's wife, hey? The big cheese himself. . . . Well, well!" He stole a glance at the slack figure of French and a moment later his voice resounded through the window as he roared instructions outside.

Silence in the window-room. The group in the corner had not moved. The Negress and French had both been revived—the black woman's eyes rolling wildly as she clung to the starched skirt of the nurse, French's face a pasty white as he half-lay in the chair listening to Gray's low-voiced words of sympathy. Gray himself seemed drained of his queer vitality.

Velie beckoned to MacKenzie, who hovered nervously at Prouty's shoulder.

"You're MacKenzie, the store manager?"

"Yes, Sergeant."

"It's time to get a move on, Mr. MacKenzie." Velie eyed him coldly. "Get a hold on yourself. Somebody's got to keep his wits about him. This is part of your job." The store manager squared his shoulders. "Now listen. This is important and it's got to be done thoroughly." He lowered his voice. "No employees to leave the building— item number one, and I'm holding you responsible for its execution. Number two, check up on all employees who are not at their posts. Number three, make out a list of all employees absent from the store to-day, with the reasons for their absence. Hop to it!"

MacKenzie mumbled submissively, shuffled away.

Velie took Lavery, who stood talking to Weaver, to one side.

"You seem to have some authority here. May I ask who you are?"

"My name is Paul Lavery, and I am exhibiting the modern furniture on display upstairs on the fifth floor.   This room is a sample of my exhibition."

"I see.   Well, you've kept your head, Mr. Lavery.   The dead woman is Mrs. French?"

Lavery averted his eyes.   "Yes, Sergeant.   It was quite a shock to all of us, no doubt.   How in God's name did she ever get—"   He stopped abruptly, worried his lip.

"Did she ever get here, you meant to say?" finished Velie grimly.   "Well now, that's a question, isn't it?   I— Just a moment, Mr. Lavery!"

He turned on his heel and walked swiftly to the door to greet a group of new arrivals.

"Morning, Inspector.   Morning, Mr. Queen!   Glad you've come, sir.   You'll find things in a rotten mess."   He stepped aside and waved a large hand at the room and its assorted occupants.   "Pretty, eh, sir?   More like a wake than the scene of a crime!"   It was a long speech for Velie.

Inspector Richard Queen—small, pert, like a white-thatched bird—followed the circuit of Velie's hand with his eyes.

"My goodness!" he exclaimed in annoyance.   "How did so many people get into this room?   I'm surprised at you, Thomas."

"Inspector."   Queen paused at Velie's deep voice.   "I thought it might—" his voice became inaudible as he murmured a few words in the Inspector's ear.

"Yes, yes, I see, Thomas."   The Inspector patted his arm.   "Tell me soon.   Let's have a peep at the body."

He trotted across the room and slipped to the far side of the wall-bed.   Prouty, his hands busy on the corpse, nodded in greeting.

"Murder," he said.   "No sign of the revolver."

The Inspector peered intently into the ghastly face of the dead woman, ran his eye over the disarranged clothing.

"Well, we'll have the boys look a little later. Keep going, Doc." He sighed and returned to Velie at the other side of the room.

"Now let's have it, Thomas. From the beginning." His little eyes roved judiciously about the men in the room as Velie rapidly outlined in an undertone the events of the past half-hour. . . . Outside a body of plainclothes men and a scattering of uniformed policemen could be seen. The patrolman, Bush, was among them.

Ellery Queen shut the door and leaned against it. He was tall and sparely built, with athletic hands, taper-fingered. He wore immaculate grey tweeds and carried a stick and a light coat. On his thin nose perched a pince-nez. Above it rose a forehead of wide proportions, white and untroubled. His hair was smoothly black. From the pocket of the coat protruded a small volume in faded covers.

He looked curiously at each person in the room—curiously and slowly, as if he enjoyed his scrutiny. The characteristics of each individual as his eyes passed from one to another he seemed to store away in a corner of his brain. His examination was almost visibly digestive. Yet it was not entirely concentrated, for he listened intently to each word of Velie's recital to the Inspector. Suddenly his eyes, in their panoramic course, met those of Westley Weaver, who stood miserably in a corner leaning against the wall.

Into the eyes of each leaped instant recognition. They started forward simultaneously, hands outstretched.

"Ellery Queen. Thank God!"

"By the Seven Virgins of Theophilus—Westley Weaver!" They wrung each other's hands with undisguised pleasure. Inspector Queen glanced their way, quizzically; then he turned back to hear the last of Velie's rumbled comments.

"It's awfully good seeing your classic features again, Ellery," murmured Weaver. His face dropped back into strained lines. "Are you—is that the Inspector?"

"In the indefatigable flesh, Westley," said Ellery. "The pater himself, with his nose to the scent.—But tell me things, boy. It's—O Tempes!—isn't it five or six years since we last met?"

"All of that, Ellery. I'm glad you're here, for more than one reason, El. It's a little comforting," said Weaver in a low voice. "This—this thing. . . ."

Ellery's smile faded. "The tragedy, eh, Westley? Tell me—how do you figure in it? You didn't kill the lady, by any chance?" His tone was jocular, but behind it was a certain anxiety which his father, ears cocked, found a little strange.

"Ellery!" Weaver's eyes met his straightforwardly. "That isn't even funny." Then the look of misery crept in again. "It's awful, El. Just awful. You haven't any idea how awful it is. . . ."

Ellery patted Weaver's arm lightly, removed his pince-nez with an absent motion. "I'll get it all in a moment, Westley. I'll hold *tête-à-tête* conversation with you later. Hang on, won't you? I see my father signaling me frantically. Chin up, Wes!" He moved away, again smiling. Weaver's eyes held a glimmer of hope as he dropped back against the wall.

The Inspector murmured to his son for a moment. Ellery made a low-voiced reply. Then Ellery strode over to the farther side of the bed and stood over Prouty, watching the medical examiner as he worked swiftly over the body.

The Inspector turned to the assembled crowd in the room. "A little quiet now, please," he said.

A thick curtain of silence dropped over the room.

6

TESTIMONY

The Inspector stepped forward.

"It will be necessary for every one to wait here," he began sententiously, "while we make some elementary but essential investigations. Let me say at once, to forestall any claims of special privilege that may be made, that this is undoubtedly a case of murder. In cases of murder, the most serious charge that can be brought against an individual, the law is no respecter either of persons or institutions. A woman is dead of violence. Somebody killed her. That somebody may be miles away at this moment, or in this room now. You can understand, gentlemen"—and his tired eyes considered the five directors especially—"that the sooner we get down to business, the better. Too much time has been lost already."

He went abruptly to the door, opened it, and called in a penetrating voice: "Piggott! Hesse! Hagstrom! Flint! Johnson! Ritter!"

Six detectives strolled into the room. Ritter, a burly man, closed the door behind him.

"Hagstrom, your book." The detective whipped out a small notebook and a pencil.

"Piggott, Hesse, Flint—the room!" He added something in a low tone. The three detectives grinned and dispersed to different portions of the room. They began a slow, methodical search of furniture, floors, walls.

"Johnson—the bed!" One of the two remaining men went directly to the wall-bed and began to examine its contents.

"Ritter—stand by." The Inspector slipped his hands into a coat pocket and withdrew his brown old snuff-box. He filled his nostrils with aromatic snuff, inhaled deeply and restored the box to his pocket.

"Now!" he said, and glared about the room at his thoroughly cowed audience. Ellery met his eye for an instant and smiled slightly. "Now! You, there!" He pointed an accusing finger at the Negress, who was staring at him with wide eyes, her skin greyish-violet with fright.

"Yassuh," she quavered, tottering to her feet.

"Your name?" snapped Queen.

"Di—Diana Johnson, suh," she whispered, gazing at him in scared fascination.

"Diana Johnson, eh?" The Inspector took a step forward, leveled his finger at her. "Why did you open this bed at twelve-fifteen today?"

"Ah—Ah had to, suh," she faltered. "Dat was—"

Lavery waved his arm hesitantly at the Inspector. "I can explain that—"

"Sir!" Lavery colored, then smiled cynically. "Go on, Johnson."

"Yassuh, yassuh! Dat was de reg'lar time fo' de exhibition, suh. Ah always comes out into dis room at a couple o' minutes befo' twelve an' gets ready fo' de exhibition, suh." The words tumbled out. "An' den, when Ah'd just got through showin' dis contraption hyah"— she indicated the divan, which seemed a combination of sofa, bed and bookcase—"Ah goes to de wall, pushes de button, and den dat—dat dead 'ooman falls out right at mah feet. . . ." She shuddered and drew a deep breath, glancing at the detective Hagstrom, who was busily taking down her words in shorthand.

"You had no idea the body was inside when you pressed the button, Miss Johnson?" demanded the Inspector.

The Negress's eyes flew wide open. "Nosuh! Ah wouldn't 'a' teched dat bed fo' a thousan' dolluhs ef Ah'd know dat!" The uniformed nurse giggled nervously. She sobered instantly as the Inspector stared in her direction.

"Very well. That's all." He turned to Hagstrom.

"Got every word?" The detective nodded, maintaining a severe silence as the old man winked fleetingly at him. Inspector Queen turned back to the group. "Nurse, take Diana Johnson to your hospital upstairs and keep her there until I give the word!"

The Negress stumbled in her eagerness to leave the window-room. The nurse followed somewhat sulkily behind.

The Inspector had Patrolman Bush summoned. The policeman saluted, answered a few questions about what had occurred on the sidewalk at the moment the body fell, and subsequently inside the window-room, and was commissioned to go back to his post on Fifth Avenue.

"Crouther!" The store detective was standing by the side of Ellery and Dr. Prouty. He now slouched forward and stared boldly at Queen. "You're the head store detective?"

"Yes, Inspector." He shuffled his feet and grinned, displaying tobacco-stained teeth.

"Sergeant Velie tells me that he instructed you to scatter your men through the main floor soon after the body was discovered. Have you attended to that?"

"Yes, sir. Got a squad of a half-dozen store detectives workin' outside, and put every available 'spotter' on the job, too," replied Crouther promptly. "But they haven't turned up anybody suspicious yet."

"Could hardly expect it." The Inspector took another pinch of snuff. "Tell me just what you found when you came in here."

"Well, Inspector, the first I knew about the murder was when one of my detectives 'phoned me upstairs in my office that something had happened outside on the sidewalk—riot or something. I came down right away and as I passed this window I heard Mr. Lavery yell for me. I ran in, saw the body layin' here, and the darky fainting on the floor. Bush, the officer on the beat, came in right after me. . I told 'em nothing ought to be touched until the Headquarters men got here, and then got right after the mobs outside, and generally kept an eye on everything until Sergeant Velie got here. I followed his orders after that, that's a fact. I—"

"Here, here, Crouther, that's plenty," said the Inspector. "Don't leave, I may be able to use you later. Short-handed enough as it is, the Lord knows. A department store!" He muttered under his breath and turned to Dr. Prouty.

"Doc! Ready for me yet?"

The kneeling police doctor nodded. "Just about, Inspector. Want me to shoot the works right here?" He seemed tacitly to question the wisdom of imparting his information before a group of laymen.

"Might as well," grunted Queen. "It can't be very enlightening."

"Don't know about that." Prouty stood up with a groan, took a firmer grip on the black cigar between his teeth.

"Woman was killed by two bullets," he said deliberately, "both from a Colt .38 revolver. Probably from the same gun—hard to tell exactly without putting them under the microscope." He held up two encarmined blobs of metal, blunted completely out of shape. The Inspector took them, turned them over in his fingers, and in silence handed them to Ellery, who immediately bent over them with a curious eagerness.

Prouty stared dreamily down at the body, plunging his hands into his pockets. "One bullet," he continued, "entered the body directly in the center of the cardiac region. Nice jagged *pericardial* wound, Inspector. Smashed the *sternum* bone, pierced the *pericardial septum*, which is the membrane separating the *pericardium* from the main body cavity, then took the logical course through—first the fibrous layer of the *pericardium*, then the serous inner layer, and finally the anterior tip of the heart, where the great vessels are. Spilled quite a bit of the yellow *pericardial* fluid, too. Bullet entered the body at an angle and it's left a fearful wound. . . ."

"Then death was instantaneous?" asked Ellery. "The second bullet was unnecessary?"

"Quite," said Prouty dryly. "Death would be instantaneous from either wound. As a matter of fact, the second bullet—maybe it's not the second, though, I can't tell of course which hit her first—bullet number two made a better job of it than even bullet number one. Because it penetrated the *precordia,* which is the region a little below the heart and above the abdomen. This is also a ragged wound, and since the *precordial* sector takes in muscles and blood-vessels of major importance, it's as vital a spot as the heart itself. . . ." Prouty stopped suddenly. His eyes strayed almost with irritation to the dead woman on the floor.

"Was the revolver fired close to the body?" put in the Inspector.

"No powder stains, Inspector," said Prouty, still regarding the corpse with a frown.

"Were both bullets fired from the same spot?" asked Ellery.

"Hard to say. The lateral angles are similar, indicating that whoever fired both bullets stood to the right of the woman. But the downward course of the bullets disturbs me. They're too much alike."

"What do you mean?" demanded Ellery, leaning forward.

"Well," growled Prouty, biting on his cigar, "if the woman were in exactly the same position when both shots were fired—assuming that both shots were fired almost simultaneously, of course—there should be a greater *downward* angle to the *precordial* wound than to the *pericardial.*

Because the *precordia* is located below the heart, and the gun would have to be aimed lower. . . . Well, perhaps I shouldn't say these things at all. There are any number of explanations, I suppose, for that difference in angle. Ought to have Ken Knowles look over the bullets and the wounds, though."

"He'll get his chance," said the Inspector with a sigh. "Is that all, Doc?"

Ellery looked up from another scrutiny of the two bullets. "How long has she been dead?"

Prouty replied promptly: "About twelve hours, I should say. I'll be able to fix the time of death more accurately after the autopsy. But she certainly died no earlier than midnight and probably no later than two in the morning."

"Through now?" asked Inspector Queen patiently.

"Yes. But there's one thing that has me a little. . . ." Prouty set his jaw. "There's something queer here, Inspector. From what I know of *precordial* wounds I can't believe that this one should have bled so little. You've noticed, I suppose, that the clothing above both wounds is stiff with coagulated blood, but not so much of it as you might expect. At least as a medical man might expect."

"Why?"

"I've seen plenty of *precordial* wounds," said Prouty calmly, "and they're messy, Inspector. Bleed like hell. In fact, especially in this case, where the hole is blasted pretty large, due to the angle, there should be pools and pools of it. The *pericardial* would bleed freely, but not profusely. But the other—I say, there's something queer here, and I thought I'd call it to your attention."

Ellery shot his father a warning glance as the old man opened his mouth to reply. The Inspector clamped his lips together and dismissed Prouty with a nod. Ellery returned the two bullets to Prouty, who put them carefully into his bag.

The police doctor unhurriedly covered the body with a sheet from the hanging bed and departed, his last words a promise to hurry the morgue wagon.

"Is the store physician here?" Queen asked.

The small dark doctor stepped uncertainly forward from a corner. His teeth gleamed as he said, "Yes, sir?"

"Have you anything to add to Dr. Prouty's analysis, doctor?" questioned Queen, with disarming gentleness.

"Not a thing, not a thing, sir," said the store physician, looking uneasily at Prouty's retreating figure. "A precise if somewhat sketchy diagnosis. The bullets entered—"

"Thank you, doctor." Inspector Queen turned his back on the little physician and beckoned imperiously to the store detective.

"Crouther," he asked in a low tone, "who's your head night-watchman?"

"O'Flaherty—Pete O'Flaherty, Inspector."

"How many watchmen are on duty here at night?"

"Four. O'Flaherty tends the night-door on the 39th Street side, Ralska and Powers do the rounds, and Bloom is on duty at the 39th Street night freight-entrance."

"Thanks." The Inspector turned to Detective Ritter. "Get hold of this man MacKenzie, the store manager, find the home addresses of O'Flaherty, Ralska, Powers and Bloom, and get 'em down here as fast as a cab will carry them. Scoot!" Ritter lumbered away.

Ellery suddenly straightened, adjusted his pince-nez more firmly on his nose, and strode over to his father. They held a whispered colloquy for a moment, whereupon Ellery quietly retreated to his vantage-point near the bed and the Inspector crooked his finger at Westley Weaver.

"Mr. Weaver," he asked, "I take it that you are Mr. French's confidential secretary?"

"Yes, sir," responded Weaver warily.

The Inspector glanced sidewise at Cyrus French, huddled exhausted in the chair. John Gray's small white hand was solicitously patting French's arm. "I'd rather not bother Mr. French at this time with questions.—You were with him all morning?"

"Yes, sir."

"Mr. French was not aware of Mrs. French's presence in the store?"

"No, sir!" The response was immediate and sharp. Weaver regarded Queen with suspicious eyes.

"Were you?"

"I? No, sir!"

"Hmmm!" The Inspector's chin sank on his chest, and he communed with himself for an instant. Suddenly his finger shot toward the group of directors on the other side of the room. "How about you gentlemen? Any of you know that Mrs. French was here—this morning or last night?"

There was a chorus of horrified noes. Cornelius Zorn's face grew red. He began to protest angrily.

"Please!" The Inspector's tone flung them back in silence. "Mr. Weaver. How is it that all these gentlemen are present in the store this morning? They're not here every day, are they?"

Weaver's frank face lightened, as if from relief. "All of our directors are active in the management of the store, Inspector. They're here every day, if only for an hour or so. As for this morning, there was a directors' meeting in Mr. French's private apartment upstairs."

"Eh?" Queen seemed pleased as well as startled. "A private apartment upstairs, you say? On what floor?"

"The sixth—that's the top floor of the store."

Ellery stirred into life. Again he crossed the floor, again he whispered to his father, and again the old man nodded.

"Mr. Weaver," continued the Inspector, a note of eagerness in his voice, "how long were you and the Board in Mr. French's private apartment this morning?"

Weaver seemed surprised at the question. "Why, all morning, Inspector. I arrived at about eight-thirty, Mr. French at about nine, and the other directors at a little past eleven."

"I see." The Inspector mused. "Did you leave the apartment at any time during the morning?"

"No, sir." The reply was snapped back at him.

"And the others—Mr. French, the directors?" pressed the Inspector patiently.

"No, sir! We were all there until one of the store detectives notified us that an accident had occurred here. And I must say, sir—"

"Westley, Westley . . ." murmured Ellery chidingly, and Weaver turned to him with startled eyes. They fell before the meaning glance of Ellery, and Weaver bit his lip nervously. He did not finish what he had begun to say.

"Now, sir." The Inspector seemed to be enjoying himself in a tired way—utterly disregarding the bewildered eyes of the many people in the room. "Now, sir! Be very careful. At what time did this notification come?"

"At twelve-twenty-five," replied Weaver in a calmer tone.

"Very well.—Every one then left the apartment?" Weaver nodded. "Did you lock the door?"

"The door closed after us, Inspector."

"And the apartment remained that way, unguarded?"

"Not at all," said Weaver promptly. "At the beginning of the conference this morning, at Mr. French's suggestion, I got one of the store detectives to stand guard outside the apartment door. He is probably still there, because his

orders were specific. In fact, I remember seeing him lounging about outside when we all rushed out to see what was
the matter down here."

"*Very* good!" beamed the old man. "A store detective,
you say? Reliable?"

"Absolutely, Inspector," said Crouther, from his corner.
"Sergeant Velie knows him, too. Jones is his name—an
ex-policeman—used to be on a beat with Velie." The Inspector looked at the Sergeant inquiringly; he nodded in
confirmation.

"Thomas," said Queen with one hand digging into his
side-pocket for a pinch of snuff, "see to it, will you? See
if this Jones fellow is still there, if he's been there all the
time, if he's seen anything, if any one tried to get into the
apartment since Mr. French, Mr. Weaver and the other
gentlemen left. And take one of the boys along to relieve
him—to relieve him, you understand?"

Velie grunted stonily and tramped out of the window-
room. As he left, a policeman entered, saluted Inspector
Queen and reported, "There's a 'phone call out there in the
leather-goods department for a Mr. Westley Weaver, Inspector."

"What's that? Call?" The Inspector turned on Weaver,
who stood miserably in a corner.

Weaver straightened. "Probably from Krafft of the
Comptroller's office," he said. "I was to give him a report
this morning, and the meeting and everything that happened afterward drove it out of my mind. . . . May I
leave?"

Queen hesitated, his glance flickering toward Ellery, who
was absently fingering his pince-nez. Ellery gave a slight
nod.

"Go ahead," the Inspector growled to Weaver. "But
come right back."

Weaver followed the policeman to the leather-goods

counter directly facing the door of the window-room. A clerk eagerly handed the telephone to him.

"Hello—Krafft? This is Weaver speaking. I'm sorry about that report— Who? Oh."

A curious change came over his face as he heard Marion French's voice over the wire. He lowered his voice immediately and bent over the instrument. The policeman, lounging behind him, surreptitiously shuffled closer, trying to catch the conversation.

"Why, what's the matter, dear?" asked Marion, a note of anxiety in her voice. "Is anything wrong? I tried to get you at the apartment, but there was no answer. The operator had to search for you. . . . I thought father had a directors' meeting this morning."

"Marion!" Weaver's voice was insistent. "I really can't stop to explain now. Something's happened, dearest— something so . . ." He stopped, seemed to be wrestling mentally with some problem. His lips tightened. "Sweetheart, will you do something for me?"

"But, Wes dear," came the girl's anxious voice, "whatever is the matter? Has anything happened to father?"

"No—no." Weaver hunched desperately over the telephone. "Be my own honey and don't ask questions now. . . . Where are you now?"

"Why, at home, dear. But, Wes, what *is* the trouble?" There was a frightened catch in her voice. "Has it anything to do with Winifred or Bernice? They're not at home, Wes—haven't been all night. . . ." Then she laughed a little. "But there! I shan't worry you, dearest. I'll take a cab and be down in fifteen minutes."

"I knew you would." Weaver almost sobbed in a tense relief. "Whatever happens, sweet, I love you, I love you, do you understand?"

"Westley! You silly boy—you've frightened me out of my wits. Good-by now—I'll be downtown in a jiffy."

There was a tender little sound through the receiver—it might have been a kiss—and Weaver hung up with a sigh.

The policeman jumped back as Weaver turned—jumped back with a broad grin. Weaver flushed furiously, started to speak, then shook his head.

"There's a young lady coming down here, officer," he said swiftly. "She'll be here in about a quarter of an hour. Won't you please let me know the moment she gets here? She's Miss Marion French. I'll be in the window."

The bluecoat lost his grin. "Well now," he said slowly, scraping his jaw, "I just don't know about that. Guess you'll have to tell the Inspector about it. *I* haven't the authority."

He marched Weaver back into the window-room against the young man's protests at the heavy hand on his arm.

"Inspector," he said respectfully, still grasping Weaver's arm, "this feller wants me to let him know when a certain young lady by the name of Miss Marion French gets here."

Queen looked up in surprise, a surprise that deepened rapidly into brusqueness. "Was that telephone call from your Mr. Krafft?" he asked Weaver.

Before Weaver could speak, the policeman interposed: "Not by a long sight, sir. 'Twas a lady, and I think he called her 'Marion.' "

"Look here, Inspector!" said Weaver hotly, shaking off the bluecoat's hand. "This is asinine. I thought the call was from Mr. Krafft, but it was Miss French—Mr. French's daughter. A—a semi-business call. And I took the liberty of asking her to come down here immediately. That's all. Is that a crime? As for letting me know when she arrives —I naturally want to spare her the shock of walking into this place and seeing her step-mother's dead body on the floor."

The Inspector took a pinch of snuff, glancing mildly from Weaver to Ellery. "I see. I see. I'm sorry, Mr.

Weaver. . . . That's right, isn't it, officer?" he snapped, whirling on the bluecoat.

"Yes, sir! Heard it all plain as day. He's telling the truth."

"And mighty fortunate for him he is," grumbled the Inspector. "Stand back, Mr. Weaver. We'll attend to the young lady when she arrives. . . . Now then!" he cried, rubbing his hands, "Mr. French!"

The old man looked up in bleary bewilderment, his eyes blank and staring.

"Mr. French, is there anything you would like to say that might clear up some of this mystery?"

"I—I—I—beg—your—pardon?" stammered French, raising his head with an effort from the back-cushion of the chair. He seemed stricken by his wife's death to the point of imbecility.

Queen regarded him with pity, looked into the eyes of John Gray, whose face was threatening, muttered, "Never mind," and squared his shoulders. "Ellery, my son, how about a careful look-see at the body?" He peered at Ellery from beneath overhung brows.

Ellery stirred. "Lookers-on," he said clearly, "see more than players. And if you think that quotation is inept, dad, you don't know your son's favorite author, Anonymous. Play on!"

7

THE CORPSE

Inspector Queen moved over to the other side of the room, where the body lay between the bed and the window. Waving aside the detective Johnson, who was rummaging among the bedclothes, the old man knelt on the floor beside the dead woman. He removed the white sheet.

Ellery bent over his father's shoulder, his gaze detached but characteristically panoramic.

The body lay in an oddly crumpled position, the left arm outstretched, the right slightly crooked beneath the back. The head was in profile, a brown toque-style hat pushed pathetically over one eye. Mrs. French had been a small slender woman, with delicate hands and feet. The eyes were fixed in a sort of bewildered glare, wide open. The mouth drooled; a thin trickle of blood, now dark and dry, streaked the chin.

The clothes were simple and severe, but rich in quality, as might be expected from a woman of Mrs. French's age and position. There was a light brown cloth coat, trimmed at the collar and cuffs with brown fox; a dark tan dress of a jersey material, with a breast and waist design of orange and brown; brown silk stockings and a pair of uncompromising brown walking shoes.

The Inspector looked up.

"Notice the mud on her shoes, El?" he asked *sotto voce*.

Ellery nodded. "Doesn't take a heap of perspicacity," he remarked. "It rained all day yesterday; remember the downpour last night? No wonder the poor lady wet her patrician feet. As a matter of fact, you can see traces of the wet even on the trimming of the toque.—Yes, dad, Mrs. French was out in the rain yesterday. Not very important."

"Why not?" the old man asked, his hands softly moving aside the collar of the coat.

"Because she probably wet her shoes and hat in crossing the sidewalk to the store," retorted Ellery. "What of it?"

The Inspector did not reply. His seeking hand plunged suddenly beneath the coat-collar and reappeared with a filmy, color-clouded scarf.

"Here's something," he said, turning the gauze-like material over in his hands. "Must have slipped down inside the coat when she tumbled out of the bed." An exclamation escaped him. On one corner of the scarf was a silk-embroidered monogram. Ellery leaned farther forward over his father's shoulder.

"*M.F.*," he said. He straightened up, frowning, saying nothing.

The Inspector turned his head toward the group of directors at the other side of the room. They were huddled together, watching his every gesture. At his movement they started guiltily and averted their heads.

"What was Mrs. French's first name?" Queen questioned the group; and as if each one had been addressed individually, there was an instant chorus of "Winifred!"

"Winifred, eh?" muttered the old man, letting his eyes return fleetingly to the body. Then he fixed Weaver with his grey eyes.

"Winifred, eh?" he repeated. Weaver bobbed his head mechanically. He seemed horrified at the wisp of silk in the Inspector's hand. "Winifred what? Any middle name or initials?"

"Winifred—Winifred Marchbanks French," stammered the secretary.

The Inspector nodded curtly. Rising, he strode over to Cyrus French, who was watching him with dull, uncomprehending eyes.

"Mr. French—" Queen shook the millionaire's shoulder gently—"Mr. French, is this your wife's scarf?" He held the scarf up before French's eyes. "Do you understand me, sir? Is this scarf Mrs. French's?"

"Eh? I— Let me see it!" The old man snatched it in a sort of frenzy from the Inspector's hand. He bent over it avidly, pulled it smooth, examined the monogram with feverish fingers—and slumped back in his chair.

"Is it, Mr. French?" pursued the Inspector, taking the scarf from him.

"No." It was a flat, colorless, indifferent negative.

The Inspector turned toward the silent group. "Can any one here identify this scarf?" He held it high. There was no answer. The Inspector repeated his question, glaring at each one individually. Of them all, only Westley Weaver averted his glance.

"So! Weaver, eh? No nonsense, now, young man!" snapped Queen, grasping the secretary by the arm. "What do the letters *M.F.* stand for—Marion French?"

The young man gulped, sent an agonized glance toward Ellery, who returned the glance commiseratingly, looked at old Cyrus French, who was mumbling to himself. . . .

"You can't believe she had anything to do—to do with it!" cried Weaver, shaking his arm free. "It's absurd—crazy! . . . You *can't* believe she had anything to do with this, Inspector. She's too fine, too young, too—"

"Marion French." The Inspector turned toward John Gray. "Mr. French's daughter, I believe Mr. Weaver said before?"

Gray nodded sullenly. Cyrus French suddenly attempted to leap from his chair. He uttered a hoarse cry. "My God, no! Not Marion! Not Marion!" His eyes blazed as Gray and Marchbanks, the directors nearest the old man, jumped to support his quivering body. The spasm lasted for a brief moment; he collapsed into his chair.

Inspector Queen returned without a word to his examination of the dead woman. Ellery had been a silent witness of the little drama, his sharp eyes flitting from face to face as it unfolded. Now he sent a glance of reassurance at Weaver, who was leaning abjectly against a table, and then stooped to pick up an object from the floor which was almost hidden by the dead woman's tumbled skirt.

It was a small handbag of dark brown suède, monogrammed with the initials *W.M.F.* Ellery sat down on the edge of the bed and turned the bag over in his hands. Curiously he lifted the flap and began to spread the contents of the bag on the mattress. He removed a small change-purse, a gold vanity-case, a lace handkerchief, a gold card-case, all monogrammed *W.M.F.*, and finally a silver-chased lipstick.

The Inspector looked up. "What's that you have there?" he asked sharply.

"Bag of the deceased," murmured Ellery. "Would you care to examine it?"

"Would I—" The Inspector glared at his son in mock heat. "Ellery, sometimes you try me beyond patience!"

Ellery handed it over with a smile. The old man examined the bag minutely. He pawed over the articles on the bed and gave up in disgust.

"Nothing there that I can see," he snorted. "And I'm—"

"No?" Ellery's tone was provocative.

"What do you mean?" asked his father with a change of tone, looking back at the contents of the bag. "Purse, vanity, hanky, card-case, lipstick—what's interesting there?"

Ellery faced about squarely so that his back hid the articles on the bed from the observation of the others. He picked up the lipstick with care and offered it to his father. The old man took it cautiously, suspiciously. Suddenly an exclamation escaped him.

"Exactly—*C*," murmured Ellery. "What do you make of it?"

The lipstick was large and deep. On the cap was a chastely engraved initial, *C*. The Inspector peered at it in some astonishment and made as if to question the men in the room. But Ellery halted him with a warning gesture and took the lipstick from his father's fingers. He unscrewed the initialed cap and twisted the body of the stick until a half-inch of red paste was visible above the orifice. His eyes shifted toward the dead woman's face. They brightened at what they saw.

He knelt quickly by his father's side, their bodies still shielding their movements from the eyes of the onlookers.

"Have a peep at this, dad," he said in an undertone, offering the lipstick. The old man looked at it in a puzzled way.

"Poisoned?" he asked. "But that's impossible—how could you tell without an analysis?"

"No, no!" exclaimed Ellery in the same low tone. "The color, dad—the color!"

The Inspector's face lightened. He looked from the stick in Ellery's hand to the dead woman's lips. The fact was self-evident—the coloring on the lips had not come from the stick in Ellery's possession. The lips were painted a light shade of red, almost pink, whereas the stick itself was a dark carmine in shade.

"Here, El—let me have that!" said the Inspector. He took the open stick and swiftly made a red mark on the dead woman's face.

"Different, all right," he muttered. He wiped off the smudge with a corner of the sheet. "But I don't see—"

"There really should be another lipstick, eh?" remarked Ellery lightly, standing up.

The old man snatched at the woman's handbag and went through it once more, hurriedly. No, there was no sign of another lipstick. He motioned to the detective Johnson.

"Find anything in the bed or the closet here, Johnson?"

"Not a thing, Chief."

"Sure? No sign of a lipstick?"

"Nope."

"Piggott! Hesse! Flint!" The three detectives stopped short in their search of the room and crossed to the Inspector's side. The old man repeated his questions. . . .

Nothing. The detectives had found no alien articles in the room.

"Is Crouther here? Crouther!" The store detective hurried over.

"Been out seeing that things were moving in the store," he announced unasked. "Everything's shipshape—boys've been hustling, that's a fact.—What can I do for you, Inspector?"

"Did you see a lipstick around here when you found the body?"

"Lipstick? No, sir! Wouldn't have touched it if I'd seen it anyway. Told everybody to leave things alone. I know that much, Inspector!"

"Mr. Lavery!" The Frenchman sauntered up. No, he had seen no sign of a lipstick. Perhaps the Negress—?

"Hardly! Piggott, send some one up to the infirmary and find out if this Johnson girl saw it."

The Inspector turned back to Ellery with a frowning brow. "Now, that's funny, isn't it, Ellery? Could some one here have appropriated the darned thing?"

Ellery smiled. " 'Honest labor,' as old Tom Dekker had it, 'bears a lovely face,' but I'm very much afraid, dad. . . . No, your efforts in the direction of finding a lipstick thief are wasted. I could almost make a nice conjecture. . . ."

"What *do* you mean, Ellery?" groaned the Inspector. "Where is it, then, if no one took it?"

"We'll come to that in the course of inexorable time," said Ellery imperturbably. "But examine the face of our poor clay again, dad—particularly the labial portion. See anything interesting aside from the color of the lipstick?"

"Eh?" The Inspector turned startled eyes to the corpse. He felt for his snuff-box and nervously took a generous pinch. "No, I can't say that I— By jiminy!" He muttered beneath his breath. "The lips—unfinished. . . ."

"Precisely." Ellery twirled his pince-nez about his finger. "Observed the phenomenon the moment I looked at the body. What amazing juxtaposition of circumstances could have caused a handsome woman still in her prime to leave her lips only half painted?" He pursed his mouth, fell into deep thought. His eyes did not leave the dead woman's lips, which showed the pinkish color of the lipstick on both the upper and lower lip, on the upper two dabs of unsmeared color and on the lower one a dab exactly in the center. Where the lipstick had not yet been smeared, the lips were a sickly purple—the color of unadorned death.

The Inspector passed his hand wearily across his brow just as Piggott returned.

"Well?"

"The colored girl fainted," reported the detective, "just as the body fell out of the wall-bed. Never saw anything, much less a lipstick." Inspector Queen draped the sheet over the body in baffled silence.

8

THE WATCHER

The door opened and Sergeant Velie entered, accompanied by a steady-eyed man dressed in black. This newcomer saluted the Inspector respectfully and stood waiting.

"This is Robert Jones, Inspector," said Velie in his deep clipped tones. "Attached to the store force, and I'll vouch for him personally. Jones was the man called by Mr. Weaver this morning to stand outside the apartment door during the directors' meeting."

"How about it, Jones?" asked Inspector Queen.

"I was ordered to Mr. French's apartment this morning at eleven," replied the store detective. "I was told to stand guard outside and see that no one disturbed the meeting. According to my instructions. . . ."

"And where did your instructions come from?"

"I understood that Mr. Weaver had 'phoned, sir," replied Jones. The Inspector looked at Weaver, who nodded, and then motioned the man to continue.

"According to my instructions," said Jones, "I strolled about outside the apartment without interrupting the meeting. I was in the sixth floor corridor near the apartment until about twelve-fifteen. At that time the door opened and Mr. French, the other directors and Mr. Weaver ran out and took the elevator, going downstairs. They all seemed excited. . . ."

"Did you know why Mr. French, Mr. Weaver and the others ran out of the apartment that way?"

"No, sir. As I said, they seemed excited and paid no attention to me. I didn't hear about Mrs. French being dead until one of the boys dropped by about a half-hour later with the news."

"Did the directors close the door when they left the apartment?"

"The door closed by itself—swung shut."

"So you didn't enter the apartment?"

"No, sir!"

"Did any one come up to the apartment while you stood guard this morning?"

"Not a soul, Inspector. And after the directors left, there was no one except the chap I told you about, who merely spilled his story and went right down again. I've been on duty until five minutes ago, when Sergeant Velie had two of his own men relieve me."

The Inspector mused. "And you're certain no one went into the apartment, Jones? It may be quite important."

"Dead certain, Inspector," replied Jones clearly. "The reason I stayed on after the directors left was because I didn't know exactly what to do under the circumstances, and I've always found it a safe bet to stand pat when something unusual happens."

"Good enough, Jones!" said the Inspector. "That's all."

Jones saluted, went up to Crouther and asked what he was to do. The head store detective, his chest held high, detailed him to help handle the crowds in the store. And Jones departed.

9

THE WATCHERS

The Inspector went quickly to the door and peered over the heads of the seething crowds on the main floor.

"MacKenzie! Is MacKenzie there?" he shouted.

"Right here!" came the faint bellow of the store manager's voice. "Coming!"

Queen trotted back into the room, fumbling for his snuff-box. He eyed the directors almost roguishly; his good humor seemed for the moment to have returned. The occupants of the room, with the exception of Cyrus French, who was still plunged in a deep lethargy of grief and indifference to what was going on, had by this time shaken off some of their horror and were growing restless. Zorn stole surreptitious glances at his heavy gold watch; Marchbanks was pacing belligerently up and down the room; Trask at regular intervals averted his head and gulped down some whisky from a flask in his pocket; Gray, his face as ashen as his hair, stood in silence behind old French's chair. Lavery was very quiet, watching with bright inquisitive eyes the least movement of the Inspector and his men. Weaver, his boyish face strained and lined, seemed to be enduring agonies. He frequently sought Ellery with pleading eyes, as if asking for help which he knew, instinctively, could not be forthcoming.

"I must ask you to have patience for a short time longer,

gentlemen," said the Inspector, smoothing his mustache with the back of his small hand. "We have a few things more to do here—and then we'll see. . . . . Ah! You're MacKenzie, I take it? Are those the watchmen? Bring 'em in, man!"

The middle-aged Scotchman had entered the window-room, herding before him four oldish men with frightened faces and fidgety hands. Ritter made up the rear.

"Yes, Inspector. By the way, I'm having the employees checked up, as Sergeant Velie instructed me to." Mac-Kenzie waved the four men forward. They shuffled a step farther into the room, reluctantly.

"Who's the head night-watchman among you?" demanded the Inspector.

A corpulent old man with fleshy features and placid eyes stepped forward, touching his forehead.

"I am, sor—Peter O'Flaherty's me name."

"Were you on duty last night, O'Flaherty?"

"Yes, sor. That I was."

"What time did you go on?"

"Me reg'lar hour, sor," said the watchman. "Ha'past five. It's O'Shane I relieve at th' desk in the night-office on th' 39th Street side. These boys here"—he indicated the three men behind him with a fat and calloused fore-finger—"they come on with me. They was with me last night, reg'lar."

"I see." The Inspector paused. "O'Flaherty, do you know what has happened?"

"Yes, sor. I've been told. And a shame it is, sor," responded O'Flaherty soberly. He stole a glance at the limp figure of Cyrus French, then jerked his head back toward the Inspector as if he had committed an indiscretion. His cronies followed his gaze, and looked forward again in exactly the same manner.

"Did you know Mrs. French by sight?" asked the Inspector, his keen little eyes studying the old man.

"I did, sor," replied O'Flaherty. "She used to come to th' store sometimes after closing when Mr. French was still here."

"Often?"

"No, sor. Not so very. But I knowed her right enough, sor."

"Hmmm." Inspector Queen relaxed. "Now, O'Flaherty, answer carefully—and truthfully. As truthfully as if you were on the witness-stand.—Did you see Mrs. French last night?"

Silence had fallen in the room—a silence pregnant with beating hearts and racing pulses. All eyes were on the broad mottled face of the old watchman. He licked his lips, seemed to reflect, squared his shoulders.

"Yes, sor," he said, with a little hiss.

"At what time?"

" 'Twas just eleven forty-five, sor," replied O'Flaherty. "Y'see, there ain't but one night entrance to th' store after hours. All th' other doors and exits are ironed up. That one door is on 39th Street, th' Employees' Entrance. There ain't no way but that t'get in or out o' the buildin'. I—"

Ellery moved suddenly, and everybody turned toward him. He smiled deprecatingly at O'Flaherty. "Sorry, dad, but I've just thought of something. . . . O'Flaherty, do I understand you to say that there is only one way into the store after hours—the Employees' Entrance?"

O'Flaherty champed his blue old jaws reflectively. "Why, yes, sor," he said. "And what's wrong about that?"

"Very little," smiled Ellery, "except that I believe there is a night freight-entrance on the 39th Street side as well. . . ."

"Oh, that!" snorted the old watchman. " 'Tain't hardly an entrance, sor. Mostly always shut. So, as I was sayin'—"

Ellery lifted a slender hand. "One moment, O'Flaherty. You say, 'Mostly always shut.' Just what do you mean by that?"

"Well," replied O'Flaherty, scratching his poll, "it's shut down tighter'n a drum all night exceptin' between eleven o'clock and eleven-thirty. So it don't hardly count."

"That's *your* point of view," said Ellery argumentatively. "I thought there must be a good reason for having a special nightwatchman at the spot all night. Who is he?"

"That's Bloom over here," said O'Flaherty. "Bloom, step out, man, and let the gentlemen look ye over."

Bloom, a sturdy middle-aged man with reddish, graying hair, stepped uncertainly forward. "That's me," he said. "Nothin' wrong in my freight department last night, if that's what you wanna know. . . ."

"No?" Ellery eyed him keenly. "Exactly why is the freight-entrance opened between eleven and eleven-thirty?"

"Fer the delivery of groceries an' meats an' such," answered Bloom. "Big turn-over every day in the store restaurant, and then there's the Employees' Restaurant too. Get supplies fresh every night."

"Who is the trucker?" interrupted the Inspector.

"Buckley & Green. Same driver an' unloader every night, sir."

"I see," said the Inspector. "Get it down, Hagstrom, and make a note to question the men on the truck. . . . Anything else, Ellery?"

"Yes." Ellery turned once more to the red-haired nightwatchman. "Tell us just what happens every night when the Buckley & Green truck arrives."

"Well, I go on duty at ten," said Bloom. "At eleven every night the truck rolls up and Johnny Salvatore, the driver, rings the night bell outside the freight door. . . ."

"Is the freight door kept locked after five-thirty?"

MacKenzie, the store manager, interrupted. "Yes, sir. It's automatically locked at closing-time. Never opened till the truck comes up at eleven."

"Go on, Bloom."

"When Johnny rings, I unlock the door—it's sheet iron —and roll 'er up. Then the truck drives inside, an' Marino, the unloader, unpacks the stuff and stores it, while Johnny and myself check it over in my booth near the door. That's all. When they're through, they take the truck out, I unroll the door, and lock it, and just stay there all night."

Ellery pondered. "Does the door remain open while the truck is being unloaded?"

"Sure," said Bloom. "It's only for a half an hour, and besides, nobody could hardly get in without one of us seeing 'em."

"You're sure of that?" asked Ellery sharply. "Positive? Swear to it, man?"

Bloom hesitated. "Well, I don't hardly see how anybody *could*," he said lamely. "Marino's out there unloading, and Johnny and me in the booth right by the door. . . ."

"How many electric lights are there in this freight room?" demanded Ellery.

Bloom looked bewildered. "Why, there's one big light right over where the truck is, and then there's a small one in my booth. Johnny keeps his headlights on, too."

"How big is this freight room?"

"Oh, about seventy-five foot deep by fifty wide. Store emergency trucks are parked there for the night, too."

"How far from your booth does the truck unload?"

"Oh, 'way in, near the back, where there's a chute from the kitchen."

"And one light in all that black expanse," murmured Ellery. "The booth is enclosed, I suppose?"

"Just a glass window facing the inside of the room."

Ellery played with his pince-nez. "Bloom, if I told you to swear that nobody could get into that freight room, past the entrance, without your seeing him, would you do it?"

Bloom smiled in a sickly fashion. "Well, sir," he said, "I don't know as I would."

"Did you see anybody get in last night while the door was open and you and Salvatore were in the booth checking over the goods?"

"No, sir!"

"But somebody might have got in?"

"I—I guess so. . . ."

"One question more," said Ellery genially. "These deliveries are made *every night*, without fail, and at exactly the same hour?"

"Yes, sir. Been that way as long as I can remember."

"Another, if you'll pardon me. Did you lock that freight door last night promptly at eleven-thirty?"

"To the dot." .

"Were you at that door all night?"

"Yes, sir. On my chair, right by the door."

"No disturbance? Didn't hear or see anything suspicious?"

"No, sir."

"If—any one—tried—to—get—out—of—the—building —by—that—door," said Ellery with startling emphasis, "you would have heard and seen him?""

"Sure thing, sir," said Bloom weakly, glancing with despair at MacKenzie.

"Very well, then," drawled Ellery, waving his arm negligently toward Bloom, "the inquisition may proceed,

Inspector." And he stepped back, making furious notes in his book.

The Inspector, who had been listening with a gradually clarifying expression on his face, sighed and said to O'Flaherty, "You were saying that Mrs. French came into the building at eleven-forty-five, O'Flaherty. Let's have the rest of it."

The head nightwatchman wiped his brow with a slightly shaking hand and a dubious glance in Ellery's direction. Then he took up the thread of his story. "Well, I sits at th' night-desk all night—never gets up, while Ralska and Powers here does the rounds every hour. That's me job, sor—an' besides I check out all those who put in overtime, like th' executive people, and such. Yes, sor. I—"

"Easy, O'Flaherty," said the Inspector, with interest. "Tell us just exactly what happened when Mrs. French arrived. You're sure it was eleven-forty-five?"

"Yes, sor. I looked at th' time-clock next th' desk, 'cause I gotta put down all arrivals on me time-sheet. . . ."

"Oh, the time-sheet?" muttered Queen. "Mr. Mac-Kenzie, will you please see that I get last night's time-sheet at once? Even before the report on the employees." MacKenzie nodded and left. "All right, O'Flaherty. Go on."

"Well, sor, through the night-door acrost th' hall I sees a taxi roll up and Mrs. French she steps out. She pays th' driver and knocks. I sees who 'tis and opens quick. She gives me a cheery good-evenin', and asks if Mr. Cyrus French was still in th' buildin'. I says no, ma'am, Mr. Cyrus French'd left early in th' afternoon, as he had, sor, carryin' a brief-case. She thanks me, stops to think a bit, then she says she'll go up to Mr. French's private apartment anyway, and starts to walk out o' th' office toward the private elevator that's only used to go up to th' apartment. I says to her, I says, Kin I get one o' the boys to run th' elevator up for her an' open th' apartment door? She says no thanks, right polite, sor, and rummages in her bag for a minute, as if to see she's got her key. Yes, she had it—she fishes it out o' her bag and shows it to me. Then she—"

"Just a moment, O'Flaherty." The Inspector seemed perturbed. "You say she had a key to the apartment? How is that, do you know?"

"Well, sor, there're only a certain number o' keys to Mr. French's apartment, sor," answered O'Flaherty, more comfortably. "S'far as I know, Mr. Cyrus French has one, Mrs. French had one, Miss Marion has one, Miss Bernice has one—me workin' here for seventeen years, I knows th' fam'ly right well, sor—Mr. Weaver has one, and there's one master-key in th' desk in my office all th' time. That's half a dozen altogether, sor. Th' master-key is in case a key is needed in an emergency."

"You say Mrs. French showed you her key before she left your office, O'Flaherty? How do you know it was the key to the apartment?" asked the Inspector.

"Easy enough, sor. Y'see, each key—they're special Yales, sor—each key has a little gold dingus on it with th' initials o' the person it belongs to. Th' key Mrs. French showed me had that on. Besides, I know th' looks o' that key; it was the right one, all right."

"One second, O'Flaherty." The Inspector turned to Weaver. "Have you your apartment-key on you, Weaver? Let me have it, please?"

Weaver extracted a leather key-case from his vest-pocket and handed it to Queen. Among a number of different keys was one with a small gold disc fused into the tiny hole at the top. On this disc were engraved the initials, W.W. The Inspector looked up at O'Flaherty.

"A key like this?"

"Just th' same, sor," said O'Flaherty, "exceptin' th' initials."

"Very well." Queen returned the key-case to Weaver. "Now, O'Flaherty, before you continue, tell me this— where do you keep your master-key to the apartment?"

"Right in a special drawer in th' desk, sor. It's there all the time, day and night."

"Was it in its place last night?"

"Yes, sor. I always looks for it special. It was there— the right key, no mistake, sor. It's got a tab on it too, with th' word 'Master' on it."

"O'Flaherty," asked the Inspector quietly, "were you at your desk all night? Did you leave your office at all?"

"No, sor!" answered the old watchman emphatically. "From th' minute I got there, at five-thirty, I didn't leave th' office until I was relieved this mornin' by O'Shane at eight-thirty. I got longer hours than him 'cause he's got more to do on his shift, with checkin' in employees and all. And as for leavin' the desk, I brings me own feed from home, even hot coffee in a thermos bottle. No, sor, I was on th' watch all night."

"I see." Queen shook his head as if to clear the mists of weariness and motioned the watchman to continue with his story.

"Well, sor," said O'Flaherty, "when Mrs. French left me office, I got up out o' me chair, went into the hall, and watched her. She went to th' elevator, opened th' door, an' went in. That's the last I saw o' her, sor. When I saw she didn't come down I thought nothin' of it, 'cause a number o' times Mrs. French has stayed overnight in Mr. French's apartment upstairs. I thought she'd done th' same this night. So that's all I know, sor."

Ellery stirred. He lifted the dead woman's handbag from the bed and dangled it before the watchman's eyes.

"O'Flaherty," he asked in a drawling voice, "have you ever seen this before?"

The watchman replied, "Yes, sor! That's th' bag Mrs. French was carryin' last night."

"The bag, then," pursued Ellery softly, "from which she took her gold-topped key?"

The watchman seemed puzzled. "Why, yes, sor." Ellery seemed satisfied and dropped back to whisper in his father's ear. The Inspector frowned, then nodded. He turned to Crouther.

"Crouther, will you please get the master-key in the office on the 39th Street side." Crouther grunted cheerfully and departed. "Now then." The Inspector picked up the gauzy scarf initialed *M.F.* which he had found on the dead body. "O'Flaherty, do you recall Mrs. French's having worn this last night? Think carefully."

O'Flaherty took the wisp of silk in his horny fat fingers and turned it over and over, his forehead wrinkled. "Well, sor," he said finally, in a hesitant tone, "I can't rightly say. Seemed to me for a minute as if I'd seen Mrs. French wear it, and then again seemed as if I hadn't. No, I couldn't rightly say. No, sor," and he returned it to the Inspector with a gesture of helplessness.

"You're not sure?" The Inspector dropped the scarf back on the bed. "Everything seem all right last night? No alarms?"

"No, sor. O' course you know th' store's wired against burglars. Quiet as a church last night. S'far as I know, nothin' happened out o' th' way."

Queen said to Sergeant Velie: "Thomas, call up the alarm central office and find out if they've a report on last night. Probably not, or we'd have heard from them by this time." Velie left, silently as usual.

"O'Flaherty, did you see any one else enter the building last night except Mrs. French? At any time during the night?" continued the Inspector.

"No, sor, absolutely not. Not a soul." O'Flaherty

seemed anxious to make this point clear, after his defection concerning the scarf.

"Ah there, MacKenzie! Let me have the time-sheet, please." Queen took from the store manager, who had just returned, a long scroll of ruled paper. He looked it over hurriedly. Something seemed to catch his eye.

"I see by your sheet, O'Flaherty," he said, "that Mr. Weaver and a Mr. Springer were the last to leave the store yesterday evening? Did you make these notations?"

"Yes, sor. Mr. Springer went out about a quarter to seven, and Mr. Weaver a few minutes after."

"Is that right, Weaver?" demanded the Inspector, turning to the secretary.

"Yes," replied Weaver in a colorless tone. "I stayed a little later last night to prepare some papers for Mr. French to-day; I believe I shaved. . . . I left a little before seven."

"Who is this Springer?"

"Oh, James Springer is the head of our Book Department, Inspector," put in mild-mannered MacKenzie. "Often stays late. A very conscientious man, sir."

"Yes, yes. Now—you men!" The Inspector pointed to the two watchmen who had not yet spoken. "Anything to say? Anything to add to O'Flaherty's story? One at a time. . . . Your name?"

One of the watchmen cleared his throat nervously. "George Powers, Inspector. No, sir, I got nothin' to say."

"Everything all right when you went your rounds? Do you cover this part of the store?"

"Yes, sir, everythin' was okay on my rounds. No, sir, I don't cover the main floor. That's Ralska's job, here."

"Ralska, eh? What's your first name, Ralska?" demanded the Inspector.

The third watchman expelled his breath noisily. "Hermann, sir. Hermann Ralska. I think—"

"You think, eh?" Queen turned. "Hagstrom, you're taking this down, of course?"

"Yep, Chief," grinned the detective, his pencil busy in his notebook.

"Now, Ralska, you were about to think something, no doubt very important," snarled the Inspector. His temper seemed frayed and raw once more. "What was it?"

Ralska held himself stiffly. "I thought I heard somethin' funny last night on the main floor."

"Oh, you did! Where, exactly?"

"Right about here—outside this window-room."

"No!" Inspector Queen grew very quiet. "Outside this window-room. Very good, Ralska. What was it?"

The watchman seemed to take heart at Queen's calmer tone. "It was just about one o'clock in the morning. Maybe a few minutes earlier. I was in the part of the store near the Fift' Avenue and 39t' Street side. This here window faces Fift' Avenue, past the night-office, so it's a good distance away. I heard a queer kind o' noise. Can't make up my mind what it was. Might 'a' been some one movin' around, might 'a' been a footstep, might 'a' been a door closin'—just don't know. Anyway, I wasn't suspicious or anything—you get so you hear noises that never happened on a night job like this. . . . But I went over in that direction and couldn't see anything wrong, so I thought it must be my imagination. Even tried a couple of the window doors. But they were all locked. Tried this one, too. So I stopped in to have a word with O'Flaherty here, and went on ahead, with my rounds. That's all."

"Oh!" Inspector Queen seemed disappointed. "So you're not certain of where the noise came from—if there was a noise?"

"Well," responded Ralska carefully, "if it was anythin'

at all it came from this section o' the floor near these big street-window displays."

"Nothing else all night?"

"No, sir."

"All right, that's all for you four men. You may go back home and catch up on your sleep. Be back here to-night for work as usual."

"Yes, sir; yes, sir." The watchmen backed out of the window-room and disappeared.

The Inspector, brandishing the time-sheet in his hand, addressed the store manager. "MacKenzie, have you given this sheet any study?"

The Scotchman replied, "Yes, Inspector—thought you might be interested and looked it over on the way."

"Fine! MacKenzie, what's the verdict? Was every employee of the store checked out regularly yesterday?" Queen's face was composed, indifferent.

MacKenzie did not hesitate. "As you can see, we have a simple check-out system—by departments. . . . I can certainly assert that every *employee* who was *in the store* yesterday checked out."

"Does that include executives and gentlemen like the Board of Directors?"

"Yes, sir—there are their names in the proper places."

"Very well—thank you," said the Inspector thoughtfully. "Please don't forget that list of absentees, MacKenzie."

Velie and Crouther at this point reëntered the room together. Crouther handed the Inspector a key, an exact replica of the one in Weaver's possession, marked "Master" on its gold disk as O'Flaherty had averred. The detective-sergeant relayed a negative report from the burglar-alarm company. Nothing unusual had occurred during the night.

The Inspector turned again to MacKenzie. "How reliable is this O'Flaherty?"

"True-blue. Would give his life for Mr. French, Inspector," returned MacKenzie warmly. "He's the oldest employee of the store—knew Mr. French in the old days."

"That's a fact," echoed Crouther, as if anxious to have his opinion considered as well.

"It has just occurred to me. . . ." Inspector Queen faced MacKenzie inquiringly. "Just how private is Mr. French's apartment? Who has access to it besides the French family and Mr. Weaver?"

MacKenzie scraped his jaw slowly. "Hardly any one else, Inspector," he replied. "Of course, the Board of Directors meet in Mr. French's apartment periodically for conferences and other business matters; but the only keys to it are in the possession of the people O'Flaherty has mentioned. As a matter of fact, it's almost peculiar how little we people know about Mr. French's apartment. In all my association with the store, and it's a matter of ten years or so, I can't recall having been in the apartment more than half a dozen times. I was thinking that only last week, when Mr. French summoned me there for some special instructions regarding the store. As for other employees—well, Mr. French has always been adamant in the matter of his privacy. Aside from O'Flaherty opening the door for the cleaning-woman three times a week, and letting her out just before he goes off duty, there's not an employee of the store who has access or occasion to visit the apartment."

"I see, I see. The apartment—we seem to be going back to that apartment," muttered the Inspector. "Well! There seems to be very little left here. . . . Ellery, what do you think?"

Ellery swung his pince-nez with unaccustomed vigor as

he regarded his father. There was a troubled glint in the depths of his eyes.

"Think? Think?" He smiled fretfully. "My ratiocinative machinery has been chiefly occupied in the last half-hour or so with a stubborn little problem." He bit his lip.

"Problem? What problem?" growled his father affectionately. "I haven't had a moment to think clearly, and you talk of problems!"

"The problem," enunciated Ellery distinctly but not loudly enough to be heard by the others, "of why Mrs. French's key to her husband's apartment is missing."

10

MARION

"Not much of a problem," said Inspector Queen. "There is no particular reason for expecting to find the key—here. Besides, I can't see that it's of much importance."

"*Alors*—we'll let it go at that," said Ellery, smiling. "I am always worried by omissions." He dropped back, searching his vest-pocket for a cigaret-case. His father eyed him sharply. Ellery rarely smoked.

A policeman pushed open the window-door at this moment and lumbered over to the Inspector. "Young lady outside giving the name of Marion French. Says she wants Mr. Weaver," he whispered hoarsely. "Scared to death at the mobs and the cops. One o' the floorwalkers is with her. What'll I do, Inspector?"

The Inspector's eyes narrowed. He shot a glance at Weaver. The secretary seemed to sense the import of the message, although he had not heard the whispered words; for he stepped forward at once.

"I beg your pardon, Inspector," he said eagerly, "but if

that's Miss French I'd like your permission to go to her at once and—"

"Amazing intuition!" cried the Inspector suddenly, his white face creasing into smiles. "Yes, I think I— Come along, Mr. Weaver. You shall introduce me to Mr. French's daughter." He turned sharply to Velie. "Carry on for a moment, Thomas. No one is to leave. I'll be back in a jiffy."

Preceded by a revitalized Weaver, he trotted out of the window-room.

Weaver broke into a run as they stepped out onto the main floor. The center of a little crowd of detectives and policemen, a young girl stood stiffly, her face drained of color, eyes wild with a nameless fear. As she caught sight of Weaver, a tremulous cry escaped her and she swayed forward weakly.

"Westley! What is the matter? These policemen— detectives—" Her arms stretched out. In full sight of the grinning police and the Inspector, Weaver and the girl embraced.

"Sweetheart! You must get hold of yourself. . . ." Weaver whispered desperately into the girl's ear as she clung to him.

"Wes—tell me. Who is it? Not—" She drew away from him with horror in her eyes. "Not—Winifred?"

She read the answer in his eyes even before he nodded.

The Inspector obtruded his elastic little figure between them. "Mr. Weaver," he smiled, "may I have the pleasure . . . ?"

"Oh, yes—yes!" Weaver stepped quickly backward, releasing the girl. He seemed astonished at the interruption, as if he had forgotten momentarily the place, the circumstances, the time. . . . "Marion dear, may I present Inspector Richard Queen. Inspector—Miss French."

Queen took the proffered little hand and bowed. Marion

murmured a perfunctory pleasance, while her large grey eyes widened in stricken interest at this tiny middle-aged gentleman with the clean white mustache who bent over her hand.

"You're investigating—a crime, Inspector Queen?" she faltered, shrinking from him, clutching at Weaver's hand.

"Unfortunately, Miss French," said the Inspector. "I'm genuinely grieved that you've had such an unpleasant reception—more than I can say. . . ." Weaver glared at him in bewildered wrath. The old Machiavelli! He had known all along what would happen! . . . The Inspector proceeded in a gentle tone. "It's your stepmother, my dear—shockingly murdered. Terrible! Terrible!" He clucked his tongue like a solicitous old hen.

"Murdered!" The girl grew very still. The hand in Weaver's twitched once, and was limp. For the instant both Weaver and the Inspector thought she would faint, and involuntarily moved forward to her aid. She staggered back. "No—thank you," she whispered. "My God —Winifred! And she and Bernice were away—all night. . . ."

The Inspector stiffened. Then his hand fumbled for his snuff-box. "Bernice, I believe you said, Miss French?" he said. "The watchman mentioned that name before, too. . . . A sister, perhaps, my dear?" he asked ingratiatingly.

"Oh—what have I— Oh, Wes dear, take me away, take me away!" She buried her face in the folds of Weaver's coat.

Weaver said, above her head, "A perfectly natural remark, Inspector. The housekeeper, Hortense Underhill, called Mr. French this morning during the conference to report that neither Mrs. French nor Bernice, her daughter, had slept at home. . . . You see, of course, that Marion— Miss French. . . ."

"Yes, yes, naturally." Queen smiled, touched the girl's arm. She started convulsively. "If you'll come this way, Miss French—? Please be brave. There is something I want you—to see."

He waited. Weaver gave him an outraged glance, but pressed the girl's arm encouragingly and led her, stumbling, toward the window. The Inspector followed, beckoning to one of the detectives nearby, who immediately took his place outside the window-door after the trio entered the room.

There was a little rustle of excitement as Weaver helped the girl into the room. Even old French, shaking as if with ague, showed a light of reason in his eyes as he spied her.

"Marion my dear!" he cried in a terrible voice.

She broke away from Weaver and fell on her knees before her father's chair. No one spoke. The men looked uneasily away. Father and daughter clung to each other. . . .

For the first time since he had come into the chamber of death, Marchbanks, brother of the dead woman, spoke.

"This—is—hellish," he said, savagely and slowly, glaring out of bloodshot eyes at the trim figure of the Inspector. Ellery, in his corner, crooked his body slightly forward, "I'm—getting—out—of—this."

The Inspector signaled to Velie. The burly Sergeant stumped across the floor and towered above Marchbanks, saying nothing, his arms hanging loosely by his sides. Marchbanks, large and corpulent, shrank before the huge detective. He flushed, muttered beneath his breath, stepped back.

"Now," said the Inspector equably, "Miss French, may I trouble you to answer a few questions?"

"Oh, I say, Inspector," protested Weaver, despite Ellery's warning flick of the finger, "do you think it absolutely necessary to—"

"I'm quite ready, sir," came the quiet voice of the girl, and she rose to her feet, her eyes a trifle red, but clearly composed. Her father had slumped back in his chair. He had forgotten her already. She smiled wanly at Weaver, who sent her an ardent glance across the room. But she kept her head averted from the sheeted corpse in the corner by the bed.

"Miss French," snapped the Inspector, flicking the gauzy scarf from the dead woman's clothes before her eyes, "is this your scarf?"

She whitened. "Yes. How does it come here?"

"That," said the Inspector dispassionately, "is what *I* should like to know. Can you explain its presence?"

The girl's eyes flashed, but she spoke calmly enough. "No, sir, I cannot."

"Miss French," went on the Inspector after a stifling pause, "your scarf was found around Mrs. French's neck, under her coat-collar. Does that convey anything to you —perhaps suggest an explanation?"

"She was wearing it?" Marion gasped. "I—I can't understand it. She—she never did that before." She glanced helplessly at Weaver, shifted her gaze and met Ellery's eyes.

They looked at each other for a startled moment. Ellery saw a slender girl with smoky hair and deep grey eyes. There was an unaccented cleanliness about the lines of her young body that made him feel pleased for Weaver's sake. She gave the impression of straightforwardness and strength of will—honest eyes, firm lips, small strong hands, a pleasingly cleft chin and a good straight nose. Ellery smiled.

Marion saw a tall athletic man with a suggestion of nascent vigor, startlingly intellectual about the forehead and lips, cool and quiet and composed. He looked thirty, but was younger. There was a hint of Bond Street about his clothes. His long thin fingers clasped a little book and he regarded her out of pince-nez eyeglasses. . . . Then she blushed slightly and her eyes wavered away toward the Inspector.

"When did you last see this scarf, Miss French?" went on the old man.

"Oh, I—" Her tone changed; she took command of herself. "I seem to remember wearing it yesterday," she said slowly.

"Yesterday? Very interesting, Miss French. Do you recall just where—?"

"I left the house directly after luncheon," she said "wearing the scarf under this coat. I met a friend at Carnegie Hall and we spent the afternoon at a recital— Pasternak the pianist. We parted after the recital and I took a 'bus down to the store. I do seem to remember wearing the scarf all day. . . ." Her brow wrinkled prettily. "I don't remember having it, however, when I returned home."

"You say you came to the store, Miss French?" interrupted the Inspector politely. "For any special reason?"

"Why—not particularly. I did think I might still catch father. I knew he was leaving for Great Neck, but I didn't know exactly when, and—"

The Inspector held up a ridiculously tiny white hand. "Just a moment, Miss French. You say your father went to Great Neck yesterday?"

"Why, yes. I understood he was to go out there for business. There's—there's nothing wrong—about that, is there, sir?" She bit her lip.

"No, no—positively no!" said the Inspector, smiling. He turned to Weaver. "Why didn't you tell me that Mr. French took a little trip yesterday, Mr. Weaver?"

"You didn't ask me," retorted Weaver.

The Inspector started, then chuckled. "One on me," he

said. "It's true enough. When did he return and why did he go?"

Weaver looked compassionately at the limp, oblivious figure of his employer. "He went early yesterday afternoon to confer with Farnham Whitney on Whitney's estate. A matter of merger, Inspector—the meeting this morning discussed just that. Mr. French told me that he was driven into the city early this morning by Whitney's chauffeur—arrived at the store at nine o'clock. Anything else?"

"Not just now." Queen turned to Marion. "Your pardon, my dear, for the interruption. . . . Now where specifically did you go when you came to the store?"

"To my father's apartment on the sixth floor."

"Indeed?" muttered the Inspector. "And why, may I ask, did you go to your father's apartment?"

"I usually go there when I'm at the store, which isn't often," explained Marion. "Besides, I was told that Mr. Weaver was there, working, and I thought—it might be nice to pay him a little visit. . . ." She eyed her father apprehensively, but he was insensible to words.

"You went there directly on entering the store? And left immediately from the apartment?"

"Yes."

"Is it possible," insinuated the Inspector very gently, "that you may have dropped your scarf in the apartment, Miss French?"

She did not reply immediately. Weaver tried frantically to catch her eye, moving his lips, framing the word "No!" She shook her head.

"Quite possible, Inspector," she said quietly.

"I see." The Inspector beamed. "Now, when did you see Mrs. French last?"

"At dinner last night. I had an appointment for the evening and left almost immediately."

"Did Mrs. French seem herself? Notice anything unusual, abnormal in her speech or actions?"

"Well. . . . She did seem worried about Bernice," Marion said slowly.

"Ah!" Queen rubbed his hands together. "Then I infer that your—step-sister, is it?—was not at home for dinner?"

"No," replied Marion after a hesitating silence. "Winifred—my step-mother told me that Bernice had gone out and would not be home for dinner. But she seemed worried nevertheless."

"She gave no indication of a reason for this worry?"

"None whatever."

"What is your step-sister's name? Is it French?"

"No, Inspector. She retains her father's name of Carmody," murmured Marion.

"I see. I see." The Inspector stood plunged in thought. John Gray shifted impatiently, whispered a word to Cornelius Zorn, who shook his head sadly and leaned resignedly against the back of French's chair. Queen paid no attention to them. He looked up at Marion. Her passive, tired little figure drooped.

"One question more for the moment, Miss French," he said, "and you may rest. . . . Can you suggest, from anything that you know of Mrs. French's background or affairs, or from anything that transpired recently—last night, yesterday, perhaps—can you suggest," he repeated, "a possible explanation for this crime? It's murder, of course," he continued hastily, before she could reply, "and I know you are naturally chary of answering. Take your time—think carefully over everything that has occurred lately. . . ." He stopped. "Now, Miss French, can you tell me anything I might wish to hear?"

There was naked silence in the room—a raw pulsing quiet that beat invisibly against the atmosphere. Ellery heard quick breaths drawn, saw bodies tense, eyes sharpen, hands twitch as, to a man, the occupants of the room with the exception of Cyrus French leaned forward, watching Marion French as she stood there, facing them.

But she said, "No," very matter-of-factly, and the Inspector's eyes flickered. Everybody relaxed. Some one sighed. Ellery noted that it was Zorn. Trask lit a cigarette nervously and let the fire die. Marchbanks sat frozen to his chair. Weaver made a little movement of despair. . . .

"Then that will be all, Miss French," returned Inspector Queen, in a tone as casual as the girl's had been. He seemed pleasantly absorbed in a contemplation of Lavery's formal cravat. "Please," he added, just as pleasantly, "do not leave the room. . . . Mr. Lavery, may I have your ear for the moment?"

Marion dropped back and Weaver sprang to her side, dragging a chair with him. She sank into it with a little smile, shading her eyes with a nerveless hand. The other snuggled secretly into Weaver's eager grasp. . . . Ellery watched them for a moment, then turned his sharp eyes on Lavery.

The Frenchman bowed, waited, fingers riffling his short beard.

11

LOOSE ENDS

"As I understand it, Mr. Lavery, you are responsible for this exhibition of modernistic house-furnishings?" Inspector Queen's voice took a fresh note.

"That is correct."

"How long has this exhibition been going on?"

"About a month, I should say."

"Your main exhibition rooms are where?"

"On the fifth floor." Lavery spread his fingers. "You see, this is more or less of a pioneer project in New York,

Inspector. I was invited to exhibit some of my creations to the American public by Mr. French and his Board, who are very much in sympathy with the movement. Most of the purely enterprising details of the present exhibition emanate from Mr. French, allow me to add."

"Just what do you mean?"

Lavery showed his teeth in a smile. "The matter of these window-exhibits, for example. That was wholly Mr. French's idea, and I do suppose it has resulted in much advertising for the establishment. Certainly the crowds have flocked from the sidewalk outside to the fifth floor exhibition rooms in such numbers that we have had to call in special ushers to handle them."

"I see." The Inspector nodded politely. "So these window-exhibits were Mr. French's idea? Yes, yes—you have just told me that. . . . How long has this particular window been dressed so, Mr. Lavery?"

"This is the—let me see—the end of the second week of the living-room-bedroom exhibit," answered Lavery, stroking his short modish beard again. "The fourteenth day, to be exact. To-morrow we were to have changed the room's contents, removed them to make way for a model dining-room."

"Oh, the windows are changed bi-weekly? Then this is the second room you have exhibited?"

"Quite so. The first was a full bedroom."

Queen mused openly. His eyes drooped with weariness; blackish pouches stood out beneath. He took a short turn up and down the room, halting once more before Lavery.

"It seems to me," he said, more to himself than to Lavery, "that this unfortunate accident and its attendant circumstances dovetail too fortuitously. . . . However! Mr. Lavery, is this window-exhibit held at the same time each day?"

Lavery stared. "Yes—yes, certainly."

"At *exactly* the same time each day, Mr. Lavery?" pursued the Inspector.

"Oh, yes!" said Lavery. "The Negress has entered this window at noon of each day ever since the institution of the exhibit."

"Very good!" The Inspector seemed pleased again. "Now, Mr. Lavery—in the month that these demonstrations have taken place, has there ever to your knowledge been one day on which the time-schedule was not adhered to?"

"No," said Lavery with positiveness. "And I am in a position to know, sir. It has been my habit to stand on the main floor behind the window-room during the Negress's demonstration every day. My lecture upstairs is not scheduled until three-thirty of the afternoon, you see."

The Inspector raised his eyebrows. "Oh, you lecture, too, Mr. Lavery?"

"But of course!" cried Lavery. "I have been told," he added gravely, "that my description of the work of the Viennese Hoffman has created something of a stir among the *monde artistique*."

"Indeed!" smiled the Inspector. "One question more, Mr. Lavery, and then I think we will have finished with you for the present.—This exhibition as a whole is not entirely a spontaneous thing? I mean," he added, "steps have been taken to make the public aware both of your window-demonstrations and of your lectures upstairs?"

"Assuredly. The publicity and advertising have been planned most carefully," rejoined Lavery. "We have circularized all the art-schools and allied organizations. The charge-accounts, I understand, have likewise been covered by personal letters from the management. The bulk of the public attention, however, has been secured by means of newspaper advertisements. Of course you have seen those?"

"Well, I rarely read department store ads," the Inspector replied hastily. "And I suppose you have received all sorts of publicity?"

"Yes—yes, indeed," and Lavery again flashed his white teeth. "If you would condescend to examine my scrap-books—"

"Hardly necessary, Mr. Lavery, and thank you for your patience. That's all."

"A moment, please.—May I?" Ellery had stepped forward, smiling. The Inspector glanced at him, waved his hand briefly, as if to say, "Your witness!" and retreated to the bed, where he sat down with a sigh.

Lavery had turned in his tracks and now stood stroking his beard, his eyes politely questioning.

Ellery did not speak for a moment. He twirled his pince-nez, looked up suddenly. "I am quite interested in your work, Mr. Lavery," he said with a disarming grimace. "Although I fear my esthetic studies have not exhausted the field of modern interior decoration. As a matter of fact, I was much interested the other day in your lecture on Bruno Paul. . . ."

"So you attended my impromptu classes upstairs, sir?" exclaimed Lavery, flushing with pleasure. "Perhaps I was a trifle enthusiastic about Paul—I know him quite well, you see. . . ."

"Indeed!" Ellery looked at the floor. "I take it that you have been in America before, Mr. Lavery—your English is quite untouched by Gallicism."

"Well, I have traveled more or less extensively," admitted Lavery. "This is my fifth visit to the States—Mr. Queen, is it?"

"I'm sorry!" said Ellery. "I am Inspector Queen's unruly scion. . . . Mr. Lavery, how many demonstrations a day are given in this window?"

"Just one." Lavery raised his black brows.

"How long does each demonstration take?"

"Thirty-two minutes exactly."

"Interesting," murmured Ellery. "By the way, is this room kept open at all times?"

"Not at all. There are some very valuable pieces in this room. It is kept locked except when it is being used for demonstration purposes."

"Of course! That was stupid of me," smiled Ellery. "You have a key, naturally?"

"A number of keys exist, Mr. Queen," answered Lavery. "The idea of the lock is more to prevent transient trespassing during the day than to keep out possible night-prowlers. It is presumed that after hours, in an establishment as well guarded as this—provided with modern burglar alarms, guards, and so on—the room would be safe enough against burglary."

"If you will pardon me for interrupting," came the mild voice of MacKenzie, the store manager, "I am in a better position to clear up the question of the keys than Mr. Lavery."

"Delighted to have you," said Ellery quickly, but he began once more to twirl his pince-nez. The Inspector, seated on the bed, preserved a watchful silence.

"We have a number of duplicate keys," explained MacKenzie, "to each of the windows. In this particular instance Mr. Lavery has one, Diana Johnson the demonstrator has one (which she leaves at the Employees' Office desk when she leaves for the day), the floorwalker on this section of the main floor and the store detectives each have one, and there is a complete set of duplicates kept in the general offices on the mezzanine floor. I am afraid very many people could have secured a key."

Ellery did not seem perturbed. He walked suddenly to the door, opened it, peered out over the main floor for a moment, and returned.

"Mr. MacKenzie, will you please summon that clerk at the leather-goods counter opposite this window?"

MacKenzie departed, returning shortly with a short, stout, middle-aged man. He was white-faced and nervous.

"Were you on duty all this morning?" inquired Ellery kindly. The man jerked his head in the affirmative. "And yesterday afternoon?" Another jerk. "Did you leave your post at any time this morning or yesterday afternoon?"

The clerk found his voice. "Oh, no, sir!"

"Very well!" Ellery spoke softly. "Did you at any time during yesterday afternoon or this morning notice any one entering or leaving this window-room?"

"No, sir." The man's tone was assured. "I've been on duty all the time; I couldn't help but notice if any one had used this room, sir. I haven't been very busy," he added, with an apologetic side-glance at MacKenzie.

"Thank you." The clerk left with eager steps.

"Well!" Ellery sighed. "We seem to be progressing, and yet nothing takes definite shape. . . ." Shrugging his shoulders, he turned once more to Lavery.

"Mr. Lavery, are these windows illuminated after dark?"

"No, Mr. Queen. The shades are drawn after every demonstration, and they are kept drawn until the following day."

"Then," and Ellery emphasized the word, "then I take it that these lighting-fixtures are dummies?"

Eyes long since dulled by waiting and wretchedness expectantly followed the direction of Ellery's arm. He was pointing toward the oddly cut, clouded-glass wall lights. The eyes all turned, too, to observe the numerous queerly shaped lamps about the room.

For answer Lavery strode to the rear wall and, after a moment's manipulation, removed one of the modernistic fixtures. The socket which should have held an electric bulb was empty.

"We have no use for lights here," he said, "so we have not installed them." With a swift movement he restored the fixture to its place on the wall.

Ellery took a decisive step forward. But then he shook his head, retreated, turned to the Inspector.

"Henceforward, or at least for the present, I shall be silent," he said, smiling, "and latinically pass for a philosopher."

12

OUT THE WINDOW . . .

A policeman pushed his way into the room, looked about as if to catch the eye of authority, was summoned peremptorily by old Queen, mumbled a few words, and departed almost as quickly as he had come.

The Inspector immediately took John Gray aside and whispered in the little director's ear. Gray nodded and went to the side of Cyrus French, who was staring blankly into space, muttering to himself. With the aid of Weaver and Zorn, Gray managed to twist French's chair around so that the old man's back was to the body. French noticed nothing. The store physician took his pulse professionally. Marion's hand was at her throat; she stood up quickly and leaned against the back of her father's chair.

Then the door opened and two white-garbed men with visored caps entered, bearing a stretcher between them. They saluted the Inspector, who jerked his thumb toward the sheeted corpse.

Ellery had withdrawn into the far corner of the room beyond the bed to hold communion with his pince-nez. He frowned at it, tapped it on the back of his hand, threw his lightcoat on the bed and sat down, taking his head between his hands. Finally, as if he had come to either an impasse or a conclusion, he produced from the pocket of his coat the volume it contained, and began to scribble hurriedly on the fly-leaf. He paid not the slightest attention to the two police doctors stooped over the dead woman.

Nor did he protest when he was unceremoniously moved by a silent, nervous man who had entered immediately behind the stretcher bearers, and who was now engaged with the help of an assistant in photographing the dead woman, her position on the floor, the bed, the handbag and other articles connected with the victim. Ellery's eyes followed the police photographer, but abstractedly.

Suddenly he snapped his little book back into his pocket and waited thoughtfully until he caught his father's eye.

"Lord, son," said the Inspector, coming over, "I'm tired. And worried. *And* apprehensive."

"Apprehensive? Come, now—don't fall into that silly frame of mind, dad. Why should you be apprehensive? This case is coming along, coming along. . . ."

"Oh, you've probably caught the murderer and hidden him in your vest-pocket," growled the old man. "I'm not worried about the murderer, I'm worried about Welles."

"Sorry!" Ellery moved closer. "Don't let Welles rile you, dad; I don't think he's as bad as you've painted him. And while he's merely heckling you, I'll be working under-cover—grasp the idea?"

"It's not half bad at that," said the Inspector. "My gosh! He's liable to walk in here any minute now, El! I never thought of that! By this time he has a telephoned report and— Yes! What is it?"

A bluecoat tramped in with a message and left.

The Inspector groaned. "Word's just come that Welles is on his way here—now we'll have arrests, interviews, grillings, reporters running over the place, and merry—"

Ellery's air of raillery vanished. He grasped his father's arm and guided him swiftly to an angle in the wall.

"If that's the case, dad, let me tell you what is in my mind—quickly." He looked around; they were fairly unobserved. He lowered his voice. "Have you reached any definite conclusions yet? I'd like to have your reactions before I tell you mine."

"Well—" the old man peered about him cautiously, then cupped his mouth in his small hands—"between you and me, son, there's something queer about the whole business. As far as details are concerned, I'm a little hazy—if you're clearer than I, it's probably because you have had something of the advantage of an observer. But as to the crime itself—the possible motive—the story behind it—I have the inescapable feeling that the murder of Mrs. French is not half so important to us as what may have necessitated the murder. . . ." Ellery nodded thoughtfully. "I have no doubt that this is a carefully planned murder. Despite the weirdness of the place, the apparent sloppiness of the crime, there is amazingly little to go on."

"What about Marion French's scarf?" asked Ellery.

"Fiddlesticks!" said the Inspector contemptuously. "Can't see that it means anything intelligible. In all probability she left it somewhere about and Mrs. French picked it up. . . . But I'll bet a cookie that the Commissioner grabs it."

"I think you're wrong there," commented Ellery. "He'll be afraid to tackle French. Don't lose sight of French's power as head of the Anti-Vice Society. . . . No, dad, for the present Welles will keep his hands off Marion French."

"Well, what have you concluded, Ellery?"

Ellery produced his small volume and turned to the flyleaf on which he had scribbled a few moments before. He looked up. "I hadn't thought about the remote nuances of the crime, dad," he said. "Although, now that you've brought it up, it seems to me that you are probably correct

about the far-reaching significance of the motive as opposed
to the crime itself. . . . No, I've been chiefly occupied
until now with more direct affairs. I have four interesting
little puzzlers to elucidate. Listen carefully.

"First, and probably most important," he began, referring to his notes, "there is the puzzle of Mrs. French's key.
We have a fair sequence of incident. The nightwatchman,
O'Flaherty, observes the victim at about eleven-fifty last
night with the gold-disked apartment key in her possession.
She is lost sight of until twelve-fifteen to-day, when she is
found dead—still in the store, but with the key missing
from the scene of the crime. The question arises, then:
Why is the key missing? It seems on the face of it a pure
matter of discovery, doesn't it? Yet—regard the possibilities. It is plausible enough at this time to suspect that the
key's disappearance is connected with the crime, more
directly with the murderer. A murderer disappears, a key
disappears. It is not difficult to imagine that they disappeared together. Now, if this is so—and for the present
let us assume that it *is* so—why did the murderer take the
key? Obviously, we can't answer that question—yet. But
—we now know that the murderer has in his possession a
key to a certain apartment—French's private apartment
on the sixth floor."

"That's so," muttered the Inspector. "I'm glad you
suggested sending one of the boys to watch that apartment
this morning."

"I had that thought," said Ellery. "But something else
disturbs me. I can't help asking myself: Doesn't the
absence of the key perhaps indicate that the body was
brought to this window from some other place?"

"I can't see that at all," objected the Inspector. "Can't
see that it has anything to do with it."

"Let's not quarrel about it," murmured Ellery. "I can
see one very, very interesting possibility that makes my

question logical and the item of Marion French's scarf seems to point the same way. I think that I'll be able to check up soon on the facts—which will put me in a position to prove more definitely what I've just postulated. . . . Let me get on to point number two.

"The natural thought one has on finding the body in this window is that the crime was committed here. Of course! Usually, one would not even stop to question it."

"It seemed funny to me, though," said the Inspector, frowning.

"Ah! It did, eh? Perhaps I can crystallize your suspicion a bit later," said Ellery brightly. "We enter, we see a body, we say: Crime was committed here. But then we stop to observe. We are told by Prouty that the woman has been dead some twelve hours. The body is found a bit after noon. That would make it a short time after midnight when Mrs. French died. In other words, when the crime was committed. Observe that in any case the crime was committed in dead of night. What is the appearance of this window at such a time—of this whole section of the building? Total darkness!"

"And—?" put in the Inspector dryly.

"You don't seem to take my dramatics very seriously," laughed Ellery. "Total darkness, I repeat. Yet we are supposing that this window is the scene of the crime. We prowl about the window, ask ourselves: Are there lights in here? If there are, that's the end of it. With the door closed, and these heavy drapes on the street side, light would be unobserved outside the window-room. We investigate and find—no, no lights. Plenty of lamps, plenty of sockets—no bulbs. I doubt, indeed, if the lamps are even wired. So—we suddenly visualize a crime in total darkness. What—you don't like that idea? Neither do I!"

"There are such things as flashlights, you know," objected Queen.

"So there are. That occurred to me. Then I asked myself: If there was a crime here, there was some logically necessary antecedent action. A crime presupposes a meeting, a probable quarrel, a murder, and in this case, disposal of the body in a *very* queer and inconvenient place—a wall-bed. . . . And all in the rays of a flashlight! As redoubtable Cyrano would remark: No, I thank you!"

"Might have carried bulbs with him, of course," muttered the Inspector, then their eyes met and they both laughed at once.

Ellery grew serious. "Well, let's leave the little matter of illumination for the present. You'll admit it reeks slightly of improbability?

"And now to that exceedingly fascinating little thing-amajig," he continued, "the lipstick engraved with the letter *C*. That's my point number three. In many ways, it's of extreme significance. The immediate conclusion is that Lipstick marked *C* does not belong to Mrs. French, whose initials, engraved on three other articles in her bag, are W.M.F. Now, Lipstick marked *C* is of a noticeably darker shade than the paint on the dead woman's lips. Which not only corroborates the premise that Lipstick marked *C* is not Mrs. French's, but also that there is *another* lipstick extant somewhere which *did* belong to Mrs. French. Follow? . . . Now where is that lipstick? It is not in this window anywhere. Therefore it is somewhere else. Did the murderer take it, along with the key? That seems silly. Ah—but haven't we a clue? Of course! For observe . . ." he paused, "the dead woman's lips. Half-finished! And of a lighter shade. What does this mean? Undoubtedly that Mrs. French was interrupted while she was dabbing at her lips with her own lipstick now missing."

"Why interrupted?" demanded the Inspector.

"Have you ever seen a woman who began to paint her lips leave them half-painted? It just isn't done. It *must* have been an interruption which prevented those lips from being entirely daubed. And a violent interruption, I'll wager; nothing short of an unprecedentedly odd occurrence would stop a woman from smearing that last red blob on the right place."

"The murder!" exclaimed the Inspector with a queer light in his eye.

Ellery smiled. "Perhaps.—But do you grasp the implication, dad? If she was interrupted by the murder or the incidents immediately preceding the murder, and the lipstick is not in this window—"

"Of course, of course!" exclaimed the old man. He sobered. "It's true, though, that the lipstick might have been taken by the murderer for purposes of his own."

"On the other hand," returned Ellery, "if it was not taken by the murderer, then it is still somewhere in or about the building. You might institute a search through six floors of this drygoods mortuary."

"Oh, impossible! But I suppose we'll have to have a try at it later."

"Perhaps it won't be necessary in about fifteen minutes," said Ellery. "At any rate, a genuinely interesting question comes up: To whom does the *C* lipstick belong, if it is not Mrs. French's? You might look into that, dad. I have an idea that the answer to that question will bring complications—*à la* Scott Welles. . . ."

At mention of the Police Commissioner's name the Inspector's features lengthened. "You'd better finish what you began, Ellery; he'll be here any minute now."

"And so I shall." Ellery removed his pince-nez and twirled it recklessly in the air. "Before we proceed to point number four, bear in mind that you're *cherchez*-ing two feminine accessories—*la lipstick de Madame, et sa clef.* . . .

"To point number four, then," continued Ellery with a faraway gleam in his eye. "For point number four we must credit the habitually sharpened perceptions of our grossly underpaid and revered medico, Sam Prouty. He thought it strange that wounds of the nature of Mrs. French's should have bled so little. At least, there was little trace of blood on her body and clothes. . . . By the way, there was also a smear of dried blood on the palm of her left hand—you noticed it, of course?"

"Saw it, all right," muttered the Inspector. "Probably clapped her hand to one of the wounds at the moment she was shot, and then—"

"And then," finished Ellery, "her hand dropped in death and the divine ichor, which by all the laws of physics, according to friend Sam, should have gushed forth, did— what? I should say," he remarked seriously after a pause, "that it obeyed the immutable laws of that exact science and did gush forth freely. . . ."

"I see what you mean . . ." murmured the old man.

"It gushed forth freely—but not in this window. In other words, we must look for an interesting combination of elements to explain away the phenomenon of two bloody revolver-wounds being practically bloodless on the discovery of the body. . . ."

"Let me sum up the indications to this point," Ellery continued swiftly. "To my mind the absence of Mrs. French's apartment key; the absence of normal illuminating-facilities in this window; the absence of Mrs. French's rightful lipstick, which she must have had almost directly before her death, since her lips are only half-painted; the absence of blood from two logically bloody wounds; the presence of Marion French's scarf; and another item of a more general but none the less convincing nature—all converge into one conclusion."

"And that is that the murder was not committed in this

window," said the Inspector, taking snuff with a steady hand.

"Exactly."

"Just what do you mean by still another item which points toward that conclusion, Ellery?"

"Has it struck you at all," answered Ellery slowly, "what an utterly preposterous setting this window-room is for the crime of murder?"

"I did think of it, as I mentioned before, but—"

"You've been too plunged into detail to get a psychological slant on this affair. Think of the privacy, the secrecy, the conveniences, that a fully planned murder requires. Here—what did the murderer have? An unlit, periodically patrolled window. Dangerous from start to finish. In the heart of the main floor, where the nucleus of the nightwatchman's staff is located. Not fifty feet from the constantly present head nightwatchman's office. Why? No, dad, it's perfectly silly! It was the first thought I had when I came in here."

"True enough," muttered the Inspector. "Yet—if it didn't take place here, why transport the body here at all *after* the murder, if that is what was done? It seems to me that almost as much danger, if not more, existed in that event as in the first. . . ."

Ellery frowned. "That had occurred to me, of course. . . . There is an explanation; there must be. I begin to see the manipulation of a fine Italian hand. . . ."

"At any rate," broke in the Inspector with a slight impatience, "so much is clear to me after your analysis: this window is certainly not the scene of the crime. I think I see—yes, of course—it's as plain as day—the apartment upstairs!"

"Oh, that!" Ellery said absently. "Naturally. Wouldn't make sense otherwise. The key, a logical place for the lipstick, privacy, illumination . . . yes, yes, the sixth floor apartment by all means. It's my next stop. . . ."

"And it's positively depressing, El!" exclaimed the Inspector, as if struck by a thought. "Imagine! That apartment has been used by five people incessantly since eight-thirty this morning, when Weaver arrived. Nobody noticed anything up there, so evidently traces of the crime were removed from the apartment before that time. Goodness—if only. . . ."

"Now don't be bothering your poor grey head with fancy!" laughed Ellery, suddenly restored to good humor. "Of course the traces of the crime have been removed. The top layer, so to speak. Perhaps even the middle layer. But away down deep, underneath, we may find—who knows? Yes, that's my next stop."

"I can't help worrying about the reason this window was used at all," frowned the Inspector. "Unless it's that time element. . . ."

"Heavens! You're becoming positively a genius, dad!" chuckled Ellery affectionately. "I've just got over solving that little problem for myself. Why was the body placed in the window? Let's apply unfailing *logos*. . . .

"There are two possibilities, either or both of which may be correct. First: to keep attention away from the *real* scene of the crime, which is undoubtedly the apartment. Second, and more logically, *to prevent the body from being discovered before noon.* The dead certainty of the daily demonstration time—which, you have reasoned, of course, was common knowledge to all New York—tenons much too snugly."

"But why, Ellery?" objected Inspector Queen. "Why delay the body's discovery until noon?"

"If only we knew that!" murmured Ellery, with a shrug. "But in a general way it seems reasonable that, if the murderer left the body to be discovered—and he knew it with certainty—at twelve-fifteen, then he had something to do *before noon* which the discovery of the body prematurely would have made dangerous or impossible. Do you follow me?"

"But what on earth—"

"Yes, what on earth," replied Ellery sadly. "What did the murderer have to do on the morning of the crime? *I* don't know."

"We're just stumbling in the dark, Ellery," said the Inspector with a faint groan. "Just staggering from premise to conclusion without a ray of light anywhere. . . . For example, why couldn't the murderer have done what he had to do last night, *in the building?* There are telephones, you know, if he had to communicate with some one. . . ."

"Are there? But—we'll have to check up on that later."

"I'll do that right away—"

"Just a second, dad," interrupted Ellery. "Why not send Velie out to that private elevator to look for traces of blood?"

The Inspector stared at him, made a fist. "Goodness! How stupidly I've managed things!" he cried. "Of course! Thomas!"

Velie stalked across the room, received an inaudible instruction, and immediately left.

"I should have thought of that before," growled the Inspector, turning back to Ellery. "Naturally, if the murder was committed in the apartment, the body had to be brought down here from the sixth floor."

"Probably find nothing," commented Ellery. "I'd pick the staircase, myself. . . . But look here, dad. I want you to do something for me.—Welles will be here any moment now. To all intents and purposes this window is the scene of the crime. He'll want to hear all the testimony all over again, anyway. Keep him down here—give me an hour upstairs alone with Wes Weaver, won't you? I must see that apartment at once. Nobody has been in it since the meeting broke up—it's been watched all the time— there *must* be something there. . . . Will you?"

The Inspector wrung his hands helplessly. "Of course, son—anything you say. You can certainly tackle it with a fresher mind than I can. I'll keep Welles down here. Want to examine that Employees' Entrance office, the freight room, and that whole section of the main floor, anyway. . . . But why are you taking Weaver?" His voice sank lower. "Ellery—aren't you playing a dangerous game?"

"Why, dad!" Ellery's eyes opened wide in honest astonishment. "What do you mean? If you've any suspicion of poor Wes, disabuse your mind of it right now. Wes and I were bunkies at school; remember that summer during which I stayed with a chum in Maine? That was Westley's father's place. I know the poor boy as well as I know you. Father's a clergyman, mother's a saint. Background clean, life's always been an open book. No secrets, no past. . . ."

"But you don't know what he's bumped into in the city here, Ellery," objected the Inspector. "You haven't seen him for years."

"Look here, dad," said Ellery gravely. "You've never made a mistake following my judgment, have you? Follow it now. Weaver's as innocent of this crime as a lamb. His nervousness is plainly connected with Marion French. . . . There! The photographer wants to talk to you."

They turned back to the group. Inspector Queen spoke to the police photographer for a few moments. Then, dismissing the man, he resolutely beckoned the Scotch store manager.

"Mr. MacKenzie, tell me—" he asked abruptly, "what is the condition of your telephone service after shopping hours?"

MacKenzie said: "All 'phones except on one trunk line

are cut off at six o'clock. That line is connected with O'Flaherty's desk at the night exit. If there are any incoming calls, he takes them. Otherwise, there is no telephone service at night."

"I see by O'Flaherty's time-sheet and report-sheet that there were no incoming or outgoing calls last night," remarked the Inspector, consulting the chart.

"You can rely on O'Flaherty, Inspector."

"Well," pursued Queen, "suppose some department is working overtime? 'Phone service kept open?"

"Yes," replied MacKenzie. "But only on written request of the head of the department.—I should add that we have very little of that sort of thing here, sir. Mr. French has always insisted that the closing hour be kept more or less strictly. Of course, there are exceptions every once in a while.—If there is no record on O'Flaherty's chart of such a request, you may be sure no lines were open last night."

"Not even in Mr. French's private apartment?"

"Not even in Mr. French's apartment," returned the store manager. "Unless Mr. French or Mr. Weaver instructs the head operator to the contrary."

The Inspector turned questioningly to Weaver, and Weaver shook his head in an emphatic negative.

"One thing more, Mr. MacKenzie. Are you aware of the last time before yesterday that Mrs. French visited the store?"

"I believe it was a week ago Monday, Inspector," replied MacKenzie after some hesitation. "Yes, I'm fairly certain. She came in to speak to me about some imported dress material."

"And she did not appear at the store after that?" Inspector Queen looked around at the other occupants of the room. There was no answer.

At this moment Velie reëntered. He whispered to his

superior and stepped back.   The Inspector turned to Ellery. "Nothing in the elevator—not a sign of blood."

A policeman stepped into the window-room and made for the Inspector.

"The Commissioner's here, Inspector."

"I'll be right out," said the Inspector wearily.   As he left the room, Ellery gave him a meaning glance.   He nodded slightly.

When he returned a few moments later, escorting the portly, pompous figure of Commissioner Scott Welles and a small army of detectives and deputies, Ellery and Westley Weaver had vanished.   And Marion French sat in her chair, clutching her father's hand, watching the window-door as if with Weaver had gone some of her heart and courage.

THE SECOND EPISODE

"As for the word CLUE, *we are indebted for its genesis to mythology. . . . Clue has descended etymologically from* CLEW *(in common with many other words of similar endings; i.e.,* TREW, BLEW, *etc.) . . . being a literal Old English translation of the Greek word for thread, directly traceable to the legend of Theseus and Ariadne and the ball of cord she gave him with which to grope his way out of the Labyrinth after killing the Minotaur. . . . A clue in the detectival sense may be of an intangible as well as a tangible nature; it may be a state of mind as well as a state of fact; or it may derive from the absence of a relevant object as well as from the presence of an irrelevant one. . . . But always, whatever its nature, a clue is the thread which guides the crime investigator through the labyrinth of non-essential data into the light of complete comprehension. . . ."*

—From WILLIAM O. GREEN'S
Introduction to
ARS CRIMINALIS
By John Strang

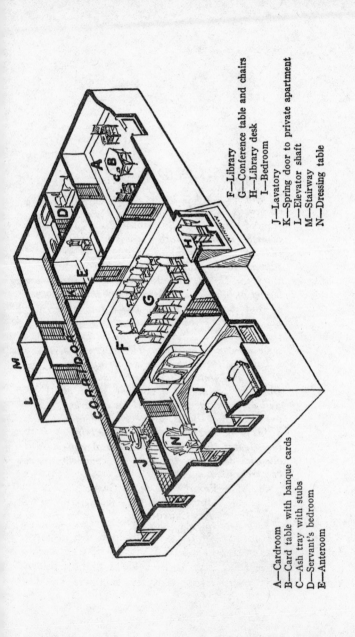

A—Cardroom
B—Card table with banque cards
C—Ash tray with stubs
D—Servant's bedroom
E—Anteroom

F—Library
G—Conference table and chairs
H—Library desk
I—Bedroom
J—Lavatory
K—Spring door to private apartment
L—Elevator shaft
M—Stairway
N—Dressing table

CORRIDOR

13

AT THE APARTMENT: *The Bedroom*

ELLERY and Westley Weaver picked their way unnoticed through the throngs on the main floor. At the rear of the store, Weaver indicated around the bend of the wall a small grilled door. A policeman stood guard with his back to the ironwork.

"That's the private elevator, Ellery."

Ellery exhibited a special police pass signed in Inspector Queen's punctilious hand. The policeman touched his cap and opened the grilled door.

Ellery noted the staircase door around the corner, then entered the elevator. He closed the door carefully, touched the button marked 6, and the elevator began to ascend. They stood in silence, Weaver's lip creased under his teeth.

The elevator was finished in bronze and ebony, with an inlaid composition-rubber floor. It was spotlessly clean. On the further wall was a low divan-like seat covered with black velvet. Ellery adjusted his pince-nez and looked about him with interest. He bent over to examine more closely the velvet seat, craned his neck at a suspicious darkening in an angle of the wall.

"Might have known Velie would overlook nothing," he thought.

The elevator clicked to a stop. The door opened automatically and they stepped out into a wide, deserted corridor. At one end of the corridor was a high window. Almost directly opposite the elevator exit was an unpaneled door of heavy mahogany. A neat small tablet, with the words:

PRIVATE
CYRUS FRENCH

was affixed to this door.

A detective in plain clothes indolently leaned against the frame. He seemed to recognize Ellery at once, for he greeted him and stepped aside.

"Going in, Mr. Queen?" he asked.

"Righto!" said Ellery, cheerfully. "Be a good man and stick it outside here while we're sniffing around the apartment. If you see any one—with authority—coming, rap on the door. If it's just anybody, shoo 'im away. Understand?"

The detective nodded.

Ellery turned to Weaver. "Let's have your key, Wes," he said in a natural tone. Without a word Weaver handed him the key-case which Inspector Queen had examined in the window not long before.

Ellery selected the gold-disked key and inserted it in the keyhole. He turned and the tumbler slipped back noiselessly. He pushed open the bulky door.

He seemed surprised at its rigid weight, for he stepped back, taking his hand from the door, and it immediately swung shut. He tried the knob. The door was again locked.

"Stupid of me," he muttered, as he again unlocked the door with the key. He waved Weaver inside the apartment before him, and then allowed the door to swing shut once more.

"Special spring lock," commented Weaver. "Why are

you surprised, Ellery? It's to insure absolute privacy. The Old Man's rather a bug on that."

"The door can't be opened from the outside without a key, then?" asked Ellery. "There's no way of fixing the bolt so that the door is temporarily unlocked?"

"The door is always as stubborn as that," said Weaver, with a fleeting grin. "Although I can't see what difference it makes."

"Perhaps all the difference in the universe," said Ellery, knitting his brows. Then he shrugged his shoulders and looked about him.

They stood in a small, almost bare anteroom with a cunningly converted skylight roof. . . . A Persian rug on the floor, a long leather-upholstered bench flanked with standing ash-trays against the wall opposite the door. . . . To the left was a single chair and a little magazine rack. And that was all.

The fourth wall was cut through for another door, smaller and not so formidable-looking.

"Not especially prepossessing," remarked Ellery. "Is this the usual taste of our multimillionaires?"

Weaver seemed to have recovered something of his natural buoyancy, now that he and Ellery were alone. "Don't misjudge the Old Man," he said hastily. "He's really a regular old duck, and knows a plain room from a fancy one. But he keeps this anteroom for the purpose of herding together the people who come to see him on business of the Anti-Vice League. This is a sort of waiting-room. Although, to tell the truth, it hasn't been used much. You know, French has an enormous suite of offices further uptown for Anti-Vice League affairs; most of that business is transacted there. I suppose, though, he couldn't resist the thought of entertaining some of his cronies here when he had the place designed."

"Any visitors of that sort lately?" inquired Ellery, his hand on the knob of the inner door.

"Oh, no! Not for several months, I think. The Old Man's been too wrapped up in the approaching merger with Whitney. Anti-Vice League has suffered, I guess."

"Well, then," said Ellery judiciously, "since there's nothing here of interest, let's proceed."

They walked into the next room, and the door swung shut behind them. This door, however, had no lock.

"This," said Weaver, "is the library."

"So I see." Ellery slouched against the door, surveying the room with open eagerness.

Weaved seemed afraid of silences. He wet his lips and said, "This is also the conference room for directors' meetings, the Old Man's hideaway, et cetera. Rather neat layout, don't you think?"

The room was at least twenty feet square, Ellery estimated, and presented a businesslike, if informal, appearance. In the center of the room stood a long mahogany table, surrounded by heavy red-leather-covered chairs. The chairs presented a ragged appearance, distributed unevenly around the table, showing signs of the haste with which the morning's meeting had been adjourned. Papers in disorderly piles were scattered over the table.

"Not usually that way," commented Weaver, noticing Ellery's grimace of distaste. "But the conference was an important one, everybody was excited, and then the news of the accident downstairs. . . . It's a wonder everything isn't in more of a mess than it is."

"Naturally!"

On the wall opposite Ellery was a severely framed portrait in oils of a ruddy-faced, masterful-jawed man, dressed in the fashion of the 'Eighties. Ellery lifted an eyebrow inquiringly.

"Mr. French's father—the Founder," said Weaver.

Under the portrait were built-in bookcases, a large comfortable-looking chair, and an end-table of modern design. An etching hung over the chair.

The wall on the corridor side and the wall near which they stood were tastefully furniture-covered. On both walls, left and right, were identically decorated doors of the swinging, rotary-hinged type. The doors were finished in a fine-grained reddish leather, studded with brass bolts.

The Fifth Avenue side of the room held a large flat-topped desk, at about five feet from the rear wall. Its shining surface held a French-style telephone, a slip of blue memorandum paper, and at the edge of the desk facing the rest of the room a half-dozen books between handsome onyx book-ends. Behind the desk the wall was pierced by a large dormer-window, draped in heavy red velvet. This window overlooked Fifth Avenue.

Ellery completed his stationary examination with a frown. He looked down at Weaver's key-case, which he still held in his hand.

"By the way, Wes," he said suddenly, "is this your own key? Ever lend it to anybody?"

"That's my own, all right, Ellery," replied Weaver indifferently. "Why?"

"I merely thought that it might be interesting to discover whether the key has ever been out of your possession."

"Nothing there, I'm afraid," said Weaver. "It's never been off my person. As a matter of fact, as far as I know, all five keys have been exclusively in their owner's possession since the apartment was built."

"Hardly," said Ellery in a dry tone. "You forget Mrs. French's." He eyed the key contemplatively. "Greatly bother you, Westley, if I appropriate yours for the time? I do believe I shall go into the business of collecting this particular type of key."

"Help yourself," replied Weaver in a small voice. Ellery detached the key from the case, which he forthwith returned to Weaver. The key he put into his vest-pocket.

"By the way," said Ellery, "is this your office too?"

"Oh, no!" replied Weaver. "I have my own office on the fifth floor. I report there in the mornings before coming up here."

"*Enfin!*" Ellery moved suddenly. "*Aux armes!* Westley, it is my earnest desire to peep into the privacy of Mr. French's bedroom. Will you oblige by leading the way?"

Weaver indicated the brass-studded door on the opposite wall. They traversed the thick-carpeted distance silently and Weaver swung the door inward. They emerged into a large squarish bedroom, with windows overlooking both Fifth Avenue and 39th Street.

The bedroom was, to Ellery's unaccustomed eyes, astonishingly modernistic in tone and decoration. Twin beds sunk almost to the floor level, both based on concentric ovals of a highly polished wood, caught the eye at once. A queerly shaped man's wardrobe and a daringly designed woman's dressing-table indicated that the room had been laid out for the use of Mrs. French as well as of her husband. Two diversions in the quietly toned but cubistic design of the walls pointed to closets within. Two chairs of unorthodox shape, a small night-table, a telephone table between the twin beds, a few bright scatter-rugs—Ellery, unacquainted with the Continental vogue at first hand, found the French bedroom a most engaging study.

On the wall toward the corridor was a door. It was partly open. Through it Ellery saw a lavatory in colored tiles as strikingly modern as the bedroom itself.

"Just what are you looking for, if you're looking for anything specific at all?" inquired Weaver.

"Lipstick. Should be here. . . . *And* key. Let's hope

it *isn't* here." Ellery smiled and stepped into the center of the room.

He observed that the beds were made up. Everything seemed in perfect order. He strode over to the wardrobe, looked at its bare top. The dressing-table caught his eye. He walked toward it as if half afraid of what he might find. Weaver followed him curiously.

The top surface of the dressing-table held few articles. A small tray of mother-of-pearl; a powder-jar; a hand-mirror. On the tray were some feminine accoutrements—tiny scissors, a file, a buffer. Nothing had the appearance of recent use.

Ellery frowned. He turned his head away, turned it back as if fascinated by the dressing-table.

"Really," he muttered, "it should be here. Of all places. The logical one. Of course!"

His fingers had touched the tray. Its shell was slightly curved at the edges. As the tray moved, something rolled off the table, where it had nestled under the tray's edge, and fell to the floor.

With a grin of triumph Ellery picked up the article. It was a small, gold-chased lipstick. Weaver came over in some astonishment to see the find. Ellery pointed to the three initials on the cap: *W.M.F.*

"Why, that's Mrs. French's!" cried Weaver.

"Dear Mrs. French," murmured Ellery under his breath. He lifted the cap of the stick and twisted. A pinkish blob of paste appeared.

"Seems to jibe," he said aloud. As if struck by a thought, he searched his coat pocket and pulled out the larger, silver-chased lipstick from the dead woman's bag in the window.

Weaver suppressed an exclamation. Ellery looked at him pointedly.

"So you recognized it, Wes?" he asked, smiling. "Now

tell me—since we're *tête-à-tête* and your innocent mind can grope trustingly in my presence. . . . To whom does this lipstick marked *C* belong?"

Weaver winced, raised his eyes to Ellery's cool ones. "To Bernice," he said slowly.

"Bernice? Bernice Carmody? The missing lady," drawled Ellery. "I suppose Mrs. French was her real mother?"

"Mrs. French was the Old Man's second wife. His daughter by his first wife is Marion. First wife died about seven years ago. Bernice came along with Mrs. French when the Old Man remarried."

"And this is Bernice's lipstick?"

"Yes. I recognized it immediately."

"Evidently," chuckled Ellery, "from the way you jumped. . . . Just what do you know, Wes, about this Bernice's disappearance? From Marion French's demeanor, I gather that she knows something. . . . Now, now, Wes —be patient with me! I'm not a lover, you know."

"Oh, but I'm sure Marion's not keeping anything back!" protested Weaver. "When the Inspector and I went out a while ago to meet her near the entrance, she told him that Bernice and Mrs. French had not slept at home. . . ."

"Not really!" Ellery was genuinely startled. "How is that, Wes? The facts, old boy, the facts!"

"This morning, just before the conference," explained Weaver, "the Old Man asked me to call his home and let Mrs. French know that he had returned from Great Neck safely. I talked to Hortense Underhill, the housekeeper— really more than a housekeeper; she's been with the Old Man for a dozen years. Hortense said that the only one up and about was Marion. This was a little after eleven. French spoke to Marion, told her the usual thing.

"At a quarter to twelve Hortense called up in something of a panic. She'd been worried over the silence of

Mrs. French and Bernice, and on going to their bedrooms had found both empty, and the beds not slept in. Which meant, of course, that both women had not been home all night. . . ."

"And what did French say to that?"

"He seemed annoyed rather than worried," replied Weaver. "Seemed to think that they had probably stayed overnight with friends. We went on with the conference, which broke up when we received the news about the—you know."

"Why on earth dad hasn't followed up that disappearance . . ." muttered Ellery with a singular facial contortion. He sprang to the telephone and ordered the store operator to summon Sergeant Velie. When Velie's voice boomed over the wire, Ellery rapidly acquainted him with the facts, advised him to let the Inspector know that he considered it imperative that Bernice be searched for immediately; and added that Commissioner Welles be kept downstairs as long as it was in Inspector Queen's power to do so. Velie grunted complete understanding and hung up.

Ellery instantly demanded the French house telephone number from Weaver, and transmitted it to the operator.

"Hello!" An indistinguishable murmur in the depths of the instrument. "Hello. This is a police officer talking. Miss Hortense Underhill? . . . Never mind that now, Miss Underhill. . . . Has Bernice Carmody returned yet? . . . I see. . . . Please! Take a cab immediately and come straight to the French store. Yes, yes, immediately! . . . By the way, has Miss Carmody a maid? . . . Very well. Bring her with you. . . . Yes, to Mr. French's private apartment on the sixth floor. Ask for Sergeant Velie when you get downstairs."

He hung up. "Your Bernice has not returned," he said mildly. "For what reason Fortunatus alone knows." He looked thoughtfully at the two lipsticks in his hand. "Was Mrs. French a widow, Wes?" he asked after a pause.

"No. She was divorced from Carmody."

"That's not Vincent Carmody, the antique dealer, by any chance?" asked Ellery, without changing expression.

"That's the man. Know him?"

"Slightly. I've been in his establishment." Ellery frowned as he regarded the lipsticks. His eyes keened suddenly.

"Now, I wonder . . ." he said, putting the gold stick aside and turning the silver one over in his fingers. He unscrewed the cap, twisted the body so that the dark red paste emerged. He kept twisting absently until the entire carmine length was visible. He tried to twist it still further. To his surprise, there was a distinct click! and the entire paste in its metal setting fell out of the silver case into his hand.

"What have we here?" he asked in honest astonishment, peering into the cavity. Weaver leaned over for a better view. Ellery tipped the case and shook it.

A little capsule about a half-inch around and perhaps an inch long fell out into his hand. It was filled with a powdery white crystalline substance.

"What is it?" breathed Weaver.

Ellery shook it, held it up to the light. "Well, sir," he said slowly, a grim smile lifting the corners of his lips, "it looks very much like heroin to me!"

"Heroin? The drug, you mean?" asked Weaver excitedly.

"Precisely." Ellery restored the capsule to the lipstick case, screwed the paste section into place, and put the lipstick into his pocket. "Nice commercial heroin. I may be wrong, but I doubt it. I'll have the stuff analyzed for me at Headquarters. Westley," and he turned squarely to French's secretary, "tell me the truth. To your knowledge is—or was—any member of the French family a drug addict?"

Weaver replied with unexpected promptitude. "Now that you've found this heroin, if that's what it is, it seems to me that I recall something queer in the conduct and actions of Bernice, especially of late. That's her lipstick, isn't it?—Ellery, I shouldn't be at all surprised if Bernice is addicted to the stuff. She's been jumpy, nervous, peaked-looking—alternated fits of gloom with spasms of hilarity. . . ."

"You're describing the symptoms, all right," said Ellery. "Bernice, eh? The lady becomes more and more interesting with every passing moment. How about Mrs. French—French himself—Marion?"

"No—not Marion!" almost shouted Weaver. Then he grinned in shame. "Sorry. No, Ellery, you forget that the Old Man is head of the Anti-Vice League—good Lord!"

"Quite a situation, eh?" smiled Ellery. "And Mrs. French was normal in that respect, you think?"

"Oh, absolutely."

"Anybody in the family besides yourself suspect that Bernice is a dope fiend?"

"I don't think so. No, I'm pretty sure no one did. Certainly not the Old Man. Marion has commented at times about Bernice's conduct and queer actions, but I'm positive she doesn't suspect—this. As for Mrs. French— well, it's hard to tell just what she thought. Always was tight-mouthed when it came to her darling Bernice. Though if she did suspect, she did nothing about it. I'm inclined to believe she was ignorant of the whole business."

"And yet—" Ellery's eyes gleamed, "it's passing strange, Westley, that the evidence should be found on Mrs. French's body—in her handbag, in fact . . . now, isn't it?"

Weaver shrugged his shoulders wearily. "My head's in a perfect whirl."

"Westley, old boy," pursued Ellery, fingering his pince-nez, "what do you think Mr. French would say if he knew there was drug-addiction in his own family?"

Weaver shuddered. "You don't know what a temper the Old Man has when he's aroused. And I think that that would arouse him——" He stopped short, looked at Ellery suspiciously. Ellery smiled.

"Time grows apace," he said with heartiness, but there was a disturbed light in his eye. "On to the lavatory!"

14

AT THE APARTMENT: *The Lavatory*

"I hardly know what we may expect to find here," said Ellery dubiously, as they stood in the glittering bathroom. "As a matter of fact, the lavatory is the last place to look. . . . Everything all right, Westley? Anything strike you as being out of place?"

Weaver answered rapidly enough, "No," but a tinge of uncertainty shaded his voice. Ellery glanced at him sharply, then around at the room.

It was long and narrow. The tub was sunken. The washbowl was slender and modern-looking. Above it hung a cunningly disguised chest. Ellery pulled open its concealed door. It held on its three glass shelves some bottles of house medicines, hair tonic, ointment, a tube of toothpaste and one of shaving cream, a safety-razor in an odd-looking wooden case, two combs, and several other articles.

Ellery slammed the door shut in a little flurry of disgust. "Come on, Wes," he growled. "I'm doddering. There's nothing here." Nevertheless, he stopped to open a door on the side. It was a closet for lavatory linens. He poked his hand into a hamper and pulled out several soiled towels.

These he examined carelessly and threw back, looking at Westley. . . .

"Well, spill it, son!" he said, pleasantly enough. "There is something on your mind. What's rotten in Denmark?"

"It's queer," said Weaver thoughtfully, pulling at his lip. "I thought it queer at the time, and now that things have happened, well—I'm thinking it's even queerer. . . . Ellery, there's something missing!"

"Missing?" Ellery's hand shot out and closed about Weaver's arm in a mighty grip. "My God, and you've kept mum! What is it that's missing, man?"

"You'll think I'm an idiot . . ." said Weaver hesitantly.

"Westley!"

"Sorry." Weaver cleared his throat. "Well, there's a razor blade missing, if you must know!" He scanned Ellery's face for a sign of levity.

But Ellery did not laugh. "A razor blade? Tell me about it," he urged, leaning against the closet door. He eyed the cabinet above the washbowl speculatively.

"I got here this morning a bit earlier than usual," began Weaver, with a worried frown. "Had to prepare for the Old Man's arrival, and there were a number of papers to straighten out for the directors' meeting. Usually, you know, the Old Man doesn't get here until ten o'clock; it's only on special occasions—like this one of the conference— that he comes earlier. . . . So I left the house in something of a hurry, intending to shave up here. I do that quite often, by the way—which is one of the reasons I keep a razor in the apartment. . . . When I got here—it was about eight-thirty—I dashed for my razor. And there wasn't any blade."

"That seems not so extraordinary," said Ellery with a smile. "You simply didn't have any in the cabinet."

"Oh, but I did!" protested Weaver. "The reason I felt something was funny was that last evening, before I left the store, I had shaved up here. I left the blade in the razor."

"Didn't you have any others?"

"No. I'd run out of them and intended to get some more. But I forgot to bring some in with me this morning. Consequently, when I wanted to scrape some of the old beard off there wasn't anything to do it with. Blade had vanished! Sounds silly, doesn't it? And I particularly left that blade in the razor yesterday because I've forgotten to restock before, and I found that you can always squeeze another shave out of the old blade."

"You mean that it had gone, absolutely? You're sure you left it in the razor?"

"Positive. I cleaned it and slipped it back."

"You didn't break it, or anything like that?"

"I tell you no, Ellery," Weaver replied patiently. "That blade was there."

Ellery's lips curved upward humorously. "A pretty problem at that," he said. "Is that why your face is fuzzed?"

"Right enough. I haven't had a chance all day to go out for a shave."

"Seems peculiar," said Ellery thoughtfully. "I mean that you should have had only one blade left in the cabinet. Where are French's blades?"

"He doesn't shave himself," replied Weaver a trifle stiffly. "He never has. Patronizes the same barber every morning."

Ellery did not comment further. He opened the cabinet and took down the wooden razor-case. He examined the plain silver razor inside, but could see nothing of interest.

"You handled the razor this morning?"

"What do you mean?"

"Did you take it out of the case?"

"Oh, no! I didn't at all. When I saw the blade was missing, I didn't even bother."

"That's *very* interesting." Ellery lifted the razor handle to the level of his eyes, holding it by the tip, careful not to touch the silver surface with his fingers. He breathed on the metal. It clouded over for an instant.

"Not the sign of a print," he commented. "Wiped away, undoubtedly." He smiled suddenly. "We begin to find signs of a presence, an apparition, a wraith here last night, old boy. Careful, wasn't he, she, or weren't they?"

Weaver laughed aloud. "Then you think my stolen blade has something to do with this mess?"

"To think," said Ellery solemnly, "is to know. . . . Keep this in mind, Westley. I believe I heard you say downstairs that you left here last night a bit before seven. The blade, then, was taken from this apartment between about seven o'clock last night and eight-thirty this morning."

"Astounding!" murmured Weaver derisively. "So that's the sort of hocus-pocus one must cultivate in order to be a detective?"

"Laugh, varlet!" said Ellery sternly. . . . He stood in a queer attitude of reflection. "I think we'll be going into the next chamber," he said in an altogether different voice. "I begin to see a tiny light. It's far off but—gossamer glimmer, nevertheless! *Allons, enfant!*"

15

AT THE APARTMENT: *The Cardroom*

He strode purposefully from the lavatory, marched through the bedroom, entered the library once more. Weaver followed, his face betraying an objective interest startlingly in variance with his nervousness of the past hour. He seemed to have forgotten something.

"What's past that door?" demanded Ellery abruptly, pointing to the second red-leather, brass-studded door on the opposite side of the room.

"That's the cardroom," replied Weaver interestedly. "Think there's something to look for, El? By George, you're getting me positively excited!" Then he stopped, his face lengthened, and he stood soberly surveying his friend.

"Cardroom, eh?" Ellery's eyes were bright. "Tell me, Wes—you were the first in the apartment this morning and you're in the best position to know—did any one who was in the library today go into any of the other rooms?"

Weaver pondered for a moment. "Except that the Old Man went into the bedroom when he got in this morning, and put his coat and hat away, nobody left the library."

"Didn't French visit the bathroom to wash up?"

"No. He was in a confounded hurry to dictate some store business and get ready for the conference."

"You were with him when he visited the bedroom?"

"Yes."

"And you're positive that none of the others—Zorn, Trask, Gray, Marchbanks—left *this room* all morning?" He took a short turn about the room. "By the way, you were here every minute of the time, I suppose?"

Weaver smiled. "I seem to be in an affirmative mood this afternoon.—Yes to both questions."

Ellery rubbed his hands together in a little spasm of glee. "The apartment, then, with the one exception of the library, is in exactly the same condition as when you arrived at eight-thirty. Excellent, most excellent, my omniscient and exceedingly helpful Westley!"

He walked briskly toward the cardroom door and pushed it open, Weaver at his heels. And Weaver cried out in sheer astonishment from behind Ellery's broad shoulders. . . .

The cardroom was smaller than both the library and the bedroom. It was paneled in walnut. Cheerful drapes hung over the single large window overlooking Fifth Avenue. A thick rug covered the floor.

But Ellery, following the line of Weaver's gaze, saw that he was staring in horror at a hexagonal, baize-covered card-table in the center of the room. A small bronze ashtray and some playing-cards, peculiarly arranged, were on the table. Two heavy folding-chairs were pushed away from the table.

"What's the trouble, Wes?" asked Ellery sharply.

"Why, that—that table wasn't there last night!" stammered Weaver. "I was in here looking for my pipe just before I left, and I'm sure. . . ."

"Not really!" murmured Ellery. "You mean the table was folded up, put away, out of sight?"

"Of course! The room was cleaned up yesterday morning by the charwoman. And those cigarets in the ashtray . . . Ellery, some one was in here after I left last night!"

"Obviously. And in the bathroom, too, if we're to believe the story of the missing razor-blade. The important thing is—why was some one in here? Just a moment." He went swiftly to the table and looked down curiously at the cards.

On both sides of the table were two small piles of cards —one stack with the faces up, the other closed. In the center of the baize were two rows of four stacks, open, with the pasteboards in descending order, as Ellery verified by investigating carefully. Between the two rows were three smaller piles.

"Banque," muttered Ellery. "Peculiar!" He looked at Weaver. "You know the game, of course?"

"No, I don't," said Weaver. "I recognized the layout of the cards as that of banque, because I've seen it played at the French house. But I don't understand the game very well; it gives me a headache. But then most card-games do. I never was much good at it."

"So I remember," laughed Ellery, "especially that night at Bloombury's when I had to sit in for you to recoup a hundred dollar I.O.U. at stud. . . . You say you've seen the game played at French's—and that's most interesting. Calls for questions, I do believe. Not many people know how to play Russian banque."

Weaver regarded Ellery strangely. His eyes went furtively to the stubs of four cigarets lying in the ash-tray. He looked back at once. "Just two people in the French household," he said in a strangled voice, "played banque."

"And they are—or were, if I must follow your past tense?" asked Ellery in a cool voice.

"Mrs. French and—Bernice."

"Oho!" Ellery whistled softly. "The elusive Bernice. . . . Nobody else play?"

"The Old Man abhors all forms of gambling," said Weaver, worrying his lips with a forefinger. "Won't play cards for anything. Doesn't know an ace from a deuce. Marion plays bridge, but only because it's something of a social necessity. She dislikes cards, and I never heard of banque before I entered French's employ. . . . But Mrs. French and Bernice were violently addicted to it. When-ever they had the opportunity they played it. None of us could quite understand it. A form of the glamorous gambling fever, I don't doubt."

"And the friends of the family?"

"Well," said Weaver slowly, "the Old Man has never been so narrow as to forbid card-playing altogether in his home. That's why this apartment, by the way, is fitted out with a cardroom. It's for the convenience of the directors—sometimes they play here between sessions. But in the house itself I have had plenty of opportunity to observe visitors and friends. I've never seen any one play banque except Mrs. French and Bernice."

"Beautiful—beautiful," said Ellery. "So symmetrically conclusive! That's the way I like things. . . ." But his brow was wrinkled with thought. "And the cigarets, old boy—tell me why you've been trying for five minutes not to look at the cigarets in the ashtray?"

Weaver flushed guiltily. "Oh!" He was silent. "I hate to say it, Ellery—I'm in the most hellish position imaginable. . . ."

"The cigarets, of course, are Bernice's brand. . . . You may as well come out with it," said Ellery wearily.

"How did you know?" cried Weaver. "But—I suppose it was clear enough to an alert . . . Yes, they're Bernice's. Her own brand. She has—had them made up for her especially."

Ellery picked up one of the stubs. It was silver-tipped, and just below the tip was printed in script the brand-name: *La Duchesse*. Ellery poked his finger among the remaining litter of stubs. His look sharpened as he noted that all, without exception, had been smoked to approximately the same length—to about a half-inch of the tip.

"Pretty thoroughly smoked out, all of them," he commented. He sniffed at the cigaret between his fingers, looked at Weaver inquiringly.

"Yes, scented. Violet, I think," Weaver said promptly. "The manufacturer provides the scent according to the specifications of his customers. I remember hearing Bernice place an order not long ago when I was over at the French's—placed it over the telephone."

"And *La Duchesse* is rare enough to have weight in an inquiry. . . . Good fortune, was it?" He talked to himself rather than to his friend.

"What do you mean?"

"No matter. . . . And, of course, Mrs. French did not smoke?"

"Why—how did you know?" demanded Weaver in surprise.

"How nicely things fit together," murmured Ellery. "So very, very nicely. And Marion—does she smoke?"

"Thank God—no!"

Ellery regarded him quizzically. "Well!" he said all at once. "Let's see what's behind this door."

He crossed the room to the wall opposite the window. A small plain door opened into a little, simply furnished bedroom. Beyond it was a tiny bathroom.

"A servant's room," explained Weaver. "Originally planned for a valet, but it's never been used to my knowledge. The Old Man isn't fussy and he'd rather have his man at the Fifth Avenue house."

Ellery made a swift examination of the two little rooms. He emerged in a moment, shrugging his shoulders.

"Nothing there, and there wouldn't be. . . ." He paused, twirling his pince-nez in the air. "We have a rather remarkable situation here, Wes. Consider: We are now in possession of three direct indications of Miss Bernice Carmody's presence in this apartment last night. Or rather two direct indications, and one—the first—of a circumstantial nature. That is—the lipstick marked *C* from Mrs. French's handbag. This is the least damaging of the three, of course, since it does not *prove* presence and might have been brought here by Mrs. French. But it must be kept in mind. Second, the game of banque, which any number of reputable witnesses, I gather, would testify, as strongly as you, was indulged in by Mrs. French and Bernice practically to the exclusion of the rest of the family and friends of the family. You noticed, didn't you, that the game has the appearance of having been interrupted at a critical stage? The way the cards are lying there—they give the distinct impression that just when the game became hotly competitive, it was stopped. . . . And third, the most critical indication of the three—the *La Duchesse* cigarets. These are so obviously Bernice's that they would be acceptable in court as admissible evidence, I'm sure, if supported by strong circumstantial evidence of a confirmatory nature."

"But what? I don't see—" cried Weaver.

"The suspicious fact that Miss Bernice Carmody has vanished," replied Ellery gravely. "Flight?" He flung the word at Weaver.

"I can't—I won't believe it," said Weaver weakly, but there was a curious relief in his voice.

"Matricide is an unnatural crime, to be sure," Ellery mused, "but is not unknown. . . . Is it possible—" His reflections were disturbed by a rapid knock at the apartment door. It was surprisingly loud, coming as it did through the three walls of the cardroom, the library, the anteroom.

Weaver looked startled. Ellery straightened with a jerk, swiftly looked around once more, then motioned to Weaver to precede him from the room. He closed the brass-studded door with gentle fingers.

"That must be your good hussif, Hortense Underhill, and the maid," said Ellery almost gayly. "I wonder if they can be the harbingers of—more evidence against Bernice!"

16

AT THE APARTMENT: *Again the Bedroom*

Weaver flung open the outer door to admit two women. Sergeant Thomas Velie loomed solidly behind them.

"Did you send for these ladies, Mr. Queen?" demanded Velie, his broad frame filling the door. "One of the boys downstairs caught 'em trying to get past the man guarding the elevator—said you sent for them. Is it all right?"

His eyes roved dourly about the apartment—as much of it as he could see from his position at the corridor door. Ellery smiled.

"It's all right, Velie," he drawled. "They'll be safe with me. . . . And how is the dear Commissioner progressing with the Inspector?"

"Got his hooks into the scarf," growled Velie, and shot a keen look at Weaver's instantly clenched fists.

"Follow up the lead I gave you over the telephone?" asked Ellery serenely.

"Yes. She's among the missing. Got two men on it already." The Sergeant's stern face cracked in a fleeting smile. "How much longer will you need the Inspector's— coöperation downstairs, Mr. Queen?"

"I'll buzz you, Velie. Fly away now, like a good little chap." Velie grinned, but his face was frozen into its customary immobility as he wheeled and made for the elevator.

Ellery turned to the two women, who were standing close together eying him apprehensively. He addressed the taller and elder of the two—a stiff, slab-figured woman in her early fifties, marble-haired and viciously blue-eyed.

"You're Miss Hortense Underhill, I take it?" he asked severely.

"That's right—Mr. French's housekeeper." Her voice was not unlike her person—thin, sharp, steely.

"And this is Miss Bernice Carmody's maid?"

The other woman, a timid little creature with faded brown hair and a plain face, started convulsively at being directly addressed and crouched closer to Hortense Underhill.

"Yes," answered the French housekeeper. "This is Miss Doris Keaton, Bernice's maid."

"Very good." Ellery smiled, stood aside with a deferential little bow. "If you'll follow me, please—?" He led the way through the red-leather door leading into the large bedroom. Weaver marched obediently behind.

Ellery indicated the two bedroom chairs. "Sit down, please." The two women sat down. Doris Keaton kept her big vapid eyes on Ellery, surreptitiously hitching her chair closer to the housekeeper's.

"Miss Underhill," began Ellery, pince-nez in hand, "have you ever been in this room before?"

"I have." The housekeeper seemed determined to out-stare Ellery. Her cold blue eyes flashed colder fire.

"Oh, you have?" Ellery paused politely without removing his gaze. "When, may I ask, and on what occasion?"

The housekeeper was undaunted by his coolness. "A peck of times. That is, so to speak. I never came, though, except at Mrs. French's request. Each time it was clothes."

"It was clothes?" Ellery seemed puzzled.

She nodded stonily. "Why, of course. They were far apart, those times, but whenever Mrs. French intended to stay here overnight, she would ask me to bring a next day's change for her. So that is how—"

"Just a moment, Miss Underhill." There was a pleasant glitter in Ellery's eyes as he reflected. "This was her usual custom?"

"So far as I know."

"When"—Ellery leaned forward—"when was the last time Mrs. French asked you to do this?"

The housekeeper did not reply at once. "I should say about two months ago," she answered finally.

"As far back as that?"

"I said two months ago."

Ellery sighed, straightened. "One of these closets, then, belonged to Mrs. French?" he asked, indicating the two modern doors set in the wall.

"Yes—that one there," she replied promptly, pointing to the concealed door nearest the lavatory. "But not only for Mrs. French's clothes—the other girls sometimes kept things in there, too."

Ellery's eyebrows shot up. "Not really, Miss Underhill!" he ejaculated. His hand caressed his jaw tenderly. "I may infer, then, that both Miss Marion and Miss Bernice sometimes used Mr. French's apartment?"

The housekeeper regarded him levelly. "Sometimes. Not very often. Only when Mrs. French was not using it, and they brought a girl friend along to spend the night—on a sort of lark, you might call it."

"I see. Have they slept here with a—a 'girl friend,' I believe you said?—recently?"

"Not that I know. Not for five or six months at least."

"Very good!" Ellery flipped his pince-nez into the air with a certain briskness. "Now, Miss Underhill, I want you to tell me quite exactly when you saw Miss Carmody last, and under what circumstances."

The two women exchanged meaning glances; the maid bit her lip and looked guiltily away. But the housekeeper retained her poise. "I *knew* that was coming," she announced in a calm voice. "But you needn't think either of my poor lambs had anything to do with this, whoever you are. They didn't and you can take that for gospel. *I* don't know where Bernice is, but be sure there's foul play been done her. . . ."

"Miss Underhill," said Ellery gently, "I'm sure this is all quite interesting, but we are in something of a hurry. If you'll answer my question—?"

"All right, if you must have it." She set her lips, folded her hands in her lap, looked at Weaver indifferently, and began. "It was yesterday.—I'd better begin right with when they woke up; it'll make easier telling.—Well, both Mrs. French and Bernice woke up at about ten o'clock yesterday morning, and the hair-dresser attended each in their rooms. They got dressed and had a bite of something. Marion had already had lunch. I served them myself. . . ."

"Pardon me, Miss Underhill," interrupted Ellery, "but did you hear what they talked about over the luncheon table?"

"I don't listen to what isn't my affair," retorted the housekeeper tartly, "so all I can tell about *that* is that they talked about a new gown being made for Bernice. And Mrs. French seemed a little absent-minded, too. She actually got her sleeve into her coffee—the poor thing! But then she was always a little funny—maybe she had a premonition of what was to come, you know?—God rest her troubled soul! . . . Well, after lunch they remained in the music-room until about two o'clock, talking and things. Don't know about what, either! But they seemed as if they wanted to be let alone. Anyway, when they came out I heard Mrs. French tell Bernice to go upstairs and dress—they were going to take a ride through the Park. Bernice went upstairs, and Mrs. French held back to tell *me* to tell *Edward Young*, the chauffeur, to get the car out. Then Mrs. French went upstairs herself to dress. But in about five minutes I saw Bernice coming down the stairs, all dressed for the street, and when she saw me she told *me* to tell her *mother*—whispered, she did—that she'd changed her mind about taking a ride in the Park and was going out to do some shopping. And she fair ran out of the house!"

Ellery seemed poignantly concerned. "Clearly if somewhat volubly told, Miss Underhill. And what would you say was the state of Miss Carmody's nerves all day?"

"Poor," replied the housekeeper. "But then Bernice has always been a high-spirited and sensitive girl. Yesterday she seemed a little more nervous than usual, though, now that I come to think of it. She was all pale and fidgety when she slipped out of the house. . . ."

Weaver moved sharply. Ellery cautioned him with a glance and motioned the housekeeper to continue.

"Well, not long after, Mrs. French came down dressed for her drive. She asked for Bernice, and I told her about Bernice's going off that way, and I gave her Bernice's message. I thought for a minute that she was going to faint—poor thing!—she got so pale and sick-looking, which wasn't like her at all, and then she took hold of herself and she said: 'All right, Hortense. Tell Young to put the car back in the garage. I shan't be going out, either . . .' and she marched right back upstairs again. Oh, yes! She did tell me, though, before she went up, to let her know the *instant* Bernice got back home. . . . Well, sir, that's the last *I* saw of Bernice, and practically the last of Mrs. French. For the poor soul stayed in her room all afternoon, came down for dinner with Marion, and then went back up to her room again. She seemed more anxious than ever about Bernice, and twice she made as if to go to the telephone, but she seemed to change her mind. Anyway, about a quarter after eleven at night she came down with her hat and coat on—yes, sir, I know you'll ask me: the brown toque and the fox-trimmed cloth coat—and she said she was going out. And go out she did. And that's the last I saw of poor Mrs. French."

"She didn't order the car?"

"No."

Ellery took a turn about the room. "And where was Miss Marion French all day?" he asked suddenly. Weaver glanced at Ellery in shocked surprise.

"Oh! Miss Marion was up bright and early—always is an early riser, the dear child—and she left the house right after luncheon, saying she had a shopping appointment with one of her friends. I think she also went to the

Carnegie Hall for the afternoon, because only the day before she showed me the tickets for a piano-playing thing by some foreigner. She does love music so, that child! She didn't get back home until about half-past five. She and Mrs. French had dinner together, and she was surprised that Bernice was absent. Anyway, right after dinner she dressed over and went out again."

"At what hour did Miss Marion French return?"

"That I can't say. I went to bed myself at eleven-thirty, after releasing the house staff for the night. Didn't see anybody come in. Mrs. French had told me not to wait up, besides."

"Not a particularly well-regulated household," murmured Ellery. "Miss Underhill, please tell me how Miss Carmody was attired when she left the house—it was about two-thirty, I presume?"

Hortense Underhill shifted restlessly in her chair. The maid still regarded Ellery with stupid, frightened eyes.

"Just about," said the housekeeper. "Well, Bernice was wearing—let me see now—her blue felt hat with the brilliant fancy, her grey chiffon dress, her grey fur-trimmed coat, and a pair of black leather pumps with rhinestone buckles. Is that what you wanted to know?"

"Precisely," said Ellery with a charming smile. He took Weaver to one side. "Wes, do you know why I've called these two worthy ladies into consultation?" he demanded in an undertone.

Weaver shook his head. "Except for the fact that you wanted to know about Bernice. . . . Oh, I say, Ellery, it wasn't that you're looking for further indications of Bernice's presence here, is it?" he asked aghast.

Ellery nodded gloomily. "We have three apparent indications of the young lady's alleged visit to the apartment, to be journalistic. . . . Something told me there were more. Indications that I might not be able to descry. The housekeeper, though—the maid, Bernice's maid—" He broke off, shook his head with impatience at his own thoughts. He turned to the waiting women. "Miss Doris Keaton." The maid jumped, stark terror in her eyes. "Don't be afraid, Miss Keaton," said Ellery mildly, "I shan't bite you. . . . Did you help Miss Bernice dress yesterday afternoon, after luncheon?"

The girl whispered: "Yes, sir."

"Would you recognize the articles of clothing, for example, that she wore yesterday, if you saw them here and now?"

"I—I think so, sir."

Ellery walked to the closet door nearest the lavatory, threw it wide—disclosing a rack hung with multicolored gowns, a silken shoe-bag tacked to the inner side of the door, and a top shelf on which lay several hat-boxes—stepped back, and said:

"There's your territory, Miss Keaton. See what you can find." He stood directly behind the girl, watching her with quick sharp flashes of his eyes. He was so absorbed in her movements that he did not even feel the presence of Weaver at his side. The housekeeper sat, a thin stone, in her chair, watching them.

The maid's fingers trembled as she rummaged among the numerous gowns on the rack. After going through the entire rack, she timidly turned to Ellery and shook her head. He motioned her to proceed.

She stood on tiptoe and lifted from the shelf the three hat-boxes. She opened these one by one and scrutinized them briefly. The first two boxes contained hats belonging to Mrs. French, she said hesitantly. This was corroborated by a frigid nod from Hortense Underhill.

The maid lifted the lid from the third box. She uttered a little choked cry and reeled backward, touching Ellery.

The contact seemed to burn her skin. She jumped away, fumbled for a handkerchief.

"Well?" asked Ellery softly.

"That's—that's Miss Bernice's hat," she whispered, biting the handkerchief nervously. "The one—she wore when she left the house yesterday afternoon!"

Ellery eyed the hat narrowly as it lay, brim to the bottom, in the box. The soft blue felt crown, due to its position, had collapsed. A glittering pin was fixed above the turned-down brim, just visible from where he stood. . . . Ellery made a brief request and the maid lifted the hat from the box and offered it to him. He turned it over in his fingers, then silently handed the hat back to the girl, who as silently took it, put her hand inside the crown, flipped the hat upside down, and deftly returned it to the box in that position. Ellery, who had been about to turn away, stiffened instantly. Nevertheless, he said nothing, watching the girl replace the three hat-boxes on the shelf.

"The shoes now, please," he said.

Obediently the maid bent over the silk shoe-rack hanging on the inside of the closet door. As she was about to remove a woman's pump, Ellery stopped her with a tap on the shoulder and turned to the housekeeper.

"Miss Underhill, will you please verify the fact that this is Miss Carmody's hat?"

He lifted a long arm, took down the box with the blue hat inside, removed the hat, and handed it to Hortense Underhill.

She examined it briefly. Unaccountably, Ellery had stepped away from the closet to stand by the lavatory door.

"It's hers," said the housekeeper, looking up belligerently. "But what that has to do with anything, *I* don't know."

"That's honest." Ellery smiled. "Will you please return it to the shelf?" As he said this, he stepped slowly forward again.

The woman, sniffing, put her hand inside the hat, inverted it, and placed it in that position in the hat-box. She carefully lifted it to the shelf and as carefully returned to her chair. . . . Weaver observed Ellery's sudden grin with a lost bewilderment.

Then Ellery did an amazing thing—a thing that brought an unbelieving stare from each of the three people watching him. He reached up to the shelf and took down the same hat-box!

He opened it, whistling a tuneless little air and, removing the much-handled blue hat, offered it to Weaver for inspection.

"Here, Wes, let's have your masculine opinion," he said cheerfully. "Is this Bernice Carmody's hat?"

Weaver regarded his friend with astonishment, taking the hat mechanically. Shrugging, he looked at the hat. "Looks familiar, Ellery, but I can't be positive. I rarely notice women's clothes."

"Hmm." Ellery chuckled. "Put the hat back, Wes old boy." Weaver sighed, grasped the hat gingerly by the crown and dropped it, brim down, into the box. He fumbled with the lid, affixed it, shoved the box back onto the shelf—for the third time in less than five minutes.

Ellery turned briskly to the maid. "Keaton, just how fastidious in her habits is Miss Carmody?" he asked, feeling for his pince-nez.

"I—I don't get you, sir."

"Does she bother you much? Does she put her own things away generally? Exactly what are your duties?"

"Oh!" The maid's eyes sought the housekeeper once more for guidance. Then she looked down at the carpet. "Well, sir, Miss Bernice was—is always careful about her clothes and things. Most always puts her hats and coats away herself when she gets in from being out. My work's more doing personal things—fixing her hair, laying out her dresses, and such."

"A *very* careful girl," put in Miss Underhill icily. "Rare and unusual, I've always called it. And Marion's the same way."

"Delighted to hear it," said Ellery with perfect gravity. "Delighted is hardly the word for it. . . . Heigh-ho, Keaton, the shoon!"

"Huh?" The girl was startled.

"Shoes—shoes, I should say."

There were at least a dozen pairs of shoes, of assorted styles and colors, protruding from separate pockets in the rack. Without exception each of the shoes lay in its compartment with the tip inside and the heel showing, hooked over the lip of the pocket.

The maid Keaton went to work. She looked over the shoes, lifting out several to examine them closely. Suddenly she snatched at a pair of black leather pumps, lying in adjacent compartments. Each pump sported a large and heavy rhinestone buckle which glittered in a shaft of sunlight as she held them up before Ellery.

"These! These shoes!" she cried. "Miss Bernice wore them yesterday when she went out!"

Ellery took them from her shaking fingers. After a moment he turned to Weaver.

"Mud splashes," he said laconically. "And here's a spot of wet. Seems indubitable!" He handed them back to the maid, who tremblingly replaced them in their compartments. . . . Ellery's eyes narrowed at once. She had put the shoes back with the heels *inside*, despite the fact that all the other shoes in the rack had the heels showing.

"Miss Underhill!" Ellery withdrew the black pumps from their pockets. The housekeeper rose sulkily.

"Miss Carmody's?" Ellery demanded, handing her the shoes.

She eyed them briefly. "Yes."

"Having reached complete agreement," drawled Ellery with a smiling change of tone, "please be so good as to return these shoes to the rack."

Without a word she obeyed. And Ellery, watching closely, chuckled to observe that she had duplicated the maid's action in putting the pumps into the rack heels first, so that the tips and buckles protruded from the pockets.

"Westley!" he said at once. Weaver approached wearily. He had been standing at a window, looking moodily down over Fifth Avenue. . . . And when Weaver replaced the pumps in the rack, he grasped the heels and stuck the shoes in tips first.

"Why do you do that?" asked Ellery as the two women, now convinced of his madness, moved uneasily away from the closet.

"Do what?" demanded Weaver.

Ellery smiled. "Easy, Hamlet. . . . Why do you put the shoes into the bag so that the heels hang over the pocket?"

Weaver stared at him. "Why, they're all that way," he said blankly. "Why should I put them in the opposite way?"

"*Alors,*" said Ellery, "*on a raison.* . . . Miss Underhill, why did you put the shoes back into the rack with the tips showing, when all the others have the heels showing?"

"Anybody would know that," snapped the housekeeper. "These black pumps have big buckles. Didn't you see what happened when Mr. Weaver put them back tips first? The buckles caught on the material of the bag!"

"Wondrous woman!" muttered Ellery. "And the others haven't any buckles, of course. . . ." He read confirmation in the housekeeper's eyes.

He left them standing before the closet and paced silently back and forth the length of the bedroom. His lips puckered fiercely as he mused. Suddenly he turned to Miss Underhill.

"I want you to look this closet over very carefully, Miss Underhill, and tell me, if you possibly can, whether anything is not there which you know should be there. . . ." He stepped back and waved his hand.

She stirred into activity, rummaging efficiently through the gowns, the hat-boxes, the shoes once more. Weaver, the maid, Ellery watched her in silence.

She paused in her work, looked undecidedly at the shoe-bag, then up at the shelf, hesitated, turned to Ellery.

"I can't be sure," she said thoughtfully, her cold eyes searching Ellery's, "but it seems to me that, while all of Mrs. French's things are here that should be here, two things of Bernice's are *not* here that should be here!"

"No!" breathed Ellery. He did not seem unduly surprised. "A hat and pair of shoes, no doubt?"

She glanced at him quickly. "How did you know? . . . Yes, that's what I thought. I remember several months ago when I was bringing down some things of Mrs. French's, Bernice asked me to take her grey toque down, too. And I did. And then there was her pair of low-heeled grey kid shoes—two tones of grey, they were—I'm fair certain I brought *those* down with me once. . . ." She turned sharply on Doris Keaton. "Are they in Miss Bernice's wardrobes at home, Doris?"

The maid shook her head with vigor. "No, Miss Underhill. I haven't seen them for a long time."

"Well, there you are. Grey felt toque, close-fitting, no trimming, and a pair of grey kid walking-shoes. They're missing."

"And that," said Ellery with a little bow that made

Miss Underhill stare, "is precisely that. Thank you so much. . . . Westley, will you escort Miss Underhill and the timidacious Keaton to the door? Tell the man outside to see that they're taken down to Sergeant Velie and kept out of the way of Commissioner Welles at least until everybody troops up here. . . . Undoubtedly, Miss Underhill, Marion French will be glad," and he bowed again to the housekeeper, "of your maternal and warming presence. *Good* afternoon!"

The instant the outer door had closed upon Weaver and the two women, Ellery ran across the library to the door of the cardroom. He entered with swift steps and stared down at the card-table with its neatly heaped piles of pasteboards and its butt-strewn ashtray. He sat down carefully in one of the chairs and examined the cards. Picking up the heavy stack of closed cards before him, he spread them out without disturbing their sequence. He frowned after a while, referred to eleven piles of cards in the center of the table. . . . Finally he rose, puzzled, defeated. He replaced all the stacks exactly as he had found them.

He was staring gloomily at the cigaret-stubs when he heard the outer door click shut and Weaver reënter the library. Ellery turned at once and left the cardroom. The red-leather door swished softly to behind him.

"Ladies taken care of?" he inquired absently. Weaver nodded almost with sulkiness. Ellery squared his shoulders, eyes twinkling. "Worrying about Marion, I'll wager," he said. "Don't, Wes. You're acting like a granny." He looked slowly about the library. His eyes came to rest after a time on the desk before the dormer-window. "I think," he announced dictatorially, sauntering toward the desk, "we'll take our ease, in a manner of speaking, and see what we can see. Rest being the sweet sauce of labor, as Plutarch so aptly says—set, Wes!"

17

AT THE APARTMENT: *The Library*

They sat down, Ellery at the comfortable swivel-chair behind the desk, Weaver in one of the leather-covered chairs at the conference table.

Ellery relaxed, letting his glance shift from wall to wall of the library, flicker over the table, the litter of business papers, the pictures on the wall, the glass top of the desk before him. . . . His glance fell idly on the slip of blue memorandum paper by the telephone. With perfect unconcern he picked it up and read it.

It was an official memorandum. On it was neatly typed a message.

Ellery reread the memorandum earnestly. He looked up at the disconsolate countenance of Weaver.

"Is it conceivable. . . ." he began. He broke off suddenly. "Tell me, Wes—when did you type this memorandum?"

"Eh?" Weaver started at the sound of Ellery's voice. "Oh, that! That's a memo I sent around to the Board of Directors. Typed it yesterday afternoon, after the Old Man left for Great Neck."

"How many copies did you make?"

"There were seven all told—one for each director, one for myself, and one for the files. This copy is the Old Man's."

Ellery spoke quickly. "How is it that I find it here on the desk?"

Weaver was surprised at the seeming inconsequentiality of Ellery's question. "Oh, I say!" he protested. "Just a matter of form. I left it here so that the Old Man could see in the morning that I'd taken care of the matter."

"And it was here—on the desk—when you left the apartment last night?" persisted Ellery.

INTER-OFFICE MEMORANDUM

C
 O   To: Mr. French ✓
  P   Mr. Gray
   Y   Mr. Marchbanks
                          Mr. Trask
                          Mr. Zorn
                          Mr. Weaver

                          Monday, May 23, 19—

A special meeting of the Board of
Directors is hereby called for the
morning of Tuesday, May the twenty-
fourth, at eleven o'clock, in the Conference Room. Do not fail to attend.
Details of the Whitney-French negotia-
tions will be discussed. It is hoped
that a final decision may be reached
officially at that time. Your presence is imperative.

Mr. Weaver is to meet Mr. French in
the Conference Room at nine a.m.
promptly to prepare the notes for
final directorial discussion.

                    [Signed] Cyrus French,

                    [Per] Westley Weaver,
                                  Sec'y.

"Well, of course!" said Weaver. "Where should it be?
Not only that, but it was *still* there when I got in this
morning." He grinned feebly.

But Ellery was serious. His eyes glittered. "You're sure

of that? . . ." He half-rose from the swivel-chair in a strange excitement. He sank back. "Seems to fit with the rest of the jigsaw," he muttered. "How beautifully it explains that one unexplained point!"

Thoughtfully he stowed the blue paper, uncreased, in a capacious wallet which he took from his breast-pocket.

"You'll say nothing of this, of course," he said slowly. . . . Weaver nodded and relapsed into apathy. Ellery bent forward, placed his elbows on the glass top, his head in his hands. He stared before him. . . . Something seemed to disturb his revery. His eyes, blank and pre-occupied, focused by degrees on the books between the onyx book-ends, standing austerely on the desk in his direct line of vision.

After a moment, as if to satisfy a mounting curiosity, he straightened up and became entirely absorbed in the titles of the books. His long arm swooped down on one of them, carried it back for closer observation.

"By the wisdom of Bibliophilus!" he murmured at last, looking up at Weaver. "What a queer collection of volumes! Does your employer make a habit of reading such heavy stuff as *An Outline of Paleontology*, Wes? Or is this a text-book hang-over from your undergraduate days? I can't recall your having a particular flair for science. It's by old John Morrison, too."

"Oh, that!" Weaver was momentarily embarrassed. "No, that's the—the Old Man's, I suppose, Ellery. His books entirely. Don't think I've ever observed the titles, as a matter of fact. What did you say—paleontology? Didn't know he went in for it."

Ellery regarded him keenly for a brief moment, then replaced the book. "And what's more—do you know," he said softly, "this *is* fetching!"

"What?" asked Weaver nervously.

"Well, bend an ear to these titles: *Fourteenth Century*

Trade and Commerce, by Stani Wedjowski. There's a rare one for you, although it is fitting that a department store magnet be interested in the history of merchanting. . . . And this one—*A Child's History of Music,* by Ramon Freyberg. A *child's* history, mind you. And *New Developments in Philately,* by Hugo Salisbury. A passion for stamps! Queer, queer, I tell you. . . . And—good heavens!—*Nonsense Anthology,* by that surpassing idiot, A. I. Throckmorton!" Ellery lifted his eyes to Weaver's troubled ones. "Dear young Dane," he said slowly, "I can understand a chronic bibliophile having this bizarre collection on his desk, for some dark purpose of his own, but I'll be immortally damned if I can make it jibe with my conception of Cyrus French, head of the Anti-Vice League and merchant prince. . . . Your employer does not impress me as having the intellectual potentialities of a paleontological field worker, who is a stamp-collecting addict, who has a passion for medieval commerce, who knows so little of music that he must read a child's history of it, and finally who indulges in the sickening horseplay of the year's best—or worst—vaudeville jokes! . . . Wes, old boy, there is more here than meets the vacillating eye."

"I'm quite at sea," said Weaver, shifting in his chair.

"And you should be, you should be, my child," said Ellery as he rose and walked over to the bookcase on the wall to his left. He lightly hummed the thematic air of *Marche Slav* as he scanned the titles of the volumes behind the glass partitions. After a moment's scrutiny he returned to the desk, where he sat down and again fingered the books between the book-ends in an absent way. Weaver's eyes followed him uneasily.

"From the books in the case," resumed Ellery, "my suspicions seem to be borne out. Nothing but works on social welfare and sets of Bret Harte, O. Henry, and Richard Harding Davis, *et al.* All of which compress nicely into the obvious intellectual stratum of your nice Old Man. Yet on the desk . . ." He mused. "And they show no signs of use," he complained, as if disturbed further by this heinous crime against literature. "In two cases, where the volumes are bound that way, the leaves are still uncut. . . . Westley, tell me truthfully, is French interested in these subjects?" He flipped his finger at the books before him.

Weaver answered immediately. "Not to my knowledge."

"Marion? Bernice? Mrs. French? The directors?"

"I can answer positively in the case of the French family, Ellery," replied Weaver, jumping from his chair and pacing up and down before the desk. "None of them reads such stuff. As for the directors—well, you've seen them."

"Gray might be interested in this preposterous mélange," said Ellery thoughtfully. "He's the type. But that child's history of music. . . . Well!"

He bestirred himself. On the fly-leaf of the little volume in his coat pocket he made a careful memorandum of the titles and authors of the desk volumes. With a sigh he dropped the pencil back into his vest pocket and once more began to stare blankly at the books. His hand played idly with one of the book-ends.

"Mustn't forget to ask French about these books," he murmured, more to himself than to Weaver, who still paced furiously up and down the room. "—Sit down, Wes! You disturb my train of thought. . . ." Weaver shrugged, sat down quiescently. "Nice things, these," Ellery said in a casual voice, indicating the book-ends. "That's a very curious bit of carving on the onyx."

"Must have cost Gray a pile of dollars," mumbled Weaver.

"Oh, they were a gift to French?"

"Gray gave them to him on his last birthday—in March.

They were imported, I know—I remember Lavery commenting on their rarity and beauty a few weeks ago."

"Did you say—March?" asked Ellery suddenly, bringing the black shining book-end closer to his eyes. "That's only two months ago, and this—" He quickly picked up the companion piece to the book-end in his hand. He placed them side by side on the glass top of the desk, all at once handling them with meticulous delicacy. He beckoned to Weaver.

"Do you see any difference between these?" he asked in some excitement.

Weaver leaned over, put out his hand to lift one of them. . . .

"Don't touch it!" said Ellery sharply. "Well?"

Weaver stood up straight. "No call to shout, Ellery," he said reproachfully. "As far as I can see, the felt under this one seems faded a little."

"Don't mind my rude manners, old son," Ellery said. "I thought that difference in shade wasn't wholly my imagination."

"I can't understand why the green felts should vary in color," remarked Weaver in a puzzled way, returning to his chair. "Those book-ends are nearly new. They must have been all right when the Old Man got them—they were, in fact. I'd have noticed the discoloration had there been one."

Ellery did not answer at once. He stared down at the two pieces of carved onyx. They were both cylindrical in shape, with the carving on the outer sides. On the under sides, where the book-ends were to be placed against the desk, were pieces of fine green felt. In the strong clear afternoon sun, streaming through the big window, one exhibited a marked difference in the shade of green.

"Here's a pretty mystery," muttered Ellery. "And what it means, if it means anything at all, I can't see at the moment. . . ." He looked up at Weaver with a glint in his eye. "Have these book-ends ever been out of this room since Gray presented them to French?"

"No," replied Weaver. "Never. I'm here every day, and I would know if they'd been moved."

"Have they ever been broken, or repaired, even here?"

"Why, of course not!" said Weaver, puzzled. "That seems sort of silly, El."

"And yet essential." Ellery sat down and began to twirl his pince-nez, his eyes riveted on the book-ends before him. "Gray's an intimate of French, I take it?" he asked suddenly.

"His best friend. They've known each other for over thirty years. They have good-natured quarrels periodically about the Old Man's obsession in the matter of white slavery, prostitution and the like, but they've always been unusually close."

"Which is as it should be, I suppose." Ellery sank into deep and concentrated thought. He did not take his eyes from the book-ends. "I wonder, now. . . ." His hand dipped into his coat pocket and emerged with a small magnifying-glass. Weaver regarded his friend in astonishment, then burst into laughter.

"Ellery! Upon my word! Just like Sherlock Holmes!" His mirth was unadulterated, inoffensive, like the man himself.

Ellery grinned sheepishly. "It *does* seem theatrical," he confessed. "But I've found it a handy little tool at times." He bent lower, applied the glass to the book-end with the darker green felt.

"Looking for fingerprints?" chuckled Weaver.

"You can never tell," said Ellery sententiously. "Although a glass isn't infallible. You need fingerprint powder to make absolutely sure. . . ." He discarded the book-end and bent the glass on its mate. As he scanned the lighter green of its felt, his hand shook convulsively.   Disregarding Weaver's cry of "What is it?" he fixed his attention rigidly on a portion of the material where the felt met the onyx, at an edge.   A thin line, so thin that to the naked eye it was like a hair, broadened slightly under the magnification of the lens.   This line, which extended all around the bottom of the book-end, was actually composed of glue —the glue with which the felt was pasted to the onyx. The second book-end also had the glue-line.

"Here, take the glass, Wes, and focus it at the juncture of felt and onyx," commanded Ellery, pointing to the under-side of the book-end.   "Tell me what you see—be careful you don't touch the surface of the onyx!"

Weaver bent over and eagerly looked through the glass. "Why, there's a sort of dust stuck in the glue—it's dust, isn't it?"

"Unorthodox-looking dust," said Ellery grimly, seizing the lens and again examining the felt at that portion of the glue-line.   In another moment he had swept the eye of the glass over the other surfaces of the book-end. He employed the same tactics with the second book-end.

Weaver uttered a short exclamation.   "I say, El, mightn't it be the same stuff you found in Bernice's lipstick?   Heroin, I think you called it!"

"Smart guess, Westley," smiled Ellery, his eye fast to the lens.   "But I seriously doubt it. . . . This will require analysis, and immediately.   Something twitters a warning message in my subconscious."

He dropped the magnifying glass on the table, thoughtfully regarded the two book-ends once more, then reached for the telephone.

"Get Sergeant Velie—yes, detective-sergeant—on the wire for me immediately."   He spoke rapidly to Weaver while he waited, receiver to ear.   "If this stuff is what I am beginning to think it is, old boy, the plot thickens like a purée. However, we'll see. Get me a good wad of absorbent cotton from the bathroom-closet, will you, Wes? Hello, hello—Velie?" he said into the telephone, as Weaver disappeared through the brass-studded door, "this is Ellery Queen speaking. Yes, from the apartment upstairs. . . . Velie, send me one of your best men at once. . . . Who? . . . Yes, Piggott or Hesse will do. At once! And mum's the word in the hearing of Welles. . . . No, you can't help—yet. Hold in, you bloodhound!" He chuckled as he hung up.

Weaver returned with a large carton filled with absorbent cotton. Ellery took it from him.

"Watch me, Wes," he announced with a laugh. "Watch carefully, because it may be necessary for you in the not remote future to testify on the witness stand as to precisely what I did here to-day. . . . Are you ready?"

"I'm all eyes," grinned Weaver.

. ."*Allay-oop!*" With a prestidigitator's flourish Ellery whipped out of the large pocket of his sack-coat a curious metal packet. He pressed a tiny button and the lid flew open, disclosing black leather pads of thin tough texture, pierced for small bits of waxed thread, each of which held a shining little instrument.

"This," said Ellery, showing his even white teeth, "is one of my most prized possessions. Given to me with the benediction of *Herr Burgomeister* of Berlin last year for the little aid I gave him in snaring Don Dickey, the American gem-thief. . . . Cunnin', isn't it?"

Weaver fell back weakly. "What on earth is it?"

"One of the handiest contraptions ever conceived by the mind of man for the use of the criminal investigator," replied Ellery, his fingers busy with the thin leather mats. "This was created especially for your humble servant through the gratitude of the Berlin mayor and the co-operator of the German central detective bureau. At my

own specifications, incidentally—I knew what I wanted.
. . . You'll observe that an almost incredible number of
articles are packed in this amazingly small aluminum container—aluminum for its lightness, by the way. Everything in it that a first-class detective might conceivably
need during a scientific investigation—on a lilliputian scale,
but strong, compact, and extraordinarily utilitarian."

"Well, I'll be damned!" exclaimed Weaver. "I didn't
know you went in for this sort of thing so seriously,
Ellery."

"Let the contents of my work-chest convince you,"
smiled Ellery. "Here we have two accessory lenses—Zeiss,
by the way,—for my pocket magnifier; stronger than
usual, you see. Here's a tiny steel tape measure with the
automatic recoil, 96-inch length, reverse side in centimeters.
Red, blue, and black crayons. Undersize drawing-compass
and special pencil. One vial each of black and white
fingerprint powder, with camel's-hair brushes and stamping
pad. Packet of glassine envelopes. Small calipers and
smaller tweezers. Collapsible probe, adjustable to various
lengths. Tempered steel pins and needles. Litmus paper
and two tiny test-tubes. Combination knife containing
two blades, corkscrew, screw-driver, awl, file, scraper.
Specially designed field-compass—and don't laugh. Not
all investigations are conducted in the heart of New York.
. . . And that's not the last by any means. Red, white
and green twine of thread-like thinness, but very strong.
Sealing-wax. Small 'lighter'—made specially for me.
Scissors. And, naturally, a stop-watch made by one of
the world's best watch-makers—a Swiss in the employ of
the German government. . . . How do you like my
traveling work-case, Wes?"

Weaver looked incredulous. "Do you mean to tell me
all those things are in that ridiculously small aluminum
container?"

"Exacty. The entire contraption is some four inches wide by six inches long, and weighs slightly less than two pounds. Thickness of a fair-sized book. Oh, yes! I forgot to mention a crystal mirror embedded in the wall of one of the aluminum sides. . . . But I'd better be getting down to work. Keep your eyes open!"

From one of the leather mats Ellery extracted the tweezers. Adjusting one of the more powerful lenses in his pocket-glass, he carefully placed the first book-end in a fixed position on the desk, held the magnifier to his eye with his left hand, and with his right painstakingly maneuvered the tweezers into the hardened glue which contained the suspicious-looking particles. He instructed Weaver to hold in readiness one of the glassine envelopes and, uprooting the almost invisible grains, placed them carefully in the envelope.

He laid down the glass and the tweezers, and sealed the envelope instantly.

"I think I've bagged them all," he said with satisfaction. "And the ones I've missed Jimmy will get. . . . Come!"

It was Detective Piggott. He closed the outer door softly and entered the library with ill-concealed curiosity.

"Sergeant said you wanted me, Mr. Queen," and his eyes were on Weaver.

"Righto. Just a sec, Piggott, and I'll tell you what to do." Ellery scribbled an inky note on the reverse side of the envelope. It read:

"DEAR JIMMY: Analyze powder-grains in envelope. Extract any additional particles in glue-line of book-end marked *A*, also analyze. Check on book-end marked *B* for similar grains. After analyzing the grains, *and not until then*, check both book-ends for fingerprints other than my own. Could bring out a print myself, but if you find any, have it 'shot' in the lab and a photoprint immediately made. 'Phone all information to me, *personally*, as soon as you've done. I'm at French apartment in French store. Piggott will tell you.

                                                        E. Q."

Marking the book-ends *A* and *B* with his red crayon, he swathed both in absorbent cotton, wrapped them in some paper Weaver found for him in the desk, and handed package and envelope to the detective.

"Take these down to Jimmy at the headquarters laboratory as fast as you can get there, Piggott," he said insistently. "Don't let anything stop you. If Velie or my father corners you on the way out, say it's on business for me. On no account let the Commissioner get wind of what you're carrying off the premises. Now scoot!"

Piggott left without a word. He was too well trained in the methods of the Queens to ask questions.

And as he slipped out of the door, he saw the shadow of a rising elevator through the frosted glass wall. He turned and sped down the emergency stairs just as the door slid open and Commissioner Welles, Inspector Queen and a small cohort of detectives and policemen stepped out.

18

SCRAMBLED SIGNS

Within five minutes the private corridor outside French's sixth floor apartment was crowded with a score of people. Two policemen stood guard at the door. Another stood with his back to the elevator, his eyes on the emergency staircase-door nearby. In the anteroom lounged several detectives smoking cigarets.

Ellery sat smiling behind French's desk in the library. Commissioner Welles puffed about the room, shouting orders to detectives, opening the doors leading off the library, peering like a myopic owl at things strange to him. Inspector Queen talked with Velie and Crouther near the

dormer-window. Weaver stood miserably in a corner, unnoticed. His eyes frequently sought the anteroom door,
beyond which he knew was Marion French. . . .

"You say, Mr. Queen," grunted Welles, out of breath,
"that the cigaret stubs and the game of—blast it! what
is it again?—banque are the only signs of this Carmody
girl's presence here?"

"Not at all, Commissioner," said Ellery gravely. "You
forget the shoes and hat in the closet. I believe I recounted
the housekeeper's identification—?"

"Yes, yes, of course!" grumbled Welles. He frowned.
"Here, you fingerprint men!" he shouted, "have you covered that little room off the cardroom?" Without waiting
for a reply, he bellowed an unintelligible order to several
photographers who were busy over the table holding the
cards and cigaret-stubs. Finally, mopping his brow, he
beckoned imperiously to Inspector Queen.

"What do you think, Queen?" he demanded. "Looks
like a pretty clear case, eh?"

The Inspector sent a sidewise glance at his son, and
smiled cryptically. "Hardly, Commissioner. We've got
to find the girl first, you know. . . . Work's barely
scratched. We haven't had the time to check a single alibi,
for example. Despite these clues pointing to Bernice Carmody, we're not at all satisfied that there isn't something
deeper. . . ." He shook his head. "At any rate, Commissioner, there's a heap of work waiting for us. Anybody
you'd like to question? We have 'em all outside in the
corridor waiting."

The Commissioner looked fierce. "No! Can't say I do
at this stage. . . ." He cleared his throat. "What's next
on your list? I've got to get down to City Hall for a
conference with the Mayor and I can't give this thing the
personal attention it deserves. Well?"

"I want to clear up a few moot points," replied Queen

dryly. "Several people out there will stand questioning. French himself—"

"French. Yes, yes. Too bad. Feel sorry for the man. Quite a blow." Welles looked around nervously and lowered his voice. "By the way, Queen, while there is not to be the slightest deviation from the highest considerations of duty, you understand, it might be—ah—wise to allow French to get home to his physician's care. . . . As for this stepdaughter business, I hope"—he paused uncomfortably—"I might say I have the feeling that this girl has made a complete getaway. You're to follow her up conscientiously, of course. . . . Too bad. I— Well! I must be going."

He turned unceremoniously on his heel, and with something like a sigh of relief tramped toward the door, followed by his bodyguard of detectives. He turned in the anteroom and shouted back, "I want a quick solution, Queen—too many unsolved homicides this past month." And he disappeared with a final quiver of his fat sides.

There was silence for several seconds after the anteroom door closed. Then the Inspector shrugged his shoulders lightly and crossed the room to Ellery's side. Ellery dragged a chair over for his father and they held a whispered conversation for many minutes. The words "razorblade," . . . "book-ends," . . . "books" . . . and "Bernice" . . . recurred at intervals. The old man's face grew longer and longer as Ellery talked. Finally, he shook his head in despair and rose.

An altercation beyond the anteroom door brought up the heads of all the men in the library. A woman's passionate voice and the gruff tones of a man intermingled. Weaver's nostrils quivered and he dashed across the room and flung open the door.

Marion French was endeavoring frantically to push past the burly figure of a detective in the anteroom.

"But I must see Inspector Queen!" she cried. "My father— Please don't touch me!"

Weaver grasped the detective's arm and violently pushed him aside.

"Get your hands off her!" he growled. "I'll teach you to handle a lady that way. . . ."

He would have attacked the amused detective if Marion had not thrown her arms around him. By this time the Inspector and Ellery had hurried up.

"Here! Ritter, stand aside!" said the Inspector. "What's the trouble, Miss French?" he asked gently.

"My—my father," she gasped. "Oh, it's cruel, inhuman. . . . Can't you see he's ill, out of his mind? For God's sake, let us take him home! He's just fainted!"

They pushed into the hallway. A crowd of people were stooping over Cyrus French, who had collapsed and lay, white-faced, still, on the marble floor. The store physician, small and dark, bent over him in distress.

"Out?" asked the Inspector with some concern.

The physician nodded. "Should be in his bed right now, sir. In a dangerous state of collapse."

Ellery whispered to his father. The old man clucked worriedly, shook his head. "Can't take a chance, Ellery. The man is ill." He signed to two detectives and Cyrus French, arms hanging limply, was carried into the apartment and laid on one of the beds. He regained consciousness a moment later, groaning.

John Gray wriggled his way past a policeman and stormed into the bedroom.

"You can't get away with this sort of thing, Inspector or no Inspector!" he cried in his high-pitched voice. "I demand that Mr. French be sent home immediately!"

"Keep your shirt on, Mr. Gray," admonished the Inspector mildly. "He's going in a moment."

"And I'm going with him," squeaked Gray. "He'll

want me, he will. I'll take this up with the Mayor, sir. I'll—"

"Shut *up*, sir!" roared Queen, his face scarlet. He whirled on Detective Ritter. "Get a cab."

"Miss French." Marion looked up, startled. The Inspector irritably took a pinch of snuff. "You may leave with your father and Mr. Gray. But please remain at home until we call this afternoon. We will want to look over the premises and perhaps question Mr. French, if he's in a condition to see us. And—I'm sorry, my dear."

The girl smiled through wet lashes. Weaver moved stealthily to her side, drew her a little apart.

"Marion dear—I'm awfully sorry I didn't lam that brute for you," he stammered. "Did he hurt you?"

Marion's eyes widened, softened. "Don't be silly, darling," she whispered. "And don't be getting mixed up with the police. I'll help Mr. Gray get father home, and stay there just as Inspector Queen ordered me to. . . . You won't be—in any trouble, dear?"

"Who? I?" Weaver laughed. "Now don't be worrying your pretty head about me.—And as for the store, I'll keep an eye on everything. Tell your father that when he can understand. . . . Do you love me?"

There was no one looking. He bent swiftly and kissed her. Her eyes glowed in answer.

Five minutes later Cyrus French, Marion French and John Gray had left the building under a police escort.

Velie lumbered over. "Got two of the boys on the trail of this Carmody girl," he reported. "Didn't want to tell you before with the Commissioner around—busy and all that."

Queen frowned, then chuckled. "All my boys are turning traitor to the City," he said. "Thomas, I want you to send somebody out on the trail of Mrs. French after she left her house last night. She walked out about eleven-fifteen. Probably took a cab, because she got here at eleven-forty-five, which would make it about right in the after-theater traffic. Got it?"

Velie nodded and disappeared.

Ellery sat at the desk again, whistling softly to himself, a faraway look in his eyes.

The Inspector had MacKenzie, the store manager, brought to the library.

"Have you checked the employees, Mr. MacKenzie?"

"A report came through from my assistant a few moments ago." Ellery listened avidly. "So far as we have been able to determine," continued the Scotchman, referring to a paper in his hand, "all employees who checked in both yesterday and today were at their posts. As for today, everything seems perfectly regular in that connection. There is, of course, a list of absentees, which I have here. If you would like to follow up on these employees, here's the list."

"We'll have a peep at it," said the Inspector, taking the list from MacKenzie. He turned it over to a detective with a command. "Now, MacKenzie, you may start the ball rolling again. Store's routine is to go on as usual, but be careful that you say nothing at all of this whole business in your publicity. Have that window on Fifth Avenue kept closed and guarded until further orders. We'll have to seal it up anyway for a time. That's all. You're free to go."

"I'd like to ask the remaining directors a question, dad, if you haven't anything to quiz them about," said Ellery, after MacKenzie had left.

"I haven't a thought in my head about them—that I could turn to account," answered Queen. "Hesse, bring in Zorn, Marchbanks and Trask. Let's have another try at 'em."

The detective returned shortly with the three directors.

They looked peaked and ragged; Marchbanks was chewing savagely at a frayed cigar. The Inspector waved his hand at Ellery and retreated a step.

Ellery rose. "Just one question, gentlemen, and then I think Inspector Queen will permit you to go about your business."

"High time," muttered Trask, biting his lip.

"Mr. Zorn," said Ellery, ignoring the attenuated and foppish Trask, "is there a regular meeting-time for your Board of Directors?"

Zorn juggled his heavy gold watch-chain nervously. "Yes—yes, of course."

"If I'm not too inquisitive, when is that meeting-time?"

"Every other Friday afternoon."

"This is routine, strictly adhered to?"

"Yes—yes."

"How is it that there was a meeting this morning—on a Tuesday?"

"That was a special meeting. Mr. French calls them as the occasion demands."

"But the semi-monthly meetings are held regardless of special meetings?"

"Yes."

"I take it, then, that there was a meeting on Friday last?"

"Yes."

Ellery turned to Marchbanks and Trask. "Is Mr. Zorn's testimony substantially correct, gentlemen?"

Both nodded their heads sullenly. Ellery smiled, thanked them, and sat down. The Inspector smiled, thanked them, and told them politely that they were free to leave. He escorted them to the door and whispered to the policeman on guard an inaudible instruction. Zorn, Marchbanks and Trask left the private corridor immediately.

"There's an interesting feller outside, El," remarked the

Inspector. "Vincent Carmody, Mrs. French's first husband. Think I'll tackle him next.—Hesse, bring in Mr. Carmody in about two minutes."

"Did you check up at all on the night freight-entrance on 39th Street while you were downstairs?" asked Ellery.

"Sure did." The Inspector took a pinch of snuff reflectively. "That's a funny place, El. With the watchman and the truckman in the little booth, it would have been pie for somebody to slip into the building, especially at night. Went over it with particular thoroughness. It certainly looks like the answer to how the murderer gained entry last night."

"It may answer the question of how the murderer got in," remarked Ellery lazily, "but it doesn't answer the question of how he got out. That exit was closed to him by eleven-thirty. If he left the building by that door, then, he must have done so before eleven-thirty, eh?"

"But Mrs. French didn't get here until eleven-forty-five, El," objected the Inspector, "and according to Prouty she was killed about midnight. So how could he have left by that door before eleven-thirty?"

"The answer to that," said Ellery, "is that he couldn't, and therefore didn't. Is there a door through which he could have slipped into the main building from the freight room?"

"Nothing to it," growled the Inspector. "There's a door 'way back in the shadows of the room. It wasn't locked—never is—because these fools took it for granted that if the outer door was locked, the inner door didn't have to be. Anyway, it heads right onto a corridor which is parallel with the corridor that runs past the nightwatchman's office, but further into the body of the main floor.* In the darkness, it must have been ridiculously easy to slip through the door, sneak down that corridor, turn the cor-

* See diagram at frontispiece.

ner, and cover the thirty feet or so to the elevator and
stairs. That's probably the answer."

"How about the master key in that office downstairs?"
asked Ellery. "Did the day-man say anything about it?"

"Nothing there," replied the Inspector disconsolately.
"O'Shane is his name, and he swears the key never left the
locked drawer during his shift."

The door opened and Hesse escorted a preternaturally
tall man with penetrating eyes and a straggly grey beard
into the room. He was handsome in a sophisticated way,
and striking. Ellery noted with interest the triangular lean
jaw. The man was dressed carelessly, but in clothes of
quality. He bowed stiffly to the Inspector and stood waiting. His eyes shifted luminously from man to man in the
room.

"I had barely a chance of talking to you downstairs, Mr.
Carmody," said the Inspector pleasantly. "There are a few
things I want to ask you. Won't you sit down?"

Carmody dropped into a chair. He nodded curtly to
Weaver as he caught the secretary's eye, but said nothing.

"Now, Mr. Carmody," began the Inspector, striding up
and down before the desk at which Ellery sat quietly, "a
few unimportant but necessary questions. Hagstrom,
you're ready?" He cocked an eye at the detective, who
nodded, notebook in hand. The Inspector resumed his
march on the rug. Suddenly he looked up. Carmody's
eyes burned deeply into thin air.

"Mr. Carmody," said the Inspector abruptly, "I understand that you are the sole owner of the Holbein Studios,
dealing in antiques?"

"That is precisely correct," said Carmody. His voice
was startling—low and vibrant and deliberate.

"You were married to Mrs. French, and divorced some
seven years ago?"

"That is also correct." There was a finality in his tones that impinged unpleasantly on the ear. He emanated an aura of complete self-control.

"Have you seen Mrs. French since your divorce?"

"Yes. Many times."

"Socially? There was no particular unpleasantness in your relations?"

"None whatever. Yes, I met Mrs. French socially."

The Inspector was slightly nettled. This witness answered exactly what he was asked, and no more.

"How often, Mr. Carmody?"

"As often as twice a week during the social season."

"And you last saw her——"

"A week ago Monday evening, at a dinner given by Mrs. Standish Prince at Mrs. Prince's home."

"You spoke to her?"

"Yes." Carmody stirred. "Mrs. French was very much interested in antiques, an interest cultivated perhaps during our marriage." The man seemed made of steel. He showed not the faintest trace of emotion. "We conversed for a time about a Chippendale chair she was particularly anxious to have."

"Anything else, Mr. Carmody?"

"Yes. About our daughter."

"Ah!" The Inspector pursed his lips, pulled at his mustache. "Miss Bernice Carmody was placed in the custody of your wife after your divorce?"

"Yes."

"You have seen your daughter periodically, perhaps?"

"Yes. Although Mrs. French secured custody of my daughter, our informal arrangement at the time of our divorce was that I might see the child at any time." A warm color floated into his voice. The Inspector regarded him quickly, looked away. He plunged into a new line of questioning.

"Mr. Carmody, can you suggest any possible explanation to account for this crime?"

"No, I cannot." Carmody grew colder at once. For no apparent reason his eyes shifted to Ellery, and held there intently for an instant.

"Had Mrs. French any enemies, to your knowledge?"

"No. She was singularly free from the profundity of character which so often breeds animosity in others." Carmody might have been talking of an utter stranger; his tone, his bearing were wholly impersonal.

"Not even yourself, Mr. Carmody?" asked the Inspector softly.

"Not even myself, Inspector," said Carmody in the same frozen tones. "If it is any concern of yours, my love for my wife dwindled during our wedded life and when it had entirely disappeared, I secured a divorce. I felt no bitterness toward her then, nor do I now. You will, of course," he added without a change in inflection, "have to take my word for that."

"Did Mrs. French seem nervous the last few times you saw her? Did anything seem to be troubling her? Did she give you any clue to a possible secret worry?"

"Our conversations, Inspector, were hardly of so intimate a nature. I noticed nothing unusual about her. Mrs. French was an extraordinarily prosaic person. Not at all the worrying kind, I can assure you."

The Inspector paused, Carmody sat quietly. Then he spoke, without warning, without passion. He merely opened his mouth and began to speak, but it was so unexpected that the Inspector started violently and took a hasty pinch of snuff to conceal his agitation.

"Inspector, you are evidently questioning me with the secret hope that I may have something to do with the crime, or that I may be in the possession of vital information. Inspector, you are wasting your time." Carmody leaned forward, his eyes strangely blazing. "Believe me when I say that I haven't the slightest interest either in the live Mrs. French—or the dead Mrs. French. Or the whole damned French tribe put together. My own concern is with my daughter. I understand that she is missing. If she is, there has been foul play. If you have any idea in your head that my daughter is a matricide, the more fool you. . . . You will be perpetrating a crime against an innocent girl if you do not immediately seek to discover Bernice's present whereabouts and the reason for her disappearance. And in that connection, you are welcome to my unstinting co-operation. If you do not look for her immediately, I shall set private detectives on her trail. I think that is all."

Carmody rose to his astonishing height and stood immovably waiting.

The Inspector stirred. "I should advise a slight softening of tone in the future, Mr. Carmody," he said dryly. "You may go."

Without another word the antique dealer turned and left the apartment.

"Well, what do you think of Mr. Carmody?" asked Queen quizzically.

"I've never known an antiquarian who wasn't queer in some way," laughed Ellery. "Cool customer, however. . . . Dad, I should very much like to see Monsieur Lavery again."

The Frenchman was pale and nervous when he was conducted into the library. He seemed excessively tired and sank into a chair at once, stretching his long legs with a sigh.

"You might have provided chairs outside in the corridor," he said reproachfully to the Inspector. "My good fortune to be the last called! *C'est la vie, hein?*" He shrugged his shoulders humorously. "May I smoke, Inspector?"

He lit a cigaret without waiting for a reply.

Ellery rose and shook himself vigorously. He looked at Lavery, and Lavery looked at him, and both smiled for no apparent reason.

"I shall be brutally frank, Mr. Lavery," drawled Ellery. "You are a man of the world. You will not be constrained by a false sense of discretion. . . . Mr. Lavery, have you ever suspected during your stay with the Frenches, that Bernice Carmody is a drug addict?"

Lavery started, regarded Ellery with alert eyes. "You have discovered that already? And without seeing the girl? My felicitations, Mr. Queen. . . . To your question, let me reply without hesitation—yes."

"Oh, I say!" protested Weaver suddenly, from his corner. "How could you know, Lavery? On such a short acquaintance?"

"I know the symptoms, Weaver," said Lavery mildly. "The sallow, almost saffron complexion; the slightly protruding eyeballs; the bad teeth; the unnatural nervousness and excitability; a certain air of furtiveness constantly maintained; the sudden hysteria and the more sudden recovery; the excessive thinness, growing more patent with every passing day—no, it was not difficult to diagnose the young lady's ailment." He turned to Ellery with a quick gesture of his thin fingers. "Let me make it perfectly clear that my opinion is just an opinion, little more. I have no definite evidence of any kind. But, short of medical advices to the contrary, I should be ready as a layman to swear that the girl is a drug fiend in an advanced stage!"

Weaver groaned. "The Old Man—"

"Of course, we're all terribly sorry about that," put in the Inspector quickly. "You suspected her of being an addict at once, Mr. Lavery?"

"From the moment I laid eyes on her," said the Frenchman emphatically. "It was a source of constant astonishment to me that more people did not observe what was so perfectly plain to me."

"Perhaps they did—perhaps they did," muttered Ellery, brows drawn taut. He brushed a vagrant thought away and addressed Lavery once more.

"Have you ever been in this room before, Mr. Lavery?" he asked, à propos of nothing.

"In Mr. French's apartment?" cried Lavery. "Why, every day, sir. Mr. French has been more than kind, and I have used this room incessantly since my arrival in New York."

"Then there is nothing more to be said," Ellery smiled. "You may now retire to your lecture-room, if it isn't too late, and carry on the grand work of continentalizing America. Good day, sir!"

Lavery bowed, showed his white teeth all around, and left the apartment with long strides.

Ellery sat down at the desk and wrote earnestly on the flyleaf of his sadly abused little book.

19

OPINIONS AND REPORTS

Inspector Queen stood Napoleonically in the center of the library, staring vindictively at the anteroom door. He muttered to himself, turning his head slowly from side to side like a terrier.

He beckoned to Crouther, the head store detective, who was assisting one of the photographers at the door of the cardroom.

"Look here, Crouther, you ought to be in a good position to know about this." The Inspector filled his nostrils with snuff. The burly store detective scraped his jaw expectantly. "Seeing that door there reminded me. What in heaven's name was French's idea in having a special spring lock put on the corridor door? Seems to me that for an apartment only occasionally used this is pretty well guarded."

Crouther grinned deprecatingly. "Now don't go bothering your head about that, Inspector. The old boy's just a bug on privacy, that's all. Hates to be interrupted—that's a fact."

"But a burglar-proof lock in a burglar-proof building!"

"Well," said Crouther, "you either have to take him that way or go nuts. Matter of fact, Inspector," he lowered his voice, "he's always been a little queer on some subjects. I can remember like today the morning I got a written order from the boss, with signatures and a lot of that bunk, requisitioning a specially made lock. That was when they were remodeling the apartment, about two years ago. So I followed my orders and had an expert locksmith manufacture the dingus on that outside door. Boss liked it pretty much, too—was happy as an Irish cop."

"How about this business of setting a man at the door?" demanded the Inspector. "Certainly that lock would keep out anybody who wasn't wanted."

"We-ell," said Crouther hesitantly, "the boss is such a bug on this privacy business that he didn't even want knocks on the door. Guess that's why he asked me for a man to stand guard every once in a while. Always kept the boys in the corridor, too—they hate the job, the whole crew of 'em. Couldn't even come into the anteroom and sit down."

The Inspector scowled down at his regulation policeman's boots for a moment and crooked his finger at Weaver.

"Come here, my boy." Weaver trudged wearily across the rug. "Just what's behind French's craze for privacy? From what Crouther tells me, this place is like a fortress most times. Who in heaven's name *is* allowed in here besides his family?"

"It's just an idiosyncrasy of the Old Man's, Inspector," said Weaver. "Don't take it too seriously. He's a good deal of an eccentric. Very few people see the inside of this apartment. Apart from myself, the immediate family, the Board of Directors, and during the last month Mr. Lavery, practically no one in the store organization is allowed in here. No, that's not quite true. MacKenzie, the store manager, is called in occasionally to get direct orders from the Old Man—was in last week, in fact. But aside from MacKenzie, this place is a complete mystery to the store forces."

"You tell 'em, Mr. Weaver," put in Crouther jocularly.

"And that's how it is, Inspector," continued Weaver. "Not even Crouther has been here in the past few years."

"Last time I saw this place before this morning," amended Crouther, "was two years ago when they were redecorating and refurnishing it." He grew red in the face at the thought of some secret injury. "That's a heck of a way to treat a head store detective, believe me."

"You ought to work for the City, Crouther," said the Inspector grimly. "Shut up and be satisfied with a soft job!"

"I should explain, if I haven't done so before," added Weaver, "that the taboo is more or less limited to employees. A great many people come here, but most of the visits are strictly by appointment with the Old Man, and his visitors come on Anti-Vice League business. Clergymen, most of them. A few politicians, not many."

"That's a fact," put in Crouther.

"Well!" The Inspector shot a keen glance toward the two men before him. "It looks mighty bad for this Carmody girl, eh? What do you think?"

Weaver looked pained and half-turned away.

"Well, I don't know about that, Inspector," said

Crouther with heavy importance. "My own ideas about this case—"

"Eh? Your own ideas?" The Inspector looked startled, then suppressed a smile. "What *are* your own ideas, Crouther? Might be of some value—never can tell."

Ellery, who had been sitting abstractedly at the desk, listening to the conversation with half-cocked ears, jammed his little volume into his pocket, rose, and sauntered idly over to the group.

"What's this? A post-mortem?" he demanded, smiling. "And what do I hear, Crouther, about an idea of yours on the case?"

Crouther looked embarrassed for a moment and shuffled his feet. But then he squared his thick shoulders and lashed out into speech, openly enjoying his rôle of orator.

"I think," he began—

"Ah!" said the Inspector.

"I think," Crouther repeated, unabashed, "that Miss Carmody is a victim. Yes, sir, victim of a frame-up!"

"No!" murmured Ellery.

"Go on," said the Inspector curiously.

"It's as plain as the nose—beg pardon, Inspector—on your face. Who ever heard of a girl bumping her own mother off? It ain't natural."

"But the cards, Crouther—the shoes, the hat," said the Inspector gently.

"Just hooey, Inspector," said Crouther with confidence. "Hell! That's no trick, to plant a pair o' shoes and a hat. No, sir, you can't tell me Miss Carmody did the job. Don't believe it and won't believe it. I go on common sense, and that's a fact. Girl shoot her own mother! No, sir!"

"Well, there's something in that," remarked the Inspector sententiously. "What do you make of Miss Marion French's scarf, while you're analyzing the crime, Crouther? Think she's mixed up in it anywhere?"

"Who? That little girl?" Crouther expanded, snorted. "Say, that's another plant. Or else she left it here by mistake. Kind o' like the plant idea, though, myself. Fact!"

"You would say, then," interpolated Ellery, "while you're on the Holmesian track, that this is a case of— what?"

"Don't get you entirely, sir," said Crouther stoutly, "but it looks darned near like a case of murder and kidnapping. Can't see any other way to explain it."

"Murder and kidnapping?" Ellery smiled. "Not a bad idea at that. Good recitation, Crouther."

The detective beamed. Weaver, who had resolutely refrained from commenting, heaved a sigh of relief when a knock on the outer door interrupted the conversation.

The policeman stationed outside opened the door to admit a weazened little man, completely bald, carrying a bulging brief-case.

"Afternoon, Jimmy!" said the Inspector cheerfully. "Got anything for us in that bag of yours?"

"Sure have, Inspector," squeaked the little old man. "Got down here as fast as I could.—Hello, Mr. Queen."

"Glad to see you, Jimmy," said Ellery, and the expression on his face was one of intense expectancy. At this moment the photographers and fingerprint investigators trooped into the library, hats and coats on, their apparatus stowed away. "Jimmy" greeted them all by name.

"Through here, Inspector," announced one of the photographers. "Any orders?"

"Not at the moment." Queen turned to the fingerprint men. "Anybody find anything?"

"Got a lot of prints," reported one of them, "but practically all came from this room. Not a one in the cardroom and none in the bedroom, except for a few stray prints of Mr. Queen's, here."

"Anything in the prints from this room?"

"Hard to say. If the room's been used all morning by this Board of Directors, chances are they're all legitimate. We'll have to get hold of these people and check their prints. Okay, Inspector?"

"Go ahead. But be nice about it, boys." He waved them toward the door. "So long, Crouther. See you later."

"Good enough," said Crouther cheerfully, and departed behind the police workers.

The Inspector, Weaver, the man called "Jimmy," and Ellery were left standing in the center of the room. The detectives personally attached to Queen lounged about in the anteroom, conversing in low tones. The old man carefully closed the anteroom door and hurried back toward the group, rubbing his hands briskly together.

"Now, Mr. Weaver—" he began.

"Perfectly all right, dad," said Ellery mildly. "No secrets from Wes. Jimmy, if you've anything to tell, tell it rapidly, graphically, and above all rapidly. Talk, James!"

"Okay," responded "Jimmy," scratching his bald pate dubiously. "What would you like to know?" His hand dived into the bag he carried and reappeared with an article painstakingly wrapped in soft tissue paper. He carefully unwrapped the package, and one of the onyx book-ends emerged. The second book-end, similarly sheathed in tissue, he placed by the side of the first on the glass top of French's desk.

"The book-ends, eh?" muttered Queen, bending forward curiously to examine the barely visible glue-lines where felt and stone met.

"In the onyx itself," ventured Ellery. "Jimmy, what were those whitish grains I sent you in the glassine envelope?"

"Ordinary fingerprint powder," replied "Jimmy," at

once. "The white variety. And how it got there, maybe you can answer—I can't, Mr. Queen."

"Not at the moment," smiled Ellery. "Fingerprint powder, eh? Did you find any more in the blue?"

"You got nearly all of them," said the little bald-headed man. "Did find a few, though. Found a bit of foreign matter, of course—some dust chiefly. But the grains are what I've told you. There's not a print on either of them, except your own, Mr. Queen."

Inspector Queen stared from "Jimmy" to Weaver to Ellery, a strange light dawning on his face. His hand fumbled nervously for his snuff-box.

"Fingerprint powder!" he said in a stunned voice. "Is it possible that—?"

"No, I've checked on what you're thinking, dad," said Ellery soberly. "This room was not entered by the police before I myself found the grains in the glue. As a matter of fact, I suspected their identity at once, but of course I wished to be certain. . . . No, if you're thinking that one of your men sprinkled the powder on these book-ends, you're mistaken. They couldn't have, possibly."

"You realize what this means, of course?" The Inspector's voice grew shrill with excitement. He took a short turn on the rug. "I have had all sorts of experience," he said, "with criminals who use gloves. That's one of the accepted habits of the law-breaking profession, it seems—maybe it's an outgrowth of fiction and newspaper exposés. Gloves, canvas, cheesecloth, felt—they're all used either to prevent leaving fingerprints or to destroy what prints may be left. But this—this is the work of a—"

"A super-criminal?" suggested Weaver timidly.

"Exactly. A super-criminal!" replied the old man. "Sounds dime-novelish, does it, El? Coming from me, too —with comparative butchers like Tony the Wop and Red McCloskey waiting for me down at the Tombs. Most cops scoff at the mere suggestion of super-criminals. But I've known them—rare and precious birds when they do crop out. . . ." He looked at his son defiantly. "Ellery, the man—or woman, for that matter—who committed this crime is not the usual criminal. He—or she—is so careful as to do the job and then, not satisfied with possibly using gloves and letting it go at that, sprinkles the room with the policeman's pet crime-detector, fingerprint powder, to bring out his or her *own* prints, in order to wipe them out of existence! . . . There isn't the slightest doubt in my mind—we're dealing with a most unusual character, a habitual criminal who's risen far above the stupidity of his generally dull-witted kind."

"Super-criminal . . ." Ellery thought for a moment, then shrugged his shoulders lightly. "It does look that way, doesn't it? . . . Commits the murder in this room, then goes about the enormously ticklish job of cleaning up afterward. Has he left prints? Perhaps. Perhaps the work he had to do was so delicate as to make it impossible for him to use gloves—there's a thought, eh, dad?" He smiled.

"Doesn't make sense, though—that last," muttered Queen. "Can't see what he might possibly have to do that he couldn't do with gloves on."

"I have a little idea about that," remarked Ellery. "But to go on. He hasn't used gloves, let us say, at least for one small but important operation, and he's certain that there are prints of his fingers left on the book-ends—which of necessity, then, are connected with what he had to do. Very well! Does he merely wipe the surface of the onyx carefully, trusting that he's eradicated all the tell-tale marks? He does not! He produces fingerprint powder, whisks it gently over all the surfaces of the onyx, one at a time, and where he sees a convolvular smudge, he immediately destroys it. In this way he's *sure* there are no fingerprints left. Smart! A little painstaking, of course—but he was gambling with his life, remember, and he took no chances. No—" Ellery said slowly, "he took—no chances."

There was a little silence, broken only by the soft swish of "Jimmy's" hand caressing his bald head.

"At least," said the Inspector impatiently, at last, "there's no sense in looking for prints anywhere about. The criminal who was clever enough to go through a rigmarole like this would be mighty sure he left none. So—let's forget it for the moment and get back to some personalities. Jimmy, wrap those book-ends up again and take them back to Headquarters with you. Better have one of the boys go along with you—let's take no chances on your, well, let's say, losing 'em."

"Right, Inspector." The police laboratory worker deftly rewrapped the book-ends in the tissue paper, stowed them away in his bag, and with a cheery, "So long!" disappeared from the room.

"Now, Mr. Weaver," said the Inspector, settling himself comfortably in a chair, "have a seat and let's hear some things about the various people we've met in the course of this investigation. Sit down, Ellery, you make me fidgety!"

Ellery smiled and seated himself at the desk, for which he seemed to have developed a curious passion. Weaver relaxed in one of the leather-covered chairs, resignedly.

"Anything you say, Inspector." He looked over at Ellery. Ellery was gazing fixedly at the books on the desk-top.

"Well, for an introduction," began the Inspector briskly, "tell us something about that employer of yours. Mighty queer cuss, isn't he? Anti-vice work made him daffy, perhaps?"

"I think you've judged the Old Man a trifle inaccurately," said Weaver tiredly. "He's the best and most generous soul in the world. If you can conceive a strange combination of Arthurian purity of nature with a definite narrowness of outlook, you'll hit close to understanding him. He's not a broad-minded man, in the generally accepted sense of the word. He has a little iron in him, too, or he wouldn't be crusading against vice. He loathes it instinctively, I think, because certainly there's never been the smallest element of scandal or criminality in his family. That's why this thing has hit him so hard. He probably foresees the ravenous way in which the newspapers will pick up the choice morsel—wife of the Anti-Vice League head mysteriously murdered, and all that. And then, too, I think he loved Mrs. French dearly. I don't think she loved him—" he hesitated, but continued loyally, "but she was always good to him in her cold, self-contained way. She was a good bit younger than he, of course."

The Inspector coughed gently. Ellery regarded Weaver with morose eyes, but his thoughts seemed far away. Perhaps on the books, for his fingers played idly with their covers.

"Tell me, Mr. Weaver," said Queen, "have you noticed anything—well, abnormal—in Mr. French's actions lately? Or better still, do you know personally of anything that might have caused him secret worry in recent months?"

Weaver was silent for a long time. "Inspector," he said at last, meeting Queen's eyes frankly, "the truth is that I know a great many things about Mr. French and his family and friends. I'm not a scandal-monger. You must understand that this is an extremely embarrassing position for me. It's hard to betray confidences. . . ."

The Inspector looked pleased. "Spoken like a man, Mr. Weaver. Ellery, answer your friend."

Ellery regarded Weaver compassionately. "Wes, old boy," he said, "a human being has been killed in cold blood. It is our business to punish the murderer who took that life. I can't answer for you—it's difficult for a straight-thinking man to spill a heap of family secrets—but if I were you, I should talk. Because, Wes"—he paused—"you're not with policemen. You're with friends."

"Then I'll talk," said Weaver despairingly, "and hope for the best.—I believe you asked about something abnormal in the Old Man's actions recently, Inspector? You've hit a truth. Mr. French *is* secretly worried and upset. Because—"

"Because—?"

"Because," said Weaver in a spiritless voice, "a few months ago an unfortunate friendship sprang up between Mrs. French and—Cornelius Zorn."

"Zorn, eh? Love-affair, Weaver?" asked Queen in a soothing voice.

"I'm afraid so," replied Weaver uncomfortably. "Though what she saw in *him*— But now I'm becoming gossipy! The fact is that they were seeing each other much too often, so much so that even the Old Man, the most unsuspicious soul that ever breathed, began to realize that something was wrong."

"Nothing definite, I suppose?"

"I don't think there was anything radically wrong, Inspector. And of course Mr. French never breathed a word of it to his wife. He wouldn't dream of hurting her feelings. But I know it touched him deeply, because once he let slip something in my presence that gave all his transparent broodings away. I'm reasonably certain that he was desperately hoping things would work out for the best."

"I thought Zorn held aloof from French in that window," mused the Inspector.

"Undoubtedly. Zorn makes no bones about his feeling for Mrs. French. She was not an unattractive woman, Inspector. And Zorn is pretty small potatoes. He broke a lifelong friendship when he began to dally with the Old

Man's wife. It's that, I think, as much as anything, that made the Old Man feel so badly."

"Is Zorn married?" put in Ellery suddenly.

"Why, yes, El," replied Weaver, facing his friend for the moment. "Sophia Zorn's a queer woman, too. I think she hated Mrs. French—not the slightest feminine sympathy in her make-up. Pretty objectionable character, that woman."

"Does she love Zorn?"

"That's hard to answer. She has an abnormal streak of possessiveness, and that may be why she was so jealous. She showed it at every opportunity and made things quite uncomfortable for all of us at times."

"I suppose," put in the Inspector with a grim smile, "it's common knowledge. Those things always are."

"Much too common," said Weaver bitterly. "It's been a hideous farce, the whole business. My God, there have been times when I was tempted to strangle Mrs. French myself for the ghastly wreck she was making out of the Old Man!"

"Well, don't make that statement when the Commissioner is around, Weaver," smiled the Inspector. "What is French's feeling for his immediate family?"

"Of course he loved Mrs. French—was uncommonly thoughtful in the little things for a man of his age," said Weaver. "As for Marion"—his eyes brightened—"she's always been the apple of his eye. A perfect love between father and daughter. . . . It's been a little unpleasant—for me," he added in a lower tone.

"So I gathered from the coldness with which you two kids habitually greet each other," remarked the Inspector dryly. Weaver flushed boyishly. "Now, how about Bernice?"

"Bernice and Mr. French?" Weaver sighed. "About what you would expect under the circumstances. If the

Old Man's anything, he's fair. Almost leans over backward in that respect. Of course, Bernice is not his daughter—he couldn't love her as he loves Marion, for instance. But he treats them exactly alike. They get equally as much of his attention, the same allowance for pin-money and clothes—not the slightest difference in their status as far as he is concerned. But—well, one is his daughter, and the other is his stepdaughter."

"And there," said Ellery with a little chuckle, "is a pointed epigram. Tell us, Wes—how about Mrs. French and Carmody? You've heard what he said—does it all fit?"

"He told the exact truth," replied Weaver at once. "He's an enigma of a man, is Carmody—cold-blooded as a fish except where Bernice is concerned. I think he'd give his shirt for her. But he treated Mrs. French after their divorce precisely as if she were an unavoidable social necessity."

"Why were they divorced, by the way?" asked the Inspector.

"Infidelity on Carmody's part," said Weaver.—"Good night! I feel like a tongue-slapping washerwoman.—Well, Carmody was so injudicious as to be caught in a hotel-room with a lady of the chorus, and though the affair was hushed up, the truth couldn't be kept from trickling out. Mrs. French, who was something of a moral virago in those days, immediately sued for divorce, and got it—and with it, custody of Bernice."

"Hardly a moral virago, Wes," remarked Ellery. "Not from the Zornian implications. Say rather—she knew what side her bread was buttered on and decided that there were more fish in the sea than a faithless husband. . . ."

"A complicated figure of speech," said Weaver, with a smile. "But I see what you mean."

"I'm beginning to get little sidelights into Mrs. French's

character," murmured Ellery. "This Marchbanks fellow—her brother, I believe?"

"And that's about all," said Weaver grimly. "Hated each other like poison. I think Marchbanks had her number. He's no glistening lily himself. Anyway, they never had much use for each other. It made it a little embarrassing for the Old Man, because Marchbanks had been on the Board for many years."

"Drinks too much, that's plain," said the Inspector. "Marchbanks and French get along all right?"

"They have very little contact socially," said Weaver. "In business, they seem to jibe nicely. But that's because the Old Man's so darned sensible."

"There's only one other member of the cast about whom I have any curiosity at the moment," said the Inspector. "And that's the dissipated-looking, fashionable gentleman of the Board named Trask. Has he any contacts with the French family other than business?"

"More 'other' than 'business,'" replied Weaver. "I may as well go the whole hog while I'm tattling. I'll need a scrubbing-brush after I'm through!—Mr. A. Melville Trask is on the Board purely as a result of tradition. His father was the original member, and it was the elder Trask's dying wish that his son succeed him. It meant loads of red tape, but finally they succeeded in dragging him in, where he's been an ornament ever since. Not a brain in his head. But shrewdness?—plenty! Because Mr. Trask has been gunning for Bernice for over a year now—ever since he was elected to the Board, as a matter of fact."

"Interesting," murmured Ellery. "What's the idea, Wes—the family fortune?"

"You've hit it exactly. Old Man Trask lost a lot in the stock market, and his son has been plunging so heavily that the report is he's near the end of his rope financially. So I guess he figured his best bet was a fortuitous marriage.

And that's where Bernice comes in. He's been hounding her, courting her, taking her out, flattering her mother for months now. He's wormed his way into the affections of Bernice—who has few enough admirers, poor kid!—so much so that they're virtually engaged. Nothing official, but that's the understanding."

"Opposition?" demanded the Inspector.

"Plenty," replied Weaver grimly. "Chiefly from the Old Man. He feels it his duty to protect his stepdaughter from a man of Trask's stamp. Trask is a cad and a rounder of the worst sort. The poor girl would lead a dog's life with him."

"Wes, what makes him so sure she'll come into money?" asked Ellery suddenly.

"Well"—Weaver hesitated—"you see, El, Mrs. French had a respectable wad herself. And, of course, it's been an open secret that when she died—"

"It would go to Bernice," said the Inspector.

"Interesting," said Ellery, rising to his full length and stretching wearily. "And for no reason at all, I'm reminded that I haven't had a bite to eat since this morning. Let's all go out for a sandwich and a sip of java. Anything more, dad?"

"Can't think of a thing," said the old man with a return to his glumness. "We'll lock up and go. Hagstrom! Hesse! Get those cigaret stubs and cards into my own bags—and the shoes and hat, too. . . ."

Ellery picked up the five books from the desk and handed them to Hagstrom.

"You might pack these, too, Hagstrom," he said. "You're taking these things to Headquarters, dad?"

"Why, of course!"

"Then, on reconsideration, Hagstrom, I'll take these books myself." The detective wrapped them carefully in a piece of brown paper he took from one of the police kits and returned them to Ellery. Weaver retrieved his hat and coat from one of the bedroom closets and the Inspector, Ellery and Weaver, preceded by the detectives, walked out of the apartment.

Ellery was the last one out. As he stood in the corridor, one hand on the knob of the outer door, he looked slowly from the apartment to the brown-papered package in his hand.

"Thus endeth," he said softly to himself, "the first lesson." His hand dropped and the door snapped shut.

Two minutes later only a lone bluecoat was left in the corridor, propped up against the door in a nondescript chair he had appropriated somewhere, reading a tabloid newspaper.

THE THIRD EPISODE

"Manhunting is by all odds the most thrilling profession in the world. Its thrills . . . are in exact proportion to the temperament of the manhunter. It reaches its completest fulfillment in the investigator who . . . observing microscopically the phenomena of a crime and collating them precisely, exercises his God-given gift of imagination and concocts a theory which embraces ALL *the phenomena and omits none, not the tiniest crumb of a fact. . . . Penetration, patience, and passion—these rarely combined qualities make the genius of criminal investigation, just as they make the genius of any profession, unless the extra-mundane arts be excepted. . . ."*

    —From THERE IS AN UNDER WORLD
       By James Redix (the Elder).

20

TOBACCO

CYRUS FRENCH's house fronted the Hudson River, on lower Riverside Drive. It was old and dusky, set well back from the Drive and surrounded by primly kept shrubbery. A low iron fence ran around the property.

When Inspector Queen, Ellery Queen and Westley Weaver entered the reception room, they found Sergeant Velie already there, engaged in earnest conversation with another detective. This man left immediately on the entrance of the small party, and Velie himself turned a perturbed face to his superior.

"We've struck oil, Inspector," he said in his calm bass. "Managed to trace the cab that picked up Mrs. French last night almost at once. It was a Yellow that patrols this neighborhood regularly. Got the driver and he remembered his fare without any trouble."

"And I suppose—" began the Inspector gloomily.

Velie shrugged. "Nothing to brag about. He picked her up right in front of the house here at about twenty after eleven last night. She told him to take her down Fifth. He followed orders. At 39th Street she told him to pull up, and then she got out. Paid him and he beat it. He did see her cross the street toward the department store. That's all."

"Not so much," murmured Ellery, "to be sure. Did he stop at all on the trip downtown—did she communicate with any one on the way?"

"I asked him that. Nothing doing, Mr. Queen. She didn't give him another order until they reached 39th Street. Of course, he did say that there was heavy traffic, and he had to stop a number of times. It's possible that somebody might have hopped in and out of the cab during a traffic wait. But the driver says no, he didn't see anything wrong."

"And if he's alert, he would have, naturally," said the Inspector, sighing.

A maid took their hats and coats, and immediately afterward Marion French appeared. She squeezed Weaver's hand, smiled wanly at the Queens, and placed herself at their disposal.

"No, Miss French, there's nothing we can do with you now," said the Inspector. "How is Mr. French?"

"Loads better." She made a little *moué* of apology. "I did act frightfully at the apartment, Inspector Queen. I know you'll forgive me—seeing father faint made me lose control of myself."

"Nothing to forgive, Marion," growled Weaver, "if I do take the words out of the Inspector's mouth. I don't think Inspector Queen quite realized how ill your father really was."

"Now, now, Mr. Weaver," said the Inspector mildly. "Miss French, do you think Mr. French will be able to see us in a half hour or so?"

"Well . . . If the doctor says so, Inspector. But goodness! Won't you sit down? I've been so upset by all this—confusion. . . ." A shadow darkened her face. The men accepted chairs. "You see, Inspector," continued Marion, "there's a nurse with daddy, and the doctor's still here. An old friend. Mr. Gray, too. Shall I see?"

"If you will, my dear. And would you mind having Miss Hortense Underhill come in for a moment?"

When Marion had left the room, Weaver excused himself and hurried after her. Her startled "Why, Westley!" could just be heard from the main hall a moment later

There was a sudden silence, then a suspiciously soft sound, and finally retreating footfalls.

"I think," said Ellery soberly, "that that was a luscious salute to the Venerian goddess. . . . I wonder why old Cyrus frowns upon Westley as a prospective son-in-law. Wants wealth and position, I suppose."

"Does he?" asked the Inspector.

"I gather so."

"Well, that's neither here nor there." The Inspector delicately took snuff. "Thomas," he said, "what have you done about Bernice Carmody? Any traces?"

Velie pulled a longer face than usual. "Just one, and it barely helps us to a start. The Carmody girl was seen yesterday afternoon leaving this house by a day watchman —special officer—who's privately employed to patrol the neighborhood. He knows the girl by sight. He saw her walk quickly down towards 72nd Street—straight down the Drive. She didn't meet any one, apparently, and was headed for a definite place, because she seemed in a hell of a hurry. He had no reason to give her more than a casual glance or two, and so couldn't tell me just how far down the Drive she went or whether she turned down a side street."

"Worse and worse." The Inspector grew thoughtful. "That girl is almighty important, Thomas," he sighed. "Put extra men on her trail if you think it's necessary. We've got to find her. I suppose you've got a complete description, clothes and all?"

Velie nodded. "Yes, and four men on her already. If there's anything at all, Inspector, we'll find it."

Hortense Underhill clumped into the room.

Ellery sprang to his feet. "Dad, this is Miss Underhill, the housekeeper. This is Inspector Queen, Miss Underhill. The Inspector has a few questions to ask you."

"That's what I'm here for," said the housekeeper.

"Um," said the Inspector, eying her keenly. "My son tells me, Miss Underhill, that Miss Bernice Carmody left this house yesterday afternoon against her mother's wishes —in fact, sneaked out behind her back. Is that correct?"

"That's correct," snapped the housekeeper, with a malevolent glance toward Ellery, who was smiling. "Though what *that* has to do with it, *I* can't see."

"No doubt," said the old man. "Was that Miss Carmody's usual procedure—to run away from her mother?"

"I haven't the faintest notion of what you're driving at, Mr. Inspector," said the housekeeper coldly. "But if you're aiming to implicate that girl . . . Well! Yes, she did that a few times a month. Slipped out of the house without a word and was gone usually about three hours. There was always a scene with Mrs. French when she returned."

"I don't suppose you know," asked Ellery slowly, "where she went at such times? Or what Mrs. French said to her when she returned?"

Hortense Underhill clicked her teeth disagreeably. "No. Neither did her mother. That's why they had a scene. And Bernice would never tell. Just sit calmly and let her mother rave. . . . Except, of course, last week. Then they *did* have a scene."

"Oh, something extraordinary a week ago, eh?" said Ellery. "And I gather that Mrs. French *did* know then?"

The housekeeper permitted an expression of surprise to flick across her hard features. "Yes, I think she did," she said more quietly than before. She favored Ellery with a suddenly interested glance. "But what it was I don't know. I think she found out where Bernice was going, and they quarreled about it."

"Just when was this, Miss Underhill?" asked the Inspector.

"A week ago Monday."

Ellery whistled softly to himself. He and the Inspector exchanged glances.

The Inspector leaned forward. "Tell me, Miss Underhill —these days on which Miss Carmody generally disappeared —do you recall whether they were all the same, or different days?"

Hortense Underhill looked from father to son, began to speak, thought for an instant, looked up again. "Now that I think of it," she said slowly, "they weren't always Mondays. I remember a Tuesday, a Wednesday, and a Thursday. . . . I do believe she went every week on consecutive days! Now, what could that mean?"

"More, Miss Underhill," replied Ellery, frowning, "than you can guess—or I, for that matter. . . . Have the bedrooms of Mrs. French and Miss Carmody been disturbed since this morning?"

"No. When I heard about the murder at the store I locked up both bedrooms. I didn't know but that—"

"That it might have been important, Miss Underhill?" said Ellery. "That was clever of you. . . . Will you please lead the way upstairs?"

The housekeeper rose without a word and walked out into the main hall and up the broad central staircase, the three men following. She stopped on the second floor and opened a door with a key from a bunch in her black silk apron-pocket.

"This is Bernice's room," she announced, and stepped aside.

They entered a large green-and-ivory bedroom, ornately furnished with period furniture. A huge canopied bed dominated the room. Despite the mirrors and colors and exotic pieces, the room was unaccountably depressing. It looked cold. The sunbeams that streamed in through the three wide windows, far from lending warmth to the ensemble, in some grotesque way only heightened the general effect of cheerlessness.

Ellery's eyes, as he stepped into the room, were not concerned with its eeriness. They focused immediately on a large, garishly carved table to the side of the bed, on which was an ashtray filled to overflowing with cigaret stubs. He quickly crossed the room and picked up the tray. Then he put it back on the table with a curious gleam in his eye.

"Was this tray with its cigaret stubs here this morning when you locked up, Miss Underhill?" he asked sharply.

"Yes. I didn't touch anything."

"Then this room hasn't been tidied since Sunday?"

The housekeeper flushed. "The room was attended to on Monday morning, after Bernice awoke," she snarled. "I will *not* hear any imputations against my household, Mr. Queen! I—"

"But why not Monday afternoon?" interposed Ellery, smiling.

"Because Bernice chased the maid out of the room after the bed was made, that's why!" snapped the housekeeper. "The girl didn't have time to empty the ashtray. I hope that satisfies you!"

"It does," murmured Ellery. "Dad—Velie—come here a moment."

Ellery silently pointed down to the cigaret stubs. There were at least thirty on the tray. Without exception the cigarets, of a flat Turkish variety, had been smoked only one-quarter of their length, and crushed out against the tray. The Inspector picked one up, and peered at a word of gilt lettering near the tip.

"Well, what's surprising about that?" he demanded. "They're the same brand as the ones on the card-table in the apartment. Girl must be frightfully nervous, though."

"But the length, dad, the length," said Ellery softly.

"However, no matter. . . . Miss Underhill, has Miss Carmody always smoked *La Duchesse?*"

"Yes, *sir*," said the housekeeper unpleasantly. "And too many for her health, too. She gets them from some Greek person with an outlandish name—Xanthos, I think it is—who makes them up on special order for young ladies of the better classes. Perfumed, they are!"

"A standing order, I suppose?"

"You suppose correctly. When Bernice's supply ran out, she merely repeated her order, which was for a box of five hundred always. . . . That's one thing about Bernice, although you mustn't take it as anything against the poor child, because too many young ladies have the same pernicious habit—but she smokes altogether too much for propriety and health, too. Her mother never smoked, nor do Marion and Mr. French."

"Yes, yes, we are aware of those facts, Miss Underhill, thank you." Ellery took a glassine envelope from his compact pocket-kit and calmly poured into it the dusty contents of the ashtray. The envelope he handed to Velie.

"You had better keep this with whatever mementoes of the case will be filed at Headquarters," he said in a sprightly tone. "I think it will prove of interest in the final summation. . . . Now, Miss Underhill, if you will please spare us just another slice of your precious time. . . ."

21

KEYS AGAIN

Ellery looked quickly about the garish room and strode over to a large door on the side wall. He opened it and uttered a low exclamation of satisfaction. It was a clothes-closet, packed with feminine garments—gowns, coats, shoes, hats in profusion.

He turned once more to Hortense Underhill, who was

regarding him with peculiar disquiet. Her lips compressed
as she saw his hand absently ruffle through the mass of
gowns hanging from the racks.

"Miss Underhill, I believe you said that Miss Carmody
was at the apartment some months ago, and hasn't been
there since?"

She nodded stiffly.

"Do you recall what she wore when she was there last?"

"Really, Mr. Queen," she said in frigid tones, "I haven't
such a memory as you evidently give me credit for. How
could I remember that?"

Ellery grinned. "Very well. Where is Miss Carmody's
apartment key?"

"Oh!" The housekeeper was genuinely startled. "That's
a funny thing, now, Mr. Queen—I mean your asking that.
Because only yesterday morning Bernice told me that she
thought she'd lost her key and asked me to get one of the
others' keys and duplicate it for her."

"Lost, eh?" Ellery seemed disappointed. "Are you certain, Miss Underhill?"

"I've just told you."

"Well, there's no harm in looking," said Ellery cheerfully. "Here, Velie, lend a hand with these duds. You
don't mind, dad?" And in a moment he and the sergeant
had attacked the closet with a furious determination, to the
accompaniment of the Inspector's chuckle and Hortense
Underhill's outraged gasp.

"You see . . ." said Ellery from clenched teeth, as he
swiftly passed his hands through coats and gowns, "people
don't generally lose things. They merely think they do.
. . . In this case, Miss Carmody perhaps searched for it in
a few obvious places and gave it up as hopeless. . . . She
probably didn't look in the right garments. . . . Ah,
there, Velie! Splendid!"

The tall sergeant held up a heavy fur coat. In his left hand gleamed a gold-disked key.

"In an inside pocket, Mr. Queen. The fur coat would make it heavy weather when Miss Carmody last used the key."

"Fair and subtle enough," said Ellery, taking the key. It was an exact duplicate of Weaver's key, which he now took from his pocket and compared with the latest discovery—a twin except for the initials *B.C.* engraved on the disk.

"Why do you want all the keys, El?" demanded the Inspector. "I can't see any good reason for it."

"You have enormous powers of perspicacity," said Ellery gravely. "Now how did you know I wanted *all* the keys? But you're perfectly right—I do, and I shall take up a collection very shortly. The reason is surely as plain as the nose on your face, as Crouther would say. . . . Don't want anybody getting into that apartment for a while, very simply."

He deposited both keys in his pocket and turned to the unpleasant housekeeper.

"Did you carry out Miss Carmody's orders about duplicating this 'lost' key?" he asked curtly.

The housekeeper sniffed. "I did not," she said. "Because now that I think of it, I don't really know whether or not Bernice was jesting with me when she said she had lost the key. And something happened yesterday afternoon that made me undecided about it, and I thought I'd wait until I saw Bernice again to ask her."

"And what was that, Miss Underhill?" inquired the Inspector, with a slow gentleness.

"Something queer, to tell the truth," she replied thoughtfully. Her eyes flashed suddenly, and her expression became remarkably more human. "I *do* want to help," she said softly. "And I am beginning to think more and more that what happened *will* help. . . ."

"You have us simply petrified with excitement, Miss Underhill," murmured Ellery, without changing expression. "Please proceed."

"Yesterday afternoon, at about four o'clock—no, I think it must have been closer to half-past three—I received a telephone call from Bernice. That was after she had left the house so mysteriously—you know."

The three men stiffened into strained attention. Velie muttered an indistinguishable curse beneath his breath, but quieted under a flashing glance from the Inspector. Ellery leaned forward.

"Yes, Miss Underhill?" he urged.

"It was most puzzling," continued the housekeeper. "Bernice had spoken to me casually about losing the key just before lunch. Yet when she called in the afternoon, the first thing she said was that she wanted her key to the apartment, and would send around for it by messenger at once!"

"Is it possible," muttered the Inspector, "that she thought you had already had a duplicate key made for her?"

"No, Inspector," said the housekeeper incisively. "It didn't sound as if she thought that at all. In fact, it seemed as if she'd utterly forgotten about having lost the key. So much so that I immediately reminded her that she'd told me about losing the key, in the morning, and having another made for her. She seemed quite distressed and said, 'Oh, yes, Hortense! Isn't it stupid of me to forget that way,' and began to say something else, when she stopped suddenly and then said, 'Don't bother, Hortense, after all, it isn't particularly important. I thought I might want to drop in at the apartment this evening.' I reminded her that she could get the use of the master-key at the night-watchman's desk if she wanted to go to the apartment so badly. But she didn't seem interested and hung up immediately."

There was a little silence. Then Ellery looked up with a great light of interest in his eyes.

"Can you remember, Miss Underhill," he asked, "just what it was that Miss Carmody began to say in the middle of the conversation, and then appeared to reconsider?"

"It's hard to be exact about it, Mr. Queen," replied the housekeeper. "But somehow I got the impression that Bernice was going to ask me to get one of the other keys to the apartment for her. Perhaps I'm wrong."

"Perhaps you are," said Ellery whimsically, "but I'd not give even the most preposterous of odds that you aren't. . . ."

"You know," added Hortense Underhill, as an afterthought, "I also got the impression, when she began to say that and stopped, that—"

"*That somebody was talking to her, Miss Underhill?*" asked Ellery.

"Exactly, Mr. Queen."

The Inspector turned a startled face toward his son. Velie moved his huge bulk lightly forward and whispered in the Inspector's ear. The old man grinned.

"Keen, keen, Thomas," he chuckled. "That's just what I was thinking, too. . . ."

Ellery flicked his finger warningly.

"Miss Underhill, I can't expect you to exhibit miracles of acuteness," he said in a serious, admiring tone. "But I should like to ask—if you're entirely certain that it was Miss Carmody talking to you over the wire?"

"That's it!" cried the Inspector. Velie smiled grimly.

The housekeeper regarded the three men with strangely limpid eyes. Something electric shot through all four.

"I don't—believe—it—was," she whispered. . . .

After a while they left the missing girl's bedroom and

entered an adjoining room. It was severer in tone and immaculately clean.

"This is Mrs. French's room," said the housekeeper in a low voice. Her acid nature seemed sweetened by a sudden realization of complex tragedy. Her eyes followed Ellery with grave respect.

"Is everything in perfect order, Miss Underhill?" asked the Inspector.

"Yes, sir."

Ellery walked over to a wardrobe and scanned its neat racks thoughtfully.

"Miss Underhill, will you please look through this rack and tell us if any of Miss Marion French's clothes are here?"

The housekeeper went through the racks while the three men looked on. She proceeded carefully, then shook her head in an unhesitating negative.

"Then Mrs. French was not in the habit of wearing Miss French's things?"

"Oh, no, sir!"

Ellery smiled with satisfaction and at once wrote a line of hieroglyphics in his makeshift notebook.

22

BOOKS AGAIN

The three men stood uncomfortably in old Cyrus French's bedroom. The nurse fluttered about in the hall, a solid door separating her from her charge. Marion and Weaver had been ordered downstairs to the drawing-room. French's physician, Dr. Stuart, a large impressive man, with a professional irascibility glared at the Queens from his post at French's bedside.

"Five minutes—no longer," he snapped. "Mr. French is hardly in a conversational condition!"

The Inspector clucked placatingly, and stared at the sick man. French lay lumpily in his great bed, nervous eyes darting from one to another of his inquisitors. One flabby white hand plucked at the silk coverlet. His face was entirely drained of color, pasty, shockingly unwholesome in appearance. His grey hair straggled over a furrowed forehead.

The Inspector stepped nearer to the bed. He bent forward and said in a low voice, "This is Inspector Queen of the police, Mr. French. Can you hear me? Do you think you are strong enough to answer a few perfunctory questions about Mrs. French's—accident?"

The quicksilver eyes ceased rolling and concentrated on the gentle grey face of the Inspector. They blinked suddenly with intelligence.

"Yes . . . yes . . ." French whispered, moistening his thin pale lips with a bright tongue. "Anything . . . to clear up this . . . ghastly business. . . ."

"Thank you, Mr. French." The Inspector leaned closer. "Is there any explanation in your mind that might account for the death of Mrs. French?"

The liquid eyes blinked, closed. When they opened, there was an expression of utter bewilderment within their reddish depths.

"No . . . none," French breathed painfully. "None . . . whatsoever. . . . She—she had . . . so many friends . . . no enemies. . . . I—it is . . . unbelievable that any one . . . should be so . . . fiendish as to . . . murder her."

"I see." The Inspector tugged at his mustache with nimble fingers. "Then you know of no one who might have had a *motive* for killing her, Mr. French?"

"No. . . ." The hoarse feeble voice gathered strength suddenly. "The shame—the notoriety. . . . It will be the death of me. . . . With all my . . . unsparing efforts to

put an end to vice . . . that this should happen to me!
. . . Hideous, hideous!"

His voice grew more and more violent. The Inspector
motioned in alarm to Dr. Stuart, who leaned quickly over
the sick man and felt his pulse. Then, in an extraordinarily
gentle voice, the physician soothed his patient until the
throaty rumblings faded off and the hand on the coverlet
unflexed and lay still.

"Have you much more?" asked the doctor in a gruff
undertone. "You must be quick, Inspector!"

"Mr. French," said Queen quietly, "is your personal
key to the store apartment always in your possession?"

The eyes rolled sleepily. "Eh? Key? Yes . . . yes,
always."

"It has certainly not left your person in the past fort-
night or so?"

"No . . . positively not. . . ."

"Where is it, Mr. French?" continued the Inspector in
an urgent soft voice. "Surely you will not mind letting us
have it for a few days, will you, sir? In the interests of
justice, of course. . . . Where? Oh, yes! Dr. Stuart,
Mr. French asks that you get the key from the key-ring in
his trousers hip-pocket. In the wardrobe, sir, the wardrobe!"

In silence the burly physician went to a wardrobe, rummaged about in the first pair of trousers that met his eye,
and returned in a moment with a leather key-case. The
Inspector examined the gold-disked key marked *C.F.*, un-
hooked it, and returned the case to the doctor, who
promptly replaced it in the trousers. French lay quietly,
eyes veiled by puffy lids.

The Inspector handed Cyrus French's key to Ellery, who
deposited it with the other keys in his pocket. Then
Ellery stepped forward and leaned over the sick man.

"Easy, Mr. French," he murmured in a soothing tone.

"We have just two or three more questions, and then you will be left to your much-needed privacy. . . . Mr. French, do you recall what books are on your desk in the library of your apartment?"

The old man's eyes flew open. Dr. Stuart growled angrily beneath his breath something about "arrant nonsense . . . silly sleuthing." Ellery's body remained in its deferential attitude, his head close to French's slack mouth.

"Books?"

"Yes, Mr. French. The books on your apartment desk. Do you recall their titles?" he urged gently.

"Books." French screwed his mouth up in a desperate effort to concentrate. "Yes, yes. . . . Of course. My favorites . . . Jack London's *Adventure* . . . *The Return of Sherlock Holmes*, by Doyle . . . McCutcheon's *Graustark* . . . *Cardigan*, by Robert W. Chambers, and . . . let me think . . . there was one other . . . yes! *Soldiers of Fortune*, by Richard Harding Davis. . . . That's it—Davis. . . . Knew Davis. . . . Wild, but a . . . a great fellow. . . ."

Ellery and the Inspector exchanged glances. The Inspector's face grew crimson with suppressed emotion. He muttered, "What the deuce!"

"You're certain, Mr. French?" persisted Ellery, leaning over the bed once more.

"Yes . . . yes. My books . . . I should know . . ." whispered the old man, annoyance sounding weakly in his voice.

"Of course! We were merely making sure. . . . Now, sir, have you ever been interested in such subjects as, let us say, paleontology—philately—medieval commerce—folk lore—elementary music?"

The tired eyes widened with puzzled amazement. The head wagged twice from side to side.

"No . . . I can't say that I am. . . . My serious read-

ing is restricted to works on sociology . . . my work for
the Anti-Vice Society . . . you know my position. . . ."

"You are positive that your five books by Davis, Chambers, Doyle and the others are on your apartment desk now,
Mr. French?"

"I—suppose so," mumbled French. "Been there . . .
for ages. . . . Ought to be. . . . Never noticed anything
wrong. . . ."

"Very well. That is quite excellent, sir. Thank you."
Ellery glanced swiftly at Dr. Stuart, who was exhibiting
marked signs of impatience. "One question, Mr. French,
and we shall leave you. Has Mr. Lavery been in your
apartment recently?"

"Lavery? Yes, of course. Every day. My guest."

"Then that will be all." Ellery stepped back and made a
hasty note on the fly-leaf of his now overscribbled little
volume. French's eyes closed, and he shifted his body
slightly, with an unmistakable relaxation that signified
complete fatigue.

"Please leave quietly," grunted Dr. Stuart. "You've
retarded his recovery sufficiently for one day."

He turned his back truculently upon them.

The three men tiptoed from the room.

But on the staircase leading to the main foyer, the Inspector muttered, "Where in time do those books come in?"

"Ask me not in mournful numbers," said Ellery ruefully.
"I wish I knew."

Thenceforth they descended in silence.

23

CONFIRMATION

They found Marion and Weaver sitting glumly in the
drawing-room, hands clasped, and suspiciously silent. The
Inspector coughed, Ellery thoughtfully scrubbed away at

his pince-nez, Velie screwed up his eyes and blinked at a Renoir on the wall.

The boy and the girl sprang to their feet.

"How—how is daddy?" asked Marion hurriedly, one slim hand to a crimson-dappled cheek.

"Resting quietly now, Miss French," replied the Inspector in some embarrassment. "Ah—a question or two, young lady, and then we will be on our way. . . . Ellery!"

Ellery came directly to the point.

"Your key to your father's apartment, Miss French—" he demanded—"is it always in your possession?"

"Why, certainly, Mr. Queen. You don't think—"

"A categorical question, Miss French," said Ellery blandly. "Your key has not left your possession in, let us say, four weeks?"

"Certainly not, Mr. Queen. It's my own, and every one else who might have occasion to go into the apartment has a key of his or her own, as well."

"Lucidly said. May I borrow yours temporarily?"

Marion half-turned toward Weaver with hesitation written in her eyes. Weaver pressed her arm reassuringly.

"Do whatever Ellery asks, Marion," he said.

Without a word Marion rang for a maid, and in a few moments turned over to Ellery another key whose only distinguishing characteristic from the keys already on his person was the neatly engraved *M.F.* on the bright disc. Ellery stowed it away with the others and murmured his thanks, retreating a step.

The Inspector promptly stepped forward.

"I must ask you what may prove an awkward question, Miss French," he said.

"I—we seem to be completely in your hands, Inspector Queen," said the girl, smiling faintly.

The Inspector stroked his mustache. "Just what has been the relationship between yourself, let us say, and your stepmother and stepsister? Amicable? Strained? Openly antagonistic?"

Marion did not answer at once. Weaver shuffled his feet and turned away. Then the girl's magnificent eyes met the old man's honestly.

"I think 'strained' expresses it exactly," she said in her clear sweet voice. "There has never been much love lost on any side of the triangle. Winifred has always preferred Bernice above me—which is of course natural—and as for Bernice, we didn't agree from the beginning. And as time went on, and—and things began to happen, the rift simply widened. . . ."

" 'Things'?" prompted the Inspector suggestively.

Marion bit her lip, flushed. "Well—just little things, you know," she said evasively. She hurried on. "All of us tried very hard to conceal our dislike for each other—for dad's sake. I'm afraid we weren't always successful. Dad is keener than people think."

"I see." The Inspector tchk-ed with concern. He straightened with a peculiarly swift movement of his body. "Miss French, do you know anything that might give us a hint to the murderer of your stepmother?"

Weaver gasped, whitened. He seemed about to voice a bitter protest. But Ellery laid a restraining hand on his arm. The girl grew still, but she did not flinch. She passed her fingers wearily across her forehead.

"I—no." It was a bare whisper.

The Inspector made a deprecating little gesture.

"Oh, please don't ask me anything more about—about *her*," she cried suddenly in an agonized voice. "I can't go on this way, talking about her, trying to tell the truth, because . . ." she spoke more quietly, " . . . because it would be in the poorest taste to calumniate that poor—dead—thing." She shuddered. Weaver boldly put his arm about her shoulders. She turned to him with a little sigh of relief and buried her face against his breast.

"Miss French." Ellery's tone was gentleness itself. "You can help us on one point. . . . Your stepsister—what brand of cigaret does she smoke?"

Marion's astonishment at the seemingly irrelevant question brought her head up with a start.

"Why—*La Duchesse.*"

"Exactly. And she smoked *La Duchesse* exclusively?"

"Yes. At least, for as long as I know her."

"Has she"—Ellery was casual—"has she any peculiarity in her method of smoking, Miss French? Any perhaps slightly unusual habit?"

The pretty brows drew closer together in a little frown. "If you mean by habit"—she hesitated—"a distinct nervousness—yes."

"Does this nervousness manifest itself in a noticeable way?"

"She smokes incessantly, Mr. Queen. And she never takes more than five or six puffs at a cigaret. She doesn't seem by nature able to smoke calmly. A few puffs, and she grinds out the long stump of tobacco still remaining almost with—viciousness. The cigarets she leaves are always bent and twisted out of shape."

"Thank you so much." Ellery's firm lips lifted in a smile of satisfaction.

"Miss French—" the Inspector took up the attack—"you left this house last night after dinner. You did not return until midnight. *Where were you during those four hours?*"

Silence. A frightened silence so suddenly fraught with hidden complications of emotion that it seemed almost of physical substance. It was a tableau created for a single moment's duration: the slight Inspector, alert, controlled, leaning forward; the straight body of Ellery, muscles completely inanimate; the vague bulk of Velie, drawn and powerful; a petrified agony on Weaver's mobile features— and the utter misery of Marion French's slender, stricken figure.

It passed in the drawing of a breath. Marion sighed, and the four men relaxed stealthily.

"I was . . . walking in . . . the Park," she said.

"Oh!" The Inspector smiled, bowed, smoothed his mustache. "Then there is nothing more to be said, Miss French. Good afternoon."

It was simply said, and the Inspector, Ellery and Velie passed from the room, into the reception hall, out of the house without another word spoken.

But it left Marion and Weaver in a dejection and apprehension so profound that they stood in their places, exactly as they had been, eyes turned away from each other, long after the outer door had snicked cleanly shut.

24

THE QUEENS TAKE STOCK

Dusk was descending on the city when Velie took leave of the Queens outside the French mansion to manipulate the official machinery already operating on the shadowy trail of the vanished Bernice Carmody.

After Velie had gone, the Inspector looked at the quiet River, looked at the darkening sky, looked at his son, who was energetically polishing his pince-nez and staring down at the pavement.

The Inspector sighed. "The air will do both of us a lot of good," he said tiredly. "I need something to clear my addled brain, anyway. . . . Ellery, let's walk home."

Ellery nodded, and side by side they sauntered down the Drive toward the corner. At the corner they turned east

and settled down to a slow, thoughtful pace. They walked another block before the silence was broken.

"This is really the first chance," remarked Ellery at last, grasping his father's arm encouragingly at the elbow, "that I've had to mull over the multitude of factors that have arisen so far. Significant factors. Telling factors, dad! There are so many they give me *mal à la tête*."

"Really?" The Inspector was depressed, morose. His shoulders sagged.

Ellery regarded him keenly. He tightened his grip on the old man's arm. "Come, dad! Buck up. I know you're at sea, but it's because of the trouble and worry you've had on your mind recently. My brain has been more than usually free from occupation lately. It's been clear enough to grasp the amazing fundamentals this case has spewed up today. Let me think aloud."

"Go ahead, son."

"One of the two most valuable clues this affair has given us is the fact that the corpse was found in the Fifth Avenue exhibition window."

The Inspector snorted. "I suppose you'll tell me now that you already know who did the job."

"Yes."

The Inspector was so taken aback that he stopped in his tracks and stared at Ellery with an expression of complete dismay and unbelief.

"Ellery! You're joking. How *could* you?" he finally managed to splutter.

Ellery smiled gravely. "Don't misunderstand me. I say I know who murdered Mrs. French. I should qualify that by saying that certain indications point with incredible consistency at one individual. I have no proof. I don't grasp one-tenth of the implications. I am entirely ignorant of the motive, the undoubtedly sordid story behind the crime. . . . Consequently, I shall not tell you whom I have in mind."

"You wouldn't," growled the Inspector, as they walked on.

"Now, dad!" Ellery laughed a little. He tightened his hold on the small package of books from French's library table, which he had carried stubbornly from the moment they had left the department store. "I have a good reason. In the first place, it's quite conceivable that I'm being misled by a series of coincidences. In that case, I should merely be making an ass of myself if I accused some one and then had to eat crow. . . . When I have *proof*—you'll know, dad, the very first one. . . . There are so many unexplained, seemingly inexplicable things. These books, for example. . . . Well!"

He said no more for a few moments as they strode through the streets.

"I began," he said at last, "with the suspicious fact that Mrs. French's body was found in the exhibition-window. And it *was* suspicious, to say the least. For all the reasons that we went over before—the lack of blood, the missing key, the lipstick and the half-painted lips, the lack of illumination, the general preposterousness of the window as the scene of the crime.

"It was quite plain that Mrs. French had not been murdered in that window. Where had she been murdered, then? The watchman's report that she had signified the apartment as her destination; the missing apartment key *which she had* when O'Flaherty saw her go toward the elevator—these suggested that the apartment should be examined at once. Which I immediately proceeded to do."

"Go on—I know all that," said Queen grumpily.

"Patience, Diogenes!" chuckled Ellery. "The apartment told the story quite graphically. Mrs. French's presence seemed indubitable. The cards, the book-ends and the story they told. . . ."

"I don't know what story they told," grunted the Inspector. "You mean that powder?"

"Not in this instance. Very well, let's forget the book-ends for the moment and go to—the lipstick which I found on the bedroom dressing-table. That belonged to Mrs. French. Its color matched the color on her half-painted lips. Women don't stop fixing their lips unless something of a tremendously serious nature intervenes. The murder? Possibly. Certainly the events leading to the murder. . . . So, for this reason and that, all of which you will know in greater detail to-morrow, I hope, I came to the conclusion that Mrs. French had been murdered in that apartment."

"I shan't argue with you, because it's probably true, although your reasons are ludicrous right now. But go ahead—get down to more concrete things," said the Inspector.

"You must grant me some premises," laughed Ellery. "I'll prove that apartment business, never fear. At this time, grant me that the apartment is the scene of the crime."

"It's granted—for the time."

"Very well. If the apartment was the scene of the crime, and the window was not, then very simply the body was removed from the apartment to the window and crammed into that wall-bed."

"In that case, yes."

"But why? I asked myself. *Why* was the body removed to the window? Why wasn't it left in the apartment?"

"To make it appear that the apartment wasn't the scene of the murder? But that doesn't make sense, because—"

"Yes, because no pains were taken to remove traces of

Mrs. French's presence, like the game of banque, the lipstick—although I'm inclined to think that leaving the lipstick was an oversight. It is evident, then, that the reason the body was removed was *not* to make it appear that the apartment was not the scene of the crime, *but to delay the discovery of the body.*"

"I see what you mean," muttered the Inspector.

"The time-element, of course," said Ellery. "The murderer must have known that at 12 o'clock sharp, every day, that window was exhibited, *and that the window was locked and unused before 12 o'clock.* I was looking for a reason to explain the removal of the body. The fact that it would not be discovered until after the noon hour gave the answer in a flash. For some reason the murderer wanted to delay the discovery of the crime."

"I can't see why. . . ."

"Not definitely, of course, but we can make a generalization that will serve the immediate purpose. If the murderer arranged it so that the body would not be found before noon, it meant that he had something to do during the morning which the discovery of the body *would have prevented him from doing.* Is that clear?"

"It follows," conceded the Inspector.

"*Allons—continuer!*" said Ellery. "At first glance, that business about having to do something which the discovery of the crime would make impossible of accomplishment, is something of a poser. However, we know certain facts. For example, no matter how the murderer entered the store, *he must have stayed all night.* There were two ways of getting in unnoticed but no way of getting out unnoticed after the murder. He could have remained hidden somewhere in the store until after closing-hours, and then stolen up to the apartment; or he could have slipped through that open freight-door on 39th Street. He certainly couldn't get out through the Employees' Entrance, because O'Flaherty was there all night, in a perfect position to see somebody leave that way. And O'Flaherty saw no one. He couldn't have got out through the freight-door, because that door was locked for the night at eleven-thirty, and Mrs. French didn't arrive until eleven-forty-five. If he had slipped out via the freight-door, he couldn't have committed the murder. Obviously! The freight-door was closed to him at least a half-hour before the woman was killed at all. So—he must have had to remain in the store all night.

"Now, that being the case, he could not escape until at least nine o'clock the next morning, when the doors were opened to the public and any one could walk out as if he were an early customer."

"Well then, why all that rigmarole about stowing the body in the window in order to prevent its discovery before noon? What for?" demanded the Inspector. "If he could get out at nine o'clock and he had something to do, why couldn't he have done it then? In that case he wouldn't care when the body was found, because he could do what was necessary immediately after nine."

"Precisely." Ellery's voice sharpened with a certain zest. *"If he were free to walk out at nine and stay out,* he would have no reason for delaying the discovery of the body."

"But, Ellery," objected the Inspector, "he *did* delay the discovery of the body! Unless—" A light dawned on his face.

"That's it exactly," Ellery said soberly. "If our murderer was in some way connected with the store, his absence would be noted or at least would be in danger of notice after a murder was discovered. By secreting the body in a place where he knew it would not be found until noon, he had all morning to watch for an opportunity to slip away and do what he had to do. . . .

"Of course, there's something else. It's an open question whether the murderer planned in advance to secrete the body in the window after killing Mrs. French in the apartment. I rather think the switch of locale was not planned on much before the crime. For this reason. Ordinarily the apartment is not entered until about ten o'clock in the morning. Weaver has his own office, and French doesn't get down until that hour. So that the murderer must have figured, in his original plan, on committing the crime in the apartment and leaving the body there. He would have ample time to get out of the building after nine and return before ten, let us say. So long as the body was found *after* he attended to his nefarious morning business, he was safe.

"But when he entered that apartment, or perhaps after he committed the crime, he saw something which made it absolutely essential for him to remove the body to the window." Ellery paused. "On the desk was a blue official memorandum. It was there all afternoon on Monday, and Weaver swears he left it there on the desk when he quit Monday evening. And it was in exactly the same position on Tuesday morning. So it was there for the murderer to see. And it said that Weaver would be there at nine o'clock! It was an innocent little memo calling a board meeting, but it must have put the murderer into something of a panic. If somebody was coming to the apartment at nine, he wouldn't have a chance to do what evidently was of desperate necessity, although we still don't know what it is. Therefore the removal of the body to the window and the rest of it. Follow?"

"Seems holeproof," grunted the Inspector, but there was a light of absorbing interest in his eye.

"There's one vital thing to be done almost immediately," added Ellery thoughtfully. "Unquestionably whoever committed the crime did not hide in the store yesterday afternoon and wait for closing hour. I'll tell you why.

The complete time-sheet is a check-up on everybody connected with this investigation. The time-sheet gives the checking-out time of everybody. *All* the people we're interested in are reported as having left the building at five-thirty or before, with the exception of Weaver and this man Springer, the head of the book department. And since they were definitely seen leaving, they couldn't obviously have *stayed* for the crime. You remember the names? Although people like Zorn, Marchbanks, Lavery and the rest do not check out, their name and time are noted when they leave the building, as was the case yesterday. Since everybody did leave, then the murderer must have got into the building by the only way left—the freight-door on 39th Street. It would be the more logical thing for the murderer to do anyway, because he could establish an alibi for the evening, and still have time to get into the store through that freight-entrance between eleven and eleven-thirty."

"We'll have to double-check everybody's movements last night," said the Inspector dolefully. "More work."

"And probably unproductive. But I agree that it's necessary. We should do that as soon as possible."

"Now." Ellery's lips twisted into a rueful smile. "There are so many ramifications to this case," he said apologetically, interrupting his line of thought. "For example—why did Winifred come to the store at all? There's a question for you! And was she lying when she told O'Flaherty that she was going to the apartment upstairs? Of course, the watchman did see her take the elevator, and it is a fair assumption that she went to the sixth floor rooms, especially since we have definite evidence of her presence there. Besides, where else could she go? The window? Preposterous! No, I think we may assume that she went directly to the private apartment."

"Perhaps Marion French's scarf was already in the window and for some obscure reason Mrs. French wished to retrieve it," suggested the Inspector, grinning wryly.

"Yes, you *don't* think," retorted Ellery. "That business of Marion's scarf has a perfectly simple explanation, I'm positive, whatever else may be mysterious about the girl. . . . But here's a point. Did Winifred French have an appointment with a particular person, in the store, in the apartment? Granted the whole affair is cloaked in mystery —a clandestine meeting in a deserted department store and all that—yet the hypothesis that the murdered woman came for a definite purpose to meet a definite person seems too inevitable to discard. In that case, then, did she know about the strange manner in which her fellow-conspirator, and as it turned out her murderer, entered the store? Or did she expect him to walk in as she did, through the regular night-entrance? Evidently not, because she made no mention of another person to O'Flaherty, which she might have done had she nothing to conceal, but gave him the distinct impression that she had dropped in for something. Then she *was* involved in some shady business, *did* know that her companion would take mysterious precautions against discovery—openly and submissively.

"Was that companion Bernice or Marion? We have reason to believe, from the mere look of things, that it might have been Bernice. The banque game, Bernice's cigarets, Bernice's hat and shoes—very significant and alarming, those last two items. On the other hand, let us examine some sidelights on the question of Bernice.

"We are fairly agreed that the murderer of Mrs. French took away Mrs. French's apartment key. This might point to Bernice on first thought, because we know she did not have her own key that afternoon—in fact, she couldn't have had her own key, since we actually found it in her closet at home to-day. Yes, it appears that if Bernice had been in that store last night, she would have taken her mother's key away. *But was she in the store?*

"The time has come, I do believe," said Ellery quizzically, "to lay that particular ghost. Bernice was *not* in the French department store last night. Perhaps I had better say at this point that Bernice is not a matricide. In the first place, despite the presence of the game of banque, which is known by many people to be a passion of both women, the presence of the cigarets betrays the frame-up. Bernice, who is a drug addict, has been indicated beyond a doubt as *always* smoking only one-quarter of the length of her *La Duchesse* cigarets, and crushing out the long stub. Yet the stubs we found were *without exception* smoked carefully down almost to the tip. This is so unnatural as to be conclusive. One or two cigarets might conceivably be found so consumed; but to find a dozen! It's no go, dad. Bernice did not smoke those cigarets we found on the card-table. And, of course, if she did not, then some one else prepared them with the obvious intention of throwing suspicion on the missing girl. Then there's the matter of the 'phone call to Hortense Underhill, presumably from Bernice. Fishy, dad—exceedingly piscine! No, Bernice didn't forget about her key so foolishly. *Somebody wanted her key badly enough to risk a call and a messenger.*"

"The shoes—the hat," murmured the Inspector suddenly, looking up at Ellery in a startled way.

"Exactly," said Ellery somberly, "very significant and alarming, as I said before. If Bernice was framed, and we find on the scene of the crime the shoes and hat she wore the day of the murder—then it simply means that Bernice has met with violence herself! She must be a victim, dad. Whether she is already dead or not I don't know. It depends on the masked story behind the crime. But certainly this deduction links the disappearance of Bernice and the murder of her mother very closely. Now why should the girl be done away with also? Perhaps, dad, if she were left at large, she might be a dangerous source of information—dangerous as far as the criminal is concerned."

"Ellery!" exclaimed the Inspector. He was trembling with excitement. "Mrs. French's murder—Bernice's kidnapping—*and she was a drug fiend. . . .*"

"I'm not particularly surprised, dad," said Ellery warmly. "You have always been quick on the scent. . . . Yes, it looks that way to me, too. Remember that Bernice walked out of her stepfather's house not only willingly, but eagerly. Is it too much to suppose that she was going —*to replenish a waning supply of drugs?*

"If that is so, and it seems a good sound possibility, then this whole case is shrouded and complicated by the manipulations—of drug distributors. I'm very much afraid we've fallen into just such a prosaic business as that."

"Prosaic your left eyebrow!" cried Inspector Queen. "Ellery, it gets clearer and clearer. And with all this rumpus about the increase in drug distribution—if we should uncover the ring that's been operating so hugely— if we should actually *nab* the ringleaders—Ellery, it will be a remarkable achievement! How I'd like to see Fiorelli's face when I tell him what's behind this!"

"Well, don't be oversanguine, dad," said Ellery pessimistically. "It may be a *tour de force*. At any rate it's sheer conjecture at this stage of the game, and we shouldn't be too uplifted by hope.

"We have another angle that helps us localize the geography of the crime even more precisely."

"The book-ends?" Inspector Queen's voice was uncertain.

"Of course. This too is based on pure reasoning, but I'll wager any one anything that in the end we find it's true.

Conclusions that fit a series of circumstances so snugly have an overwhelmingly high percentage of probability in their favor. . . .

"Westley Weaver avers positively that the onyx book-ends have neither been repaired nor removed from the apartment library since they were presented to French by John Gray. In examining the book-ends we find a noticeable difference in the color of the green felt, or baize, pasted on the bases, the under surfaces. Weaver offers the suggestion that something is wrong. Why? Because this is the first time he has noticed the differing shades of green. He has seen those book-ends for months. He is certain that when the book-ends were new the felts were alike in color, that they must have been alike all along.

"As a matter of fact, while there is no evidential method whereby we may tell when exactly that lighter felt appeared, there is one corroboration." Ellery stared thoughtfully at the pavement. "The book-end with the lighter felt was newly glued. That I would take my oath on. The glue, while powerful in action and already quite hard, retained a viscidity and suspicious stickiness that told the story at once. And the powder grains stuck in the glue-line—no, the evidence is there. The book-ends were handled last night by the criminal. We might suspect Mrs. French, perhaps, if not for the fact that the fingerprint powder was used. That's the work of your 'supercriminal,' dad, not of an elderly society lady." He smiled.

"Let's try to link book-ends and crime more closely." He squinted ahead in a little tempest of silence. The old man trudged by his side, eyes on the changing street vista. "We enter the scene of the crime. We find many things of a peculiar nature there. The cards, the lipsticks, the cigarets, the shoes, the hat, the book-ends—all out of tune with normality. We have linked every element except the book-ends directly with the crime. Why, in the face of the possibilities—why not the book-ends too? I can furnish excellent hypotheses commensurate with known facts. The fingerprint powder grains, for one thing. Accessories of crime. And a crime was committed. We find the grains stuck in a newly glued felt, which is also suspiciously different in shade from its fellow. Certainly it is against all reason to say that the felts might have been differently colored from the beginning. Not with such an expensive and unique pair of book-ends. And the difference was never noticed before. . . . No, the human probabilities all point to the conclusion that last night some one removed the original felt from the first book-end, pasted on a new piece of felt, sprinkled fingerprint powder to bring out any prints that might be on the book-end, removed the fingerprints, and inadvertently left some minute grains in the fresh glue-line of the piece."

"You've proved it to my satisfaction," said the Inspector. "Go on."

"*Alors!*. I examine the book-ends. They are of solid onyx. Furthermore, the only change in their composition is the removal of the original felt from one of them. I conclude therefore that the book-end was *not* repaired in order to hide something inside or because something was extracted from its interior. There is no interior. Everything is on the surface.

"With this in mind, I ask myself: What other reason could have caused the repair of the onyx piece, if it was not to hide traces of a secretion or a removal? Well, there's the crime itself. Can we tie the crime and the fixing of the book-ends into one knot?

"Yes, we can! Why should a felt be removed and another substituted? *Because something happened to that felt which, if the felt were left as it was, would have betrayed traces of a crime.* Remember that the murderer's most pressing need was to keep knowledge of the murder from every one until he had delivered the all-important message during the morning. And he knew that that library would be tenanted at nine o'clock in the morning, that if anything were wrong with the book-end it would be noticed in all probability."

"Blood!" exclaimed the Inspector.

"You've hit on it," replied Ellery. "It could scarcely be anything else but bloodstains. It would have to be something of a directly suspicious nature, or the murderer would not have taken all the trouble he did. The cards, the other things—these in themselves would never suggest a murder before the body was found or foul play even suspected. But blood! That's the water-mark of violence.

"So I reasoned that in some way blood soaked the felt, and the murderer was compelled to change the felt and dispose of the tell-tale bloody one."

They walked on in silence for a long time. The Inspector was buried in thought. Then Ellery spoke once more.

"You see," he said, "I was progressing with commendable rapidity in the reconstruction of the physical elements of the crime. And, when I had reached the conclusion about the blood-soaked felt, immediately another isolated fact leaped into my mind. . . . You remember Prouty's suspicions in connection with the lack of blood on the corpse? And our instant deduction that the murder must have been committed somewhere else? Here was the missing link."

"Good, good," murmured the Inspector, reaching excitedly for his snuff-box.

"The book-ends," went on Ellery rapidly, "were obviously of no importance in the crime *until* they became blood-soaked. After that, of course, the whole chain of incident was a logical outgrowth—changing the felt, handling the book-ends, and then applying the powder to efface prints made necessary by the handling. . . .

"Then, I reasoned, the staining of the book-end was an accident. It was standing innocently on the glass-topped desk. How could the blood have got on it? There are two possibilities. The first is that the book-end was used as a weapon. But this is indefensible, because the wounds were the result of revolver-shots, and there are no signs of a *striking* blow with such a bludgeon as the book-end might have made. Then the only remaining possibility is that the blood got on it inadvertently. How might this have occurred?

"Easily. The book-end is on the glass-topped desk. The only way blood could get on the bottom of the book-end, where the blood would show ineffaceably, would be by its *trickling across the glass* and soaking into the material. But you see what this gives us."

"Mrs. French was sitting at the desk when she was shot," announced the old man gloomily. "She was shot below the heart. She fell into the chair and got another in the heart itself. The blood from the first wound gushed out before she fell. The blood from the second wound trickled out as she lay across the table—and soaked into the felt."

"And that," said Ellery, smiling, "is a perfect recitation. Remember that Prouty is sure that the *precordial* type of wound particularly would bleed profusely. That's probably what happened. . . . Now we can further reconstruct the crime. If Mrs. French sat at the desk and was shot in the heart, then her murderer was in front of her and shot across the desk. It must have been at a distance of several feet, because there are no powder marks on the woman's clothes. We can perhaps compute the approximate height of the murderer by determining the angle at which the bullets entered the body. But I have little faith in this, because there is no exact way of judging just how far the bullets traveled, or in other words how far from Mrs. French the murderer stood when he fired. And an error of inches would throw off all our calculations as to his height, considerably. You might get your firearms expert, Kenneth Knowles, on the job, but I don't think much will come of it."

"Neither do I," sighed the Inspector. "Nevertheless, it's comforting to be able to place the crime so precisely. It all hangs together, Ellery—a nice bit of reasoning. I'll get Knowles to work immediately. Is there anything else, son?"

Ellery said nothing for an appreciable moment. They turned into West 87th Street. Half-way up the block stood the brownstone old house in which they lived. They quickened their steps.

"There's a heap more, dad, that I haven't gone into, because of this and that," Ellery said absently. "The signs were all there, for the world to see. They needed intelligent assembly, however. You're probably the only one on the scene who has the mental potentiality for piecing them together. The others . . . And you're exceptionally dulled by care." He smiled as they reached the brownstone steps of their dwelling.

"Dad," he said, one foot on the lowest step, "on one phase of this investigation I am entirely at sea. And that—" he tapped the package under his arm, "is the five books I plucked from old French's desk. It seems silly to suppose that they can have anything to do with the murder, and yet—I have the queerest feeling that they can explain so much if we worm out their secret."

"You've gone slightly daffy with concentration," growled the Inspector, laboriously ascending the stairs.

"Nevertheless," remarked Ellery, inserting a key into the lock of the big carved old-fashioned door, "this night is dedicated to a sedulous analysis of the books."

THE FOURTH EPISODE

"Oriental police set far smaller store by the criminal alibi than do Occidentals. . . . We know only too well what warped cunning is capable of . . . and prefer to probe emotions and instincts rather than crack down highly glazed stories. This is undoubtedly explained by the difference in psychology of the two racial strains. . . . The Oriental is notoriously more suspicious than the Occidental, dealing with fundamentals rather than superficials. . . . Where the Western world is inclined to shout a lusty BANZAI! *in acclamation of its more successful rogues, we cut off their ears, or put them in stocks for milder crimes, or behead them for major ones—but always pointing out by example (with true Japanese subtlety, perhaps?) the overwhelming ignominy of the punishment. . . ."*

—From the Preface to the English edition of A THOUSAND LEAVES, *By* Tamaka Hiero.

25

ELLERIUS BIBLIOPHILUS

THE hearth of the Queen domicile was housed in one of the West 87th Street's lingering brownstones. That the Queens chose to live among the unvarnished woods of a generation dead and gone was a commentary upon the powerful influence of son upon father. For Ellery, whose collection of well-used books, whose dilettante's knowledge of antiquities, whose love for the best of the past, overwhelmed his natural leaning toward the comforts of the modern age, stood firmly against the Inspector's groaning indictment of "dustiness and mustiness."

You might expect, therefore, that the Queens lived on the top floor of this sprawling old mansion, and that the door was of time-softened oak (on which appeared their only concession to expediency—a placard labeled "The Queens"), and that when you were admitted by gypsy-blooded Djuna, an odor redolent of old leather and masculinity would assail the nostrils.

There was an anteroom hung with a vast tapestry (the gift of the Duke of —— in return for the Inspector's services in a matter preserved in silence). The anteroom was opulently Gothic, and it was Ellery's will again which prevented the Inspector from consigning it, period furniture and all, to the auction rooms.

And there was the living-room and library. Dotted with books, massed with books. Oak-ribbed ceiling— huge natural fireplace with a broad oak mantel and curious old ironwork—the Nuremberg swords crossed martially above—old lamps, brasswork, massive furniture. Chairs, divans, footstools, leather cushions, ashstands—a veritable fairyland of easy bachelordom.

Off the living-room was the bedroom, a chaste and comfortable rest-place.

The whole was presided over by small, volatile Djuna, the orphan boy adopted by Inspector Queen during his lonely years when Ellery was attending the University. Djuna's world was limited to his beloved patron and their common dwelling-place. Valet, cook, housekeeper and on occasion confidant. . . .

At nine o'clock of the morning of Wednesday, the twenty-fifth of May—the day after the discovery of Mrs. Winifred French's lifeless body in the French establishment—Djuna was setting the table in the living-room for a late breakfast. Ellery was conspicuous by his absence from the room. The Inspector sat grumpily in his favorite armchair, staring at Djuna's twinkling brown hands.

The telephone bell rang. Djuna grasped the instrument.

"For you, Dad Queen," he announced pompously. "It's the District Attorney."

The old man plodded across the room to the telephone.

"Hello! Hello, Henry. . . . We-e-ell, a little progress. Something tells me Ellery is on the scent. In fact, he told me so himself. . . . What? . . . Yes, as far as I'm concerned it's a devil's brew. Can't make head or tail of it. . . . Oh, go on with your blarney, Henry! I'm talking straight. . . . The situation is briefly this."

The Inspector spoke for a long time in a voice fluctuating between despair and excitement. District Attorney Henry Sampson listened carefully.

"And that," concluded the Inspector, "is where it stands at this moment. Something tells me Ellery is up to one of his familiar tricks. He was up half the night poring over those infernal books. . . . Yes, certainly, I'll keep you posted. May need you soon at that, Henry. Ellery performs miracles at times, although I'd wager my next year's pay that— Oh, go on back to your work, you ferret!"

He hung up the receiver in time to greet a prodigiously yawning Ellery who fumbled with his necktie and endeavored to keep the folds of his dressing-gown together simultaneously.

"So!" growled the Inspector, plumping into his chair. "What time did you get to bed, young man?"

Ellery finished the delicately dual operation and reached for a chair, digging Djuna surreptitiously in the ribs.

"No scolding now," he said, reaching for a piece of toast. "Have breakfast yet? No? Waiting for the sluggard? Regale yourself with this Olympian coffee—we can talk as we eat."

"What time?" repeated the Inspector inexorably, sitting down at the table.

"To be temporal," said Ellery, his mouth full of coffee, "it was three-twenty A.M."

The old man's eyes softened. "Shouldn't do that," he mumbled, reaching for the percolator. "It'll fag you."

"Essential." Ellery drained his cup. "There are things to do, Sire. . . . Have you heard anything this morning?"

"Plenty that means nothing," said the Inspector. "I've been at that 'phone since seven. . . . Got a preliminary autopsy report from Sam Prouty. Nothing to add to what he said yesterday except that there are absolutely no signs of drug poisoning or addiction. The woman was certainly not a 'dope.' "

"Interesting, and not necessarily uninformative," smiled Ellery. "What else?"

"Knowles, the firearms man, was vague enough to make it unexciting. He claims that he couldn't place the distance the bullets traveled before they entered the body, exactly to the foot. The angles are easily determined, but from his calculations the murderer might be anywhere from five to six feet in height.   Not very illuminating, eh?"

"Hardly.   We'll never convict anybody on that kind of evidence.   But I can scarcely blame Knowles.   These things are rarely absolute.   How about the absentees from the store yesterday?"

The Inspector scowled.   "Had one of the boys checking up with MacKenzie all yesterday evening.   Just had Mac-Kenzie on the wire.   Everybody accounted for, not a thing suspicious or unexplained.   And as for this Carmody girl, poor Thomas had his strings out all night.   Combed the neighborhood.   Contacted the Missing Persons Bureau.   I tipped him off on the drug business, and the Narcotic Squad's been busy checking up on known dives.   Nothing doing.   Not a trace of her."

"Just dropped out of existence. . . ."   Ellery frowned, poured himself another cup of coffee.   "I'll confess the girl has me worried.   As I said yesterday, all signs point to her having been done away with.   If not done away with, then certainly held very securely in a remote hide-out.   If I were the murderer, I think I'd add her to my list of victims. . . .   There's just a bare chance that she may be alive, dad.   Velie must redouble his efforts."

"Don't worry about Thomas," said the Inspector grimly. "If she's alive, he'll find her in time.   If she's dead— Well!   He's doing all he can."

The telephone bell rang again.   The Inspector answered. "Yes, this is Inspector Queen talking. . . ."   His tone changed magically.   It dripped formality.   "Good morning, Commissioner.   What can I do for you? . . . Well, sir, we're getting along very nicely.   We've gathered together a heap of threads, and it's not twenty-four hours since we found the body. . . . Oh, no!   Mr. French has been a bit upset about the whole affair.   We've gone quite easy on him—nothing to worry about there, sir. . . . Yes,

I know. We're making it as comfortable for him as we can under the circumstances. . . . No, Commissioner. Lavery has an absolutely unimpeachable reputation. A foreigner, of course. . . . What's that? Absolutely no! . . . We have a perfectly natural explanation for that scarf of Miss Marion French's, sir. Well, I'm relieved too, to tell the truth, Commissioner. . . . Quick solution? Commissioner, it will be quicker than that! . . . Yes, sir, I know. . . . Thank you, Commissioner. I'll keep you posted."

"And that," said the Inspector in a deadly voice, as he hung up the receiver carefully and turned a livid face toward Ellery, "is a sample of the blank-dangest, extra-soft-boiled, unmitigated blatherskite of a mud-hen of a police commissioner that this or any city ever had!"

Ellery laughed aloud. "You'll be frothing at the mouth if you don't control yourself. Every time I hear you rave about Welles I'm reminded of that sage Germanic dictum: 'Who fills an office must learn to bear reproach and blame.'"

"On the contrary, I'm getting soft words from Welles," said the Inspector, in a calmer tone. "He's frightened out of his wits about this French affair. French wields a lot of power for a harmless old reformer, and Welles doesn't like the possibilities. Did you hear the absolute nonsense I salved him with over the 'phone? Sometimes I think I've lost my self-respect."

But Ellery was suddenly plunged in thought. His eyes had spied the five books from French's desk, which now lay on an end-table nearby. With an indistinct murmur of sympathy, he rose and sauntered over to the table, fingering the books affectionately. The old man's eyes narrowed.

"Out with it!" he said. "You've discovered something in those books!" He hopped out of his chair suspiciously.

"Yes, I think I have," replied Ellery slowly. He picked

up the five books and carried them to the breakfast-table.
"Sit down, dad. My work last night wasn't entirely
wasted."

They sat down. The Inspector's eyes were bright and
curious as he chose one of the books at random and riffled
its pages aimlessly. Ellery watched him.

"Suppose, dad," said Ellery, "you take up these five
books and go through them. Here's the situation. You
have five volumes, the only fact to go on being that they're
queer books for a certain person to possess. You're looking
for a reason to explain why those five books are where they
are. Go to it."

He lit a cigaret thoughtfully and leaned back in his
chair, blowing smoke at the paneled ceiling. The Inspector seized on the volumes and attacked them singly. When
he had finished with one, he took up the next, and so on
until he had examined all five. The wrinkles on his forehead deepened. He looked up at Ellery out of very
puzzled eyes.

"Danged if I can see anything remarkable in these books,
Ellery. There doesn't seem to be a point of similarity
among them."

Ellery smiled, drew his body forward abruptly. He
tapped the books with a long forefinger for emphasis.
"That's exactly why they *are* remarkable," he said. "There
doesn't seem to be a point of similarity. And in fact,
except for one little link, they *haven't* any points of
similarity."

"You're talking Greek," said the Inspector. "Elucidate."

For answer Ellery rose and disappeared into the bedroom.
He reappeared in a moment with a long slip of paper on
which were copiously inscribed in a weird series of scrawled
characters a body of notes.

"This," he announced, reseating himself at the table, "is

the result of last night's séance with the ghosts of five authors' brain-children. . . . Lend ear, Father Queen.

"The books, by title and author, are as follows—just to make the analysis entirely clear: *New Developments in Philately*, by Hugo Salisbury. *Fourteenth Century Trade and Commerce*, by Stani Wedjowski. *A Child's History of Music*, by Ramon Freyberg. *An Outline of Paleontology*, by John Morrison. And finally, *Nonsense Anthology*, by A. I. Throckmorton.

"Let's analyze these five books.

"Number one. The titles have not the slightest connection with each other. Because of this fact, we can discard any thought that the *subject matter* of the books is relevant to our investigation.

"Number two. The dissimilarity is further heightened by a number of small points. For example, all the covers are of different colors. True, there are two blues, but they are of distinct hues. The sizes are different: three of the books are oversize, and all of these oversizes have differing dimensions: one of the books is a pocket edition; the last book is of average size. The bindings are different: three of them are of cloth, but of different grain; one of them is a de luxe leather binding; one of them is bound in linen. The inner format is different. In two cases the paper is light India in shade; in the other three white is used. Of the white different weights are apparent. The type-style, on examination, although I know little enough about such technical matters, is in each instance different. The number of pages differs also—and their actual enumeration elicits no intelligible message. They mean nothing. . . . Even in price they show dissimilarity. The leather-covered book is listed at ten dollars; two others are five; the fourth is three-fifty, and the pocket edition is a dollar and a half. The publishers are different. The dates of issue and number of editions are different. . . ."

"But Ellery—of course—they're more or less obvious . . ." objected the Inspector. "Where does this
lead you?"

"In an analysis," returned Ellery, "nothing is too trivial
to be overlooked. They may mean nothing and they may
mean a heap. In any case, they are definite facts about
these five books. And if they point to nothing else, they
certainly indicate that physically the books differ in practically every respect.

"Number three—and this is the first exciting development—the right-hand top corner of the back inside leaf—
let me repeat that: the right-hand top corner of the back
inside leaf—has the notation in hard pencil of a date!"

"A date?" The Inspector snatched one of the books
from the table and turned to the back inside leaf. There,
in the upper right-hand corner, was a tiny penciled date.
He examined the other four books and they exhibited in
exactly the same places similar penciled dates.

"If," continued Ellery calmly, "you arrange these dates
arbitrarily in their chronological order this is the result:

4/13/19—
4/21/19—
4/29/19—
5/7 /19—
5/16/19—

"By consulting the calendar I discovered that these dates
represent, progressively as I have given them: Wednesday,
Thursday, Friday, Saturday, and Monday."

"That's interesting," muttered the Inspector. "Why is
Sunday omitted?"

"A valuable little point," said Ellery. "In four cases we
have consecutive days of the week, one week apart. In
one case a day—Sunday—is skipped. That this is an oversight on the part of the dater is not likely; that a book is
missing is impossible, because the number of days between

the first four dates is eight, and the fifth is increased only to nine. Plainly, then, Sunday was omitted for the reason that Sunday is generally omitted—it is a non-working day. What the work is I haven't at the moment an answer for. But we may take the irregularity in the case of the Sunday omission as a logical irregularity which you will find in any part of the business world."

"Follows," commented the Inspector.

"Very well. We now come to point number four. And this is of considerable interest. Dad, take up the five books and read the titles in the chronological order of their dates."

The old man obeyed. "*Fourteenth Century Trade and Commerce,* by Stani Wedjowski. The—"

"One moment," interrupted Ellery. "What's the date on the back inside leaf?"

"April thirteenth."

"What day is April thirteenth?"

"Wednesday."

Ellery's face lit up triumphantly. "Well?" he cried. "Don't you see the connection?"

The Inspector looked slightly nettled. "Darned if I do. . . . The second one is *Nonsense Anthology,* by A. I. Throckmorton."

"Date and day?"

"Thursday, April twenty-first. . . . The next is *A Child's History of Music,* by Ramon Freyberg—Friday, April twenty— By jinks, Ellery! Friday, April twenty-ninth!"

"Yes, go on," said Ellery approvingly.

The Inspector concluded rapidly. "*New Developments in Philately,* by Hugo Salisbury—and that's *Saturday,* May seventh. . . . And the last one is *An Outline of Paleontology,* by John Morrison—*Monday,* of course. . . . Ellery, this is really amazing! In every case the *day* coincides with the first two letters of the author's last name!"

"And that's one of the major results of my all-night session," smiled Ellery. "Pretty, isn't it? *Wed*jowski— Wednesday. *Th*rockmorton—Thursday. *Fr*eyberg—Friday. *Sa*lisbury—Saturday. And *Mo*rrison—Monday, with Sunday obligingly omitted. Coincidence? Hardly, hardly, dad!"

"There's dirty work at the crossroads, all right, my son," said the Inspector with a sudden grin. "This doesn't make any impression on me as far as the murder is concerned, but it's mighty interesting nevertheless. Code, by George!"

"If the murder is worrying you," retorted Ellery, "harken to my point number five. . . . We have five dates so far. April thirteenth, April twenty-first, April twenty-ninth, May seventh, and May sixteenth. Let us suppose, for the sake of blessed argument, that there is a sixth book somewhere in limbo. Then, by all the laws of probability, that sixth book, if it exists, should bear a date eight days from Monday the sixteenth of May, which is—"

The Inspector leaped to his feet. "Why, this is extraordinary, Ellery," he cried. "Tuesday, May twenty-fourth —the day of . . ." His voice fell flatly in a curious disappointment. "No, that's not the day of the murder; it's the day *after* the murder."

"Now, dad," laughed Ellery, "don't go moping so soon because of a little thing like that. It *is* extraordinary, as you say. If a sixth book is extant, then it bears the date of May twenty-fourth. If we can do nothing else at this time, we can certainly suppose the existence of that sixth book. The continuity is too compelling. Things don't merely happen that way. . . . This problematical sixth book gives us our first definite link between the books and the crime. . . . Dad, has it occurred to you that our criminal had to *do* something on Tuesday morning, the twenty-fourth of May?"

The Inspector stared at him. "You think the book—"

"Oh, I think so many things," said Ellery ruefully, rising and stretching his lean figure. "But it does seem to me that we have every reason to believe in the existence of a sixth book. And there is only one possible clue to that sixth book. . . ."

"It's author's name begins with *Tu*," said the Inspector quickly.

"Exactly." Ellery gathered up the tell-tale volumes and stowed them carefully away in a drawer of a large desk. He returned to the table and looked thoughtfully down at his father's grey head with its tiny pink bald spot.

"All night," he said, "I have felt that one person alone can furnish me—willingly—with the missing information. . . . Dad, there is a story behind these codified books, and the story is undoubtedly tied up with the crime. I am so positive of that that I'll bet you a dinner at Pietro's."

"I don't bet," growled the Inspector, twinkling, "at least with you, you dunderhead. And who's this know-it-all?"

"Westley Weaver," replied Ellery. "And he doesn't know it all. I believe that he is withholding some information which to him is meaningless, but which to us may mean a solution of the mystery. I believe that if for any reason he is deliberately withholding this information, that reason concerns Marion French. Poor Wes thinks Marion is up to her knees in the muck of this thing. And perhaps he's right—who knows? At any rate, if there's one person in this whole investigation whom I trust implicitly it's Westley. He's a little dense at times, but he's the real thing. . . . I do believe I'll have a little chat with Westley. It may do us all good to have him down here for a round-table discussion."

He took up the telephone and gave the number of the French store. The Inspector watched him dubiously as he waited.

"Wes? This is Ellery Queen. . . . Can you jump into a

cab, Westley, and come down to my place for a half-hour or so? It's quite important. . . . Yes, drop everything and come over."

26

THE TRAIL TO BERNICE

The Inspector prowled about the apartment in a fever of restlessness. Ellery completed his toilet in the bedroom and listened calmly to his father's occasional outbursts of invective against fate, crime and police commissioners. Djuna, silent as ever, removed the breakfast things from the living-room table and retired to his kitchenette.

"Of course," said the Inspector in a more lucid moment, "Prouty did say that he and Knowles were pretty sure Mrs. French was sitting down when the second shot was fired. That corroborates part of your analysis, anyway."

"It helps," said Ellery, struggling with his shoes. "Expert testimony never hurt any trial, especially when the experts are men like Prouty and Knowles."

Queen snorted. "You haven't seen as many trials as I have. . . . But what gets me is that revolver. Knowles says the bullets are from one of those black .38 Colts that you can buy for a dime a dozen from any 'fence.' Of course, if Knowles could get hold of the gun, he could absolutely establish that the bullets were shot from it, because they still retain enough barrel marks of a unique character to make identification positive. Incidentally, they're both from the same gun. But how on earth can we get hold of it?"

"You're riddling," said Ellery. "I don't know."

"And without the gun we're terribly short of vital evidence. It isn't in the French store—the boys have searched from cellar to roof. Then the murderer took it away with him. Too much to expect that we'll ever get our hands on it."

"Well," remarked Ellery, putting on a smoking-jacket, "I shouldn't be so positive. Criminals do stupid things, dad, as you know better than I. Although I will admit that—"

The doorbell rang imperiously and Ellery started in astonishment. "Why, that can't be Westley so soon!"

The Inspector and Ellery went into the library and found a very dignified little Djuna ushering William Crouther, the French store detective, into the room. Crouther was flushed and excited; he began to speak at once.

"Morning, gentlemen, morning!" he cried genially. "Resting up after a hard day, eh, Inspector? Well, I think I've got something you'll be interested in—yes, sir, that's a fact."

"Glad to see you, Crouther," lied the Inspector, while Ellery's eyes narrowed as if in anticipation of the news Crouther had to transmit. "Sit down, man, and tell us all about it."

"Thank you, thank you, Inspector," said Crouther, sinking into the Inspector's sacred armchair with an explosive sigh. "I haven't been exactly sleeping myself," he announced as a preliminary, chuckling. "Did considerable flat-footing last night and I've been on the go since six this morning."

"Honest toil requireth no reward before heaven," murmured Ellery.

"Eh?" Crouther seemed puzzled, but a grin spread over his florid face as he fumbled in his breast-pocket and produced two oily cigars. "Little joke, eh, Mr. Queen? Smoke, Inspector? You, Mr. Queen? . . . Don't mind if I do myself." He lit the cigar and flicked the burnt match carelessly into the fireplace. A pained spasm passed over the face of Djuna, who was removing the last traces of the breakfast meal from the table. Djuna was tyrannical when his household was upset. He cast a venomous glance at Crouther's broad back and stumped away into the kitchenette.

"Well, Crouther, what is it?" demanded the Inspector with a crackle of impatience in his voice. "Spill it, spill it!"

"Right you are, Inspector." Crouther lowered his voice mysteriously, leaning forward toward the two men and emphasizing his forthcoming remarks with the butt of his fuming cigar. "What do you think I've been doing?"

"We haven't the slightest idea," said Ellery, with interest.

"I've—been—on—the—trail—of—Bernice Carmody!" whispered Crouther in a vibrant bass voice.

"Oh!" The Inspector was patently disappointed. He regarded Crouther morosely. "Is that all? I've got a squad of my best men on the same job, Crouther."

"Well," said Crouther, leaning back and flicking ashes on the carpet, "I didn't exactly expect you to kiss me at that statement, Inspector—that's a fact. . . . But," his voice lowered cunningly again, "I'll bet your men didn't get what I got!"

"Oh, you got something, did you?" asked the Inspector quickly. "Now, that *is* news, Crouther. Sorry I was so hasty. . . . Just what is it you've dug up?"

Crouther leered triumphantly. "The trail of the girl out of the city!"

Ellery's eyes flickered with sincere surprise. "You got that far, did you?" He turned to his father with a smile. "That seems to be one on Velie, dad."

The Inspector looked disgruntled and curious at the same time. "I'll be hanged for a rascal!" he muttered. "How did you do it and what's the dope exactly, Crouther?"

"It was this way," said Crouther promptly, crossing his legs and puffing smoke into the air. He seemed to be enjoying himself hugely. "I've worked all along—with due

respect to you and your boys, Inspector—on the idea that
this Bernice Carmody was done away with. Kidnapped,
murdered—I don't know—but somethin' like that. I felt
that she didn't do the job, although the signs do point to
her, and that's a fact. . . . So I took the liberty of
snoopin' around the French house last night and seeing
what I could see about how the girl got out of the place.
Saw this housekeeper up there and she told me what she
told you, I guess. Don't mind, Inspector? . . . Anyway,
I found out too about that 'special' who saw her walkin'
down the Drive toward 72nd Street. That set me going,
and before I got stuck I'd traced her a long way. I found
a cruising cab-driver who said he picked up a woman of
her description on West End Avenue and 72nd. Private
cab, it is; and I guess I was just lucky, that's all. This
whole business of trailing is part luck and part perspiration—fact, ain't it, Inspector?"

"Ummh," said the Inspector sourly. "You've certainly
put one over on Tom Velie. What then? Get any more?"

"Sure did!" Crouther relit his cigar. "Driver took the
girl to the Hotel Astor. She told him to wait for her.
She went into the lobby and in about two minutes came
out again with a tall blond man dressed kind of swell, and
carrying a suitcase. They piled into the cab. Driver said
the girl seemed kind of scared, but she didn't say anything,
and the tall man told him to take 'em for a drive through
Central Park. In the Park, just about the middle, man
tapped on the window and told the driver to stop—they
were goin' to get out. That was what made the driver
kind of leery, anyway—couldn't ever remember anybody
payin' off in the middle of the Park. But he didn't say
anything, and the blond gent paid the fare and told him
to drive off. He did, but not before he'd caught a look at
the girl's face. She was pale and sort of half-shot—looked
drunk, he said. So he just moved off slow and careless, and

kept his eyes open. And sure enough, he saw the pair of 'em go over to a parked car not fifty feet away, get in, and right away the car shot out of the Park goin' uptown!"

"Well," said the Inspector in a hushed voice, "that's quite a story. We'll have to look over this cab-driver. . . . Did he catch the license-number of the car?"

"Too far away," said Crouther, scowling for an instant. Then his face cleared. "But he wasn't too far away to spot the fact that it had a Massachusetts license-plate."

"Excellent, Crouther, excellent!'" cried Ellery suddenly, springing to his feet. "Thank goodness some one has kept his head about him! What kind of car was it—did your man see?"

"Yep," grinned Crouther, expanding under the praise. "Closed car—sedan—dark blue—and a Buick. How's that?"

"Mighty nice work," said the Inspector grudgingly. "How did the girl act on the trip over to the other automobile?"

"Well, the driver couldn't see so well," said Crouther, "but he did tell me that the girl sort of stumbled and the tall man grabbed her arm and sort of forced her."

"Slick, slick!" muttered the Inspector. "Did he catch a glimpse of the driver in the closed car?"

"Nope. But there must have been some one in the Buick, because our man says the couple climbed into the back, and then the car streaked it right out of the Park."

"How about this tall blond man, Crouther?" asked Ellery, puffing furiously at his cigaret. "We should be able to get a fairly complete description of him from the taxicab driver."

Crouther scratched his head. "Never thought of askin' the guy," he confessed. "Here, Inspector—how about your boys taking it up from where I've left off? I got plenty of work at the store, now that things are shot to pieces down there. . . . Want this driver's name and address?"

"Certainly." The Inspector wrestled inwardly with a spiritual problem as Crouther wrote out the name and address. When the store detective handed it to him it was evident that virtue had won, for he smiled weakly and stretched out his hand. "Let me congratulate you, Crouther. That was a good night's work!"

Crouther pumped the Inspector's hand up and down heartily, grinning. "Glad to help, Inspector—that's a fact. Just goes to prove that us boys on the outside *do* know a thing or two, eh? I always say—"

The doorbell trilled, relieving the Inspector of the embarrassment of having his hand held. Ellery and the old man looked at each other for a fleeting instant. Then Ellery sprang toward the door.

"Expecting company, Inspector?" asked Crouther broadly. "Don't want to butt in. I guess I'd better—"

"No, no, Crouther, stay right where you are! I have an idea you may come in handy," called Ellery rapidly, as he made for the door in the anteroom.

Crouther beamed and sat down again.

Ellery threw open the door. Westley Weaver, his hair rumpled, a worried look on his face, walked hurriedly into the apartment.

27

THE SIXTH BOOK

Weaver shook hands all round, expressed surprise at the presence of Crouther—who shuffled his feet awkwardly and grinned—rubbed his face with one nervous hand, and then sat down, waiting. He eyed the Inspector apprehensively.

Ellery, noting this, smiled. "No cause for neurosis, Wes," he said gently. "This isn't quite a third degree.

Have a cigaret, make yourself comfortable, and listen for a moment."

They drew chairs around the table. Ellery looked at his fingernails thoughtfully.

"We've been muddling over those books I picked up on the desk in French's apartment," he began. "And we've discovered some interesting things there."

"Books?" exclaimed Crouther in a bewildered way.

"Books?" echoed Weaver, but his tone was flat and unconvincing.

"Yes," repeated Ellery, "books. The five volumes that you saw me puzzling over. Westley," and he looked full into the young man's eyes, "I have an idea that somewhere at the back of your mind is a lump of information that we can use. Information about these volumes. To be perfectly frank, I noticed a queer hesitancy on your part when I first got my hooks into them. Just what are your scruples—if you have any—about this story I've laid to you—if there is a story?"

Weaver flushed violently, began to stammer. "Why, Ellery, I never—"

"Look here, Wes." Ellery leaned forward. "There's something on your mind. If it's Marion, let me tell you here and now that none of us has the slightest suspicion of the girl. There may be something behind her nervous attitude, but whatever it is, it isn't criminal, and probably has little to do directly with the murder of Mrs. French. . . . Does that sweep away any scruples in your mind?"

Weaver stared at his friend for a long time. The Inspector and Crouther sat quietly. Then the young man spoke —in a different voice this time, a voice colored with a new confidence. "Yes, it does," he said slowly. "Marion *has* been on my mind, and her possible connection with the affair has made me not quite so frank as I might have been. And I do know something about those books."

Ellery smiled with satisfaction. They waited in silence for Weaver to collect his thoughts.

"You've had occasion," said Weaver at last, lapsing into a clear narrative tone, "to mention a man by the name of Springer. I believe his name arose when you were looking over the nightwatchman's chart, Inspector. You remember that on Monday evening Springer didn't leave the building until seven o'clock, and that I followed him out directly after. These facts were recorded on O'Flaherty's chart."

"Springer?" Ellery frowned. The Inspector nodded. Weaver looked hesitantly at Crouther and then turned to the Inspector. "Is it all right—?" he began in some embarrassment.

Ellery replied at once for his father. "Perfectly, Wes. Crouther has been in on the case from the beginning, and I imagine he may be of help in the future as well. Go ahead."

"Very well, then," said Weaver. Crouther sank back into his chair complacently. "About two months ago—I forget the exact date—the Accounting Department brought to the attention of Mr. French certain suspicious irregularities in the Book Department. Springer, of course, is head of the department. The irregularities were of a financial nature, and it was thought that receipts were not commensurate with the volume of business. It was a confidential matter, and the Old Man was quite upset about it. There was nothing definite in the Accounting Department's suspicions, and because the whole business was vague, the accountants were ordered to forget all about it temporarily, and the Old Man asked me to conduct a little private investigation of my own."

"Springer, hey?" scowled Crouther. "Funny I didn't hear about it, Mr. Weaver."

"Mr. French didn't believe," explained Weaver, "that

too many people should know about it. The suspicions were just nebulous enough to call for secrecy. And because I handle most of the matters connected with the Old Man personally, he turned to me rather than to any one else. . . . I couldn't, of course," continued Weaver wearily, "do any scouting around during the working day. Springer himself was always there. So I was compelled to do my investigating after hours. I had been checking up sales slips and records for about three or four days in the Book Department, after everybody had left the building, as I thought, when one evening I got wind of something queer. I might say that my few nights' snooping hadn't got me anywhere—everything seemed all right."

The Queens and Crouther were listening now with strained attention.

"The night I've referred to," went on Weaver, "I was about to enter the Book Department when I noticed an unusual brightness—a number of lamps were lit up. My first thought was that somebody was working overtime, and when I looked in cautiously the thought seemed corroborated. It was Springer, alone, pottering about in the aisles of the Department. I don't know exactly what made me keep out of sight—perhaps it was the fact that I was already suspicious of him—but I did, and watched curiously to see what he was doing.

"I saw him go over to one of the wall-shelves, after looking around with a furtive air, and swiftly take down a book. He took a long patent pencil from his pocket and, opening the book somewhere at the back, he made a rapid notation with the pencil. He snapped the book shut, made some sort of mark on the back-board, and immediately placed the book on a different shelf. I noted that he seemed quite anxious about *how* he placed the book; he fussed with it for several moments before he seemed satisfied. And that was all. He entered his private office in the rear and reappeared shortly after wearing his hat and coat. He then walked out of the Department, almost brushing by me as I stood huddled in a little alcove in the shadow. A few moments later the lights, except for one or two bulbs kept lit all night, snapped out. I found out later that he had checked out the regular way, informing the nightwatchman that he was through for the night, and that O'Flaherty should have the switch for the book section turned off."

"That doesn't seem so flukey to me," said Crouther. "Probably just part of his job."

"When you're looking for suspicious activity," said the Inspector vaguely, "you can generally find it."

"I had something of the same thought," replied Weaver. "It was a trifle peculiar to find Springer working overtime in the first place—the practice is rather discouraged by Mr. French. But then the incident itself might be perfectly innocent. I did go over to that shelf after Springer had gone and inquisitively I took down the book he had just placed there. I turned to the back and on an inside leaf I found in pencil a date and a street-and-number address."

"An address?" Both Ellery and the Inspector exclaimed simultaneously. "What was it?" demanded the Inspector.

"I forget just now," said Weaver, "but I have a note of it in my pocket. Would you like—?"

"Never mind the address at the moment," said Ellery with a curious calm. "I'm not quite clear on this matter of the five books I took from French's desk. Are they the actual books Springer marked?"

"No, they're not," replied Weaver. "But perhaps I had better give you my story in something like a sequence of incidents. It's rather complicated. . . . After noticing the date and address, which I couldn't figure out at all as far as a possible meaning was concerned, I examined the back-board on which I had seen Springer write something.

I found it was merely a light pencil-line under the name of the author."

"That back-board fascinated me from the moment you mentioned it," mused Ellery. "Are you sure, Westley, that the mark was under the *entire* name? Wasn't it perhaps under *the first two letters?*"

Weaver stared. "Why, so it was," he cried. "But how on earth could you know, Ellery?"

"Guess-work," said Ellery negligently. "But it follows. No wonder," he said, turning to his father, "I couldn't get more out of these books, dad. They aren't the originals. . . . Go on, Wes."

"I had no reason then," continued Weaver, "to take decisive action about that book. I merely noted the address and date and, after slipping the book back into the exact place in which Springer had originally set it, I went about my business of checking up on Springer's records. As a matter of fact, I forgot about the whole thing. It wasn't until the following week—nine days, to be exact—that the incident was recalled to my mind."

"Springer did the same thing, I'll bet!" cried Crouther.

"Bravo, Crouther," murmured Ellery.

Weaver smiled fleetingly and went on. "Yes, under the same circumstances Springer did the same thing, and because I had gone down into the Book Department on my regular nightly check-up, I caught him at it again. This time I was puzzled to note that he repeated his performance of the week before in every detail. And the business still didn't register any meaning in my mind. I merely jotted down the address and date once more—they were different from the previous week's, incidentally—and went about my business. It wasn't until the third week—after eight days had passed—that my suspicions began to function a little more actively."

"Then," said Ellery, "you took a duplicate of the book,

and the book was *Fourteenth Century Trade and Commerce,* by a gentleman named Stani Wedjowski."

"Correct," said Weaver. "On that third occasion, it came to me that the addresses were of vital importance. What that importance was I had no idea. But I realized that the books were there for some purpose, and I decided to try a little experiment. In the case of the Wedjowski book, after Springer had gone I got another copy of the book, marked the date in the back for reference, made a private note of the new address, and took the duplicate book back upstairs with me to study. Perhaps, I thought, there's something *about* this book that will enlighten me. I left the original exactly where Springer had placed it, naturally.

"I studied that book until I was blue in the face. I couldn't make a thing of it. And I repeated my tactics for the next four weeks—Springer did his mysterious little job every eight days, I noticed—and studied my duplicate books very assiduously. They didn't make sense, and I was getting desperate. I might add that all this time I had been keeping tabs on Springer's records, and I was just beginning to see light. Springer was taking advantage of the one flaw in the departmental system, and was falsifying his accounts in a devilishly clever manner. And then I knew that the books must have some significance—whether connected with my own investigation or not I didn't know. But I had no doubt now that they signified something crooked.

"At any rate, by the sixth week I was quite desperate. This was Monday evening—the night of the murder, although I had no idea of what was going to happen within a few hours. I watched Springer as usual, saw him go through the customary ritual, and leave. But this time I meant to do a daring thing. *I took the original book.*"

"Good for you!" cried Ellery. He lit a cigaret with unsteady fingers. "Brilliant, in fact. Go on, Wes; this is tremendously exciting." The Inspector said nothing; Crouther regarded Weaver with a new respect.

"I duplicated the markings in another book exactly and placed it where Springer had left the original, which I took away with me. I had to do these things in a hurry, because I meant to follow Springer that night to see if I could get any clue from his movements. I was in luck, because he had stopped to chat with O'Flaherty. As I dashed out of the building, Springer's latest book under my arm, I was just in time to see him turn the corner on Fifth Avenue."

"Regular detective," remarked Crouther admiringly.

"Well, hardly," laughed Weaver. "At any rate I followed Springer's wandering trail all evening. He had dinner alone in a Broadway restaurant and then went to a movie. I stuck to his trail like the fool I am, I suppose, because he did nothing at all suspicious, telephoned no one, spoke to no one, all evening. Finally, about midnight, he got home—he lives in the Bronx in an apartment house. I watched that house for an hour—even pussyfooted up to the floor on which his apartment is. But Springer stayed in. And so I finally went home, still carrying Springer's book, but no wiser when I left him than when I'd begun to follow."

"Nevertheless," said the Inspector, "you showed good judgment in sticking to him."

"What's the title of that sixth book and where is it? How does it happen that I didn't find it among the five others in French's apartment? You put the five books there, of course?" asked Ellery rapidly.

"One at a time," pleaded Weaver, smiling. "The book is *Modern Trends in Interior Decoration,* by Lucian Tucker. . . ." Ellery and the Inspector exchanged glances at Weaver's mention of the author's name. "You didn't find it among the other five because I didn't leave it there. I took it home with me. You see, I felt all along that the duplicates weren't important. It was evidently the originals that counted. Perhaps I was wrong, but I certainly figured that the sixth, being an original, was more precious than the other five. So I put it in a safe place Monday night when I got home—my own bedroom. As for the five, the reason I kept them at the store was that I was studying them at odd moments and wanted them handy. I didn't want to bother the Old Man about them and the whole business, because he was having his hands full negotiating this merger with Whitney, and he always leaves details to me, anyway. So I merely slipped each book, as I got it, between the book-ends on the Old Man's desk. I also took away one of the Old Man's books to keep the count similar, and merely hid them in the bookcase, behind odd volumes there. In this way, by the end of five weeks the Old Man's five books had entirely disappeared into the bookcase, and the duplicates of Springer's books were between the book-ends. I meant to explain if the Old Man noticed the new volumes on his desk, but he didn't, so I didn't bother. Those 'favorites' of his are mere atmosphere, anyhow; he'd got so accustomed to seeing them there on his desk that he sort of took it for granted they were still there, even though he was up and about that desk every day for weeks. It often happens that way. . . . As for Springer noticing the strange books on the desk, that was impossible. Springer never had occasion to come to Mr. French's apartment."

"Then I take it," demanded Ellery, with a creeping light of animation in his eyes, "that you put the five books between the book-ends week for week? In other words, that the first book, the Wedjowski thing, was on that desk six weeks ago?"

"Exactly."

"That's *most* interesting," said Ellery, and subsided in his chair.

The Inspector stirred into action. "Here, Weaver, let's have a look at those addresses. You have them on you, I think you said?"

For answer, Weaver took a small notebook from his breast-pocket and extracted a slip of paper. The Inspector, Ellery and Crouther bent curiously over to read the seven addresses.

"Well, I'll be——" The Inspector's voice was hushed, quietly throbbing. "Ellery, do you know what these are? Here are *two* addresses that Fiorelli's boys have had under suspicion for weeks as depots for the distribution of dope!"

Ellery dropped back thoughtfully, while Crouther and Weaver stared at each other. "I'm not particularly surprised," said Ellery. "Two, eh? That means all seven are probably dope-distributing headquarters . . . changed from week to week . . . clever, no doubt about it!" Suddenly he started forward. "Wes!" he almost shouted, "the sixth address! Where is it? Quickly!"

Weaver hastily produced another memorandum. The address was a number on East 98th Street.

"Dad," said Ellery at once, "this is remarkable luck. Do you realize what we've in our hands? *Yesterday's dope depot!* The date—May twenty-fourth—Tuesday—the trail is so hot it sparks!"

"By the lord Harry," muttered the Inspector, "you're right. If that 98th Street place should still be tenanted— I can't see why not——" He sprang to his feet and reached for the telephone. He gave the number of Police Headquarters and in a moment was speaking to Sergeant Velie. He spoke rapidly, had his call switched to the office of the Narcotic Squad. He spoke tersely to Fiorelli, head of the Squad, and hung up.

"I've just tipped off Fiorelli and they're going to raid that 98th Street address immediately," he said briskly, taking a pinch of snuff with practiced fingers. "They're taking Thomas with them, and they'll stop here to pick us up. I want to be in on this one!" His jaw stiffened grimly.

"Raid, hey?" Crouther rose and tightened his muscles. "Mind if I go along, Inspector? Be a picnic for me—that's a fact!"

"No objection at all, Crouther," said the Inspector absently. "You deserve a bit of the show, anyway. . . . Fiorelli has raided those two addresses I recognized, but in each case the birds had shut up shop and disappeared. Let's hope they haven't had time in this case!"

Ellery opened his mouth as if to speak, then clamped his lips together very firmly. He became thoughtful at once.

Weaver seemed confounded by the bombshell he had caused to explode. He subsided limply in his chair.

28

UNRAVELING THREADS

They all looked at Ellery in sudden disquiet. Crouther, his mouth half-open, shut it and began to scratch his head. Weaver and the Inspector shifted heavily in their chairs at the same instant.

Ellery without a word stepped into the kitchenette. His low voice was heard murmuring to Djuna. Ellery reappeared, fumbled for his pince-nez and began to twirl it idly. "The uneasy thought just struck me—and yet," his face brightened, "it isn't so bad at that!"

He replaced his glasses on his thin nose and rose to his feet, pacing leisurely up and down before the table. Djuna slipped out of the kitchenette and left the apartment.

"While we're waiting for the squad wagon," Ellery said, "we may as well go over some of the ground, in the light of these newest disclosures of Westley's.

"Does anybody doubt now that French's is being used as an important medium for drug distribution?"

He challenged them lightly with his eyes. An angry glare lit up Crouther's heavy features.

"Say, Mr. Queen, that's pretty rough on me," he barked. "I'm not denying this Springer guy is a crook—don't see how it could be otherwise—but how do you figure out a dope ring's been operating right under our noses at the store?"

"Keep your shirt on, Crouther," said Ellery mildly. "They've merely put one over on the French establishment. What an opportunity," he went on, in the tone of one who finds much to admire, "for a drug ring! Using a no doubt simple code, which is already fairly clarified in my mind, transmitting it through innocent books, and setting the whole business in the respectable domain of the head of the Anti-Vice League himself! That's a stroke of genius, that is. . . . Look here. There can't be an alternative. We find at intervals of eight days—the only exception being one of nine, and this is plausibly accounted for by the intervention of Sunday—the head of the Book Department marking an address in—and this is one of the beautiful elements of the scheme—in little-used, stodgy books. . . . Did you notice that the date in each book was *not* the date when Springer prepared it? No, in every case it was for the day *following*. The book marked Wednesday, by the author whose name began with *WE*, was placed on the *same* shelf . . . it was the same shelf every week, wasn't it, Wes?"

"Yes."

"The book marked for Wednesday, then, was placed on the same shelf as all the others on Tuesday evening. The Thursday book on Wednesday evening the week following, and so on. What could this possibly mean? Obviously, that Springer didn't allow too much time to elapse between the evening he prepared the book with the address and *the time it was to be picked up!*"

"Picked up?" demanded the Inspector.

"Of course. Everything points to a well-constructed plan of operation in which Springer's main job was to inform some one of an address through the medium of a book. If Springer could inform that problematical person or persons by word of mouth, why the complicated book-code system? No. The probability is that Springer knows the people who come in to pick up his doctored volumes, but that they, being mere pawns, don't know him. But this is really beside the point. The crux of the matter is that Springer would not allow the prepared book to linger on the shelf too long. It might be purchased; the address in it might inadvertently be noticed by a stranger. Dad, if you were in Springer's place, how would you arrange *the time* when the book should be picked up?"

"Seems clear. If Springer prepared it at night, then he would have it picked up in the morning."

Ellery smiled. "Exactly. What risk then does he run? He writes the address in the book after hours, when the book cannot be removed that night in a legitimate way by an outsider; and the very next morning the appointed messenger takes it from its place on the shelf—a place of course set definitely when the plan was originally concocted. The chances are, in fact, that the messenger arrives as early as possible the next morning—perhaps as soon as the store opens, at nine o'clock. He browses around, goes over to the shelf finally, picks up the book he knows about in advance through a sign which I'll explain in a moment, pays for it in the regular way and walks out with his information under his arm—safe, clean and ridiculously easy.

"Now! There are a few inferences to be drawn. We must suppose that when the messenger arrives in the morning he has no contact with Springer—really, everything points to this complete alienation between Springer and the messenger, with one or both ignorant of the other's identity. Then the only clue the messenger has to the book fixed the night before is a code, or system, arranged beforehand. That's just common sense. But what could the code be? And that is the beautiful part of the plan.

"Why, I asked myself, was it necessary to the plan to have the author's name—at least its first two letters—coincide with the first two letters of the day on which the book was to be picked up by the messenger? The question is answered if we suppose complete ignorance of detail on the part of the messenger. If, when he got his job, his first instructions, he was told the following, then the whole procedure becomes clear: 'Every week you are to call at the French Book Department for a book which will contain an address. The book will be on the top shelf of the fourth tier of book-racks situated in such and such a place in the Department. The book will always be on that shelf. . . . Now. Every week you are to call on a different day. Eight days apart, to be exact. Except when Sunday intervenes, and then it will be nine days—from the preceding Saturday to the following Monday. Let us say the morning you are due to call for the book is a Wednesday. Then the book you should pick up will be by an author whose last name begins with a *WE*, to correspond to the *WE* of Wednesday. To make identification absolutely positive, and to get you out of the Book Department as quickly as possible, so that you will not be compelled to rummage through every book on that shelf, a light pencil-mark will appear on the first two letters of the author's name, positively identifying the proper volume. You pick up the book, look at the back inner leaf to make sure the address is there, then buy the book and walk out of the store.' . . . Does that sound plausible?"

There was a vehement chorus of assents from the three men.

"It's a devilishly ingenious scheme," said Ellery thoughtfully, "if a little complicated. Really, though, the complications iron themselves away with the passage of time. The beauty of the plan is that the messenger needs his instructions *only once*, the first time, and he can carry on indefinitely, for months, without a slip-up. . . . The next Thursday he has to look for a pencil-mark on a book whose author's last name begins with *TH;* the Friday following, an *FR;* and so on. What the messenger does with the book when he gets it is debatable. From the look of things, this is a highly centralized society of drug distributors, with the pawns in the game knowing as little as possible about the business at hand, probably being kept in complete ignorance of the ringleader or leaders. The question naturally arises—"

"But why," asked Weaver, "that period of *eight* days? Why not merely every week on the same day?"

"A good question, and it has, I think, a simple answer," replied Ellery. "These people were taking not the slightest chance of a slip-up. If a certain person came into the Book Department at nine o'clock *every Monday*, he might after a time be noticed and remarked on. But coming in on a Monday, then a Tuesday, then a Wednesday, all a week and a day apart, there was little likelihood that he would be remembered."

"My God, what a racket!" muttered Crouther. "No wonder we never got wind of it!"

"Clever's no name for it," sighed the Inspector. "Then you think, Ellery, that the addresses are all local 'joints' for the selling of the dope?"

"No question about it," said Ellery, lighting another cigaret. "And while we're remarking about cleverness, how does this strike you? The ring never uses the same address twice! That's patent from the different address each week. And it's apparent, too, that their system of distribution makes it a methodical weekly affair. Your Narcotic Squad has a chance to ferret out a drug depot if it's used week after week; people notice suspicious activity, perhaps; the address and the word go around through the grapevine of the underworld. But how can your Squad ever get on the track of a gang which uses a *different* depot every week? Why, the scheme is amazing. As it is, Fiorelli did get wind of two of the addresses through informers or stool-pigeons; the fact that he didn't get any other shows how holeproof the plot really is. And of course, when he raided the places, he found the ring gone—cleared out. They probably have an afternoon *soirée* week after week and dismantle the place immediately after the last customer's gone.

"Now consider how safe the ring really is. They must have a regular channel of communication with their customers—and I suspect it's a limited list. Too many would be dangerous by their very numbers. That means, then, that the customers are wealthy, probably society people, who get a weekly tipoff by telephone, we'll say—just an address. They know the rest. And what can the customer do? What does he *want* to do? We all know the desperate, uncontrollable craving of the addict for his drug. Here he has a safe source of supply, and what's more important, a regular source of supply. No—the customers aren't blabbing. What could be sweeter?"

"It staggers the imagination," muttered the Inspector. "What a plan! But if we clean them up this time—!"

"I need only refer to the well-known cup and the better-known lip," laughed Ellery. "However, we'll see.

"Some questions arise, as I began to say a few moments

ago, more directly applicable to the murder. We may certainly presume that Bernice is—or was—one of the ring's customers. And I do believe that shady, mysterious motive of which we haven't been able to grasp the merest shadow, is beginning to emerge into daylight. Winifred French was not an addict. She carried in her bag a lipstick belonging to Bernice and filled with heroin. . . . And carried it to her death. A strong line of incident, dad! Very, very strong. . . . Interesting, isn't it, especially since we haven't been able to discover any other motive for the crime? But motive won't mean much in the unraveling of this case, I'm afraid; the big job is to corral the murderer and also to round up the drug ring. A dual task which presents to my deduction-weary mind a suggestion of difficulty. . . .

"Another question. Is Springer pawn or king in this drug game? My guess is—he's on the inside, knows all the facts, but is not top man. And the question naturally arises, too—did Mr. Springer fire the lethal weapon aimed at Mrs. French's heart? I'd rather not go into that at the moment.

"And finally, doesn't this business of the drug ring indicate that Winifred's murder—and Bernice's disappearance—are integral parts of the same crime, rather than two unrelated crimes? I think it does, but I cannot see how we shall ever get to the truth of the matter unless—a certain eventuality occurs. Deponent being temporarily out of wind, deponent will sit down and think of the case *in toto*."

And Ellery, without another word, seated himself and worried his pince-nez in a thoroughly absent manner.

The Inspector, Weaver and Crouther sighed all at once.

They were sitting that way, silently, looking at each other, when a short siren blast from the street below announced the arrival of Fiorelli, Velie and the raiding party.

29

RAID!

The police van, crammed with detectives and officers, rushed through the West Side, headed uptown. Traffic opened magically before its wailing siren. Hundreds of eyes followed its reckless course wonderingly.

The Inspector shouted to a grim and chagrined Velie, above the roar of the exhaust, Crouther's story of the lone taxicab driver and the mysterious automobile with the Massachusetts license-plate. The Sergeant gloomily promised an immediate check-up on the chauffeur's story and dissemination of the new information to all his operatives on the trail of the vanished girl. Crouther sat chuckling by his side as Velie took from the Inspector's hand the name and address of the cab-driver.

Weaver had been excused, and with the arrival of the van had left to return to the French store.

Fiorelli sat quietly chewing his fingernails. His face was haggard and feverish as he pulled the Inspector to one side.

"Had a bunch of boys beat it up to the 98th Street address beforehand to surround the house," he boomed hoarsely. "Not taking any chances on their doing a fade-away. The boys are keeping under cover, but they won't let a rat slip through the net!"

Ellery sat calmly in the van, watching the crowds jump into view and disappear. His fingers thrummed a rhythmic tattoo on the iron mesh obscuring the view.

The powerful truck turned into 98th Street and dashed eastward. The neighborhood thickened, grew squalid. As the van plunged further toward the East River the on-rushing scene became one of ramshackle buildings and ramshackle humanity. . . .

At last the police car ground to a stop. A man in plain clothes had stepped suddenly from a doorway into the middle of the street, pointing meaningly toward a low, two-story building of rotten wood and peeled paint, leaning crazily over the sidewalk as if the slightest convulsion of nature would topple it, a brittle wreck, into the gutter. The front door was closed. The windows were heavily shaded. The house looked tenantless, lifeless.

With the first grinding of the van's brakes, a dozen men in plain clothes ran into view from odd corners and doorways. Several in the dilapidated backyard of the house drew guns and advanced on the rear of the building. An avalanche of policemen and detectives poured out of the truck, headed by Fiorelli, Velie and the Inspector, Crouther close behind, and ran up the crumbling wooden steps to the front door.

Fiorelli pounded fiercely on the cracked panels. There was not a whisper of audible response. At a sign from Inspector Queen Velie and Fiorelli put their formidable shoulders to the door and shoved. The wood splintered and the door cracked back, revealing a dim, musty interior, a broken old chandelier, and a flight of uncarpeted steps leading up to a second floor.

The police streamed into the building, investing both floors simultaneously, opening doors, pushing into corners, guns ready.

And Ellery, sauntering leisurely behind, openly amused at the psychology of the gaping mob which had miraculously gathered outside the house, kept back by the clubs of several bluecoats, saw at once that the raid was a failure.

The house was empty, without the least sign of occupancy.

30

REQUIEM

They stood about in one of the dusty, deserted rooms— an old-fashioned parlor, with the battered remains of a

Victorian fireplace mutely proclaiming its fall upon evil days—and talked quietly. Fiorelli was beside himself with impotent rage. His dark beefy face was the color of slate; he kicked a charred piece of wood across the room. Velie looked glummer than usual. The Inspector took the unsuccessful termination of the raid more philosophically. He inhaled snuff and sent one of the detectives in search of a caretaker, or superintendent, if there was one to be found in the neighborhood.

Ellery said nothing.

The detective returned shortly with a strapping, livid Negro.

"Do you take care of this house?" asked the Inspector brusquely of the Negro.

The Negro removed his rusty derby and shuffled his feet. " 'Spects so, yassuh!"

"What are you—janitor, superintendent?"

"Kinda, suh. Ah takes care of a whole passel o' houses on dis block. Rents 'em fo' de ownahs when a tenant comes 'long."

"I see. Was this house occupied yesterday?"

The Negro bobbed his head vigorously. "Yassuh! 'Bout fo'-five days ago party comes 'long an' rents de whole house. Da's wha' de agent says when he brung 'm down. Paid de agent cash money fo' a month. Saw it wiv mah own eyes."

"What sort of man was the tenant?"

"Kinda shortish an' had a long black mustache, suh."

"When did he move in?"

"De nex' day—Sunday, Ah don' doubt. Van come moseyin' down wiv some fu'niture."

"Did you see the name of the van company on the truck?"

"Nosuh, sho' didn't. Dey weren't none. One o' dese

open trucks wiv de sides covuhed wiv black ta'paulin. No name on de truck a-tall."

"Did you see the man with the black mustache around much?"

The Negro scratched his short woolly thatch. "Nosuh, kain't say Ah did. Don't believe Ah seed him a-tall till yestiddy mo'nin'."

"How was that?"

"Dat's when he moved out agin, suh. Didn't say nuffin' to me, but jes' about eleven o'clock in de mo'nin' de same truck she rolls up to de do' and de two drivuhs dey goes into de house an' purty soon dey stahts pilin' de fu'niture out o' de house an' into de truck. Didn't take 'em long— dey wan't much fu'niture, an' den Ah sees de boss-man come out o' de house, say sumpin' to de drivuhs, an' walk away. De truck went away, too. Yassuh, an' de boss-man jes' flung dat key de agent gave'm right out deah on de stoop o' de house befo' he walked off. Yassuh."

The Inspector spoke in a low voice to Velie for a moment, then turned back to the Negro.

"Did you see anybody go into the house during the four days?" asked the Inspector. "Especially Tuesday afternoon —yesterday?"

"Why—yassuh, yestiddy, but not befo'. Mah old 'ooman, she sets out yonduh gen'ally all day, an' she told me las' night dat dey was a whole raft o' white folks comin' up to dat empty house all yestiddy aftuhnoon. Dey was all kinda put out when dey saw de house was closed. Oh, 'bout a dozen of 'em. Dey all went away quick."

"That'll do," said the Inspector slowly. "Give your name and address and the name of the realty company you're working for to that man over there, and keep your mouth tight about all this. Remember!"

The Negro stiffened, mumbled, stammered the required

information to a detective of the Narcotic Squad, and shuffled rapidly from the room.

"Well, that settles it," said Inspector Queen to Velie, Fiorelli, Ellery and Crouther, who were grouped together. "They got wind and beat it. Something made 'em suspicious and they had to clear out—didn't even have time to distribute the dope to their customers. There must be a dozen mighty sick addicts in the city to-day."

Fiorelli made a disgusted gesture. "Aw, let's fade," he growled. "They got a jinx on me, that gang."

"Tough luck," said Crouther. "That must have been fast work."

"I'm going to trace that truck, if I can," said Velie. "Want to help, Crouther?" He smiled sardonically.

"Hey, lay off," said Crouther good-naturedly.

"Don't quarrel, now," sighed the Inspector. "You might try, Thomas, but I have a notion that's a privately owned truck that operates only on the ring's jobs. And I suppose that now the gang is scared off, we'll not pick up their trail again in a hurry. Eh, Ellery?"

"I suggest," said Ellery, speaking for the first time since the raid, "that we go home. We've met our Waterloo for—" he smiled sadly—"to put it mildly, the nonce."

Fiorelli and Velie mustered the squad of officers and took the police van back to Headquarters, leaving a bluecoat on guard outside the 98th Street shack. Crouther, poking Velie slyly in the ribs as the burly Sergeant swung into the truck, departed early for the French store.

"They'll be sendin' out an alarm for me," he grinned. "After all, I got a job."

He hailed a cruising taxicab which headed west and south. The Queens followed suit in another cab.

Ellery took out his thin silver watch in the car and stared at its dial with amused eyes. The Inspector regarded him in a puzzled way.

"I can't see why you want to go home," he grumbled. "I'm a long time overdue at my office now. There must be a pile of work on my desk. I've missed the morning line-up for the first time in months, and I suppose Welles has called again, and——"

Ellery stared fixedly at his watch, a faint smile on his lips. The Inspector subsided, muttering.

Ellery paid the cab-driver when the taxi drew up before their brownstone on 87th Street, herded his father gently upstairs, and did not speak until Djuna had closed the door behind them.

"Ten minutes," he announced with satisfaction, snapping the watchcase shut and returning the watch to his vest-pocket. "That's average time, I should say, from 98th Street and the River to 87th Street on the other side." He grinned and threw off his light coat.

"Have you gone fay?" gasped the Inspector.

"Like a fox," said Ellery. He took up the telephone and called a number. "French's? Connect me with Mr. Springer in the Book Department. . . . Hello, Book Department? Mr. Springer, please. . . . What? Who is this speaking? . . . Oh, I see. . . . No, it's quite all right. Thank you!"

He hung up.

The Inspector was twisting his mustache in an agony of apprehension. He glared at Ellery. "Do you mean to say that Springer's——" he began in a thunderous voice.

Ellery seemed not perturbed. "I'm so glad," he said with sly simplicity. "Mr. Springer, according to his young lady assistant, was taken suddenly ill not five minutes ago and left in something of a hurry, saying he would not return to-day."

The old man sank into his chair worriedly. "How under heaven could I have anticipated this?" he said. "I surely thought he'd keep until later in the day. Return, he said, did he? We'll never set eyes on him again!"

"Oh, but you shall," said Ellery gently.

And quoth Ellery: " 'Preparation is half the battle, and nothing is lost by being on one's guard.' The good Spanish don uttered a homely truth there, padre!"

31

ALIBIS: MARION-ZORN

Muttering imprecations upon the elusive head of James Springer, the Inspector departed for a flying visit to Headquarters, leaving Ellery hunched comfortably before the open dormer-window, smoking and thinking. Djuna, in his uncanny simian way, sat motionless on the floor at his feet, unblinking in the soft glare of sunlight streaming into the room. . . . When the Inspector returned two hours later Ellery, still smoking, was seated at the desk reading over a batch of notes.

"Still at it?" asked Queen with quick concern, hurling his hat and coat toward a chair. Djuna noiselessly picked them up and hung them in a closet.

"Still at it," rejoined Ellery. But there was a deep wrinkle between his brows. He rose, looked reflectively at his notes, then with a sigh replaced them in the desk and shrugged his shoulders. The wrinkle disappeared, dissolved smoothly into small fine lines of humor as he caught sight of his father's worried mustache and high color.

"Nothing new downtown?" he asked sympathetically. He sat down at the window again.

Queen paced nervously up and down the rug. "Little enough. Thomas has looked up that cab-driver of Crouther's—and we've driven up another blind alley, it seems. The man gave us a pretty clear description of this tall blond abductor, and of course we've flashed wires through the entire East. Particularly Massachusetts. With a description of the car and Bernice Carmody. Now I suppose we'll have to wait. . . ."

"Umm." Ellery flicked the ashes from his cigaret. "Waiting won't bring Bernice Carmody back from the grave," he said in sudden earnestness. "And there's still a chance she may be alive. . . . I shouldn't confine my search to the northeast, dad. This gang is clever. They may have pulled the old license-plate trick. They may actually have headed south, changed cars—any one of a dozen things. In fact, if you found Bernice Carmody, dead or alive, right here in New York City, it wouldn't surprise me in the least. After all, the trail ended in Central Park. . . ."

"Thomas has his eyes open and his beaters out," said the Inspector disconsolately. "And he's up to the tricks as well as you, my son. If there's the faintest spoor, he'll follow it—and get not only the girl but the men too."

"*Cherchez la femme*," said Ellery lightly. . . . He sat musing. The Inspector placed his hands behind his small back and strode up and down, eying Ellery in a puzzled manner meanwhile.

"Marion French called me at Headquarters," he stated suddenly.

Ellery's head lifted slowly. "Yes?"

The old man chuckled. "I thought that would get you! . . . Yes, the girl called several times this morning while I was here, and when I finally got to the office she seemed quite feverish with—well, not excitement exactly, but anticipation. So, being thoughtful of you, my son— which is more than you can say about yourself, incidentally —I asked her to meet me here."

Ellery merely smiled.

"I suppose Weaver's been talking to her," continued the Inspector grumpily.

"Dad!" Ellery laughed outright. "Occasionally you positively startle me with your insight. . . ."

The doorbell rang, and Djuna ran to answer it. Marion French, dressed in a severe black suit and a pert little black hat, her chin set at a charmingly defiant angle, stood outside.

Ellery sprang to his feet, his fingers straying to his tie. The Inspector stepped forward quickly and opened wide the anteroom door.

"Come in, come in, Miss French!" He was all smiles and fatherliness. Marion smiled bewilderingly at Djuna and greeted the Inspector in a grave undertone as she walked into the living-room. She blushed at Ellery's warm words of welcome. And sat down in the Inspector's own armchair at his magnanimous command, perched on the edge of the leather seat, hands tightly clasped, chiseled lips firm.

Ellery stood by the window. The Inspector drew up a chair and sat close to the girl, facing her.

"Now, what is it you wanted to talk to me about, my dear?" he asked in a conversational tone.

Marion's glance flew timidly to Ellery and returned. "I— It's about—"

"About your visit to Mr. Zorn's place Monday evening, Miss French?" inquired Ellery, smiling.

She gasped. "Why—why, you knew!"

Ellery made a deprecatory gesture. "It is hardly knowledge. Some call it guessing."

The Inspector's eyes bored into hers. But his voice was gentle now. "Has Mr. Zorn a hold over you—or is it a matter more directly concerned with your father, my dear?"

She stared from one to the other as if she could not believe her ears. "To think—" She laughed a trifle hysterically. "And I thought all the while that it was a deep, dark secret. . . ." A shadow seemed to lift from her face all at once. "I suppose you want a coherent story. You have heard, Westley tells me—" she bit her lip and crimsoned—"I shouldn't have said that—he told me *particularly* not to say we'd discussed this. . . ." Both the Inspector and Ellery laughed aloud at her *naïveté.* "At any rate," she went on, smiling faintly, "I gather that you've heard about—about my stepmother and Mr. Zorn. . . . Really, it was more gossip than anything else!" she cried. She calmed immediately. "But I wasn't sure. And we all tried—so hard—to keep the nasty rumors from father. I'm afraid we weren't entirely successful." Fear suddenly flamed in her eyes. She stopped short and looked down at the floor.

Ellery and the Inspector exchanged glances. "Go on, Miss French," said the Inspector in the same soothing tone.

"Then"—she spoke more rapidly now—"I overheard, quite by accident, something that confirmed part of the rumors. Nothing—it hadn't gone far, their affair, but it was getting dangerous. Even I could see that. . . . That's the way things were on Monday."

"You told your father?" asked Queen.

She shivered. "Oh, no! But I had to save daddy's health, his reputation, his—his peace of mind. I didn't even take Westley into my confidence. He would have forbidden me to do—what I did. I called on Mr. Zorn—and his wife."

"Go on."

"I went to their apartment. I was frankly desperate. It was just after dinner and I knew they'd both be at home. And I wanted Mrs. Zorn to be there, because she knew—and she was as jealous as a witch. She'd even threatened—"

"Threatened, Miss French?" demanded the Inspector.

"Oh, it was nothing, Inspector," said Marion hurriedly, "but it told me that she knew what was going on. And it was as much her fault that Mr. Zorn fell in love with—with Winifred as anything. Mrs. Zorn is—oh, quite awful. . . ." She smiled wanly. "You'll think me a scandalous gossip. . . . But before both of them I accused Mr. Zorn, and—and told him it must stop. Mrs. Zorn flew into a terrible rage and began to swear. All her spite turned against Winifred. She threatened dire things. Mr. Zorn tried to argue with me, but—I suppose the weight of two women railing at him just sapped his strength. He left his apartment in a huff—left me with that awful woman. She looked almost insane . . ." Marion shuddered. "So I became a little frightened and—well, I suppose it *was* a good deal like running. I could hear her screaming even in the corridor. . . . And—and that's all, Inspector Queen, that's all," she faltered. "When I left the Zorns' apartment it was a little after ten. I felt weak and sick. I really did walk in the Park, as I told you yesterday at the store. I walked and walked until I thought I'd drop from exhaustion, and then I went home. It was just about midnight."

There was a little silence. Ellery, watching the girl impassively, turned his head away. The Inspector cleared his throat.

"You went directly to bed, Miss French?" he asked.

The girl stared at him. "Why, what do you mean? . . . I—" Fright gleamed again in her eyes. But she said courageously, "Yes, Inspector, I did."

"Did any one see you come into the house?"

"No—no."

"You saw no one, spoke to no one?"

"No."

The Inspector frowned. "Well! At any rate, Miss French, you did the right thing—the only thing—in telling us about it."

"I didn't want to," she said in a small voice. "But

Westley, when I told him to-day, said I must. And so—"

"Why didn't you want to?" asked Ellery. It was the first time he had spoken since Marion had begun her story.

The girl did not speak for a long moment. Finally, with a determined expression, she said: "I'd rather not answer that, Mr. Queen," and rose.

The Inspector was on his feet instantly. He escorted her to the door in an animate silence.

When he returned, Ellery was chuckling. "As transparent as any angel," he said. "Don't frown so, dad. Have you checked up on our good friend Cyrus French?"

"Oh, that!" The Inspector looked unhappy. "Yes, I had Johnson working on it last night. Got his report this morning. He was at Whitney's in Great Neck, all right. I understand he had a slight attack of indigestion about nine o'clock Monday night. Retired immediately."

"Coincidence?" Ellery grinned.

"Eh?" Queen scowled. "At any rate, that accounts for him."

"Oh, yes?" Ellery sat down and crossed his long legs. "Purely as an intellectual exercise," he said mischievously, "it does nothing of the kind. You see, old Cyrus retires at nine. Let us assume that he wishes to return to New York without the knowledge of his host. Suddenly. That night. He slips out of the house and goes trudging down the road. . . . Hold! Did any one see him leave so early in the morning in Whitney's car?"

The Inspector stared. "The chauffeur, of course—man who drove him into the city. Johnson told me French left long before any one else was up. But the chauffeur!"

Ellery chuckled. "Better and better," he said. "Chauffeurs can be hushed. It has been done. . . . Our worthy anti-vicious magnate, then, slips out of the house; perhaps his accomplice, the chauffeur, even drives him down to the station secretly. There's a train about that hour. I know, because I took one three weeks ago Monday night when I returned from Boomer's. And it's only a half-hour or so into Penn Station. In time to slip through the freight-door. . . ."

"But he'd have to stay all night!" groaned the Inspector.

"Granted. But then there's a sagacious chauffeur to alibi one. . . . You see how simple it is?"

"Oh, tosh!" exploded the Inspector.

"I didn't say it wasn't," said Ellery, eyes twinkling. "But it's something to bear in mind."

"Fairy-tales!" growled the Inspector, and then they laughed together. "I've arranged to get those alibis, by the way. I called Zorn from the office and told him to come down here. I want to see how his story checks up with Marion French's. And what he did after ten last night."

Ellery lost his bantering air. He looked dissatisfied, rubbed his forehead wearily. "It might be wise," he said, "to get all those alibis clear, at that. Mightn't be a bad idea to get Mrs. Zorn down here, too. And I'll emulate the Stoics meanwhile."

The Inspector made a number of telephone calls, while Djuna went rapidly through telephone directories, and Ellery slumped into an easy-chair and closed his eyes. . . .

A half-hour later Mr. and Mrs. Zorn sat in the Queen living-room side by side, facing Inspector Queen. Ellery was far off in a corner, almost hidden by a jutting book-case.

Mrs. Zorn was a large-boned woman, well fleshed and rosy. Her too-golden hair was cut in a severe, startling bob. She had cold green eyes and a large mouth. She looked, at first glance, under thirty; on closer observation, faint crinkles around her chin and eyes added ten years to her appearance. She was dressed in the height of fashion and carried herself with an air of arrogance.

Despite Marion's story, Mr. and Mrs. Zorn seemed on the most amicable of terms. Mrs. Zorn acknowledged her husband's introduction of the Inspector with regal graciousness; she punctuated each remark to Zorn with a sweet "My dear. . . ."

The Inspector examined her shrewdly with his eyes, and decided not to mince words.

He turned first to Zorn. "I have called you, as a logical step in this inquiry, to explain your movements on the night of Monday past, Mr. Zorn."

The director's hand strayed to his bald pate. "Monday night? The night—of the murder, Inspector?"

"Exactly."

"Are you insinuating—" Rage leaped into his eyes behind their heavy gold-rimmed spectacles. Mrs. Zorn made the least gesture with a finger. Zorn calmed magically. "I had dinner," he said, as if nothing had happened, "at our apartment with Mrs. Zorn. We stayed in all evening. At ten o'clock or so I left the apartment and went directly to the Penny Club on Fifth Avenue and 32nd Street. I met Gray there and we discussed the Whitney merger for a half-hour or so. I developed a headache and told Gray I thought I'd try to walk it off. We said good-night and I left the Club. I did take a long walk up the Avenue and, in fact, walked all the way home to 74th Street."

"And what time was that, Mr. Zorn?" asked the Inspector.

"I should say about a quarter to twelve."

"Was Mrs. Zorn up—did she see you?"

The large rosy woman chose to reply for her husband. "No, Inspector, no indeed! I had dismissed the servants for the night a little after Mr. Zorn left the apartment, and I'd gone to bed myself. I fell asleep almost immediately, and didn't hear him come in." She smiled, exhibiting huge white teeth.

"I'm afraid I don't quite understand how—" began the Inspector courteously.

"Mr. Zorn and I have separate sleeping apartments, Inspector Queen," she said, dimpling.

"Umm." The Inspector turned once more to Zorn, who had sat perfectly still during this colloquy. "Did you meet any one you knew during your walk, Mr. Zorn?"

"Why—no."

"When you entered your apartment house, did any of the house personnel see you?"

Zorn fumbled with his massive red mustache. "I'm afraid not. There's only a night-man at the switchboard after eleven, and when I came in he was absent from his post."

"The elevator, I suppose, is of the self-service type?" asked Queen dryly.

"Yes—that's correct."

The Inspector turned to Mrs. Zorn. "At what time did you see your husband in the morning—Tuesday morning?"

She raised her blond brows archly. "Tuesday morning—let me see. . . . Oh, yes! It was ten o'clock."

"Fully dressed, Mrs. Zorn?"

"Yes. He was reading his morning paper when I came into our living-room."

The Inspector smiled, quite wearily, and rose to take a short turn about the room. Finally he stopped before Zorn and fixed him with a stern eye. "Why haven't you told me about Miss French's visit to your apartment Monday evening?"

Zorn grew very still. The effect of Marion's name on Mrs. Zorn was startling. The color drained from her face and her pupils dilated tigerishly. It was she who spoke.

"That ———!" she said in a low passionate voice. But her body was tense with anger. The mask of politeness fell from her face and revealed an older woman—shrewish, cruel.

The Inspector seemed not to hear. "Mr. Zorn?" he said.

Zorn moistened his lips with a nervous tongue. "That's true—true enough. I didn't see that it had anything to do. . . . Yes, Miss French visited us. She left about ten o'clock."

The Inspector made an impatient movement. "You talked about your relations with Mrs. French, Mr. Zorn?" he asked.

"Yes, yes. That's it." The words tumbled out, gratefully.

"Mrs. Zorn flew into a rage?"

The woman's eyes darted cold green fire. Zorn mumbled, "Yes."

"Mrs. Zorn." The eyes became veiled. "You went to bed shortly after ten Monday night and did not leave your chamber until ten o'clock the following morning?"

"Right, Inspector Queen."

"In that case," concluded the Inspector, "there is nothing more to be said—now."

When the Zorns had departed, the Inspector saw that Ellery was sitting in his forgotten corner laughing silently to himself.

"I fail to see the joke," said the old man ruefully.

"Oh, dad—the mess and mire of it!" cried Ellery. "*La vie c'est confusée!* How beautifully events belie each other. . . . What do you make of your late interview?"

"I don't know what you're talking about," growled the Inspector, "but I know one thing. *Any one* who can't be accounted for by the visual evidence of witnesses between eleven-thirty o'clock Monday night and a little after nine on Tuesday morning might have done this job. Let's take a hypothetical case. Suppose X is a possibility as the murderer. X is not seen after eleven-thirty Monday night. He says he went home and went to sleep. There is no witness. Suppose he didn't go home. Suppose he slipped into the French store through that freight entrance. And got out the next morning at nine. Returned home, sneaked into his apartment without any one seeing him, and then reappeared about ten-thirty or so, letting lots of people see him. The presumption is that he slept home all night and therefore couldn't have committed the crime. Yet physically it was possible. . . ."

"Too true, too true," murmured Ellery. "Well, evoke the next victim."

"He should be here any moment now," said the Inspector, and went into the bathroom to bathe his perspiring face.

32

ALIBIS: MARCHBANKS

Marchbanks glowered. He bore himself with the sullenness of a man who nurses a grudge. He snapped at the Inspector and ignored Ellery. He deposited his stick and hat on the table with a bang, rudely refusing to allow Djuna to take them from him. He sat down uninvited and drummed nastily on the arm of the chair.

"Well, sir," thought the Inspector, "we'll have at *you*." He took a pinch of snuff with deliberation, regarding Marchbanks curiously. "Marchbanks," he said in curt tones, "where were you Monday evening and night?"

The dead woman's brother scowled. "What's this—a third degree?"

"If you choose to make it so," retorted the Inspector, in his most unpleasant voice. "I repeat—where were you Monday night?"

"If you must know," said Marchbanks bitingly, "I was out on Long Island."

"Oh, Long *Island!*" The Inspector seemed duly impressed. "When did you go, where did you go, and how long did you stay?"

"You people always insist on a 'story,' " wheezed Marchbanks, setting his feet solidly on the rug. "Very well. I left town at about seven o'clock Monday evening. In my car. . . ."

"You drove yourself?"

"Yes. I—"

"Anybody with you?"

"NO!" shouted Marchbanks. "Do you want my story or don't you? I—"

"Continue," said the Inspector judicially.

Marchbanks glared. "As I began to say—I left town Monday evening at seven in my car. I was bound for Little Neck—"

"Little Neck, eh?" interpolated the Inspector exasperatingly.

"Yes, Little Neck," stormed Marchbanks. "What's wrong in that? I had been invited to a small party at the house of a friend of mine there—"

"His name?"

"Patrick Malone," replied Marchbanks resignedly. "When I got there, I found no one at home except Malone's man. He explained that at the last moment Malone had been called away on business and had had to call off the party. . . ."

"Did you know that such an eventuality might occur?"

"If you mean did I know that Malone was going to be called away—yes, in a way. He'd mentioned the possibility of it over the 'phone to me earlier in the day. At any rate, I saw no use in staying, so I left at once and proceeded off the main road to my own shack, a few miles farther on. I keep it for occasional jaunts into the Island. I—"

"Have you any servants there?"

"No. It's a small place and I prefer solitude when I'm out that way. So I slept there overnight and returned to the City in the morning by car."

The Inspector smiled sardonically. "I suppose you met no one all night or in the morning who might verify your statements?"

"I don't know what you mean. What are you driving at—?"

"Yes or no?"

". . . No."

"What time did you get to the City?"

"About ten-thirty. I rose rather late."

"And what time was it Monday evening when you reached your friend Malone's place and spoke to his valet?"

"Oh, I should say about eight or eight-thirty. I don't recall exactly."

The Inspector sent a mutely humorous glance across the room to Ellery. Then he shrugged his shoulders. Marchbanks' florid face darkened and he rose abruptly.

"If you have nothing more to ask me, Inspector Queen, I must be going." He picked up his hat and stick.

"Ah! Just one other thing. Sit down, Marchbanks." Marchbanks reluctantly reseated himself. "How do you account for the murder of your sister?"

Marchbanks sniggered. "I thought you'd ask that. Up a tree, eh? Well, I'm not surprised. The police of this city are—"

"Answer my question, please."

"I don't account for it, and I can't account for it!" cried Marchbanks suddenly. "That's your business! All I know is that my sister has been shot to death, and I want her murderer sizzling in the Chair." He stopped, out of breath.

"Yes, yes, I realize your natural desire for revenge," said the Inspector tiredly. "You may go, Mr. Marchbanks, but keep in town."

33

ALIBIS: CARMODY

Vincent Carmody was the next caller. His reticence was as marked as usual. He folded his astonishing length and sat down quite noiselessly in the inquisitorial chair. And sat waiting.

"Ah—Mr. Carmody," began the Inspector uneasily. The antique-dealer disdained to reply to what was obviously a question of fact. "Ah—Mr. Carmody, I've called you in for a little consultation. We are checking up on the movements of everybody connected directly or indirectly with Mrs. French. Purely as a matter of form, you understand. . . ."

"Ummm," said Carmody, his fingers in his straggly beard.

The Inspector dipped hastily into his old brown snuffbox. "Now, I should be happy, sir, to hear an account of your movements on Monday night—the night of the murder."

"The murder." Carmody said it negligently. "Not interested in that, Inspector. What about my daughter?"

The Inspector stared with growing irritation at Carmody's expressionless lean face. "Your daughter's search is being conducted by the proper authorities. We haven't found her yet, but we have new information which is likely to produce results. Please answer my question."

"Results!" Carmody said it with surprising bitterness. "I know what that word means in the police vocabulary.

You're stumped and you know it. I'll put my own detective on the case."

"Will you *please* answer my question?" grated the Inspector.

"Keep cool," said Carmody. "Don't see what my movements on Monday night have to do with the case. I certainly didn't kidnap my own daughter. But if you must have it, here it is.

"Late Monday I received a telegram from one of my scouts. He reported the discovery of practically a house full of early American pieces in the wilds of Connecticut. I invariably investigate finds of that nature personally. I took the train at Grand Central—the 9:14. Changed at Stamford and didn't get to my destination until nearly midnight. It's far off the beaten path. Had the address and immediately called on the people who owned the furniture. Nobody home, and I still don't know what went wrong. Had no place to stay—no hotel there—and had to return to the city. Couldn't make a decent connection and didn't get back to my apartment until four in the morning. That's all."

"Not quite, Mr. Carmody." The Inspector mused. "Did any one see you when you returned to the city—at your apartment, perhaps?"

"No. It was too late. Nobody up. And I live alone. I had my breakfast at the apartment dining-room at ten o'clock. The head-waiter will identify me."

"No doubt," said the Inspector disagreeably. "Meet any one on your trip who might remember you?"

"No. Unless the conductor of the train."

"Well!" Queen slammed his hands behind his back and regarded Carmody with open distaste. "Please make a note of all your movements and mail it to me at Headquarters. One question more. Do you know that your daughter Bernice is a drug addict?"

Carmody leaped out of his chair snarling. In an instant he had been transformed from bored reticence to contorted fury. Ellery half-rose from his chair in the corner; it appeared for a moment as if the antique-dealer might strike the Inspector. But the old man stood very still, examining Carmody coolly. Carmody, fists clenched, subsided in his chair.

"How did you find that out?" he muttered in a strangled voice. The muscles rippled under the skin of his dark triangular jaw. "I didn't think any one knew—except Winifred and me."

"Ah, so Mrs. French knew it too?" queried the Inspector instantly. "Had she known it long?"

"So it's out," growled Carmody. "Good God!" He raised a haggard face to Queen. "I've known it for about a year. Winifred—" his face hardened—"Winifred didn't know it at all. Eyes of the mother, and all that," he added bitterly. "Rot! She thought chiefly of herself. . . . So I told her—two weeks ago. She didn't believe it. We quarreled. But at the end she knew—I saw it in her eyes. I had talked to Bernice countless times about it. She was shameless. She would not divulge the source of her drug supply. In desperation I turned to Winifred. I thought Winifred might succeed where I had failed. I don't know any more . . ." His voice dropped to a whisper. "I was going to take Bernice away—somewhere—anywhere—cure her. . . . And then Winifred was murdered and Bernice —gone. . . ." His voice died away. Huge welts stood out under his eyes. The man was suffering—how deeply, by what perverse psychology only Ellery, sitting quietly in his corner, realized.

And then, without another sound, without so much as a word of explanation, Carmody sprang to his feet, snatched his hat, and dashed from the Queen apartment. The Inspector, at the window, saw him running wildly down the street, hat still clutched in his hand.

34

ALIBIS: TRASK

Trask was a half-hour late for his appointment at the Queen apartment.   He appeared indolently, indolently greeted the two Queens, indolently sank into the chair, indolently applied a match to his cigarette, which was stuck rakishly in a long jade holder, and indolently awaited the Inspector's questions.

Where was he Monday night?   Oh, about town—vaguely, with an idle gesture of his arm.   He tweaked the points of his mustache.

Where "about town"?   Well, really—can't remember. Some night-club or other at first.

At what time?   Must have started about eleven-thirty.

Where was he before eleven-thirty?   Oh, he'd been disappointed by some friends, and had dropped into a Broadway theater at the last moment.

What was the name of the night-club?   Really, don't recall it.

What did he mean by "not recalling it"?   Well—to tell the truth, he had some bootleg liquor and it must have contained dynamite—ha, ha!   Put him out like a light. Got awfully drunk.   Didn't remember anything except dashing cold water on his face at ten o'clock Tuesday morning in the lavatory of the Pennsylvania Station.   All mussed up, too.   Must have had an awful night of it. Probably kicked out of the night-club in the morning. And all that.   Just had time to dash home and get into some fresh clothes.   Then the directors' meeting at the French store.

"Beautiful!" muttered the Inspector, eying Trask as if he were an obnoxious little animal.   Trask flicked the ashes from his cigarette in the general direction of a tray.

"Trask!"   The whip in Queen's voice brought the tall,

dissipated director's body up with a start. "Are you sure you can't remember what night-club you were in?"

"I say now," drawled Trask, sinking back, "you scared me that time, Inspector. I've told you no. Went completely out of my head. Don't recall a thing."

"Well, that's just too bad," grunted the Inspector. "If I'm not disturbing you, Trask—do you know that Bernice Carmody was a habitual drug-user?"

"Not really!" Trask sat up straight. "Then I *was* right!"

"Oh, you suspected it?"

"A number of times. Bernice was queer quite frequently. Showed all the symptoms. I've seen plenty of 'em." He brushed a speck of ash from his gardenia with languid distaste.

The Inspector smiled. "Which didn't daunt you from going ahead with your contemplated engagement to Miss Carmody?"

Trask looked virtuous. "Oh, no—really! I'd intended to cure her after we were married. Without her family's knowledge, and all that. Too bad—too bad," he sighed. He sighed again.

"What has your relationship been with Cyrus French?" demanded the Inspector impatiently.

"Oh, that!" Trask brightened. "Absolutely of the best, Inspector. You—er—you would rather expect a chap to get along with his future father-in-law. Haw-haw!"

"Get out of here," said the Inspector distinctly.

35

ALIBIS: GRAY

John Gray folded his gloves neatly, deposited them in his rich black derby, and handed them with a cheerful smile to Djuna. Then he shook hands decorously with the

Inspector, nodded to Ellery with just the proper note of heartiness, and obediently seated himself at the Inspector's request.

"Well!" he chuckled, smoothing his white mustache. "Very charming household, I see. Very! And how is the investigation proceeding, Inspector? Tchk, tchk!" He chattered like a spry old parrot, his twinkling eyes never still.

The Inspector cleared his throat. "A little matter of check-up, Mr. Gray. Routine. I haven't inconvenienced you by this summons?"

"Not at all, not at all," said Gray amiably. "I've just come from a visit to Cyrus—Cyrus French, I should say—and he's much better, by the way, much better."

"That's nice," said the Inspector. "Now, Mr. Gray, just to make it legal—can you account for your movements on Monday night?"

Gray looked blank. Then he smiled slowly. Then he burst into an infectious chuckle. "I see, I see! Clever, Inspector, quite clever. You want to be sure of everything. Very interesting! I suppose every one is coming in for a similar quiz?"

"Oh, yes!" said the Inspector reassuringly. "We've had a number of your colleagues on the carpet today already." They both laughed. Gray became politely serious.

"Monday night? Let me see." He plucked his mustache thoughtfully. "Of course! Monday night I spent the entire evening at my Club. The Penny Club, you know. Had dinner there with some of my cronies, played billiards—the usual thing. At about ten o'clock, I believe, or perhaps a little after ten, Zorn—you remember Zorn, of course, one of my fellow-directors—Zorn dropped in for a chat. We discussed the coming merger, the details of which we were to work out in conference the next morning

with French and the rest, and about a half-hour later Zorn
left, complaining of headache."

"Well, that tallies nicely," said Queen, with a grin.
"Because Mr. Zorn was here not long ago and told us about
your meeting at the Penny Club."

"Really?" Gray smiled. "Then I gather there is little
left to be said, Inspector."

"Not quite, Mr. Gray." The Inspector clucked cheerfully. "You see, just to keep the record straight—how did
you spend the rest of the evening?"

"Oh! In a commonplace manner, sir. I left the Club
at about eleven and walked home—I live not far from
there, on Madison Avenue. Simply went home and to
bed."

"You live alone, Mr. Gray?"

Gray grimaced. "Unfortunately, being a misogynist,
I have no family, Inspector. An old servant keeps house
for me—I live in an apartment hotel, you know."

"Then your housekeeper was up when you returned
from the Club, Mr. Gray?"

Gray spread his hands briefly. "No. Hilda had left on
Saturday evening to visit a sick brother in Jersey City, and
did not get back until Tuesday afternoon."

"I see." The Inspector took snuff. "But surely *some
one* saw you get home, Mr. Gray?"

Gray looked startled, then he smiled again one of his
twinkling smiles. "Oh, you want me to establish my—
alibi, is it, Inspector?"

"That's what it's called, sir."

"Then there's nothing more to be said," replied Gray
happily. "Because Jackson, the night-clerk, saw me when
I entered the building. I asked for mail and stood chatting
with him for several minutes. Then I took the elevator
to my suite."

The Inspector's face brightened. "Then really," he said,

"there *is* nothing more to be said.   Except—" his face lengthened momentarily—"what time was it when you stopped talking with this night-clerk and went upstairs?"

"Just eleven-forty.   I remember glancing at the clock above Jackson's desk to compare it with my own watch."

"And where is your hotel, Mr. Gray?"

"Madison and 37th, Inspector.   The *Burton*."

"Then I think—   Unless, Ellery, you would like to ask Mr. Gray a question or two?"

The aged little director turned quickly, in open surprise. He had forgotten the presence of Ellery, who was sitting quietly in his corner listening to the conversation.   Gray looked expectant as Ellery smiled.

"Thank you, dad—I *have* something to ask Mr. Gray, if we're not keeping him too long?"   He looked questioningly at their visitor.

Gray expostulated.   "Not at all, Mr. Queen.   Anything I can do to help you—"

"Very well, then."   Ellery hoisted his lean length from the chair and stretched his muscles.   "Mr. Gray, I'm going to ask you a peculiar question.   I rely upon your discretion to preserve silence, for one thing, and upon your undoubted loyalty to Mr. French and your concern in his bereavement to answer frankly."

"I'm entirely at your service."

"Let me present a hypothetical case," continued Ellery rapidly.   "Let us suppose that Bernice Carmody was a drug addict. . . ."

Gray frowned.   "A drug addict?"

"Exactly.   And let us suppose further that neither her mother nor her stepfather suspected her malady and condition.   Then let us suppose that Mrs. French suddenly discovered the truth. . . ."

"I see, I see," murmured Gray.

"The hypothetical question arising from this hypotheti-

cal case is: What do you think Mrs. French would do?"
Ellery lit a cigaret.

Gray grew thoughtful. Then he looked into Ellery's
eyes. "The first thing that occurs to me, Mr. Queen," he
said simply, "is that Mrs. French would *not* confide in
Cyrus."

"That's interesting. You know them both so well. . . ."

"Yes." Gray set his small wrinkled jaw. "Cyrus has
been a lifelong friend. I know—or knew—Mrs. French
perhaps as well as any one acquainted with the French
family. And I am certain, familiar as I am with Cyrus's
character and Mrs. French's knowledge of his character,
that she would not dare to tell him such a thing. She would
keep it strictly to herself. She might possibly inform Carmody, her first husband. . . ."

"We needn't go into that, Mr. Gray," said Ellery. "But
why would she keep it a secret from French?"

"Because," said Gray frankly, "Cyrus is hypersensitive
on the subject of vice, particularly drug addiction. You
must remember that most of his latter years have been
devoted to wiping out as much of this sort of vice in the
City as possible. To find it in his own family would, I
firmly believe, unbalance him. . . . But, of course," he
added quickly, "he doesn't know; I'm positive Mrs. French
would keep a thing like that to herself. She might try to
cure the girl secretly, perhaps. . . ."

Ellery said clearly: "One of the major reasons for Mrs.
French's silence in a case like this would be, I suppose, that
she was aiming to secure for her daughter a generous slice
of her husband's fortune?"

Gray started uncomfortably. "Well . . . I don't . . .
Yes, if you must have the truth, I think that is so. Mrs.
French was a calculating—not necessarily unscrupulous,
mind you—but a calculating and very practical woman. I
believe that, motherlike, she was determined that Bernice

come in for a good share of Cyrus's estate when Cyrus should pass on. . . . Is there anything else, Mr. Queen?"

"That is," said Ellery, smiling, "quite sufficient. Thank you immeasurably, Mr. Gray."

"Then," said the Inspector, "that will be all."

Gray looked relieved, accepted his coat, hat and gloves from Djuna, murmured polite adieux, and left.

The Inspector and Ellery heard his light quick step on the staircase as he descended to the street.

36

"THE TIME HAS COME . . ."

The Queens had dinner in silence. Djuna served in silence, and in silence cleared the table afterward. The Inspector dipped into the browned interior of his snuff-box and Ellery held communion with first a cigaret, then a pipe, then a cigaret again. In all this time no word was spoken. It was a silence of sympathy, not infrequent in the Queen household.

Finally Ellery sighed and stared into the fireplace. But it was the Inspector who spoke first.

"As far as I am concerned," he said with a grim disappointment, "this day has been entirely wasted."

Ellery raised his eyebrows. "Dad, dad, you grow more irascible with every passing day. . . . If I didn't know how upset and overworked you've been of late, I'd be annoyed with you."

"At my obtuseness?" demanded the Inspector, twinkling.

"No, at the lapse of your usual mental vigor." Ellery twisted his head and grinned at his father. "Do you mean to say that today's incidents have meant nothing to you?"

"The raid flat, Springer skipped, nothing tangible from the alibis of these people—I can't see any cause for celebration," retorted the Inspector.

"Well, well!" Ellery frowned. "Perhaps I'm over-sanguine. . . . But the whole thing is so clear!"

He sprang to his feet and began to rummage in his desk. He produced his voluminous sheets of notes and thumbed rapidly through them under the Inspector's wearied and bewildered eyes. Then he slapped them back into their receptacle.

"It's all over," he announced, "all over but the shouting and—the proof. I have all the threads—or rather, all the threads which lead inexorably to the murderer of Mrs. French. They don't make solid proof, such as is demanded by our venerable courts of law and our prosecuting system. What would you do in a case like that, dad?"

The Inspector wrinkled his nose in self-disgust. "I take it that what's been a hopeless maze to me has been a clear thoroughfare to you. That rankles, son! I have raised up a Frankenstein to haunt my old age. . . ." Then he chuckled and laid a slightly infirm hand on Ellery's knee.

"Good lad," he said. "I don't know *what* I'd do without you."

"Shucks." Ellery blushed. "You've gone sentimental, too, dad. . . ." Their fingers met covertly. "Now, look here, Inspector! You've got to help me to a decision!"

"Yes, yes. . . ." Queen dropped back, embarrassed. "You've got a case, an explanation and no proof. What to do. . . . Bluff, my son. Bluff as if you'd raised the pot before the draw on a pair of fours and then found real opposition staring at you. Raise again!"

Ellery looked thoughtful. "I've been tottering on the edge . . . Christmas!" His eyes brightened with a sudden thought. "How stupid I've been!" he cried at once. "I've a beautiful card up my sleeve and I've forgotten all about it! Bluff? We'll just about sweep our slippery friend off our slippery friend's feet!"

He yanked the telephone toward him, hesitated, then

turned it over to the Inspector, who was regarding him with gloomy fondness.

"Here's a list," he said, scribbling on a piece of paper, "of some people of importance. Will you blow the conch, dad, while I begin a memorization of these pesky notes?"

"The time is—" asked the Inspector submissively.

"To-morrow morning at nine-thirty," replied Ellery. "And you might call the D.A. and tell him to close in on our friend Springer."

"Springer!" cried the Inspector.

"Springer," replied Ellery. And thereafter there was silence, broken periodically by the voice of the Inspector on the telephone.

PARENTHESIS AND CHALLENGE

I have often found it a stimulating exercise in my own reading of murder fiction to pause at that point in the story immediately preceding the solution, and to try by a logical analysis to determine for myself the identity of the criminal. . . . Because I believe that numerous gourmets of this species of fictional delicacy are as interested in the reasoning as in the reading, I submit in the proper spirit of sportsmanship an amiable challenge to the reader. . . . Without reading the concluding pages, Reader—Who killed Mrs. French? . . . There is a great tendency among detective-story lovers to endeavor to "guess" the criminal by submitting to the play of a blind instinct. A certain amount of this is inevitable, I will admit, but the application of logic and common sense is the important thing, the source of the greater enjoyment. . . . Whereupon I state without reservation that the reader is at this stage in the recounting of *The French Powder Mystery* fully cognizant of all the facts pertinent to the discovery of the criminal; and that a sufficiently diligent study of what has gone before should educe a clear understanding of what is to come. *A rivederci!*   E. Q.

THE LAST EPISODE

"Forty years in the service of the SÛRETÉ, *one might hazard, would dull the edge of one's zest for the hunt. Thank the good Lord, this is not so! at least in my own case, which has been as full of interest, I dare say, as the next. . . . There was the admirable Henri Tencqueville, who cut his throat before my very eyes when we cornered him in his Montmartre hideaway . . . and Petit Charlot, who shot two of my faithful lads to death and bit off a piece of the good Sergeant Mousson's nose in the* mêlée *before he was subdued. . . . Ah, well! I grow tender in reminiscence, but . . . I would make the point that even to-day, old and enfeebled as I am, I would not give up the thrill of that final* coup de main, *that last stage of the chase when the quarry, panting and desperate, has his back to the wall—no, not for all the everlasting delights of the Turkish heaven! . . ."*

—From THE MEMOIRS OF A PREFECT,
   By Auguste Brillon.

37

MAKE READY!

THEY came in one by one—furtive, curious, impassive, bored, reluctant, openly nervous. Quietly they came in, conscious of the tight police cordon, of a quivering strain in the atmosphere, of shrewd eyes that noted and calculated their least movement—conscious most of all of grim over-hanging disaster, to whom and with what dire effects they did not know and could only guess.

It was nine-thirty of the fateful Thursday morning. The door through which they shuffled in silence was the door marked PRIVATE: CYRUS FRENCH. . . . They passed inside through the bare lofty anteroom, into the heavy quiet of the library, sat down in incredible camp-chairs set up martially facing the dormer-windows.

They crowded the room. In the front row sat old Cyrus French himself, a white and trembling figure. His fingers were desperately entwined in the fingers of Marion French by his side. Westley Weaver, harried face gaunted by sleeplessness, occupied the seat next to Marion's. To French's left was Dr. Stuart, the old man's physician, watching his patient with a professional pantherishness. By Stuart's side sat John Gray, dapper and birdlike, occasionally leaning over the doctor's bulky abdomen to talk into the sick man's ear.

In the row behind were Hortense Underhill, the housekeeper, and Doris Keaton, the maid. Both sat rigidly, whispering to each other out of the corners of their mouths, peering about with frightened eyes.

In serried ranks. . . . Wheezing Marchbanks; the portly Zorn fingering his watch-chain; a befurred and aromatic Mrs. Zorn dispensing smiles to the grave Frenchman, Paul Lavery, who stroked his short beard; Trask, a flower in his lapel, but utterly pale, with enormous leaden rings under his eyes; the antique-dealer Vincent Carmody, a saturnine figure, uncompromising, somber, even in his chair towering above the heads of the company; mild-mannered Arnold MacKenzie, the general manager of the store; Diana Johnson, the Negress who had discovered Mrs. French's dead body; the four watchmen—O'Flaherty, Bloom, Ralska, Powers. . . .

There was little conversation. Each time the anteroom door opened people twisted about in their seats, craned, jerked their eyes back to the window again with guilty side-glances toward each other.

The conference-table had been pushed against the wall. In a row of chairs before the table sat Sergeant Thomas Velie and William Crouther, chief of the store's detective force, talking in undertones; scowling Salvatore Fiorelli, of the Narcotic Squad, bright black eyes snapping at some inexpressible thought, his scar pulsing slowly beneath the swarthy skin; "Jimmy," the little bald-headed operative of the Headquarters fingerprint department. At the anteroom door stood Patrolman Bush, relegated to the important post of guardian of the door. A cloud of detectives, among them Inspector Queen's favorite operatives—Hagstrom, Flint, Ritter, Johnson, and Piggott—massed along the wall directly opposite the conference-table. At each corner of the room stood a silent officer in blue, cap in hand.

Neither Inspector Queen nor Ellery Queen had yet put in his appearance. People whispered this information to each other. They looked sidelong at the anteroom door, against which Bush's broad back was set.

Gradually, tangibly, another silence came over the scene. Whispers trembled, wavered, ceased. Glances became more furtive, chair-twistings more frequent. Cyrus French coughed violently; he doubled up in agony. Dr. Stuart's eyes flickered with a vague anxiety. Weaver bent far to the side when the old man's paroxysm had passed; Marion looked startled; soon their heads were close together, touching. . . .

Crouther scraped his hand over his face. "What the hell is holdin' up the works, Sergeant?" Velie shook his head gloomily. "What's it all about?"

"Got me."

Crouther shrugged.

The silence thickened. Every one grew still as stone. . . . The silence grew more embarrassing with each passing moment—a silence that swelled, breathed, became alive. . . .

Then Sergeant Velie did a strange thing. His spatulate forefinger, resting on his knee, tapped three distinct times, in rhythm. Not even Crouther caught the signal, and Crouther was at Velie's side. But the officer on guard, who had been watching the Sergeant's hand for minutes, immediately sprang into motion. All eyes flashed instantly upon him, grasping at this sign of life, of happening with a pitiful eagerness. . . . The policeman went to the desk, which was shrouded by a light tarpaulin, and bending far over carefully removed the covering. He stepped back, folded the tarpaulin neatly, retreated to his corner. . . .

But he was already forgotten. As if the sheer rays of a searchlight had been trained upon the desk, every one in the room eyed the objects revealed with a fascination drawn from the deepest crevices of his being.

They were many, and heterogeneous. Ranged in orderly rows along the glass top, each with a small labeled card before it, were the gold lipstick marked *W.M.F.*, which Ellery had found on the bedroom dressing-table; the silver-chased lipstick with the *C* monogram from the dead woman's bag in the exhibition-window; six keys with gold discs—the keys to the apartment, five of which bore the initials of Cyrus French, Winifred Marchbanks French, Marion French, Bernice Carmody, Westley Weaver, and the sixth the word Master; the two carved onyx book-ends, lying with a small jar of white powder and a camel's-hair brush between them; the five strange volumes which Ellery had found on French's desk; the shaving-set from the lavatory cabinet; two ashtrays filled with cigaret stubs— one set much shorter in length than the other; the gauzy scarf initialed *M.F.*, taken from the neck of the victim; a board on which were tacked the cards from the cardroom table, laid out exactly as they had first appeared to the police; the slip of blue memorandum paper which was checked off at Cyrus French's typewritten name; the blue hat and the walking shoes from the bedroom closet which Hortense Underhill and Doris Keaton had identified as having been worn by Bernice Carmody the day she disappeared; and a black .38 Colt revolver, with the two now rusty-looking splatters of metal which had been the lethal bullets lying near the muzzle.

Quite by itself, prominently in view of the audience, lay a pair of dull, steely manacles—a symbol and a portent of what was to come. . . .

And there they reposed, the silent clues garnered during the investigation frankly open to the gaze of the uneasy guests of Ellery Queen. Again they stared, whispered.

But this time they had not long to wait. A slight commotion in the corridor outside became plainly audible in the library. Sergeant Velie lumbered to his feet and went quickly to the anteroom door, motioning Patrolman Bush aside. He disappeared, the door swinging shut behind him.

Now the door became the focal point of those half-angry, bewildered eyes—that door behind which the deep murmur of several voices kept up a short mysterious litany.

. . . And as if it had been cut cleanly by a knife, the voices broke off and an instant of silence fell before the knob of the door was rattled, the door was pushed inward, and eight men stepped into the room.

38

THE END OF ALL THINGS

It had been Ellery Queen's hand on the knob—a subtly changed young man with drawn features and a sharpened glance that swept the room once and then returned to the anteroom.

"Before me, Commissioner," he murmured, holding the door wide. Commissioner Scott Welles grunted, pushed his heavy body into view. Three tight-lipped men in plain clothes—his bodyguard—flanked him as he crossed the room toward the desk.

Next to appear in full sight of the assembled company was a strangely altered Inspector Richard Queen, holding himself rigidly erect. He was pale. He followed the police commissioner in silence.

After Queen came District Attorney Henry Sampson and his assistant, the red-haired Timothy Cronin. They were whispering to each other, paying no attention to the occupants of the room.

Velie, making up the rear, carefully closed the anteroom door, flipped Bush back to his post with a curt finger, and dropped into his chair beside Crouther. The store detective looked up at him inquiringly; Velie said nothing and settled his big body. Both men turned to watch the newcomers.

There was a little flurry of conversation as Ellery Queen and his companions stood near the desk at the head of the room. Inspector Queen indicated one of the leather-padded conference chairs immediately to the right and a little behind the desk, as the seat to be occupied by the Commissioner. Welles seemed a sadder and wiser man—he sat down without a word, his eyes on Ellery's quiet figure before the desk.

The three guards disposed themselves with the other detectives at the side of the room.

Inspector Queen himself sat down in a big chair to the left of the desk, with Cronin at his side. The District Attorney dropped into a chair next to the Commissioner. Desk in the center, its varied articles beckoning attention. On either side two chairs with official occupants. And dominating the scene . . .

The stage was set.

Ellery Queen, cynically examining the room and its occupants once more, expressed himself as satisfied at the Commissioner's brusque question. Ellery stepped behind the desk and stood with his back to the dormer-windows. His head was lowered, his eyes on the desk-top. His hand strayed to the glass, hovered over the book-ends, played with the jar of white powder. . . . He smiled, straightened, raised his head, removed his pince-nez glasses, looked calmly at his hushed audience, waited. . . . Not until there was absolute silence did he speak.

"Ladies and gentleman." Prosy beginning! Yet something vaguely eerie shivered through the air; it was a simultaneous sigh from many breasts.

"Ladies and gentlemen. Sixty hours ago Mrs. Winifred French was shot to death in this building. Forty-eight hours ago her body was found. This morning we have assembled at a private Waterloo to name her murderer." Ellery had spoken quietly; now he paused for the slightest instant. . . .

But after that sigh *en masse* even breaths seemed to be drawn with care. No one spoke; no one whispered. They merely sat and waited.

A cutting edge slipped into the tone of Ellery's voice.

"Very well! A few preliminary explanations are required. Commissioner Welles—" he turned slightly toward Welles, "it is with your permission that I conduct this unofficial inquest?"

Welles nodded, once.

"Then let me explain," continued Ellery, turning back to his auditors, "that I am merely taking the place of Inspector Queen, who is unable to take charge because of a minor throat ailment which makes long speaking difficult and painful. Correct, sir?" He bowed very solemnly in the direction of his father. The Inspector grew even paler than before, nodded wordlessly. "Further," Ellery went on, "if I shall at any time use the personal 'I' in my discourse this morning, you are to understand that it is merely for convenience—that in reality I shall be describing the investigatory processes of Inspector Queen himself."

He halted abruptly, threw a challenging glance about the room, met nothing but wide eyes and ears, and plunged at once into an analysis of the French murder case.

"I shall take you through our investigation of this crime, ladies and gentlemen," he began in a sharp decisive tone, "step by step, deduction by deduction, observation by observation, until I arrive at what is an inevitable conclusion. Hagstrom, you are taking this down?"

Eyes followed the direction of Ellery's glance. At the side of the room where the detectives were congregated, Detective Hagstrom was seated, pencil poised above a stenographic notebook. Hagstrom bobbed his head.

"What transpires here this morning," explained Ellery pleasantly, "will become part of the official dossier of the case. Enough of asides!" He cleared his throat.

"Mrs. Winifred Marchbanks French was discovered dead —killed by two bullets, one in the heart and one in the *precordial* region below the heart—on Tuesday at fifteen minutes or so past noon. When Inspector Queen arrived upon the scene he noted several facts which led him to believe that"—he paused—"the exhibition-window on the main floor was *not* in effect the place where the crime was committed."

The room was deathly still. Fascination, fear, aversion, grief—the gamut of emotions played upon those intent white faces. Ellery Queen went on, rapidly.

"There were five component elements in this initial investigation," he said, "that pointed to the conclusion that the murder was not committed in the window.

"The first was the fact that, while on Monday night Mrs. French had in her possession her personal key to this apartment, the key was missing from her person and effects Tuesday morning, on the discovery of her dead body. O'Flaherty, the head nightwatchman, testified that she had the key at eleven-fifty Monday night when she left his cubbyhole to take the elevator upstairs. Yet it was gone. Search of the store and premises left the key still unfound. What was the inference? That the key and the crime were in some way connected. How? Well, the key appertained to the apartment. If it was missing, wasn't there an indication that the apartment also entered into the crime somewhere? At least there was enough suspicion to be gleaned from the missing key to warrant a belief that the apartment *might have been* the scene of the crime."

Ellery paused; his lips twitched with fleeting amusement at the frowning faces before him.

"Captious reasoning? I see the disbelief on your faces. Yet bear it in mind. The fact of the key's being missing meant nothing of itself—but when it was added to the four other facts of which I shall speak, it took on significance indeed."

He swung back into his main narrative.

"The second element was a grotesque and even amusing one—you will see, incidentally, that the detection of crime is not built upon weighty salient factors, but upon just such incongruities as I shall have occasion to mention this morning. . . . I refer to the fact that the crime must have been committed a short time after midnight. This was simply calculated from Dr. Prouty's report—Dr. Prouty is the Assistant Medical Examiner—that Mrs. French had been dead some twelve hours when she was found.

"If Mrs. French had been shot to death in the window-room at a little past midnight, ladies and gentlemen," continued Ellery, with a twinkle in his eye, "her murderer must have committed his crime either in total darkness or by the feeble illumination of a pocket-torch! For there were no lighting fixtures that worked in the room—in fact, no bulbs—and the room was not even wired. Yet we were forced to suppose that the murderer met his victim, talked with her, perhaps quarreled with her, then shot her unerringly in two vital spots, disposed of her body in the wall-bed, cleaned up the blood-stains and what not—all in a room at best illuminated by a flashlight! No, it was not reasonable. Wherefore Inspector Queen, quite logically, I believe, concluded that the crime was not committed in the exhibition-window."

There was a little rustle of excitement. Ellery smiled, continued.

"This, however, was not the only reason for his belief. There was a third point. And that was the lipstick—the long, silver-chased lipstick—monogrammed C, found in Mrs. French's handbag by her body. That this lipstick obviously was not Mrs. French's I shall not discuss at this point. The pertinent factor was that it contained lip-rouge of a decidedly darker shade of red than the lip-rouge on the dead woman's lips. But this meant that Mrs. French's own lipstick—with which she daubed the lighter rouge on her lips—should be somewhere about. But it was not! Where could it be? Perhaps the murderer took it? That sounded rather nonsensical. The most plausible explanation seemed to be that the missing lipstick was somewhere else in the building. . . . Why somewhere else in the building?—why not at Mrs. French's home, or at least outside the store?

"For this very good reason. That Mrs. French's lips—her dead mute lips—which were painted with the lighter shade of red, indicated that she had not completed her application of the rouge! There were two dabs on either side of her upper lip, and another small dab in the center of her lower lip. The rouge had not been smeared—it had patently been applied with a finger and left that way. . . ." Ellery turned toward Marion French. He said gently, "How do you apply your lip-rouge, Miss French?"

The girl whispered: "Just as you described, Mr. Queen. Three pats, one on each side of the upper lip and one in the center of the lower lip."

"Thank you." Ellery smiled. "We had, then, visible evidence of a case where a woman began to paint her lips and did not complete the operation. But this was unnatural, remarkable. There are very few things that will keep a woman from finishing this delicate task. Very, very few! One of them might be a violent interruption of some kind. A violent interruption? But there was murder committed! Was that the interruption?"

He changed his tone, forged ahead. "It seemed likely. But in any case, those lips had not been painted in the window-room. Where was the lipstick? That we found it later in the apartment was merely confirmation. . . .

"Point number four was physiological. Dr. Prouty was puzzled by the fact that there was so little blood on the corpse. Both wounds—one particularly—should have bled considerably. The *precordial* region contains many blood-vessels and muscles which would have been badly torn by the passage of the bullet, which left a ragged wound. Where was the blood? Had the murderer cleaned it up? But in the dark, or semi-darkness, he could not possibly have removed all traces of the copious blood-flow from those wounds. Whereupon we were compelled once more to conclude that that blood had flowed—*somewhere else.* Which meant that Mrs. French had been shot somewhere else than in the window-room.

"And the fifth point was a psychological one which I fear"—he smiled sadly—"would not carry much weight in a court of law. Nevertheless to me it was quite overwhelming in its indication. For the mind rebelled at the thought that the window-room was the scene of the crime. It was preposterous, dangerous, asinine from the point of view of a potential murderer. A meeting and a murder connote secrecy, privacy—any number of exact requirements. The window-room afforded none of these. The room is not fifty feet away from the head nightwatchman's office. That area is well-patrolled at periodic intervals. Revolver-shots had to be fired—and none was heard. No! Both Inspector Queen and myself felt—for the five reasons I have given you, no single one of which was conclusive, but which were collectively significant—that the crime was not committed in the window-room."

Ellery paused. His audience was following the story with eager, panting concentration. Commissioner Welles regarded Ellery with a new light in his small eyes. The Inspector was sunk deeply in thought.

"If not the window," continued Ellery, "where then? The key pointed to the apartment—the required privacy, illumination, a logical place for the use of lipstick—certainly the apartment seemed the best possibility. So Inspector Queen, relying upon my discretion and discernment, since he himself could not leave the window-room where the preliminary investigation was still going on,

asked me to go to the apartment and see what I could see.
Which I did, with interesting results. . . .

"The first thing I found in the apartment was Mrs.
French's own lipstick, lying on the bedroom dressing-
table." Ellery picked up the gold lipstick from the desk
and held it up for a moment. "This lipstick proved at
once, of course, that Mrs. French had been in the apartment on Monday night. The fact that it was lying under
the curved edge of a mother-of-pearl tray on the dressing-
table and was quite hidden, showed that it had probably
been overlooked by the murderer. In fact, the murderer
had no reason even to look for it, because he did not apparently observe that the lipstick in Mrs. French's bag and
the coloring on her lips were not identical." Ellery replaced the glittering metal case on the desk.

"Now, I found the lipstick on the dressing-table. What
did this mean? It seemed rather plain that Mrs. French
had been using the stick at that dressing-table inside when
she was interrupted. But the fact that the lipstick was still
there on the table when I found it pointed, it seemed to me,
to the fact that Mrs. French was not shot in the bedroom.
What was the interruption, then? Obviously, either a
knock on the outer door or the noise of the murderer
entering the apartment. It was not the latter, for the murderer had no key to the apartment, as I shall soon prove.
Then it must have been a knock at the door. Then,
too, Mrs. French must have been expecting it, for it so disturbed her, or it was so important to her, that she immediately put down her lipstick, neglecting to complete the
daubing of her lips, and hurried through the library and
into the anteroom to admit her nocturnal visitor. Presumably she opened the door, the visitor entered, and they
went into the library where Mrs. French stood behind the
desk and the visitor stood to the right, facing her—that is,
Mrs. French stood where I am standing now and the mur-

derer stood about where Detective Hagstrom is sitting at this moment.

"How do I know this?" went on Ellery rapidly. "Very simply. On examining the library, I discovered that these book-ends, which lay on the desk"—he lifted the two onyx book-ends carefully and exhibited them—"had been tampered with. The green felt sheathing of one of them was lighter in shade than its mate. Mr. Weaver volunteered the information that the book-ends were only two months old, having been presented to Mr. French by Mr. Gray on the occasion of Mr. French's last birthday, and that he had observed them at that time in perfect condition, with the felts exactly alike in color. Furthermore, the book-ends had never left the room, or in fact the desk itself. Apparently, then, the change of felt had occurred the night before. And that was proved when, on examining the felt under a powerful glass, I noted some scattered grains of a white powder stuck in the glue-line where felt and onyx met!

"The glue was still a trifle viscid," said Ellery, "showing that it had been very recently applied. The grains, on examination, by myself cursorily and on analysis by the official fingerprint expert, proved to be ordinary fingerprint powder, such as is used by the police. But the use of fingerprint powder predicated a crime. There were no fingerprints on the onyx. That meant the fingerprints had been removed. Why the powder, then? Obviously, first to sprinkle the surface in order to bring out what fingerprints might be there, and second to remove the ones found. So much was evident.

"But the larger question arose—why were these book-ends handled at all?" Ellery smiled. "It was an important question, and its answer told an important story. Well, we now knew that they were handled in order to change the felt on one of them. *But why had that felt been changed?*"

His eyes challenged them mischievously. "There was only one logical answer. *To hide or remove a trace of the crime.* But what could such a trace be—one that would necessitate carefully ripping off a whole felt, running down to some department in the store which stocks felts and baizes (with what risk you may imagine!), bringing back the felt and some glue, and finally pasting the new protector on the book-end? It must be a damaging trace indeed. The most damaging trace of a crime which I can conceive is—blood. And that was the answer.

"For Dr. Prouty had stated positively that much blood had flowed. Then I had found the exact spot where Mrs. French's heart-blood had poured out of her body! I proceeded to reconstruct that incident. The book-ends were on the far edge of the desk, opposite the place where I am now standing. The blood must have come, then, from a position similar to mine at this moment. If we suppose that Mrs. French had been shot as she stood here, the first bullet striking above the abdomen in the *precordial* region, then the blood spurted out directly on the glass top of the desk and trickled across to the book-end, soaking it in gore. Whereupon she must have collapsed in the chair, falling forward just as the second bullet, fired from the same spot, hit her directly in the heart. This also bled a little. Only one book-end was affected—the one nearer the center of the table. It was so bloody that the murderer was compelled to remove the felt altogether and substitute a new one. Why he felt compelled to hide this trace of the crime I shall go into later. As for the different shade of the new felt—it is an optical fact that colors are more difficult to distinguish truly by artificial light than by daylight. At night, no doubt, the two shades of green seemed identical. With the aid of the sun I immediately detected the difference. . . .

"You see now how we concluded exactly where Mrs.

French was when she was murdered. As for the position of her assailant, it was determined from the angle of the wounds themselves, which were pointing to the left and quite ragged, indicating that the murderer stood rather sharply to the right."

Ellery paused, patting his lips with a handkerchief. "I have strayed a little from the main line of my exposition," he said, "because it was necessary to convince you that I now had genuine proof that the murder had been committed in the apartment. Until the discovery of the tampered book-ends I could not be sure, despite the fact that I found these cards and cigaret-stubs"—he displayed them briefly—"in the cardroom next door."

He put down the board on which the cards were tacked. "We found the cards lying on the table there arranged in such a manner as to indicate immediately that a game of Russian banque had been interrupted. Mr. Weaver testified that the cardroom had been tidy the evening before, that the cards had not been there. That meant, of course, that some one had used them during the night. Mr. Weaver further attested to the fact that of all the French family and their friends and acquaintances, Mrs. French and her daughter Bernice Carmody were the only ones addicted to the game of banque—that in fact it was well known in many quarters how passionately devoted to it they were.

"The cigaret-stubs in the ashtray on the table bore the brand-name *La Duchesse*—again identified by Mr. Weaver as Miss Carmody's brand. It was scented with her favorite *odeur*, violet.

"It seemed, then, that Mrs. French and Miss Carmody had both been in the apartment Monday night, that Miss Carmody had smoked her unusual cigarets, and that they had played a game of their beloved banque.

"In the bedroom closet we found a hat and a pair of shoes identified by Miss Underhill, the French housekeeper, and Miss Keaton, a maid in the French employ, as having been worn by Miss Carmody on Monday, the day of the murder, when she left the house and was not seen again. Another hat and another pair of shoes were missing from the closet, seeming to indicate that the girl had changed the damp ones she was wearing for the dry ones that were missing.

"So much for that." Ellery paused and looked about him, eyes glittering strangely. There was not the slightest sound from his audience. They seemed mesmerized, intent only on watching the slowly rising structure of damning evidence.

"To make an all-important point . . . Now that I knew that the apartment was the scene of the crime, the question inevitably arose: *Why was the body removed to the window downstairs?* What purpose did it serve? For it must have served some purpose—we saw too many signs of cunning, coördinated scheming to believe that the murderer was an arrant lunatic, doing things for no reason at all.

"The first alternative was that the body was removed to make it appear that the apartment was not the scene of the murder. But this did not follow from the facts, for if the murderer wished to remove all traces of the crime from the apartment, why did he not also remove the banque game, the cigaret-stubs, the shoes and the hat? True, if the body were not discovered or the murder not suspected, the finding of these articles would indicate no crime. But the murderer could not hope to conceal the body forever. Some day, somehow, it would be found, the apartment gone over, and the cards, cigarets and other things would point to the apartment as the place where the murder was committed.

"So, it was evident that the body was removed for another reason entirely. What could that be? The answer came after thought—*to delay the discovery of the body*. How was this arrived at? Simple mental arithmetic. The exhibition was held every single day at noon sharp. This was an unvarying rule. The window was not entered until noon. These facts were common knowledge. If the body were hidden in that wall-bed the murderer had absolute assurance that it would not be discovered before twelve-fifteen. There was the good sharp reason ready made for us—the only gleam of light in the whole muddle, which was complicated by such questions as why the window was used at all when it had so many obvious disadvantages, and so on. So we had no doubt that the murderer took the trouble of carrying the body down six flights of stairs and into the exhibition-room because he knew that the body would not be found all the next morning.

"Logically, then, the question followed: Why did the murderer desire to delay the discovery of the body? Think it over and you will see that there can be only one convincing reason—because he had to do something on Tuesday morning which the discovery of the body would have rendered dangerous or even impossible!"

They were hanging on his words now breathlessly.

"How could this be?" asked Ellery, his eyes sparkling. "Let's shift to a new tack for the moment. . . . No matter how the murderer entered the store, he must have stayed all night. He had three ways to enter, but no way to get out unobserved. He could have hidden in the store during the day; he could have come in after hours by the Employees' Entrance; or he could have slipped into the building by the freight-door at eleven o'clock at night while the commissary truck was unloading the food supplies for the next day. The chances were that this last was the method used, for O'Flaherty had seen no one enter by his door, and coming in at eleven at night was better for the murderer's purpose than having to stay in the store from five-thirty until midnight.

"But how to get out? O'Flaherty reports no one left by his door; all other exits were locked and bolted; and the freight-door on 39th Street was closed at eleven-thirty, fifteen minutes before Mrs. French even arrived at the store and a half-hour before she was murdered. So the criminal had no recourse but to stay in the store all night. Then he could not escape until nine the next morning, when the doors were opened to the public. At that time he could walk out of the store as if he were an early customer.

"But here another factor entered. If he could walk out of the store at nine, a free man, why couldn't he also attend to whatever business he had without the rigmarole of taking the body to the window in order to secure a delay? The point is that he *did* transfer the body. Then he *couldn't* walk out of the store at nine, a free man. He *needed* that delay. He had *to stay in the store even after nine!*"

Simultaneously there came a short gasp from different quarters of the room. Ellery looked around quickly, as if anxious to determine exactly who had been shocked into astonishment and perhaps fear.

"I see that several of you catch the inference on the wing," he said, smiling. "There could be only one reason to explain why our murderer had to stay in the store even after nine—and that is that *he was connected with the store!*"

This time incredulity, suspicion, dread were written on all those plastic faces. Every one drew unconsciously away from his neighbor, as if suddenly aware of the many persons which this last indictment might implicate.

"Yes, that is where we arrived finally," continued Ellery in an unemotional voice. "If our mysterious criminal were an employee of the store or connected with the store in some official or even unofficial capacity, his absence on the discovery of a murder would certainly be noted. He could not afford to have his absence, which was evidently of paramount importance, noted. He was in a difficult position. The memorandum note"—he exhibited the blue slip on the desk before him—"left on this desk by Mr. Weaver overnight told the murderer that both Mr. Weaver and Mr. French would be in the apartment at nine o'clock the next morning. If he left the body in the apartment, the murder would be discovered at nine, the hue and cry raised, and he would never get his chance to slip out of the store and attend to his secret business. And even telephone calls might be watched. So he had to make sure the body was not discovered until he had time to slip away, or even telephone (for this would be untraceable if there was no reason to check calls). The only method which he knew would surely delay the discovery of the body was to hide it in the window-room. Which he did, and quite successfully.

"By this time we were able to clear up finally that minor point of how the murderer entered the building. We had the Monday time-chart. Our murderer must be, we said, an employee of the store or in some way connected with it. Yet the time-chart showed that every one had checked out regularly before or at five-thirty. Then the murderer must have entered the building by the freight-door, as the only means left.

"One other point, while we are on the subject of the murderer's desire to delay the discovery of the body. . . . It occurred to me, as no doubt it has occurred to you, that our mysterious criminal ran uncommon risks and embarked on numerous voyages of complication when he began to clean up the mess after his crime. For example—that he carried the body downstairs. But that is explained by the fact that he had to have time in the morning to attend to this vague business, an item, incidentally, which we have not as yet explained. Also—why did he go to the trouble of securing a new felt, carefully mopping up the blood, and so on? Again this is answered by the need for time in the morning, and the fact that if a bloody book-end were found by Mr. Weaver, let us say, at nine o'clock a crime would be suspected at once, and undoubtedly the criminal's chance of getting his business done would be seriously jeopardized. Evidently then, what he had to do was of the most pressing importance—so pressing that he could not run the risk of the crime's even being suspected before that business was attended to. . . ."

Ellery paused and referred to a sheaf of paper which he took from his breast-pocket. "We must leave for the moment our general conclusion that the person we are seeking is connected officially or semi-officially with this establishment," he said at last. "Please bear that statement in mind while I veer off into another lane of speculation entirely. . . .

"I brought to your attention a few moments ago four concrete evidences of the presence of Miss Bernice Carmody in this apartment on Monday night. These were, in the order in which we found them, the game of banque exclusively indulged in by Miss Carmody and her mother; the *La Duchesse* cigarets, violet-scented, known to be Miss Carmody's special brand; Miss Carmody's hat, which she was observed wearing on Monday afternoon when she disappeared from sight; and her shoes, which fit the same description.

"Now I shall show you that, far from proving that Miss Carmody was present here on Monday night, they prove exactly the contrary," continued Ellery briskly. "The banque game contributes nothing to our little refutation; the cards lay there in a legitimate array, and we must leave them for the present.

"The cigarets, however, present a more illuminating view of my contention. These"—he held up one of the ashtrays on the exhibit-table—"these cigaret-stubs were found on the table in the cardroom." He lifted one of the stubs from the tray and held it high. "As you can see, this cigaret has been almost entirely consumed—in fact, only the small strip which bears the brand imprint is left. Without exception, each of the ten or twelve cigarets in this ashtray have been uniformly smoked to the same tiny stub.

"On the other hand, in Miss Carmody's bedroom at the French house we found these stubs." He exhibited the second ashtray, picking out one of the cigarets from its cluttered, dusty depths to show to his audience. "You will observe that in the case of this stub, the cigarets, also a *La Duchesse* of course, has been little more than one-quarter consumed—Miss Carmody evidently having taken only five or six puffs before crushing the remainder in the tray. Every stub in this tray from Miss Carmody's bedroom has been similarly treated.

"In other words," he said with a bare smile, "we find the amusing phenomenon of two sets of cigarets, both presumably smoked by the same person, exhibiting distinctly opposite physical remains. On investigating, we discovered that Miss Carmody, for reasons soon to be clarified, is extremely nervous—so much so that none of those persons who know her best can recall any occasion on which she has not smoked her favorite cigarets in exactly this wasteful, convulsive manner.

"What is the inference?" A perceptible pause. "Merely that Miss Carmody did *not* smoke the cigarets we found on the cardroom table; that they were smoked or prepared by some one else who did not know Miss Carmody's unvarying method of throwing away cigarets one-quarter consumed. . . .

"Now, as for the shoes and hat," Ellery said without allowing his auditors time in which to digest this latest pronouncement, "we found further signs of a tampering hand. The appearance of things is that Miss Carmody was here Monday night, having been wet by the rain of the afternoon and evening, and that before leaving the apartment she changed her soaked hat and shoes, putting on others from the small stock of her clothing already in the bedroom closet. *But* we discovered that the hat had been inserted in a hat-box with its brim to the bottom. And that the shoes had been stuck into the shoe-bag with their heels projecting from the pocket.

"In testing the habituary nature of such a procedure, we considered that an overwhelming percentage of women put their hats away in hat-boxes with the crowns *to the bottom* and the brims to the top; also that when shoes have large buckles, as this pair has, they are put away with the heels inside, so that the buckles will not catch on the material of the bag. Yet both articles denoted this peculiar ignorance of feminine custom. Here the inference is also obvious— Miss Carmody did not put away those shoes and the hat; *a man did.* For it is the masculine custom to put hats away with the brim downward; and a man would not grasp the significance of the buckle. All the shoes in the rack had the heels showing, because none happened to have buckles; whoever put Miss Carmody's shoes in the rack automatically followed suit, which a woman would not have done.

"Now these points, taken by and of themselves, are, I will confess, rather weak and inconclusive. But when you put the three together, the evidence is too strong to be overlooked—it was not Miss Carmody who smoked the cigarettes and put away shoes and hat, but some one else— a man."

Ellery cleared away a huskiness in his throat. His tone was barbed with earnestness, despite a growing hoarseness.

"There is another item of considerable interest in this last connection," he continued. "In examining the lavatory inside, Mr. Weaver and I ran across an intriguing theft. A safety-razor blade of Mr. Weaver's, which he had used after five-thirty Monday afternoon and had cleaned and restored to the case because it was his last blade and he knew he would have to shave in the morning—this blade, I say, was missing on Tuesday morning. Mr. Weaver, who was busy Monday night and consequently forgot to put in a new supply of blades, came to the apartment Tuesday morning early—at eight-thirty, in fact, because he had to clear up some business and reports before the arrival of Mr. French at nine. He intended to shave in the apartment. The blade, which he had put away only the late afternoon before, was gone. Mr. French, let me explain, does not keep a razor, never shaving himself.

"Now why was the blade gone? Of course, it was plain that the blade must have been used Monday night or early Tuesday morning before Mr. Weaver arrived here. Who could have used it? One of two people—Mrs. French or her murderer. Mrs. French could have used it as a cutting instrument of some sort; or her murderer could have used it.

"Of the two alternatives, surely the second is more tenable. Remember that the criminal was constrained by circumstances to pass the night in the store. Where could he stay with most safety? Certainly in the apartment itself! He could not roam about the dark floors, or even hide among them with as great a margin of safety as in the apartment—not with the watchman prowling about all night! Now—we find a blade used. It suggests normally the process of shaving. Well, why not? We know that the murderer had to make an appearance in the morning as an employee or official of the store. Why shouldn't he shave while he was temporarily occupying the apartment?

It predicates a cold-blooded personality, but that is an argument for rather than an argument against it. Why is the blade missing? Evidently something happened to it. What could have happened to it? Did it break? Why not! The blade had been used a few times; it was brittle. A little extra force in screwing the parts of the razor together, and the blade might easily have snapped. Let us suppose that this happened. Why didn't the murderer merely leave the broken blade? Because the murderer is a canny scoundrel and in his own way an excellent psychologist. If a broken blade remains it is more likely to be recalled that it was *not* broken at a former date than to take it for granted that the blade *was* broken at that former date. If the blade is missing there is no incentive to suspicion or memory. An altered object is a more vigorous mental stimulant than a missing one. At least, that is what I should have thought if I had been in the murderer's place; and in effect I believe the person who planned this affair did the correct thing in taking away the blade—correct according to his lights. The proof is that Mr. Weaver thought little or nothing of the missing blade until I probed it out of him; and then it was only because I brought to the investigation an unprejudiced, impersonal observation."

Ellery grinned a little. "I have been working on presumptions and more or less feeble deductions, as you can see; yet if you put together all the scattered, flimsy facts which I have outlined in the past ten minutes, I think you will see that common sense simply cries out that the blade was used for shaving, that it was broken, and that it was taken away. We find no evidence that the blade might have been used for anything but its legitimate purpose; and this only strengthens the contention. Let me leave this line of thought temporarily and go to another, altogether different, and in its way one of the most significant in the entire investigation."

There was a surreptitious rustling of bodies in hard chairs, a quick intake of breaths. The eyes on Ellery did not waver.

"It may have come to you," he said in a quiet, merciless voice, "that more than one person could have been implicated in this affair; that, perhaps, if Miss Carmody did not put away her shoes and hat—disregarding the damning evidence of the cigarets—she still might have been present; for another—a man—could have disposed of the shoes and hat while she stood by or did something else. I shall disprove that with the most gratifying expedition."

He put his palms flat on the desk, leaned slightly forward. "Who, ladies and gentlemen, had rightful access to this apartment? Answer: The five possessors of the keys. That is—Mr. French, Mrs. French, Miss Carmody, Miss Marion French, and Mr. Weaver. The master key in O'Flaherty's desk was closely guarded, and no one could have got it without either his knowledge or the knowledge of the day man, O'Shane. And no such knowledge exists, which makes it plain that the master key in no way enters our calculations.

"Of the six keys *in esse*, as it were, we are now able to account for five. Mrs. French's is missing. All the others are absolutely accounted for as having been exclusively in the possession of their owners. Mrs. French's key has been sought for by the combined cunning of the detective force. It is still missing. In other words, it is not on these premises, despite the fact that O'Flaherty positively avers that Mrs. French had it in her possession when she entered the store Monday night.

"I told you at the beginning of this impromptu demonstration that the murderer probably took that key. Now

I tell you not only that he took it, but that *he had to take it*.

"We have one confirmation in fact that the criminal *wanted* a key. On Monday afternoon, some time after Miss Carmody left the French house furtively, Miss Underhill, the housekeeper, received a telephone call. The caller claimed to be Miss Carmody. The caller asked Miss Underhill to have Miss Carmody's key to the apartment ready, that a messenger would be sent for it at once. Yet only the very same morning, Miss Carmody had told Miss Underhill that she had lost her key, she thought, and asked Miss Underhill to secure one of the other keys and make a duplicate for her!

"Miss Underhill doubts that the caller was Miss Carmody. She is ready to swear that some one stood by the telephone at the other end and prompted the caller's reply when Miss Underhill reminded the caller about the lost key and the morning's instructions. The caller then hung up in some confusion. . . .

"What is the inference? Surely that the caller was not Miss Carmody, but a hireling or accomplice of the murderer, who prompted the call in order to secure a key to the apartment!"

Ellery drew a long breath. "I leave you for the moment to your own cogitations on the interesting reflections this incident raises. . . . Now let me conduct you through a logical maze to another conclusion—the one with which I began this branch of my thesis.

"Why did the murderer want a key? Obviously, to secure a means of access to the apartment. He could not get in except through the agency of a second person who possessed a key, if he had not one himself. Presumably he expected to be admitted to the apartment by Mrs. French, but in the careful planning of the crime the possession of a key for himself might conceivably be important, and this explains the call and the projected 'messenger.' But to the case in point!

"The criminal killed Mrs. French in the apartment. Now that he had a corpse and knew that he must take it down into the window-room, for the various reasons I have given, he pulled up with a sudden thought. He knew that the door to the apartment had a spring lock that snapped shut. He had no key, having failed in his effort to get hold of Bernice Carmody's. He must carry the body out of the apartment. Yet he had much to do in the apartment afterward—clean up the evidences of blood, 'plant' the shoes and hat, the banque game and cigarets. As a matter of fact, even if he cleaned up the room and 'planted' the false evidence before he took the body down, he still needed means of reëntry into the apartment. He had to pussyfoot through the store for the felt, the glue, and other paraphernalia needed to fix the book-ends. How was he to get back into the apartment? He also meant to sleep in the apartment, apparently—again, how was he to get back? You see, whether he took the body downstairs before or after he cleaned up, he still needed a means of reëntry to the apartment. . . .

"His first thought must have been to insert something between the door and the floor to keep the springed door from clicking shut. But what about the watchmen? He must have thought: 'The watchmen make rounds through this corridor by the hour. They will be sure to notice a partly open door and investigate.' No, the door had to be closed. But—a thought! Mrs. French had a key, her own key—the one by which she herself entered the apartment. He would use that. We can picture him opening her bag while she lay, bleeding and dead, across the desk, finding the key, putting it into his own pocket, picking up the corpse and leaving the apartment, now certain of a means of reëntering it when he was through with his grisly task.

"*But*"—and Ellery smiled grimly—"he had to bring the key back upstairs with him, obviously, to get into the apartment again. Therefore we didn't find it on the body. True, he might have gone upstairs, done his cleaning up, and then taken the key downstairs again. But—of course that's inane—how would he get back again? Besides, the danger he would encounter—taking still another chance of being detected on the main floor getting into the window. . . . It was dangerous enough the first time, but that was inescapable. No, he probably figured that the best thing he could do would be to pocket the key and dispose of it when he left the building in the morning. True, he might have left it in the apartment, on the card-table for example. But the fact that it isn't in the apartment shows that he took it away with him—he had two alternatives and chose one of them.

"We find then—" Ellery paused for the merest instant—"that our criminal committed the murder *without accomplices.*

"I see doubt on some faces. But surely it is quite clear. If he had an accomplice, he wouldn't have been forced to take the key at all! . . . He would have carried the body downstairs, and his accomplice would have remained in the apartment to open the door for him when he was finished downstairs. Don't you see? The very fact that he had to take the key shows that it was a one-man job. I might be confronted with the objection: 'Well, it could have been two people at that, because both might have carried the body downstairs.' To that I reply with certainty, 'No!' because it would have involved a double risk —two people would have been easier to detect by a watch-man than one. This crime is well thought out—the author of it would never have taken this unnecessary chance of discovery."

Ellery stopped abruptly and stared down at his notes. No one moved. When he looked up there was a tightness about his lips that revealed an inward strain whose cause no one there could guess.

"I have now reached the point, ladies and gentlemen," he announced in a calm flat voice, "where I can go to some length in describing our elusive criminal. Would you care to hear my description?"

He looked about the room, challenging them with his eyes. Bodies rigid through excitement sagged in reaction. Every one averted his head. There was no sound from them.

"I take it that you would," said Ellery in the same flat voice, which contained a note of amused menace. "Very well, then!"

He leaned forward, eyes glittering. "Our murderer is a man. The tactics employed in putting the shoes and hat into the closet plus the evidence of the missing blade point to this masculinity. The physical energy required in disposing of the body and the rest; the mental agility, with its recurrent traces of hard common sense; the cold-bloodedness, the unscrupulosity—all these point unerringly to a masculine figure with, if you will, a fairly heavy beard which requires daily shaving."

They followed the movements of his lips with bated breaths.

"Our man worked alone, without accomplices. The deductions from the missing key, which I have gone into at great length, point to this."

There was not a tremor of movement in the room.

"Our lone man is connected with the store. The removal of the body to the window downstairs and all its attendant complications, which I have also expounded at some length, prove this."

Ellery relaxed slightly. Again he looked about the room with a little smile. He applied his handkerchief to his lips, glanced slyly at Commissioner Welles, who sat perspiring and alert in his chair; at his father, who was slumped in an attitude of weariness, one fragile hand shielding his eyes; at the motionless detectives to his left; at Velie, Crouther, "Jimmy," and Fiorelli to his right. Then he began once more.

"On one point," he said dryly, "we have as yet reached no definite conclusion. I refer to the nature of the business which the murderer considered so imperative as to require special attention Tuesday morning. . . .

"Which brings me to the most absorbing subject of the five books which we discovered on this desk—that interesting mélange of paleontology, elementary music, commerce of the *moyen age,* philately, and bad vaudeville jokes."

Ellery launched into a short, graphic description of the five strange volumes, the markings, Weaver's story of Springer's duplicity, the revelation that the addresses were drug-distributing depots, and finally the unsuccessful raid on the house at the 98th Street address, taken from the sixth book in Weaver's possession.

"When Springer prepared the sixth book," continued Ellery, to his ever-tensing audience, "we can assume that he had no suspicion that the book-code was being tampered with or known to an outsider. If he had, he would not have prepared the book and left it for Mr. Weaver's investigating fingers. So that, when Springer left the store on Monday night, followed by Mr. Weaver, he did not know that this sixth book, *Modern Trends in Interior Decoration,* by Lucian Tucker, was in our young amateur detective's possession. And since Springer met and spoke to no one all evening, even when he arrived at his Bronx apartment (for we have checked up through the telephone company and found that he did not make any telephone calls when he got home), he could not therefore have known that the book-system had been tampered with until, at the very earliest, the next morning, Tuesday, when he returned to work. In other words, after the murder. If we presume that not Springer, but some one else, would have been apprised by an outsider of the discovery of the code system, we must not forget that the only method by which any one could have communicated with another about the matter from the store would be by telephoning, since he could not leave the store during the night. And we discovered that the telephone service at this store is cut off at night, with the exception of one trunk line leading to O'Flaherty's desk; and this was not used, according to O'Flaherty's own testimony.

"Then we are forced to conclude that it was impossible for any one in the store Monday night and early Tuesday morning to have communicated with Springer or any one else about the missing sixth book, which Weaver took away with him."

Ellery forged ahead rapidly. "The fact that the system of dope distribution was disorganized the next morning, Tuesday—as it was, for the sudden abandonment of the 98th Street house on Tuesday afternoon is clear evidence— could have been due only to some one of the drug ring discovering during the night that the system was being tampered with. I repeat here the fact that Springer went ahead on Monday evening with his regular task of codifying the sixth book, showing that up to that time the ring considered their system safe. Yet by next morning they had become alarmed and fled the 98th Street rendezvous, even before catering to their addict-customers. Again, then, the logical explanation is that it was during the previous night that some one discovered something wrong.

"This discovery could have been caused only by, first, noticing the absence of the sixth book from its accustomed shelf in the Book Department Monday night after Weaver left—the last one to check out of the store; second, finding the five duplicate books on Mr. French's desk Monday night; or third, both. We must conclude therefore that, since the disorganization did take place the morning after the crime, it could have only been ordered by some one who made one or both of these discoveries Monday night. Some one—to amplify—who must have been in the store after Springer and Weaver left, and who therefore could not get out of the store or communicate with any one until at least nine o'clock Tuesday morning."

Dawning comprehension shone from several faces before him. Ellery smiled. "I see that some of you are anticipating the inevitable conclusion. . . . Who in the store that night was in a position to make one or both of these bibliographical discoveries? The answer is: the murderer, the man who killed Mrs. French in the room in which the five books were prominently in sight. Is there anything about the murderer's subsequent actions which proves that he *did* make the discovery of the five books in the apartment? Yes, there is. The fact that the murderer removed the body to the window-room in order to give himself time next morning to attend to his 'business'—which until this point has been obscure. . . .

"The deductive chain, ladies and gentlemen," said Ellery in a curiously triumphant voice, "is too strong and perfectly welded to be anything but truth. *The murderer warned the drug ring Tuesday morning.*

"In other words, to add an element to our growing description—our murderer is a man, who worked alone, who is connected with the store, and who belongs to a large, well-organized drug ring."

He paused, fingered the five books on the desk with sensitive fingers. "Furthermore, we are now in a position to add another qualifying item to the growing description of the murderer.

"For had our drug-distributing murderer been present in the French apartment *before* the night of the murder —and by 'before' I mean at any time within five weeks prior to the fatal night—he would have seen the books on the table, would have become suspicious, would have at once ordered the cessation of the book-code operations in the Book Department. And since up to the very night of the murder the book system was still in effect, it follows most gracefully that the murderer had not been in the French library for between one and five weeks before Monday night last. . . . We have confirmation that it was the murderer again who saw those books on the desk. For in examining and later fixing the damaged book-ends, he could scarcely have missed seeing—and understanding to his horror the significance of—the five volumes. . . .

"As a matter of fact," continued Ellery swiftly, "there is no difficulty in deducing that the murderer, upon seeing the incriminating books on this desk, immediately stole downstairs to the Book Department with a flashlight to determine whether the sixth book had been tampered with also. And of course he would have found it gone—the climax-capping discovery which would make it imperative for him to get word to his confederates that the game was up. This is a decently reasonable conjecture which very soon, I am happy to announce, we shall be able to check more positively!"

And with this he stopped short, mopped his forehead with his handkerchief, and polished the lenses of his pince-nez with absent fingers. This time a ripple of conversation disturbed the quiet atmosphere, beginning in a minor cadence that swelled to excited proportions, only to cease abruptly when Ellery lifted a hand for silence.

"To make the analysis complete," he resumed, restoring his glasses to his nose, "I shall now become perhaps objectionably personal. For I mean to take up, one by one, each of you and measure you by the yardstick I have constructed in this analysis!"

Instantly the room was a babel of exclamations, expressions of anger, resentment, bewilderment, uncomfortable self-interest. Ellery shrugged his shoulders, turned toward Commissioner Welles. The Commissioner said "Yes!" in a decisive tone and glared at the people assembled before him. They subsided, muttering.

Ellery turned back to his audience with a half-smile. "Really," he said, "I have not sprung my greatest surprise by any means. So there is little cause for protest on the part of any one here—or should I say nearly any one? At any rate, let's begin this fascinating little game of elimination.

"From the first unit on my yardstick—the fact that the murderer is a man—" he said, "we may at once absolve, even as an intellectual exercise, Miss Marion French, Miss Bernice Carmody, and Mrs. Cornelius Zorn.

"The second unit—that this man worked alone—is irrelevant and useless to determine identity, so we will proceed to the third unit, which is that the murderer, a man, is connected with this establishment. And to the fourth, which is that the murderer has not been in this apartment within the past five weeks.

"There is, first, Mr. Cyrus French." Ellery bowed insouciantly to the feeble old millionaire. "Mr. French is certainly connected with this establishment. Mr. French, further, could have committed the crime, if you judge physical possibility a factor. I demonstrated privately not long ago that, had Mr. French bribed the chauffeur of his host, Mr. Whitney, to take him into the City from Great Neck on Monday night and forget about it, he could have arrived at this apartment in sufficient time to slip through the freight entrance and into the apartment. He was not seen again, except by the chauffeur, after he retired to his room in the Whitney house at nine o'clock Monday night complaining of a slight indisposition.

"However—" Ellery smiled at the purpling face of French—"Mr. French has certainly been in this room within the past five weeks—every day, in fact, for years. And if this seems inconclusive, Mr. French, rest easy. For there is another reason, that thus far I have purposely neglected to mention, which makes your culpability a psychological impossibility."

French relaxed, a vague smile lifting the corners of his tremulous old mouth. Marion squeezed his hand. "Now," said Ellery busily, "Mr. John Gray, donor of the entangled book-ends and close friend to the French family. You, Mr. Gray," he said gravely, directly addressing the spruce old director, "are eliminated on a number of counts. Although you are connected with the store in a very important capacity, and although your absence on Tuesday morning would have been seriously noticed, you too have been a frequent visitor to these rooms during the past five weeks; in fact, you attended a meeting here on Friday, I believe. And you had an alibi for Monday night which we checked up and found stronger than even you believe. For not only does the night-man at your hotel desk confirm your statement that you were talking with him at eleven-forty Monday night, making it impossible for you to have entered the store, but another person, unknown to you—a fellow-resident at the same apartment hotel—saw you enter your suite at eleven-forty-five. . . . Even without this we could not seriously have entertained a thought of your guilt, for we had no reason to believe that your friend the night-clerk is anything but an honest man. No more reason, in fact, than that Mr. Whitney's chauffeur, in the case of Mr. French, is dishonest.   In Mr. French's case I merely mentioned the bribe as an eventuality, improbable but certainly within the realm of possibility."

Gray sank back with a curious sigh, dug his small hands into the pockets of his coat.   Ellery turned to red-faced, nervous Cornelius Zorn, who was fumbling with his watch-chain.   "Mr. Zorn, your alibi was weak, and you could have, with perjured testimony on the part of Mrs. Zorn, committed the murder.   But although you are a prominent official of the store, you too have been in this room at least once weekly for many months.   And you, too, as well as Mr. French and Mr. Gray, are further absolved by this psychological inadmissibility of which I spoke before.

"Mr. Marchbanks," continued Ellery, turning to the heavy-set, lowering brother of the dead woman, "your story about the automobile trip to Long Island and staying overnight at your house in Little Neck, unseen by any one who might vouch for your presence, also made it phys-ically possible for you to have returned to the city in time to get into the store and commit the murder.   But you needn't have been so irate yesterday—you are absolved too by this secret point of mine, besides being eliminated, as a regular attendant here at the directorial conferences, on the same account as Mr. Zorn.

"And Mr. Trask—" Ellery's tone hardened slightly— "although you were drunk and rolling about the streets—" Trask's jaw dropped in vapid astonishment— "on Monday night and Tuesday morning, you, too, are set free by my yardstick, as well as by my as yet undivulged item."

Ellery paused, looked contemplatively at the stony, dark features of Vincent Carmody.   "Mr. Carmody.   In many respects you deserve our apologies and genuine commisera-tions.   You were entirely eliminated from our speculations by the fact that you are in no way connected with the store.   Had you committed the murder, despite your story of the night trip to Connecticut, which was unsubstantiated and might have been false, there would have been no necessity for taking the body of Mrs. French downstairs to the window-room. Because you could have walked out of the store at nine o'clock unrestrained by any fear that your absence might be noticed. You did not belong in the store at all. You, too, incidentally, are eliminated further by my charming and mysterious little point.

"And now," continued Ellery, turning to the disturbed Gallic features of Paul Lavery, "we come to you. Don't be afraid!" he smiled—"you didn't commit the crime! I was so certain that I did not even bother to ask you for a statement of your movements on Monday night. You have been in this apartment daily for weeks. Besides, you came here directly from France only a short time ago—it was quite beyond the area of probability to suspect you, therefore, of being embroiled in a gang of drug-peddlers operating with intense organization in this city and country. And you, too, cannot very well be our murderer, since you do not logically measure up to my last point, still withheld. And, if I were to be minutely psychiatric, I might add that a man of your refined and Continental intelligence would never have committed the regrettable mistakes which got our esteemed mysterioso into trouble. For I do believe that, out of all of us, you alone would have been man-of-the-world enough to know how a woman puts her hat into a hat-box, and how she stores buckled shoes in a shoe-bag. . . .

"We have now," continued Ellery pleasantly, but there was a feverish glitter in his eye, "narrowed the field of inquiry considerably. We might discuss, of course, Mr. MacKenzie, the general manager, who is an employee of the store. No, no! Mr. MacKenzie, don't rise to protest—we've eliminated you already. Because of this last point of ours, which is almost ready for exposition, and because you have been in this apartment within five weeks. But any of the hundreds of employees of the store who have *never* been in this apartment and whose movements Monday night are unaccounted for, might be the murderer. We'll come to that in a moment. At this time, ladies and gentlemen—" Ellery made a sharp sign to Patrolman Bush at the anteroom door, who immediately bobbed his head and went out, leaving the door open behind him—"at this time I wish to present to you a gentleman who until now has been more or less of an unknown quantity; no less a personage than—" there was a flurry at the outer door; it opened and Bush entered, followed by a detective who held a white-faced man, manacled, tightly by the elbow— "Mr. James Springer!"

Ellery retreated slightly, a grim smile on his face. The detective escorted his prisoner to the front of the room, where two chairs were immediately set by one of the attendant policemen. The two men sat down, Springer holding his manacled hands limply in his lap, staring steadfastly at the floor. He was a middle-aged man with sharp features and grey hair; a livid bruise on his right cheek was mute evidence of a recent scuffle.

Everybody in the room stared at nim wordlessly. Old French was speechless with rage at the sight of the employee who had betrayed him. Weaver and Marion both laid restraining hands on his shaking arm. But there were no words in that audience—only hot eager glances, and in one case a frozen steady immutability. . . .

"Mr. Springer," said Ellery quietly—yet his voice exploded like a shell in the strained atmosphere of the room— "Mr. Springer has been kind enough to turn State's evidence. Mr. Springer, who ran away with the deluded thought that he might successfully evade the police, was caught the very day he attempted to escape because we were prepared for it. Mr. Springer's capture has been kept very quiet. Mr. Springer has cleared up many little items of procedure which we could not possibly have deduced.

"For example, that the murderer is his chief in the drug ring, which even now is being scattered and pursued throughout the country. That the murderer is the right-hand man of the eloquently termed 'master mind' of the drug ring in this city. That Miss Bernice Carmody, who we discovered by investigation was probably a drug addict in an advanced stage, had come under the influence of the heroin habit, had met by devious ways the 'master mind,' had been introduced to the code-system, had become so dependent upon the drug that she willingly solicited new customers from her social circle, becoming in a way therefore almost a member of the ring. That Miss Carmody's pernicious addiction was unsuspected by her family until, as we know, her father, Mr. Carmody, began to suspect and told his former wife, Mrs. French, what he suspected; and Mrs. French, observing, saw that it was true. That Mrs. French, in her assertive way, directly accused her daughter of addiction and finally broke down the girl's weakened will until she confessed everything—including the name of the man connected with the French store who was supplying her directly with her own drugs. That Mrs. French, who we may suppose did not inform her husband of the true state of affairs because of his violent aversion to this form of vice, on Monday took away from Miss Carmody the newly replenished supply of drugs which she kept in the false bottom of her specially made lipstick. That Mrs. French further forced her daughter to make an appointment for her with this man, this employee in her husband's store, for Monday night at midnight, secretly, to plead with him for her daughter—to force him, by threats of disclosing to the police what she now knew about the drug organization, to loose his grip on her daughter and allow the girl to be cured secretly by her mother. That this appointment was made on Sunday through Miss Carmody. That this man immediately reported the alarming state of affairs to his chief, the ubiquitous 'master mind,' who in his customary cold-blooded fashion commanded him to kill Mrs. French, who by now, in turn, was in possession of too much vital information to be allowed to live; and also to do away with Miss Carmody, who had proved a weak cog in the machine and must also be disposed of. That this man, under threat of being killed himself, laid his plans and made his appointment. That he entered secretly through the freight-door, which as an employee of the store he knew was open at that exact half-hour each night. That he waited until midnight in a store lavatory and then made his way stealthily to the apartment on the sixth floor, knocked, and was admitted by Mrs. French, who had arrived a few minutes before. That she stood by the desk, as we deduced, and they argued; that he was not aware of the heroin-filled lipstick in her bag, or he would have taken it; that without hesitation he shot and killed Mrs. French, who bled profusely, the blood staining the book-end; that on bending over the desk he saw the five books, and realized that some one had been tampering with the code-system; that he saw the blue memorandum announcing the arrival next morning at nine of Mr. Weaver and Mr. French; that he realized he could not communicate with any one of the ring about this latest unforeseen development, because he was unable to get out before the next morning and could not telephone; that he therefore decided to hide the body in the exhibition-window, which would give him ample time next morning to slip away and warn his gang, for if the body were left in the apartment and discovered at nine, he would be unable for precautionary reasons to leave the building; and finally that he disposed of the body where we found it. Also that on his way back he stopped at the Book Department on the main floor and confirmed his suspicion that the sixth book was also missing. That he took Mrs. French's key back with him, having been unsuccessful in his attempt to get Bernice Carmody's that afternoon by the ruse of the telephone call. Finally, that he cleaned up the apartment, fixed the book-end, 'pianted' the evidence against Miss Carmody, stayed overnight, shaved in the morning, broke the blade and took it away with him; and slipped out shortly after nine, emerging with the early shoppers only to reënter the building at once through the regular Employees' Entrance, in order to be checked in officially. And that he managed soon after to sneak off and warn his gang leader of the discovery of the book-system. . . ."

Ellery cleared his throat, went on relentlessly. "Mr. Springer was also kind enough to clear up the matter of Miss Carmody's abduction. With the action of Mrs. French on Sunday of taking away her store of the drug, the girl became desperate and got in touch with the murderer. This fitted in with his plans—he told her to come to a rendezvous in the lower part of the city for a new supply. She went on Monday afternoon and was promptly abducted, being taken by confederates to a Brooklyn hideaway and murdered. Her clothes were confiscated and brought back to our murderer, who had as yet committed no capital crime. These clothes the murderer brought with him to the apartment Monday night—the hat and shoes, tied up innocently in a small parcel, but wet a trifle with rain to make the deception perfect.

"There is only one thing more to explain before proceeding to the much-wished-for *dénouement*. . . . And that is the reason for 'planting' the banque game, cigarets, shoes and hat to make it appear as if Bernice herself had been implicated in the crime. And this, too, was outlined—under protest—by Mr. Springer, who has been just a cog—an important cog, perhaps—in the vicious wheel. . . .

"The murderer left evidences of Miss Carmody's presence because she had necessarily vanished. Since she had been murdered and would be missing, there was a logical reason for connecting the two events—the disappearance of the girl and the murder of her mother. It would seem perhaps as if the girl had committed the crime. Since this was untrue, the murderer felt that it might confuse the police and put them off the real track. The murderer did not really hope that the deception would be successful for long—it was merely another red herring drawn across the trail, and anything which would lead the scent away from him in another direction he felt was desirable. And the actual 'framing' required little enough trouble and work. The cigarets he secured from Xanthos', Miss Carmody's tobacconist, since she had once told him where she secured her private supply. The banque he knew about from Miss Carmody, also. The rest was child's play. . . ."

They were sitting on the edge of the hard camp-chairs now, straining forward to catch every syllable. Occasionally they looked at each other in a puzzled manner, as if unable to see clearly to the end of the analysis. Ellery brought them back to attention with his next words.

"Springer!" The name cracked out sharply. The prisoner started, paled, looked up furtively. His eyes fell at once to the carpet he had been studiously observing. "Springer, have I given your story faithfully—and completely?"

The man's eyes fluttered in a sudden agony, rolled in their sockets, wildly seeking a face in the swaying crowd before him. When he spoke, it was in a husky monotone, barely audible to those avid ears.

"Yes."

"Very well, then!" exclaimed Ellery, leaning forward, his tone keenly triumphant. "I have still to expatiate upon that unspoken point which I termed mysterious a few moments ago. . . .

"You will recall that I spoke of the book-ends and the few grains of powder stuck in the glue between the onyx and the new felt. That powder was ordinary fingerprint powder.

"From the moment that I was certain of the nature of the powder, the veils dissipated before my eyes and I sensed the truth. We thought at first, ladies and gentlemen," he continued, "that the use of fingerprint powder by the criminal indicated a very superior sort of murderer—a supercriminal, in fact. One who would use the implements of the police's own trade—it was a natural thought. . . .

"But"—and the word lashed into them with deadly emphasis—"there was another inference to be drawn—an inference which in a fell swoop eliminated all suspects but one. . . ." His eyes flashed fire; the hoarseness disappeared from his voice. He leaned forward carefully, over the desk with its litter of clues, holding them with the magnetism of his personality. "All suspects—but one . . ." he repeated slowly.

After a pregnant moment he said: "That one is the man who was employed by this store; who had not been in this room for at least five weeks; who attempted to put us off the track of himself by getting an accomplice without a record to give false information about the 'movements' of Bernice Carmody, who was already dead, in fact; who at the same time was clever enough to say, when he saw that we believed Miss Carmody to have been 'framed,' that he thought so, too, despite the fact that he himself had done the framing; who was present—the only suspect to be present, by the way—when the full story of the codified books and the culpability of Springer was told, and who took the very first opportunity of warning Springer to flee, realizing that, with Springer caught, he himself was in serious danger; *who, most important of all, was the only personality connected with this investigation to whom the use of fingerprint powder was natural and thoroughly logical. . . .*"

He stopped abruptly, eyes fixed with interest, expectancy, the eagerness of the chase, upon one corner of the room.

"*Watch him, Velie!*" he cried suddenly, in a piercing voice.

Before they could turn, before they could grasp the significance of the scene enacted before them so swiftly and vitally, there came the sounds of a short violent struggle, a bull-like bellow of rage, the hoarse panting of breaths, and finally one sharp stupendous deafening report. . . .

Ellery stood limply, wearily in his fixed position at the desk. He did not move while they rushed concertedly from all sides of the room to the quiet spot where the body of a man lay, already stiff in death, in a pool of blood.

It was Inspector Queen who reached that contorted body first, by a lightning leap; who knelt quickly on the carpet, motioning aside the red-faced, heaving figure of Sergeant Velie; who turned the convulsed corpse of the suicide over; who muttered in words inaudible even to the nearest spectator:

"No legal evidence—and the bluff worked! . . . Thank God for a son. . . ."

The face was the face of the head store detective, William Crouther.

THE END